THE SECRET SCIENCE ALLIANCE

→ AND THE **COPYCAT CROOK**

ELEANOR DAVIS

BLOOMSBURY

NEW YORK   LONDON   OXFORD   NEW DELHI   SYDNEY

DEDICATED TO KINO SCHOOL AND EVERYONE
WHO HAS EVER LEARNED AND TAUGHT THERE

The Secret Science Alliance and the Copycat Crook

Created, written & drawn by Eleanor Davis
Inked by Drew Weing
Colored by Joey Weiser & Michele Chidester
Lettered by Bryant Paul Johnson
Art direction & book design by John Lind

Text and illustrations © 2009 by Eleanor Davis.

First published in the United States of America in 2009
by Bloomsbury Children's Books
www.bloomsbury.com

Produced for Bloomsbury Children's Books by Kitchen, Lind & Associates LLC
www.kitchenandlind.com

Bloomsbury is a registered trademark of Bloomsbury Publishing Plc

For information about permission to reproduce selections from this book, write to
Permissions, Bloomsbury Children's Books, 1385 Broadway, New York, New York 10018
Bloomsbury books may be purchased for business or promotional use. For information on bulk
purchases please contact Macmillan Corporate and Premium Sales Department at specialmarkets@macmillan.com

Library of Congress Cataloging-in-Publication Data
Davis, Eleanor.
Secret science alliance and the copycat crook / by Eleanor Davis. — 1st U.S. ed.
p.   cm.
Summary: Eleven-year-old Julian Calendar thought changing schools would mean leaving his "nerdy"
persona behind, but instead he forms an alliance with fellow inventors Greta and Ben and works with
them to prevent an adult from using one of their gadgets for nefarious purposes.
ISBN-13: 978-1-59990-142-8 · ISBN-10: 1-59990-142-0 (hardcover)
ISBN-13: 978-1-59990-396-5 · ISBN-10: 1-59990-396-2 (paperback)
1. Graphic novels. [1. Graphic novels. 2. Inventors—Fiction. 3. Schools—Fiction. 4. Clubs—Fiction.
5. Individuality—Fiction. 6. Youths' writings.] I. Title.
PZ7.7.D38Sec 2010   [Fic]—dc22   2008045399

ISBN: 978-1-59990-895-3 (e-PDF)

Printed in China by Toppan Leefung Printing Ltd, Dongguan, Guangdong
(hardcover) 10 9 8 7 6
(paperback) 20 19 18 17 16 15 14

All papers used by Bloomsbury Publishing, Inc., are natural, recyclable products made from wood grown in well-managed forests.
The manufacturing processes conform to the environmental regulations of the country of origin.

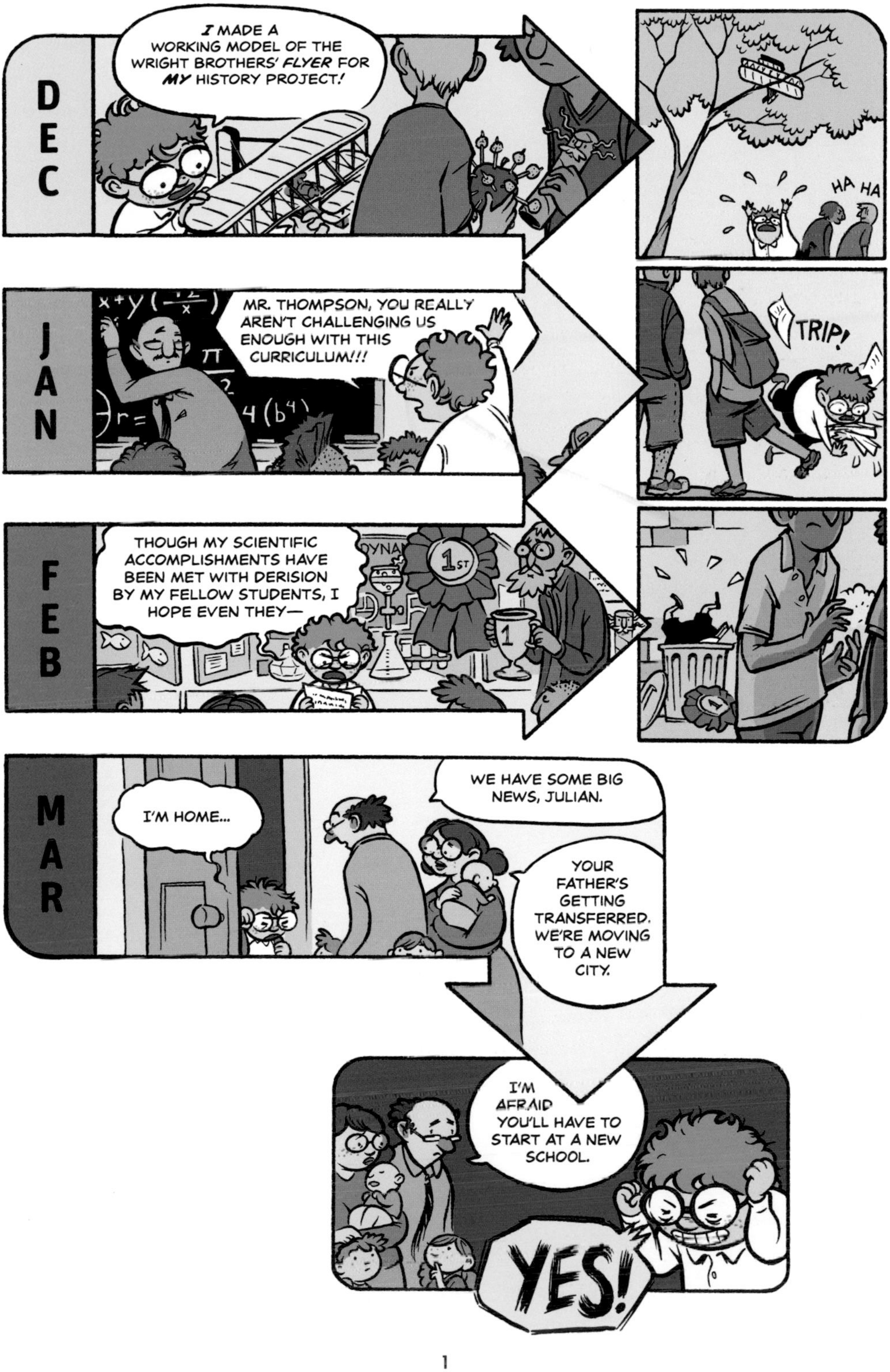
DEC
I MADE A WORKING MODEL OF THE WRIGHT BROTHERS' FLYER FOR MY HISTORY PROJECT!
HA HA
JAN
MR. THOMPSON, YOU REALLY AREN'T CHALLENGING US ENOUGH WITH THIS CURRICULUM!!!
TRIP!
FEB
THOUGH MY SCIENTIFIC ACCOMPLISHMENTS HAVE BEEN MET WITH DERISION BY MY FELLOW STUDENTS, I HOPE EVEN THEY—
MAR
I'M HOME...
WE HAVE SOME BIG NEWS, JULIAN.
YOUR FATHER'S GETTING TRANSFERRED. WE'RE MOVING TO A NEW CITY.
I'M AFRAID YOU'LL HAVE TO START AT A NEW SCHOOL.
YES!

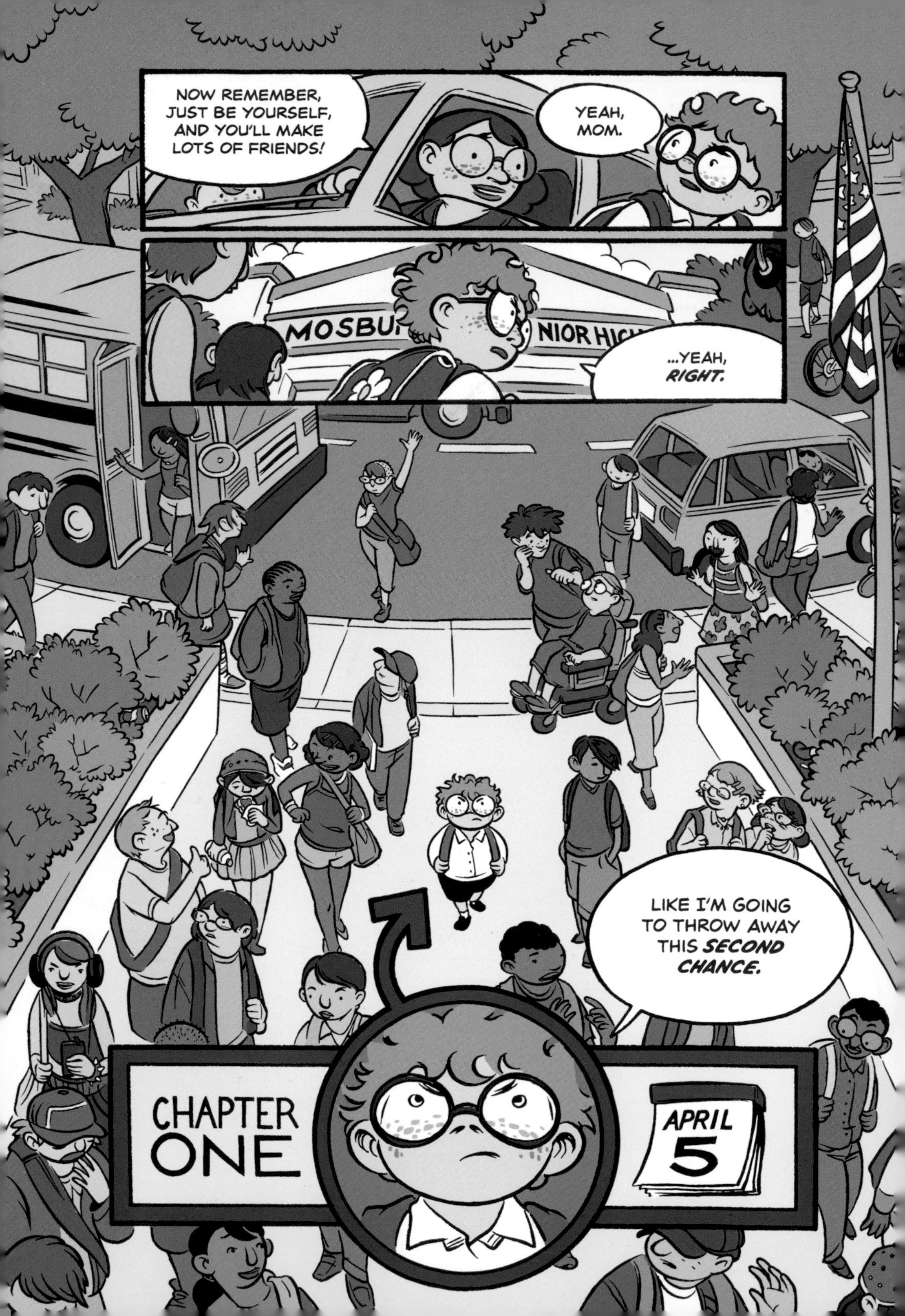
NOW REMEMBER, JUST BE YOURSELF, AND YOU'LL MAKE LOTS OF FRIENDS!
YEAH, MOM.
MOSBU
NIOR HIG
...YEAH, *RIGHT.*
LIKE I'M GOING TO THROW AWAY THIS *SECOND CHANCE.*
CHAPTER ONE
APRIL 5

THE SECRET SCIENCE ALLIANCE

AND THE COPYCAT CROOK

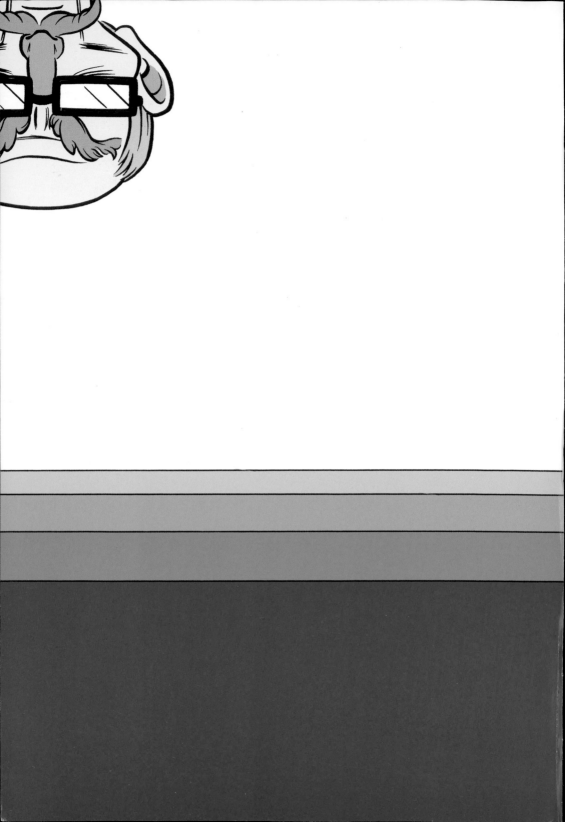

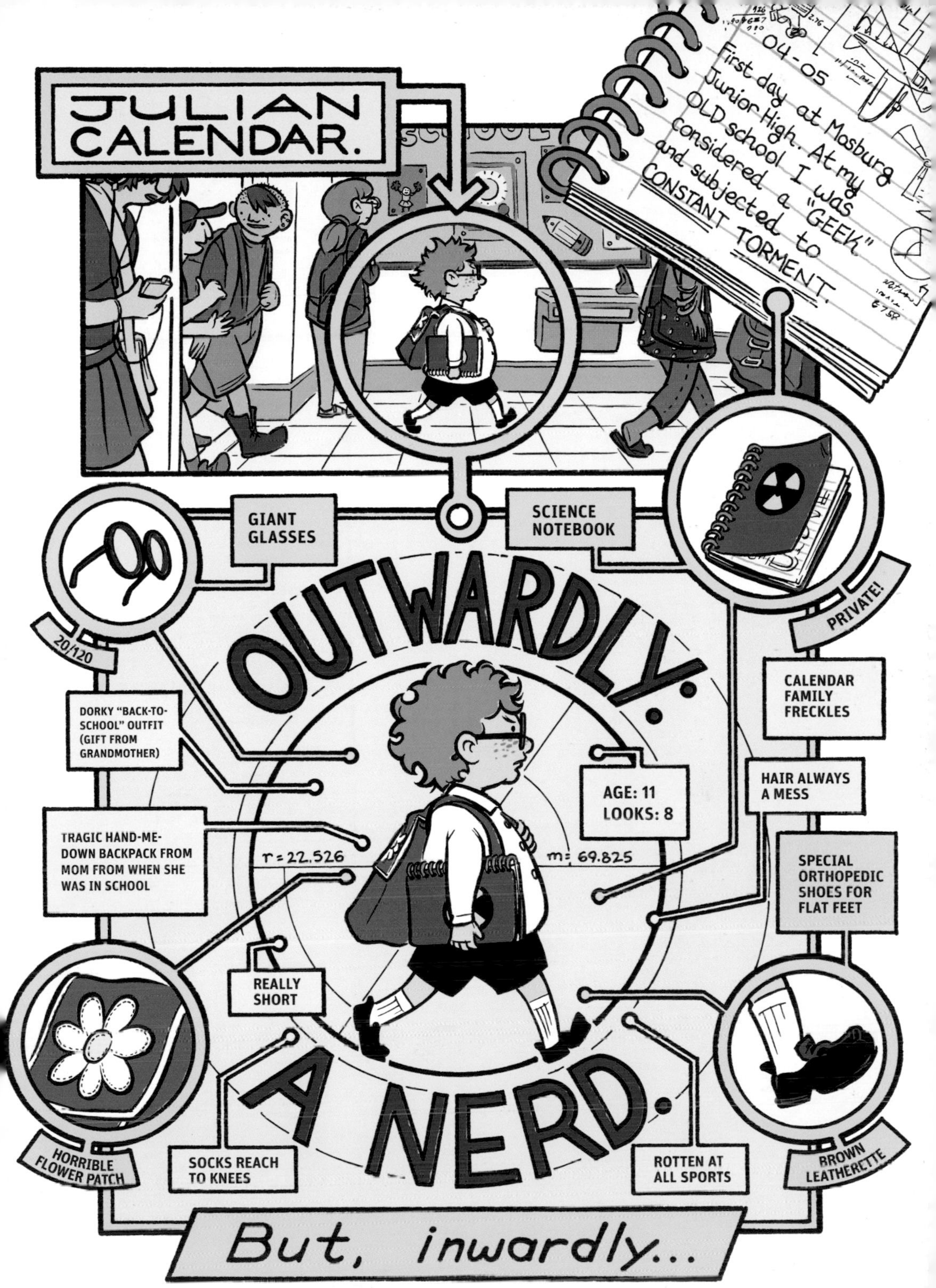
JULIAN CALENDAR.
04-05
First day at Mosburg Junior High. At my OLD school I was considered a "GEEK" and subjected to CONSTANT TORMENT.
GIANT GLASSES
20/120
SCIENCE NOTEBOOK
PRIVATE!
OUTWARDLY:
DORKY "BACK-TO-SCHOOL" OUTFIT (GIFT FROM GRANDMOTHER)
CALENDAR FAMILY FRECKLES
AGE: 11
LOOKS: 8
HAIR ALWAYS A MESS
TRAGIC HAND-ME-DOWN BACKPACK FROM MOM FROM WHEN SHE WAS IN SCHOOL
r = 22.526
m= 69.825
SPECIAL ORTHOPEDIC SHOES FOR FLAT FEET
REALLY SHORT
A NERD.
HORRIBLE FLOWER PATCH
SOCKS REACH TO KNEES
ROTTEN AT ALL SPORTS
BROWN LEATHERETTE
But, inwardly...

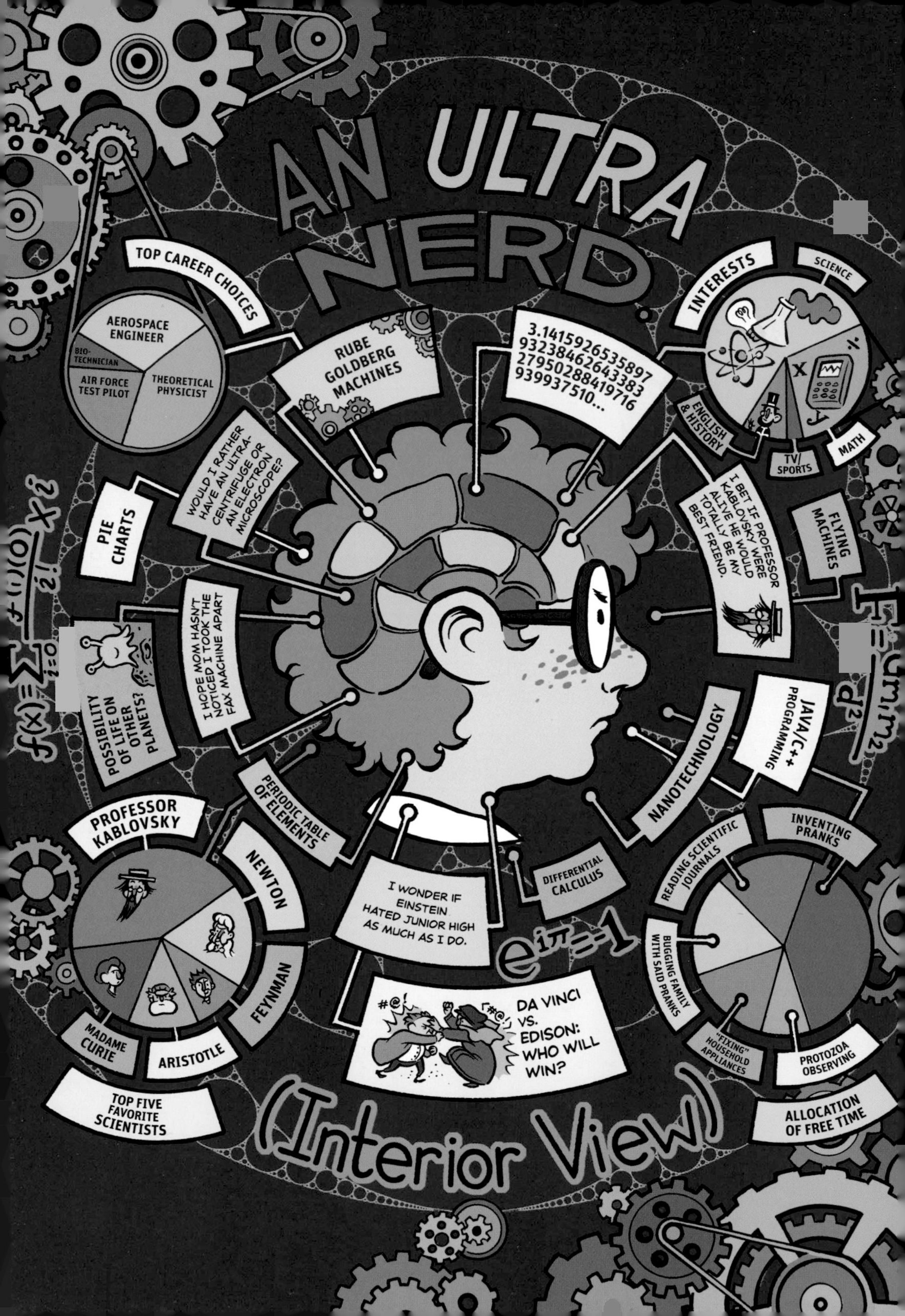
AN ULTRA NERD
(Interior View)
TOP CAREER CHOICES
AEROSPACE ENGINEER
BIO-TECHNICIAN
AIR FORCE TEST PILOT
THEORETICAL PHYSICIST
RUBE GOLDBERG MACHINES
3.14159265358979323846264338327950288419716939937510...
INTERESTS
SCIENCE
ENGLISH & HISTORY
TV/SPORTS
MATH
WOULD I RATHER HAVE AN ULTRA-CENTRIFUGE OR AN ELECTRON MICROSCOPE?
PIE CHARTS
I BET IF PROFESSOR KABLOVSKY WERE ALIVE HE WOULD TOTALLY BE MY BEST FRIEND.
FLYING MACHINES
I HOPE MOM HASN'T NOTICED I TOOK THE FAX MACHINE APART
POSSIBILITY OF LIFE ON OTHERS PLANETS?
JAVA/C++ PROGRAMMING
NANOTECHNOLOGY
PERIODIC TABLE OF ELEMENTS
PROFESSOR KABLOVSKY
NEWTON
FEYNMAN
ARISTOTLE
MADAME CURIE
TOP FIVE FAVORITE SCIENTISTS
I WONDER IF EINSTEIN HATED JUNIOR HIGH AS MUCH AS I DO.
DIFFERENTIAL CALCULUS
$e^{i\pi}=-1$
#@!
#@!
DA VINCI VS. EDISON: WHO WILL WIN?
INVENTING PRANKS
READING SCIENTIFIC JOURNALS
BUGGING FAMILY WITH SAID PRANKS
"FIXING" HOUSEHOLD APPLIANCES
PROTOZOA OBSERVING
ALLOCATION OF FREE TIME

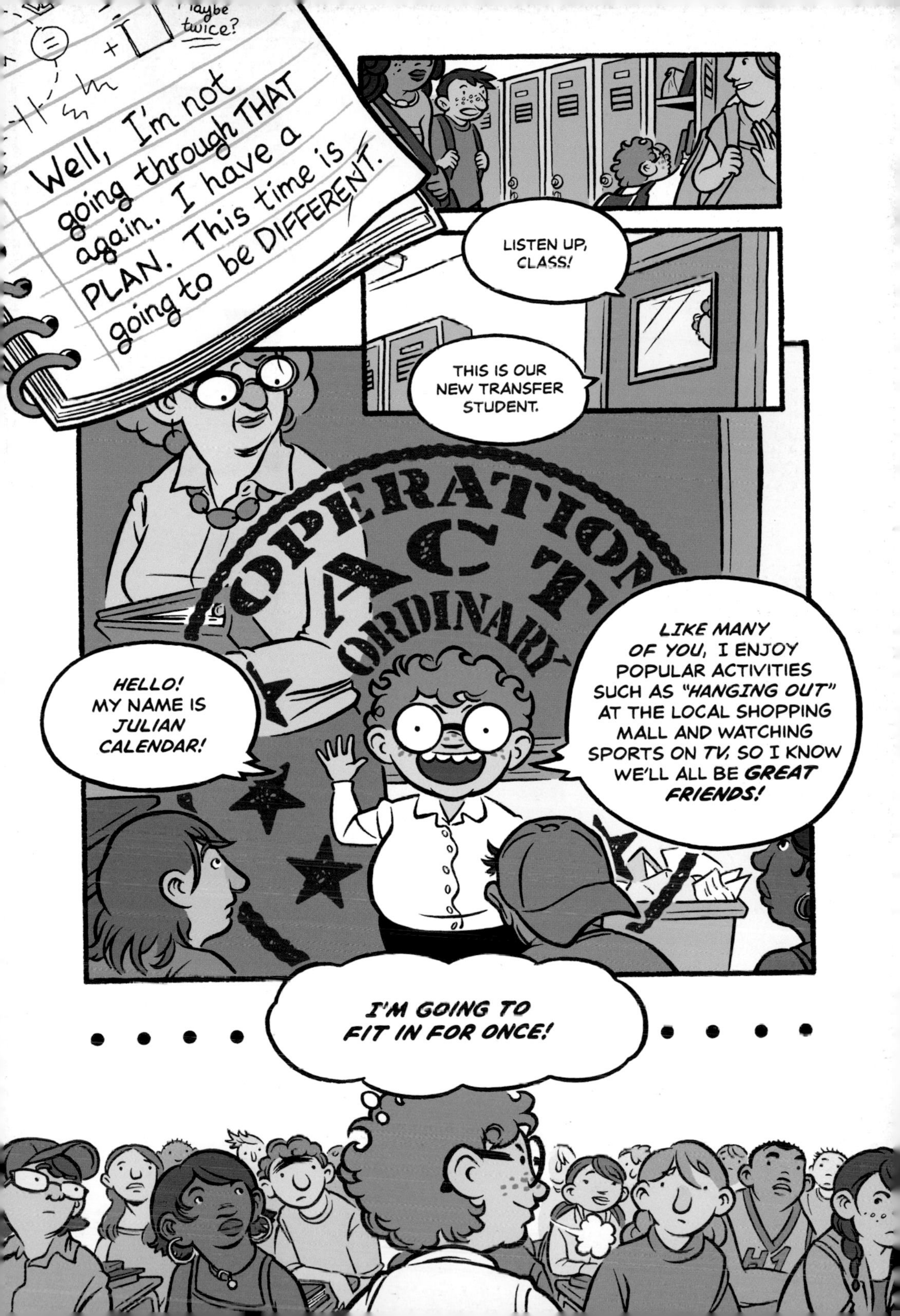
Maybe twice?
Well, I'm not going through THAT again. I have a PLAN. This time is going to be DIFFERENT.
LISTEN UP, CLASS!
THIS IS OUR NEW TRANSFER STUDENT.
OPERATION ACT ORDINARY
HELLO! MY NAME IS JULIAN CALENDAR!
LIKE MANY OF YOU, I ENJOY POPULAR ACTIVITIES SUCH AS "HANGING OUT" AT THE LOCAL SHOPPING MALL AND WATCHING SPORTS ON TV, SO I KNOW WE'LL ALL BE GREAT FRIENDS!
I'M GOING TO FIT IN FOR ONCE!

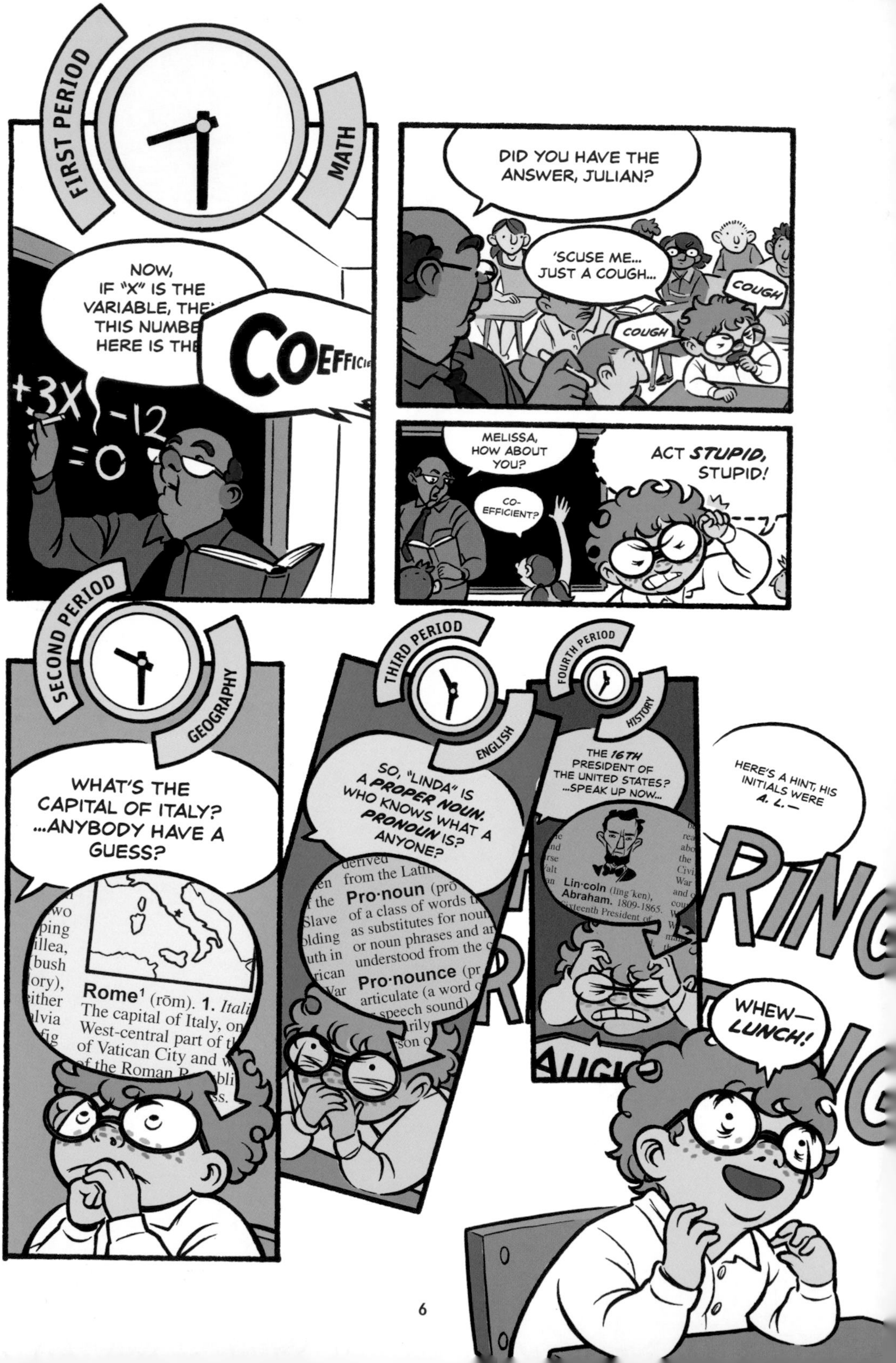
FIRST PERIOD
MATH
NOW, IF "X" IS THE VARIABLE, THEN THIS NUMBER HERE IS THE
COEFFICI
+3X -12 =0
DID YOU HAVE THE ANSWER, JULIAN?
'SCUSE ME... JUST A COUGH...
COUGH
COUGH
MELISSA, HOW ABOUT YOU?
CO-EFFICIENT?
ACT STUPID, STUPID!
SECOND PERIOD
GEOGRAPHY
WHAT'S THE CAPITAL OF ITALY? ...ANYBODY HAVE A GUESS?
Rome[1] (rōm). 1. Itali
The capital of Italy, on
West-central part of th
of Vatican City and w
of the Roman R
THIRD PERIOD
ENGLISH
SO, "LINDA" IS A PROPER NOUN. WHO KNOWS WHAT A PRONOUN IS? ANYONE?
derived
from the Latin
Pro·noun (prō
of a class of words t
as substitutes for noun
or noun phrases and ar
understood from the c
Pro·nounce (pr
articulate (a word o
speech sound)
FOURTH PERIOD
HISTORY
THE 16TH PRESIDENT OF THE UNITED STATES? ...SPEAK UP NOW...
Lin·coln (lĭng'kən), Abraham. 1809-1865. Sixteenth President of
HERE'S A HINT, HIS INITIALS WERE A. L.—
RING
WHEW— LUNCH!

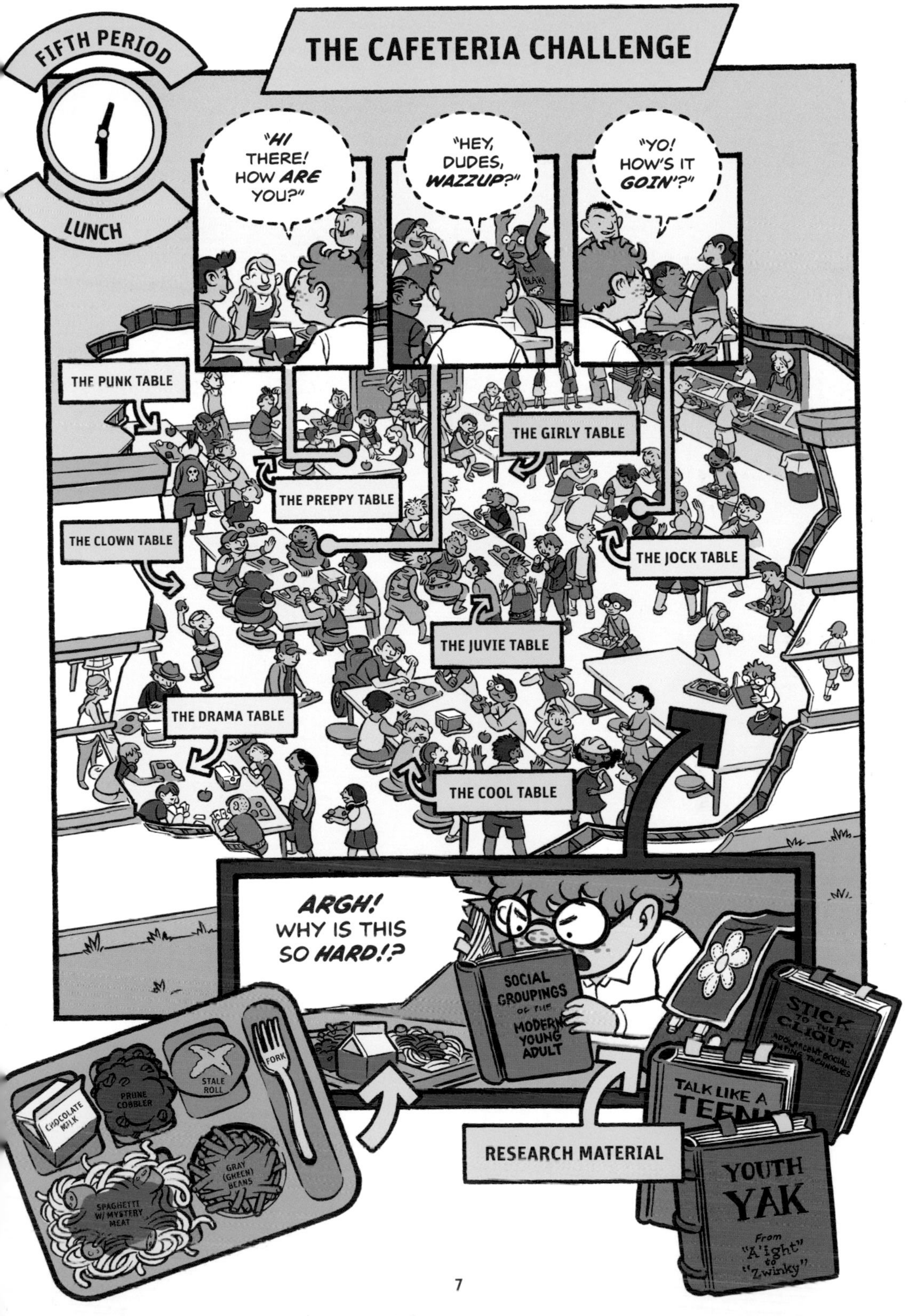
FIFTH PERIOD
LUNCH
THE CAFETERIA CHALLENGE
"HI THERE! HOW ARE YOU?"
"HEY, DUDES, WAZZUP?"
"YO! HOW'S IT GOIN'?"
THE PUNK TABLE
THE PREPPY TABLE
THE GIRLY TABLE
THE CLOWN TABLE
THE JOCK TABLE
THE JUVIE TABLE
THE DRAMA TABLE
THE COOL TABLE
ARGH! WHY IS THIS SO HARD!?
SOCIAL GROUPINGS OF THE MODERN YOUNG ADULT
STICK TO THE CLIQUE: ADOLESCENT SOCIAL BONDING TECHNIQUES
TALK LIKE A TEEN
YOUTH YAK From "A'ight" to "Zwinky"
RESEARCH MATERIAL
CHOCOLATE MILK
PRUNE COBBLER
STALE ROLL
FORK
GRAY (GREEN) BEANS
SPAGHETTI W/ MYSTERY MEAT

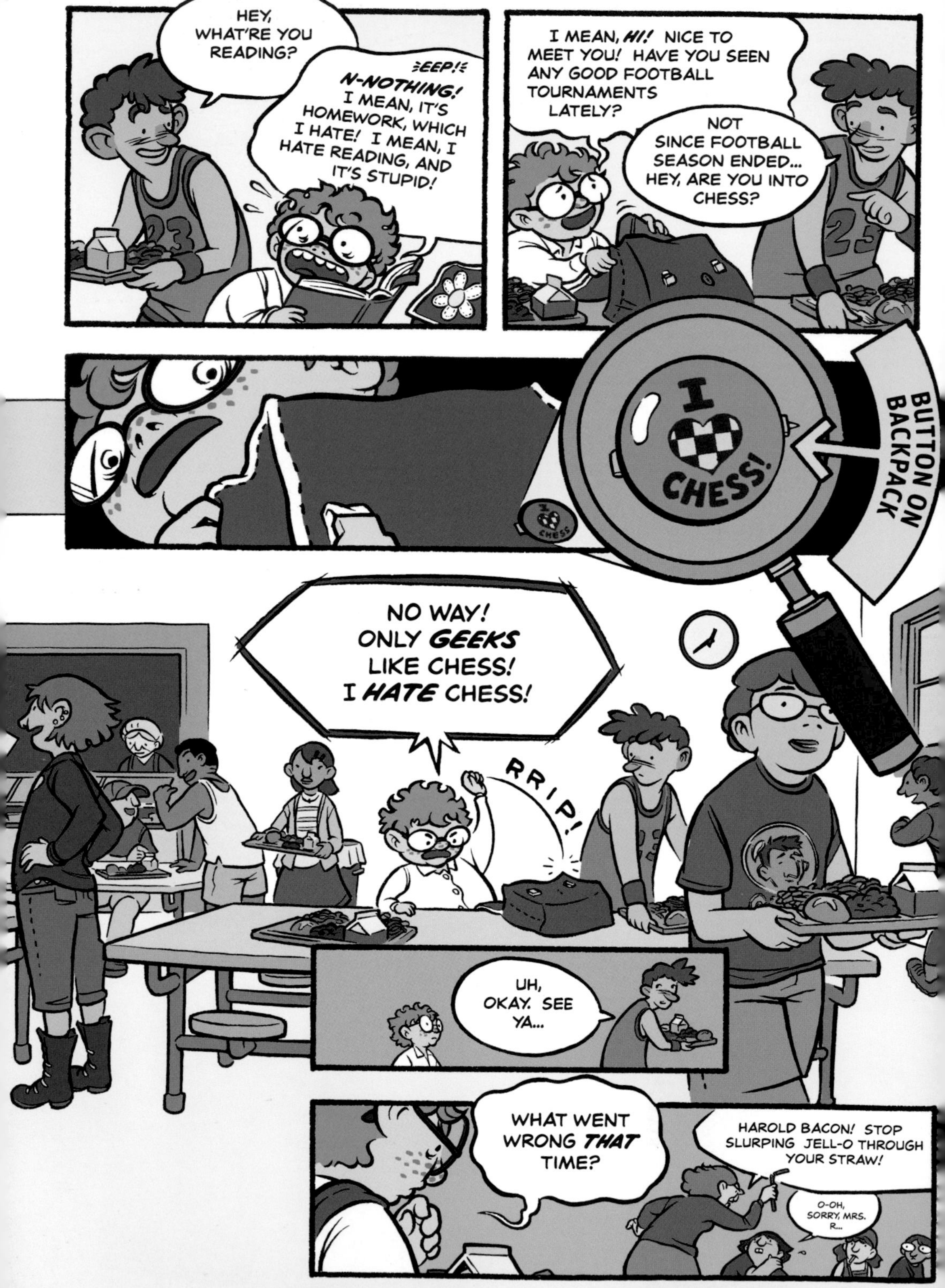
HEY, WHAT'RE YOU READING?
EEP!
N-NOTHING! I MEAN, IT'S HOMEWORK, WHICH I HATE! I MEAN, I HATE READING, AND IT'S STUPID!
I MEAN, HI! NICE TO MEET YOU! HAVE YOU SEEN ANY GOOD FOOTBALL TOURNAMENTS LATELY?
NOT SINCE FOOTBALL SEASON ENDED... HEY, ARE YOU INTO CHESS?
I ♥ CHESS!
BUTTON ON BACKPACK
NO WAY! ONLY GEEKS LIKE CHESS! I HATE CHESS!
RRIP!
UH, OKAY. SEE YA...
WHAT WENT WRONG THAT TIME?
HAROLD BACON! STOP SLURPING JELL-O THROUGH YOUR STRAW!
O-OH, SORRY, MRS. R...

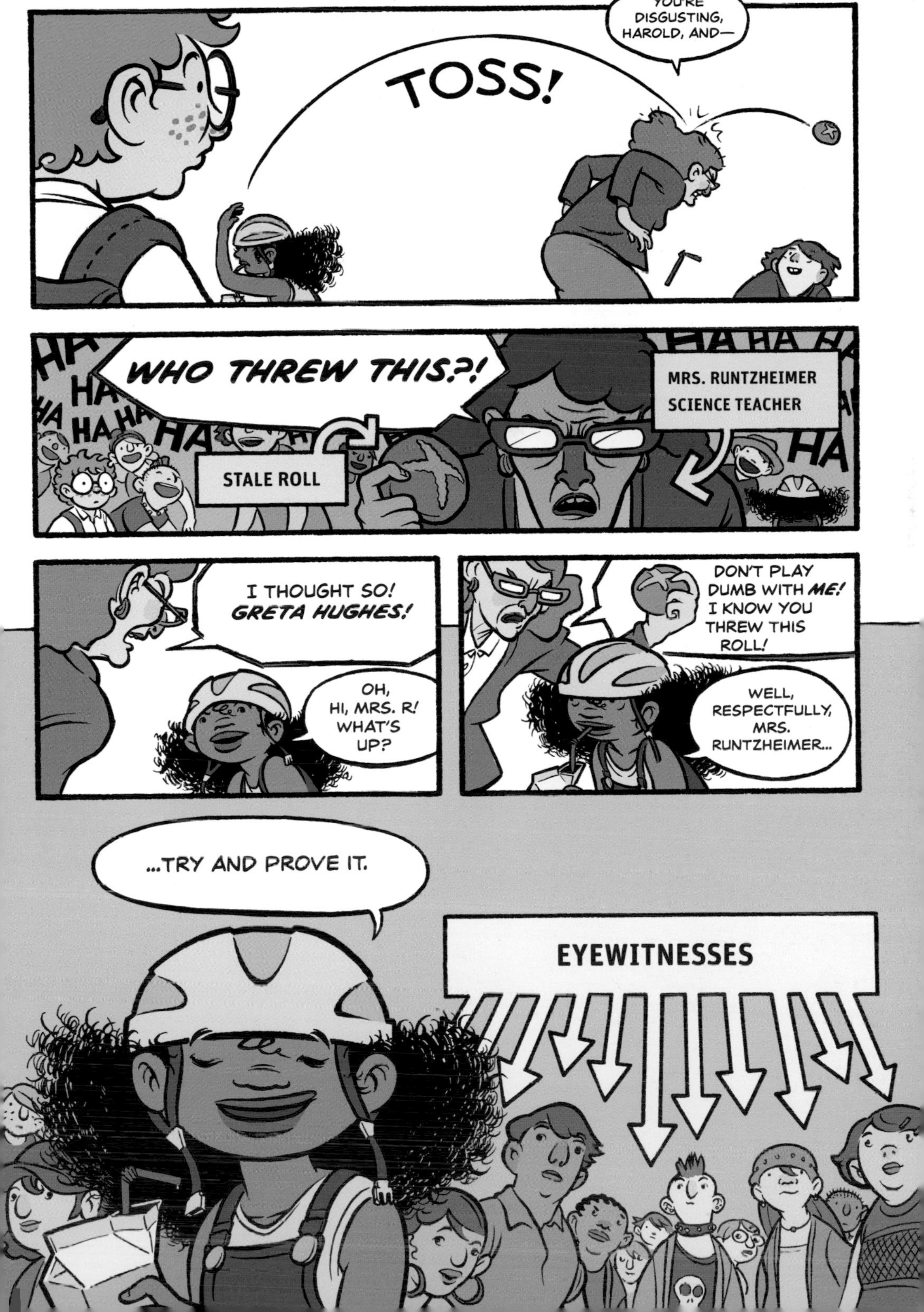

YOU'RE DISGUSTING, HAROLD, AND—
TOSS!
HA HA HA HA HA HA HA HA HA HA HA HA
WHO THREW THIS?!
MRS. RUNTZHEIMER
SCIENCE TEACHER
STALE ROLL
I THOUGHT SO! *GRETA HUGHES!*
OH, HI, MRS. R! WHAT'S UP?
DON'T PLAY DUMB WITH *ME!* I KNOW YOU THREW THIS ROLL!
WELL, RESPECTFULLY, MRS. RUNTZHEIMER...
...TRY AND PROVE IT.
EYEWITNESSES

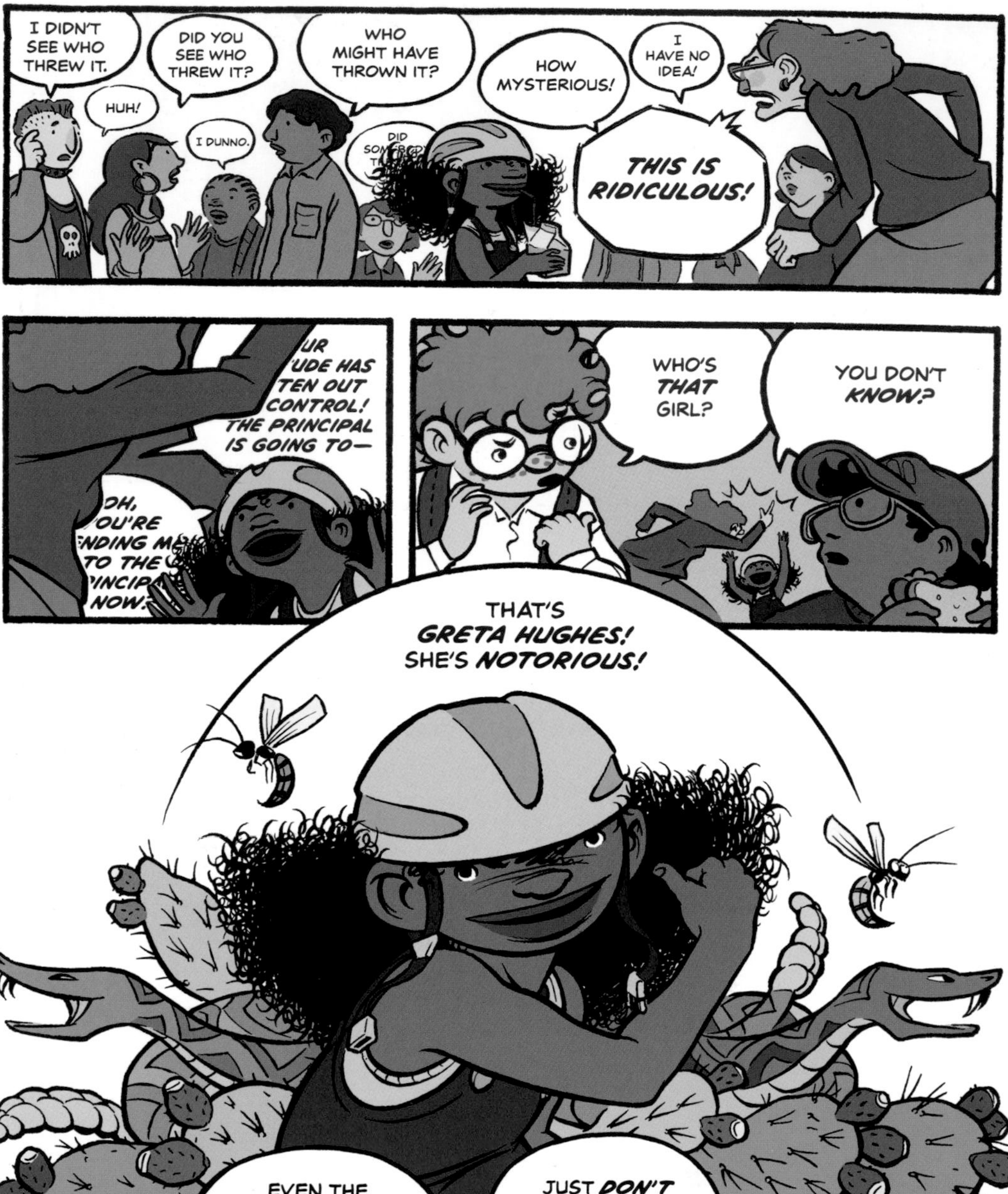
I DIDN'T SEE WHO THREW IT.
HUH!
DID YOU SEE WHO THREW IT?
I DUNNO.
WHO MIGHT HAVE THROWN IT?
DID
HOW MYSTERIOUS!
I HAVE NO IDEA!
THIS IS RIDICULOUS!
UR
UDE HAS
TEN OUT
CONTROL!
THE PRINCIPAL IS GOING TO—
OH,
OU'RE
NDING M
TO THE
INCIP
NOW.
WHO'S THAT GIRL?
YOU DON'T KNOW?
THAT'S GRETA HUGHES! SHE'S NOTORIOUS!
EVEN THE TEACHERS ARE AFRAID OF HER!
JUST DON'T GET ON HER BAD SIDE!

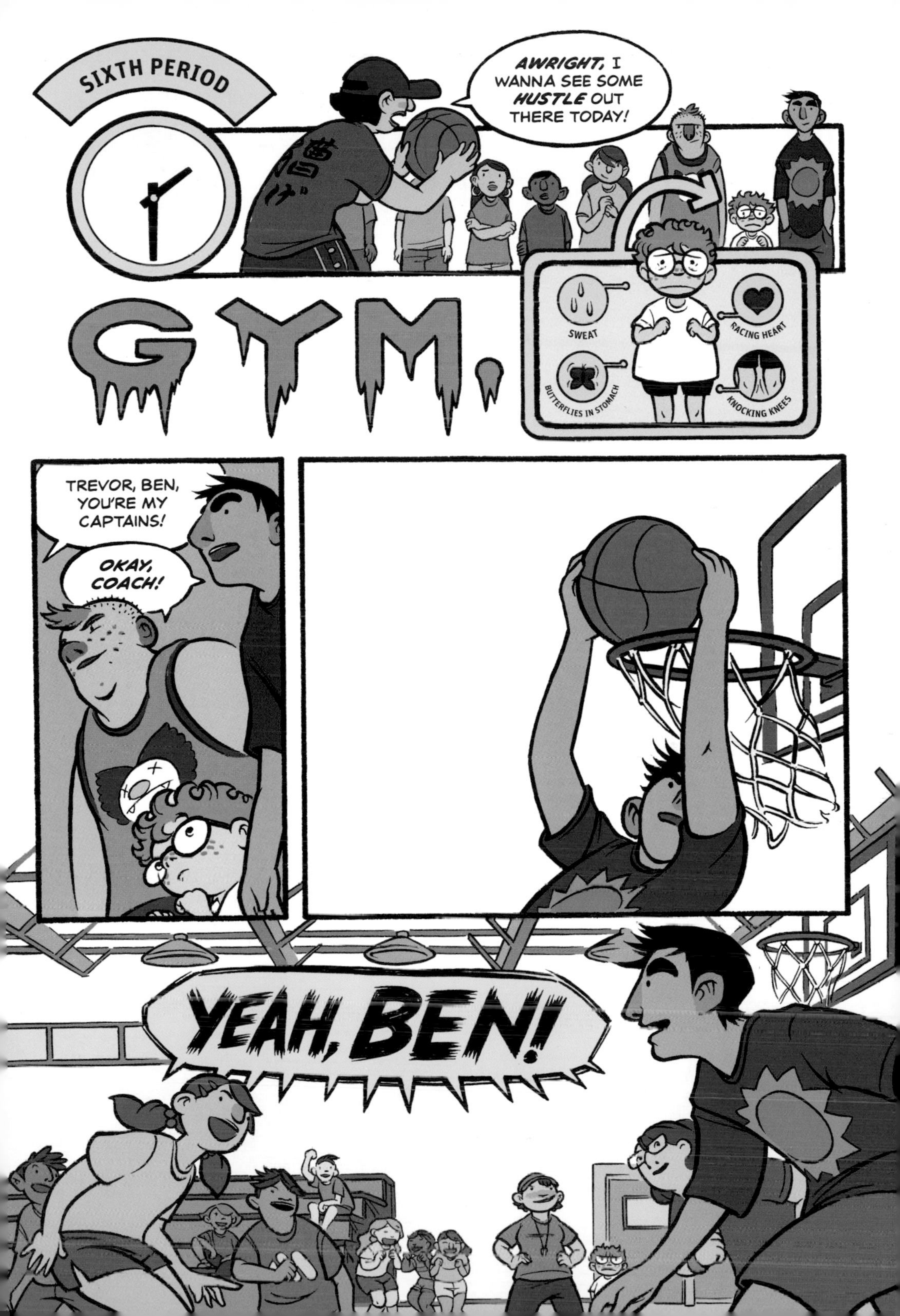
SIXTH PERIOD
AWRIGHT, I WANNA SEE SOME HUSTLE OUT THERE TODAY!
GYM.
SWEAT
RACING HEART
BUTTERFLIES IN STOMACH
KNOCKING KNEES
TREVOR, BEN, YOU'RE MY CAPTAINS!
OKAY, COACH!
YEAH, BEN!

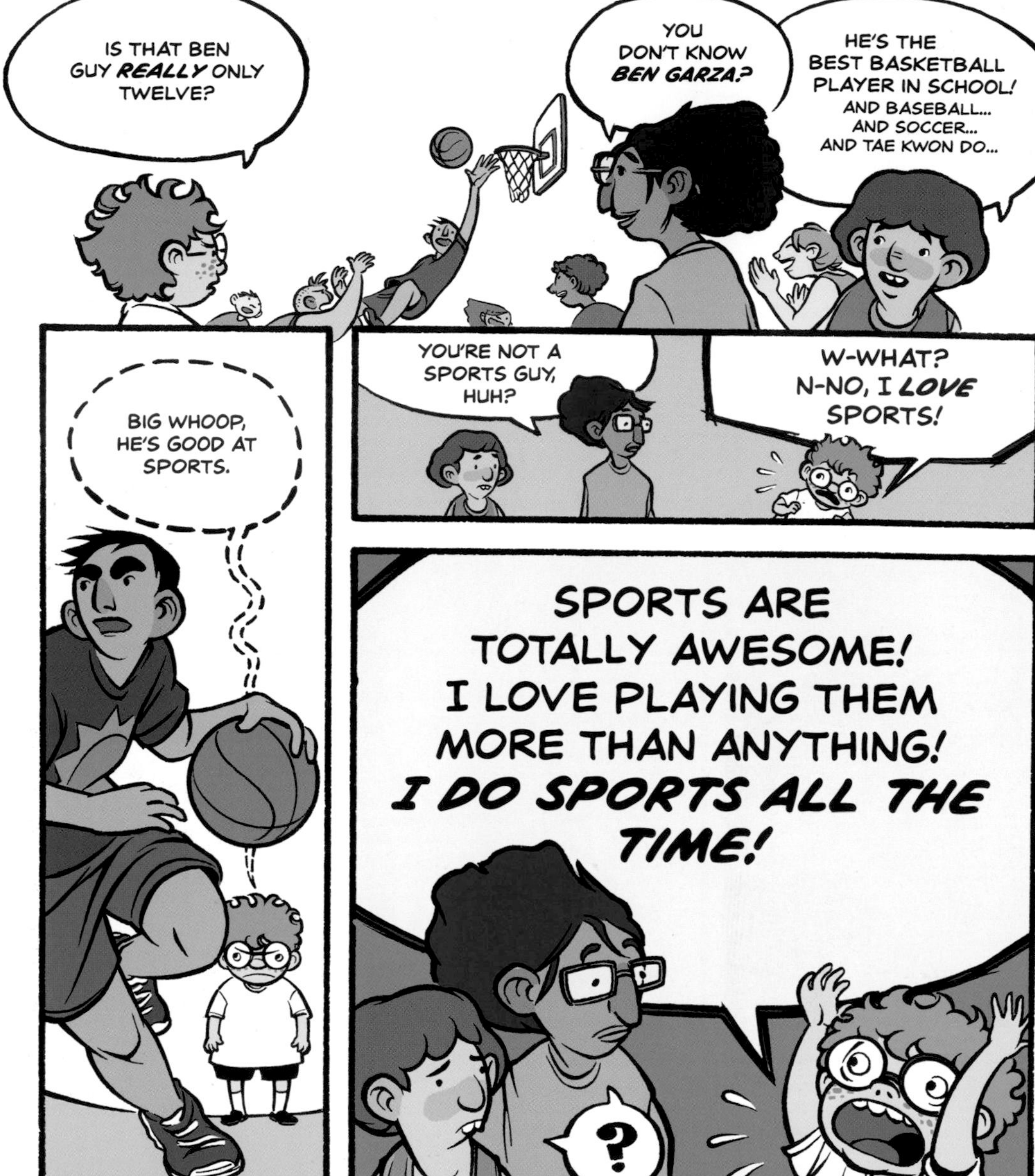
IS THAT BEN GUY *REALLY* ONLY TWELVE?
YOU DON'T KNOW *BEN GARZA?*
HE'S THE BEST BASKETBALL PLAYER IN SCHOOL! AND BASEBALL... AND SOCCER... AND TAE KWON DO...
BIG WHOOP, HE'S GOOD AT SPORTS.
YOU'RE NOT A SPORTS GUY, HUH?
W-WHAT? N-NO, I *LOVE* SPORTS!
SPORTS ARE TOTALLY AWESOME! I LOVE PLAYING THEM MORE THAN ANYTHING! *I DO SPORTS ALL THE TIME!*
?
OKAY, CALENDAR, GET IN THERE!
AHH NO!

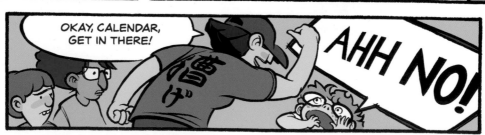

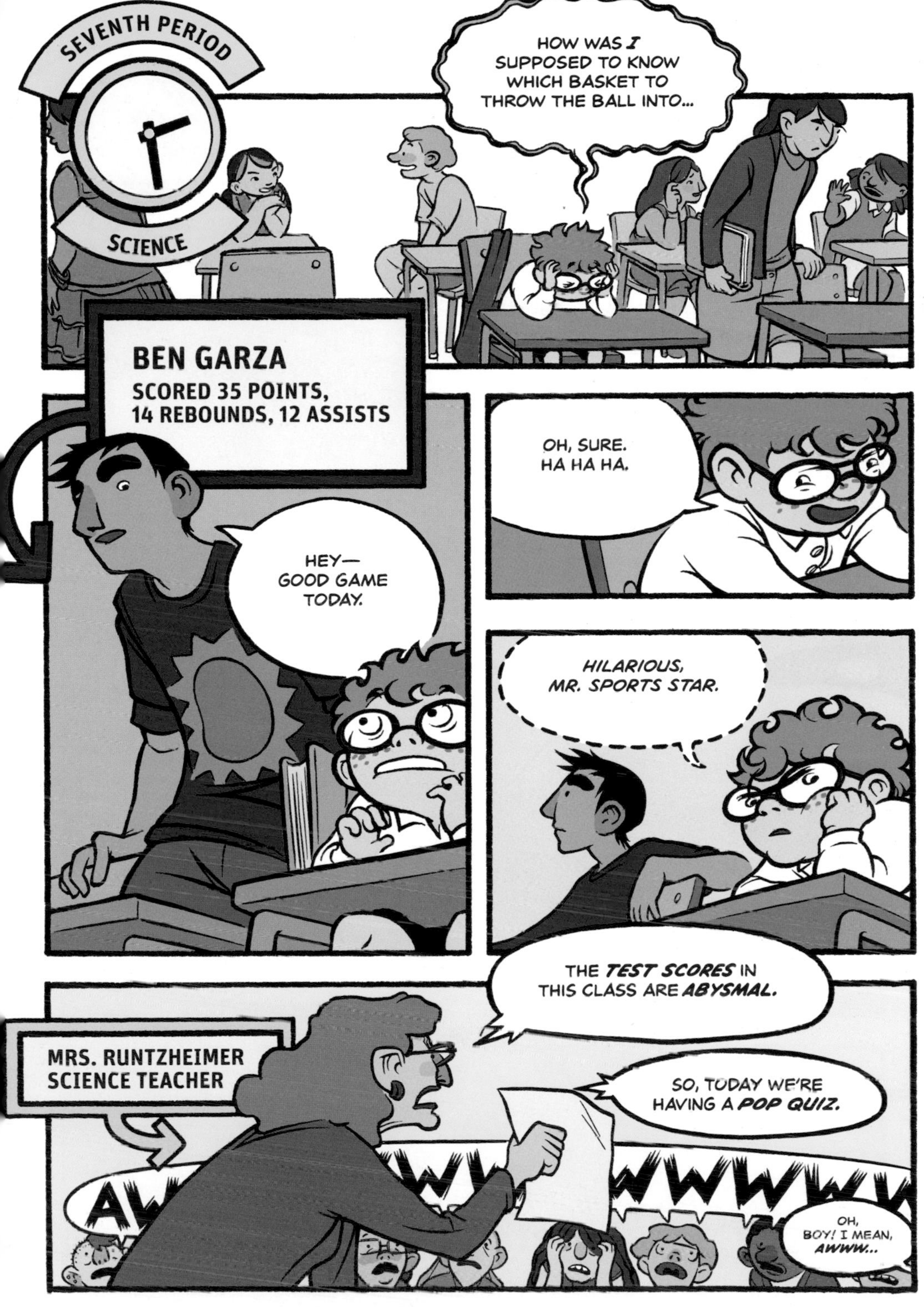
SEVENTH PERIOD
SCIENCE
HOW WAS *I* SUPPOSED TO KNOW WHICH BASKET TO THROW THE BALL INTO...
BEN GARZA
SCORED 35 POINTS, 14 REBOUNDS, 12 ASSISTS
HEY— GOOD GAME TODAY.
OH, SURE. HA HA HA.
HILARIOUS, MR. SPORTS STAR.
THE ***TEST SCORES*** IN THIS CLASS ARE ***ABYSMAL.***
MRS. RUNTZHEIMER
SCIENCE TEACHER
SO, TODAY WE'RE HAVING A ***POP QUIZ.***
AW
WWWWWWW
OH, BOY! I MEAN, ***AWWW...***

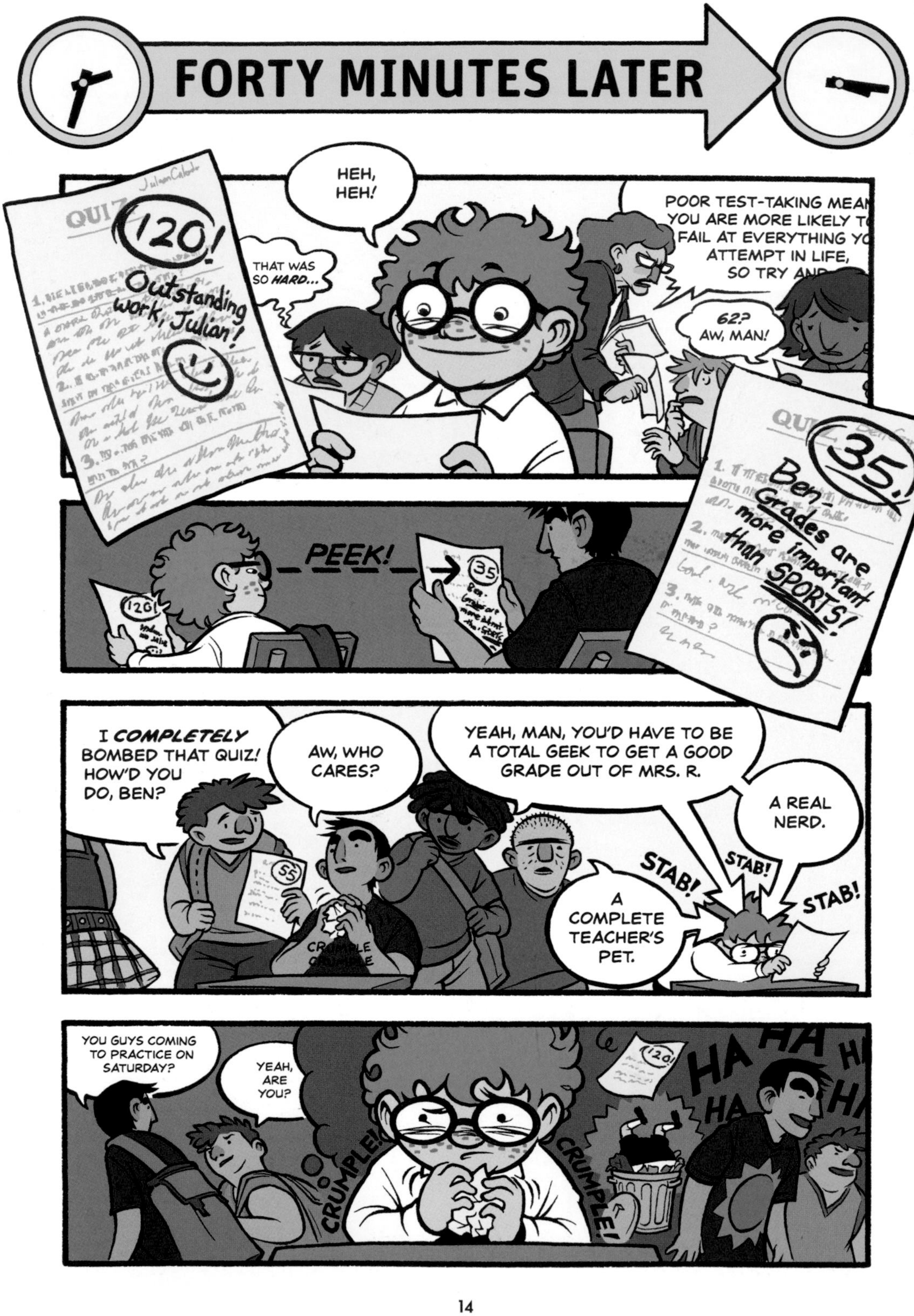

FORTY MINUTES LATER
HEH, HEH!
THAT WAS SO HARD...
QUIZ
120!
Outstanding work, Julian!
POOR TEST-TAKING MEAN
YOU ARE MORE LIKELY T
FAIL AT EVERYTHING YO
ATTEMPT IN LIFE,
SO TRY AN
62? AW, MAN!
35.
Ben- Grades are more important than SPORTS!
PEEK!
I COMPLETELY BOMBED THAT QUIZ! HOW'D YOU DO, BEN?
AW, WHO CARES?
YEAH, MAN, YOU'D HAVE TO BE A TOTAL GEEK TO GET A GOOD GRADE OUT OF MRS. R.
A REAL NERD.
A COMPLETE TEACHER'S PET.
STAB!
STAB!
STAB!
YOU GUYS COMING TO PRACTICE ON SATURDAY?
YEAH, ARE YOU?
CRUMPLE!
CRUMPLE!
HA HA HA HA

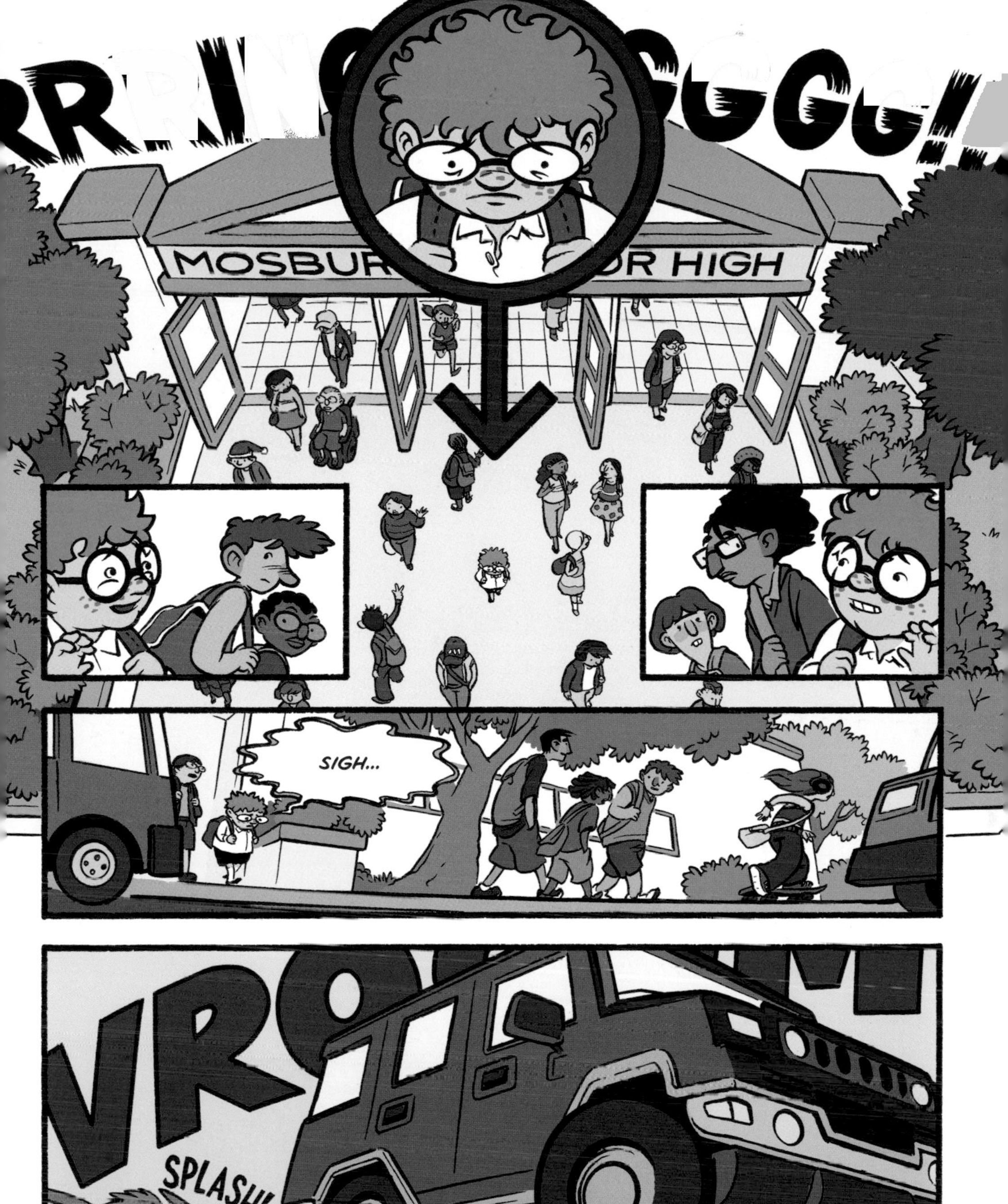
SIGH...
SPLASH!

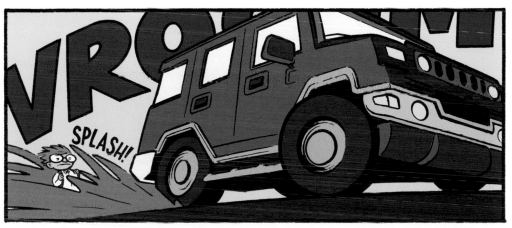

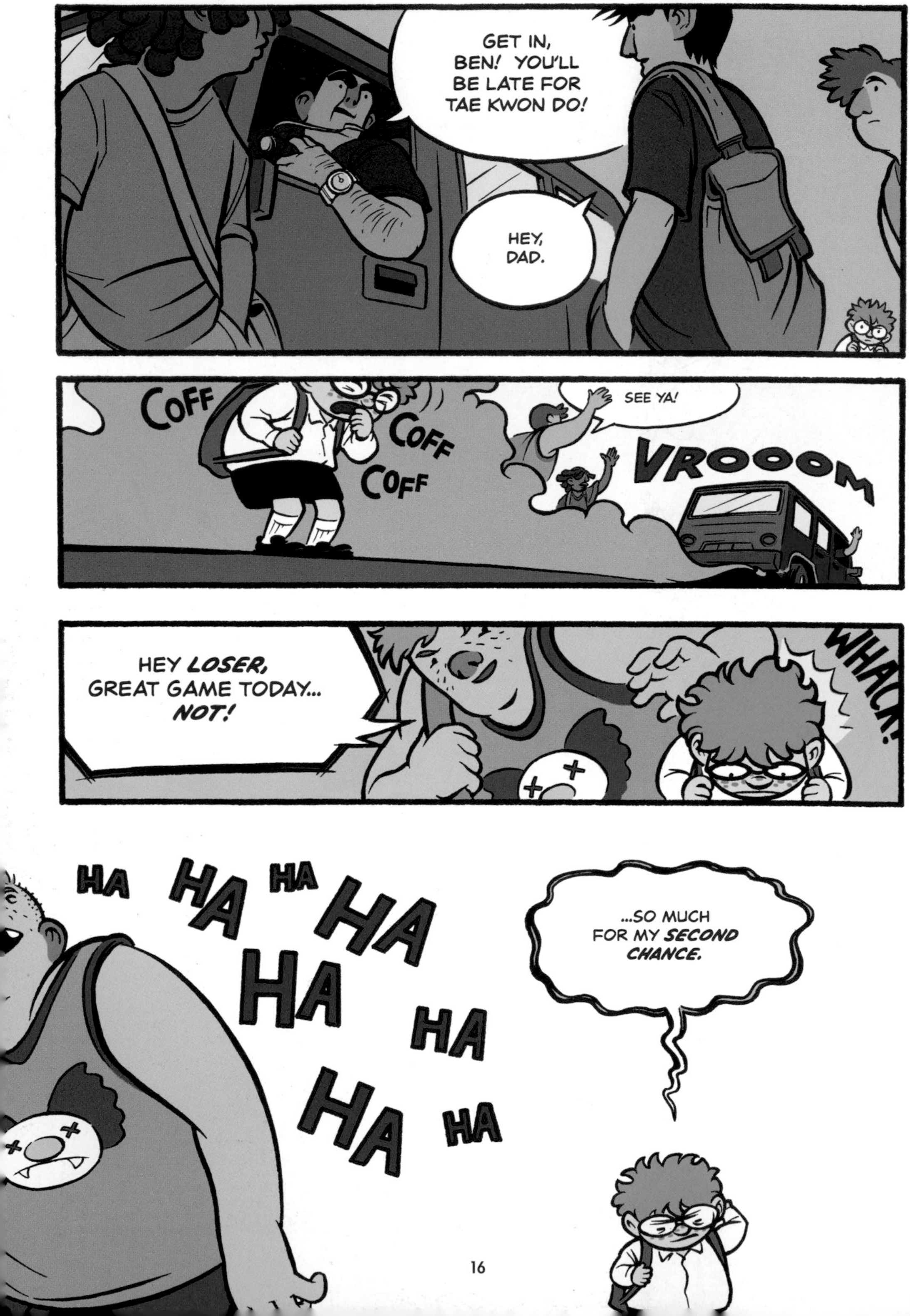
GET IN, BEN! YOU'LL BE LATE FOR TAE KWON DO!
HEY, DAD.
COFF
COFF
COFF
SEE YA!
VROOOM
HEY *LOSER,* GREAT GAME TODAY... *NOT!*
WHACK!
HA HA HA HA HA HA HA HA
...SO MUCH FOR MY *SECOND CHANCE.*

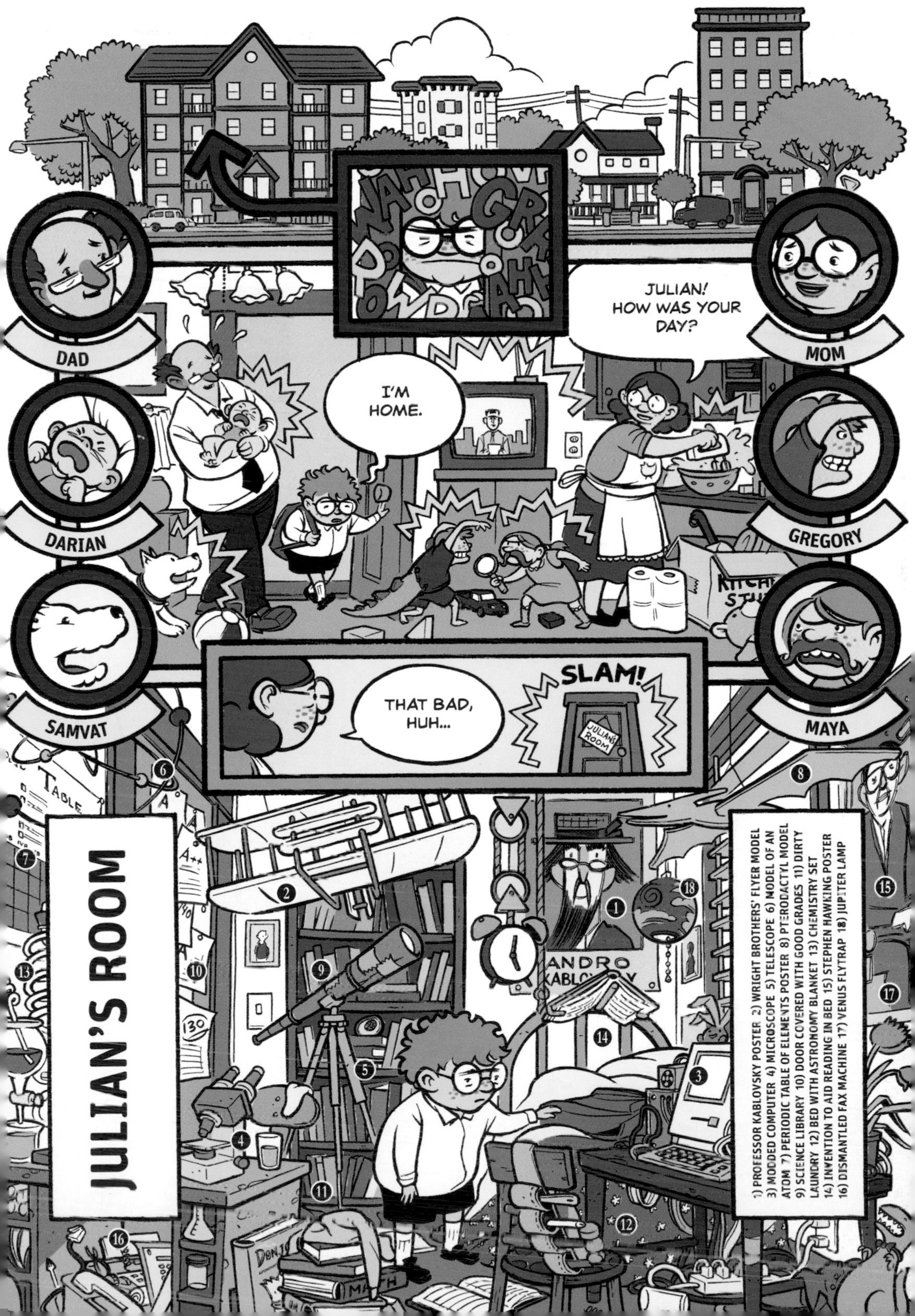
DAD
MOM
JULIAN! HOW WAS YOUR DAY?
I'M HOME.
DARIAN
GREGORY
SAMVAT
MAYA
THAT BAD, HUH...
SLAM!
JULIAN'S ROOM
JULIAN'S ROOM
1) PROFESSOR KABLOVSKY POSTER 2) WRIGHT BROTHERS' FLYER MODEL 3) MODDED COMPUTER 4) MICROSCOPE 5) TELESCOPE 6) MODEL OF AN ATOM 7) PERIODIC TABLE OF ELEMENTS POSTER 8) PTERODACTYL MODEL 9) SCIENCE LIBRARY 10) DOOR COVERED WITH GOOD GRADES 11) DIRTY LAUNDRY 12) BED WITH ASTRONOMY BLANKET 13) CHEMISTRY SET 14) INVENTION TO AID READING IN BED 15) STEPHEN HAWKING POSTER 16) DISMANTLED FAX MACHINE 17) VENUS FLYTRAP 18) JUPITER LAMP

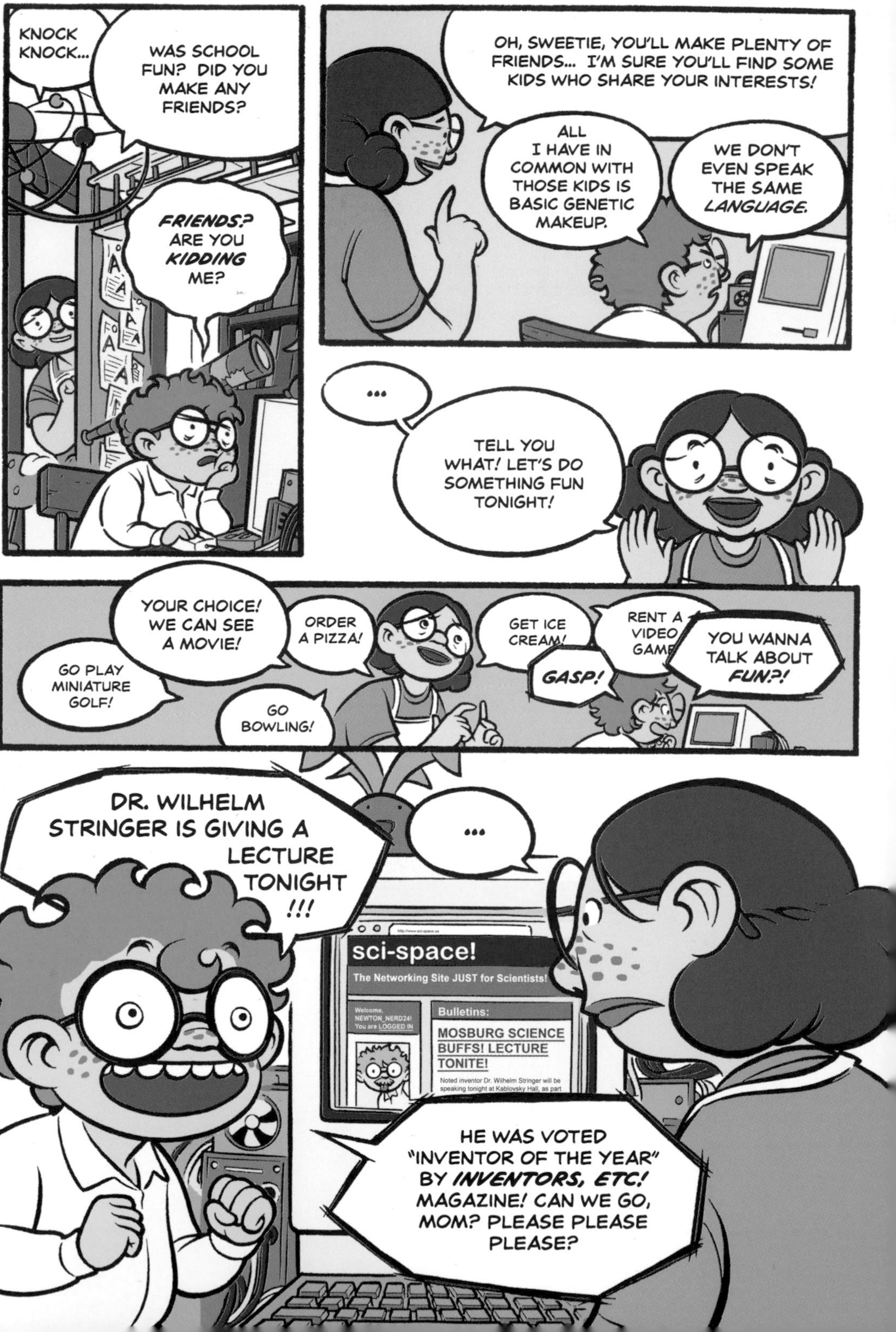

KNOCK KNOCK...
WAS SCHOOL FUN? DID YOU MAKE ANY FRIENDS?
FRIENDS? ARE YOU KIDDING ME?
OH, SWEETIE, YOU'LL MAKE PLENTY OF FRIENDS... I'M SURE YOU'LL FIND SOME KIDS WHO SHARE YOUR INTERESTS!
ALL I HAVE IN COMMON WITH THOSE KIDS IS BASIC GENETIC MAKEUP.
WE DON'T EVEN SPEAK THE SAME LANGUAGE.
...
TELL YOU WHAT! LET'S DO SOMETHING FUN TONIGHT!
YOUR CHOICE! WE CAN SEE A MOVIE!
GO PLAY MINIATURE GOLF!
ORDER A PIZZA!
GO BOWLING!
GET ICE CREAM!
RENT A VIDEO GAME
GASP!
YOU WANNA TALK ABOUT FUN?!
DR. WILHELM STRINGER IS GIVING A LECTURE TONIGHT !!!
...
sci-space!
The Networking Site JUST for Scientists!
Welcome, NEWTON_NERD24! You are LOGGED IN
Bulletins:
MOSBURG SCIENCE BUFFS! LECTURE TONITE!
Noted inventor Dr. Wilhelm Stringer will be speaking tonight at Kablovsky Hall, as part
HE WAS VOTED "INVENTOR OF THE YEAR" BY INVENTORS, ETC! MAGAZINE! CAN WE GO, MOM? PLEASE PLEASE PLEASE?

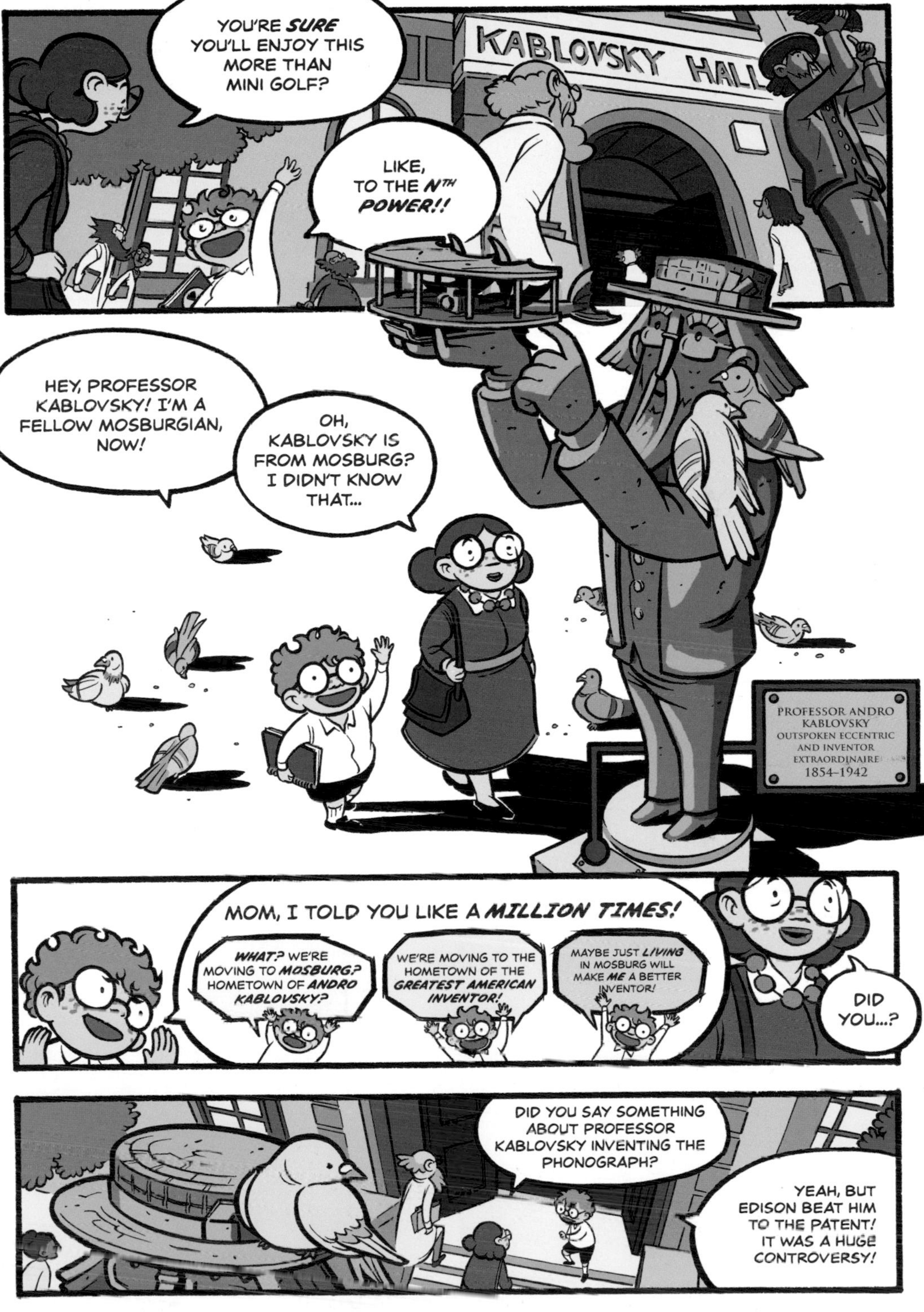
KABLOVSKY HALL
YOU'RE **SURE** YOU'LL ENJOY THIS MORE THAN MINI GOLF?
LIKE, TO THE N^{TH} **POWER!!**
HEY, PROFESSOR KABLOVSKY! I'M A FELLOW MOSBURGIAN, NOW!
OH, KABLOVSKY IS FROM MOSBURG? I DIDN'T KNOW THAT...
PROFESSOR ANDRO KABLOVSKY OUTSPOKEN ECCENTRIC AND INVENTOR EXTRAORDINAIRE 1854–1942
MOM, I TOLD YOU LIKE A **MILLION TIMES!**
WHAT? WE'RE MOVING TO **MOSBURG?** HOMETOWN OF **ANDRO KABLOVSKY?**
WE'RE MOVING TO THE HOMETOWN OF THE **GREATEST AMERICAN INVENTOR!**
MAYBE JUST **LIVING** IN MOSBURG WILL MAKE **ME** A BETTER INVENTOR!
DID YOU...?
DID YOU SAY SOMETHING ABOUT PROFESSOR KABLOVSKY INVENTING THE PHONOGRAPH?
YEAH, BUT EDISON BEAT HIM TO THE PATENT! IT WAS A HUGE CONTROVERSY!

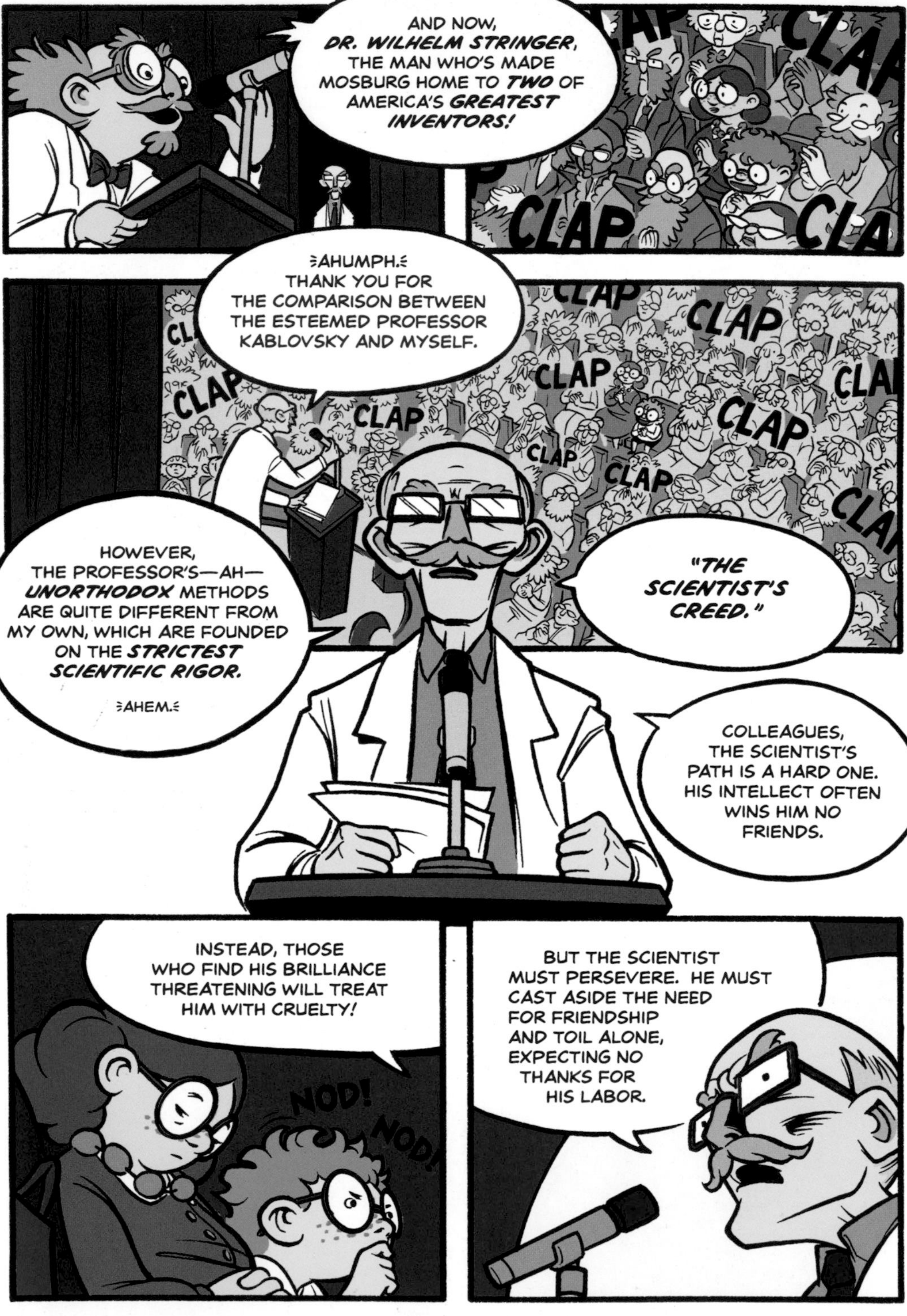
AND NOW, *DR. WILHELM STRINGER*, THE MAN WHO'S MADE MOSBURG HOME TO *TWO* OF AMERICA'S *GREATEST INVENTORS!*
CLAP CLAP CLAP CLAP
AHUMPH. THANK YOU FOR THE COMPARISON BETWEEN THE ESTEEMED PROFESSOR KABLOVSKY AND MYSELF.
CLAP CLAP CLAP CLAP CLAP CLAP CLAP
HOWEVER, THE PROFESSOR'S—AH— *UNORTHODOX* METHODS ARE QUITE DIFFERENT FROM MY OWN, WHICH ARE FOUNDED ON THE *STRICTEST SCIENTIFIC RIGOR.*
AHEM.
"THE SCIENTIST'S CREED."
COLLEAGUES, THE SCIENTIST'S PATH IS A HARD ONE. HIS INTELLECT OFTEN WINS HIM NO FRIENDS.
INSTEAD, THOSE WHO FIND HIS BRILLIANCE THREATENING WILL TREAT HIM WITH CRUELTY!
NOD! NOD!
BUT THE SCIENTIST MUST PERSEVERE. HE MUST CAST ASIDE THE NEED FOR FRIENDSHIP AND TOIL ALONE, EXPECTING NO THANKS FOR HIS LABOR.

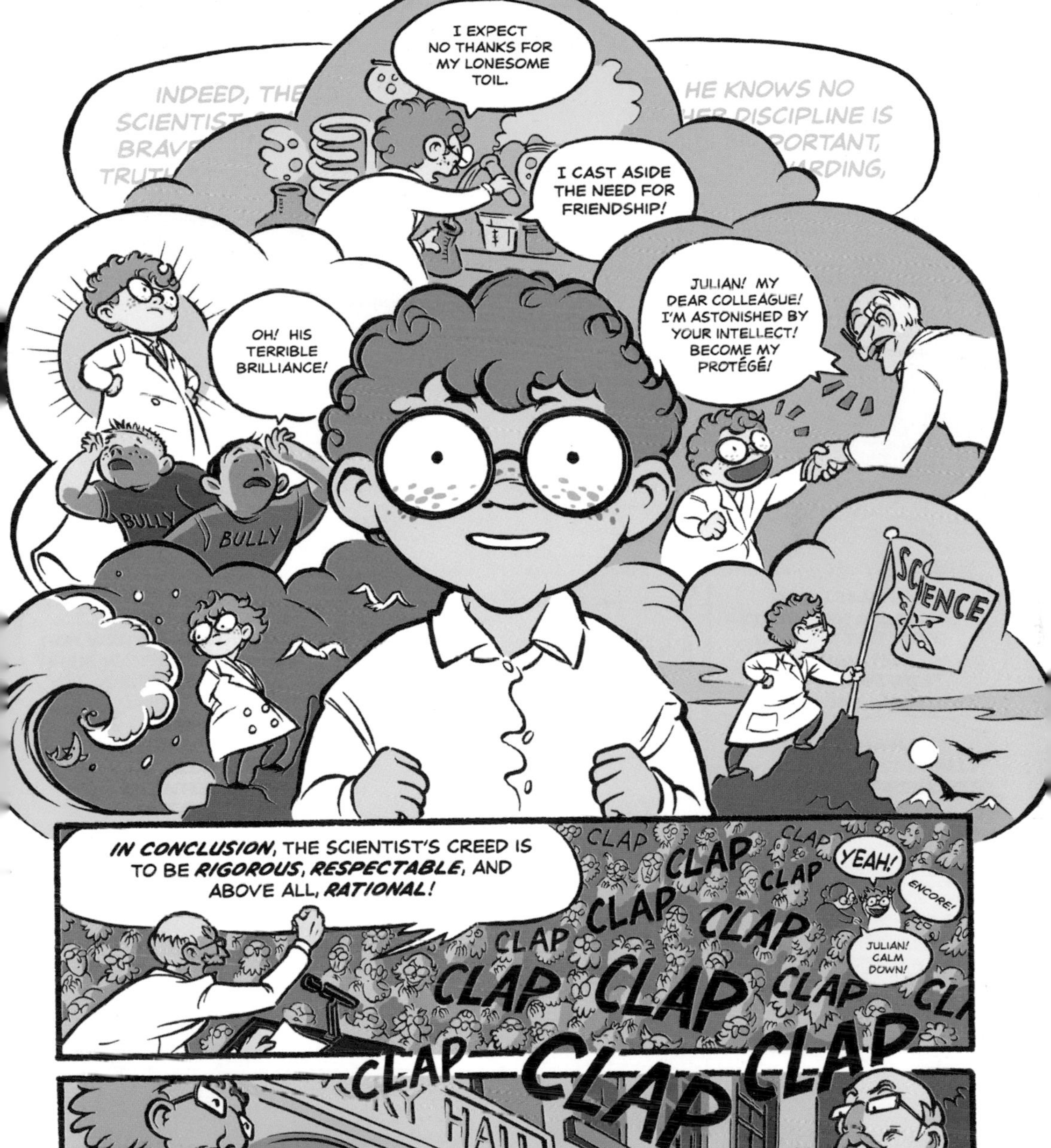
INDEED, THE
I EXPECT NO THANKS FOR MY LONESOME TOIL.
HE KNOWS NO
I CAST ASIDE THE NEED FOR FRIENDSHIP!
OH! HIS TERRIBLE BRILLIANCE!
BULLY
BULLY
JULIAN! MY DEAR COLLEAGUE! I'M ASTONISHED BY YOUR INTELLECT! BECOME MY PROTÉGÉ!
SCIENCE
IN CONCLUSION, THE SCIENTIST'S CREED IS TO BE RIGOROUS, RESPECTABLE, AND ABOVE ALL, RATIONAL!
CLAP CLAP CLAP CLAP CLAP CLAP CLAP CLAP CLAP CLAP
YEAH!
ENCORE!
JULIAN! CALM DOWN!
CLAP CLAP CLAP
HALL
DR. STRINGER!
DR. STRINGER

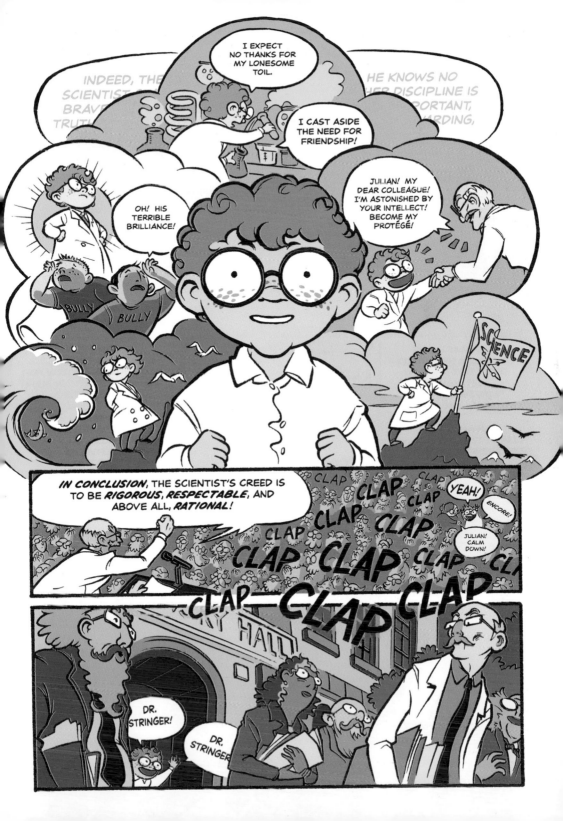

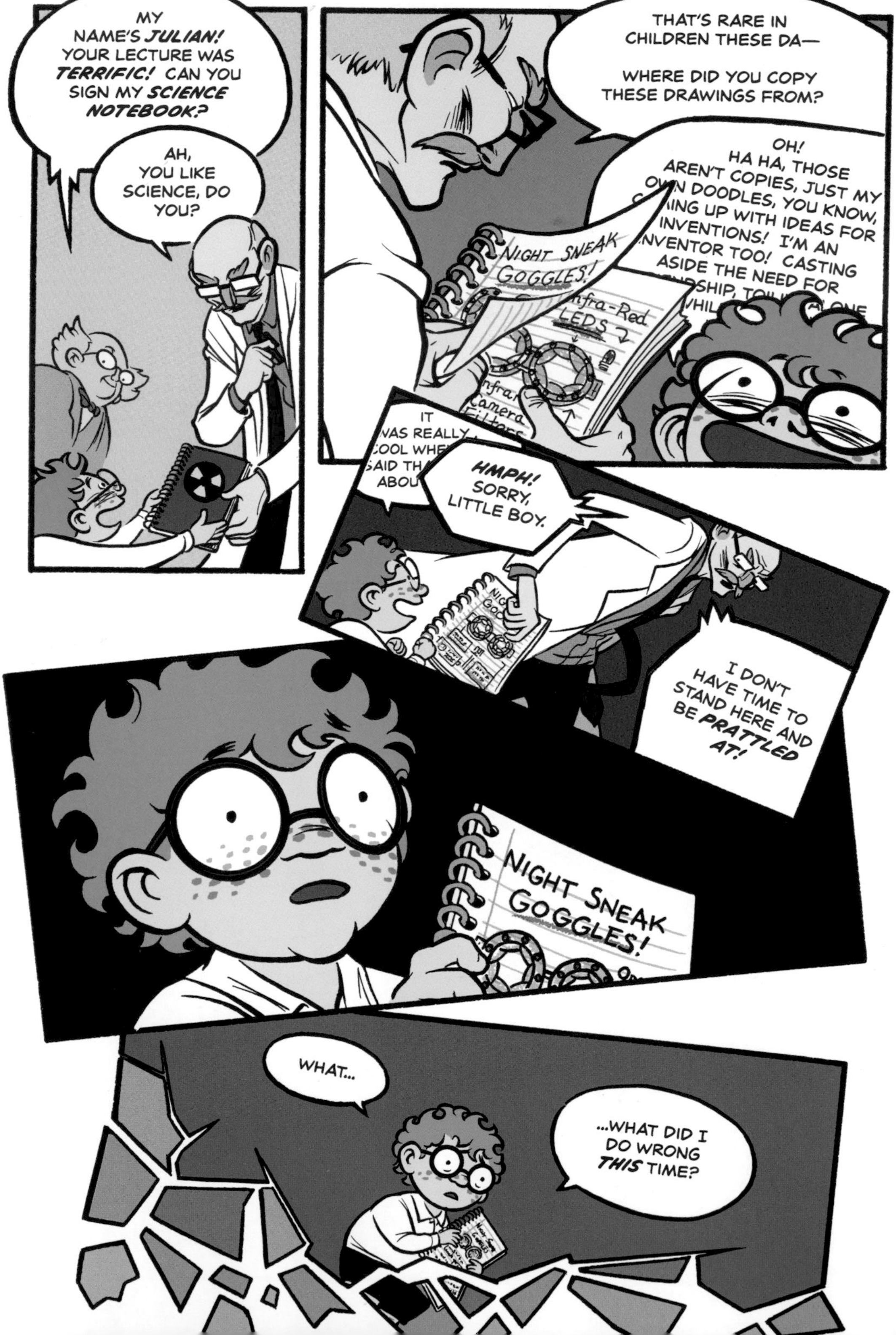
MY NAME'S ***JULIAN!*** YOUR LECTURE WAS ***TERRIFIC!*** CAN YOU SIGN MY ***SCIENCE NOTEBOOK?***
AH, YOU LIKE SCIENCE, DO YOU?
THAT'S RARE IN CHILDREN THESE DA—
WHERE DID YOU COPY THESE DRAWINGS FROM?
OH!
HA HA, THOSE
AREN'T COPIES, JUST MY
INVENTIONS! I'M AN
INVENTOR TOO! CASTING
ASIDE THE NEED FOR
NIGHT SNEAK GOGGLES!
LEDS
IT
HMPH! SORRY, LITTLE BOY.
I DON'T HAVE TIME TO STAND HERE AND BE ***PRATTLED AT!***
NIGHT SNEAK GOGGLES!
WHAT...
...WHAT DID I DO WRONG ***THIS*** TIME?

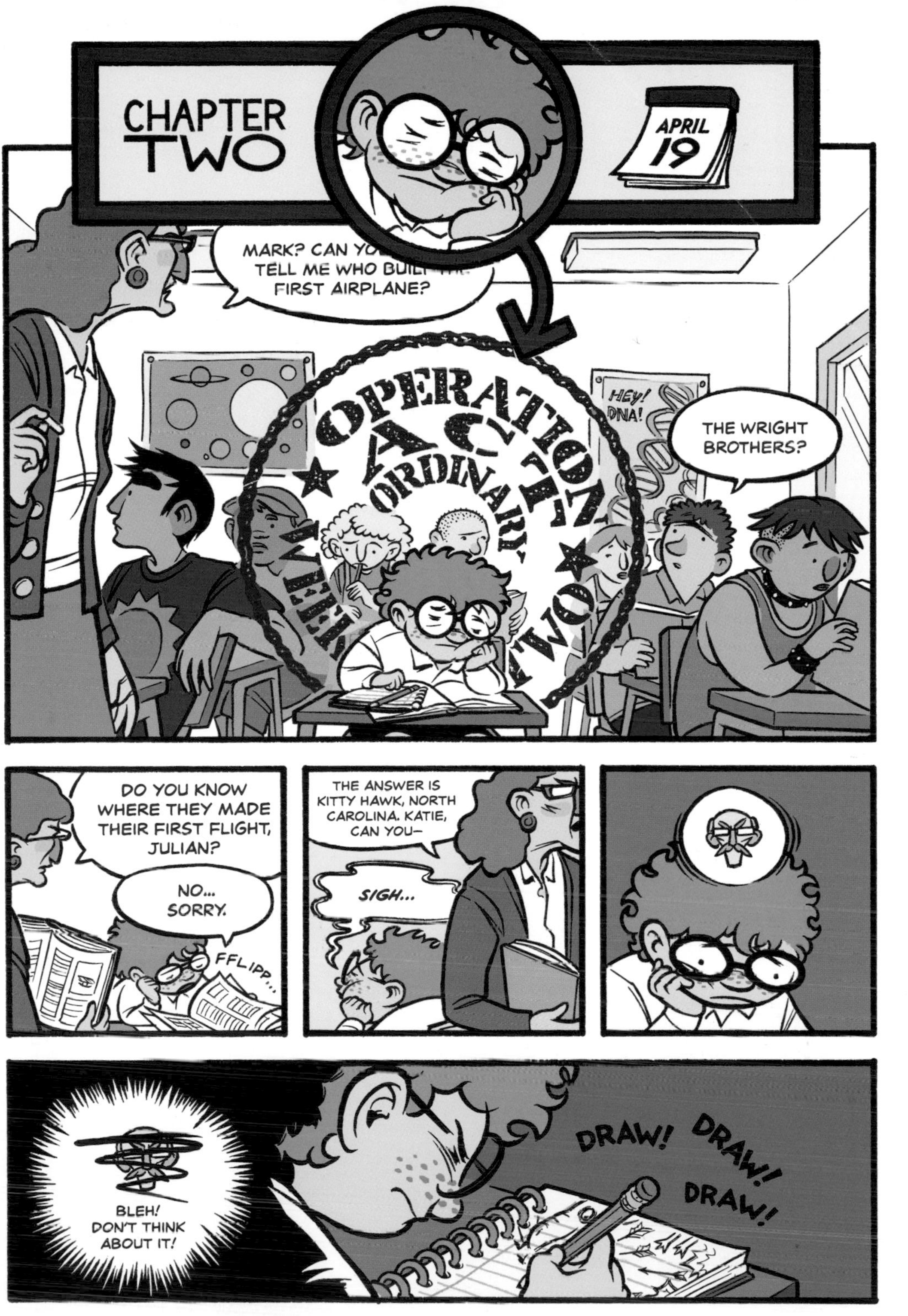
CHAPTER TWO
APRIL 19
MARK? CAN YOU TELL ME WHO BUILT THE FIRST AIRPLANE?
OPERATION ACT ORDINARY
WEEK TWO
HEY! DNA!
THE WRIGHT BROTHERS?
DO YOU KNOW WHERE THEY MADE THEIR FIRST FLIGHT, JULIAN?
NO... SORRY.
FFLIPP...
THE ANSWER IS KITTY HAWK, NORTH CAROLINA. KATIE, CAN YOU—
SIGH...
BLEH! DON'T THINK ABOUT IT!
DRAW! DRAW! DRAW!

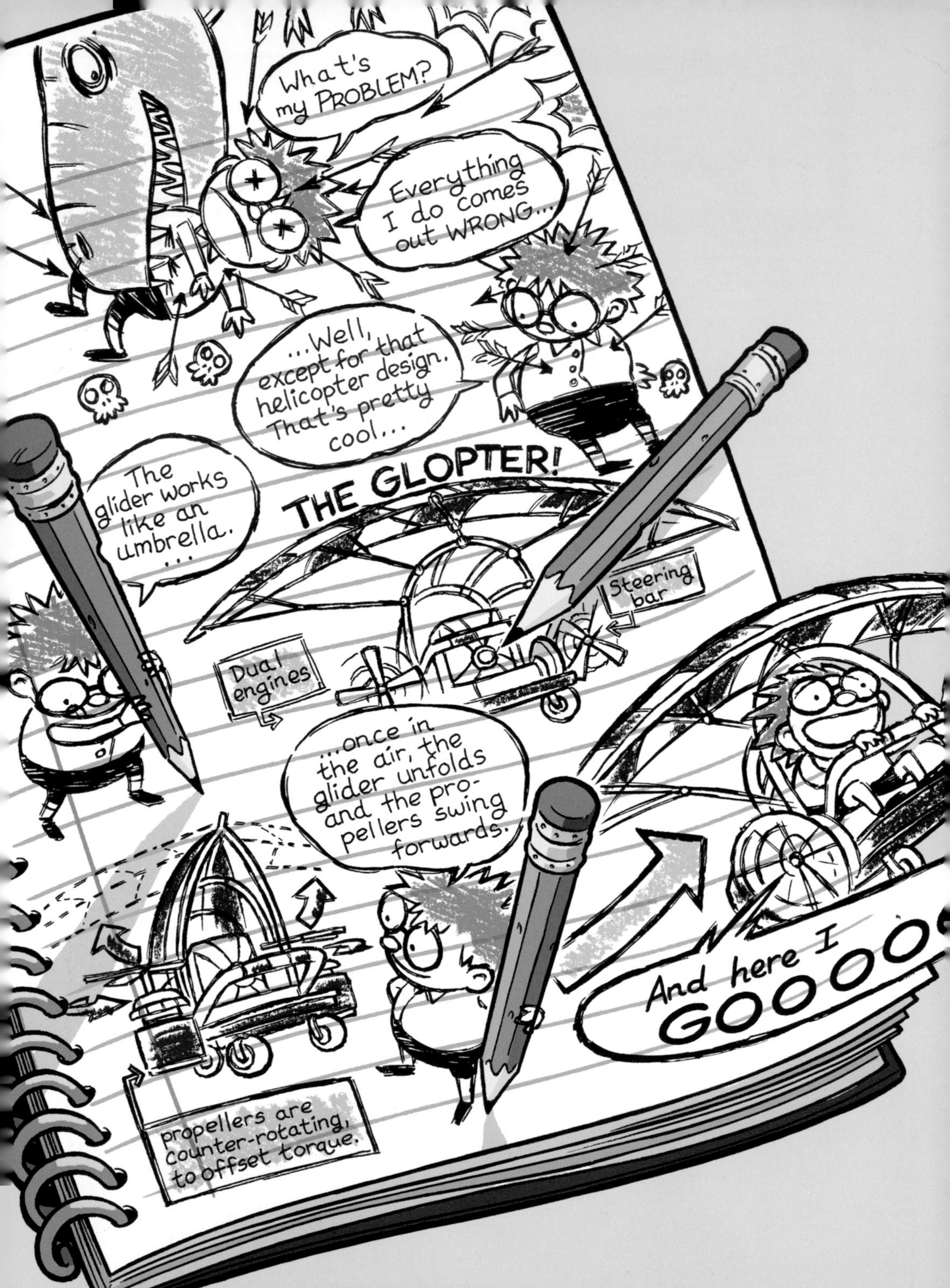
What's my PROBLEM?
Everything I do comes out WRONG...
...Well, except for that helicopter design. That's pretty cool...
The glider works like an umbrella. ...
THE GLOPTER!
Steering bar
Dual engines
...once in the air, the glider unfolds and the propellers swing forwards.
propellers are counter-rotating, to offset torque.
And here I GOOOOO

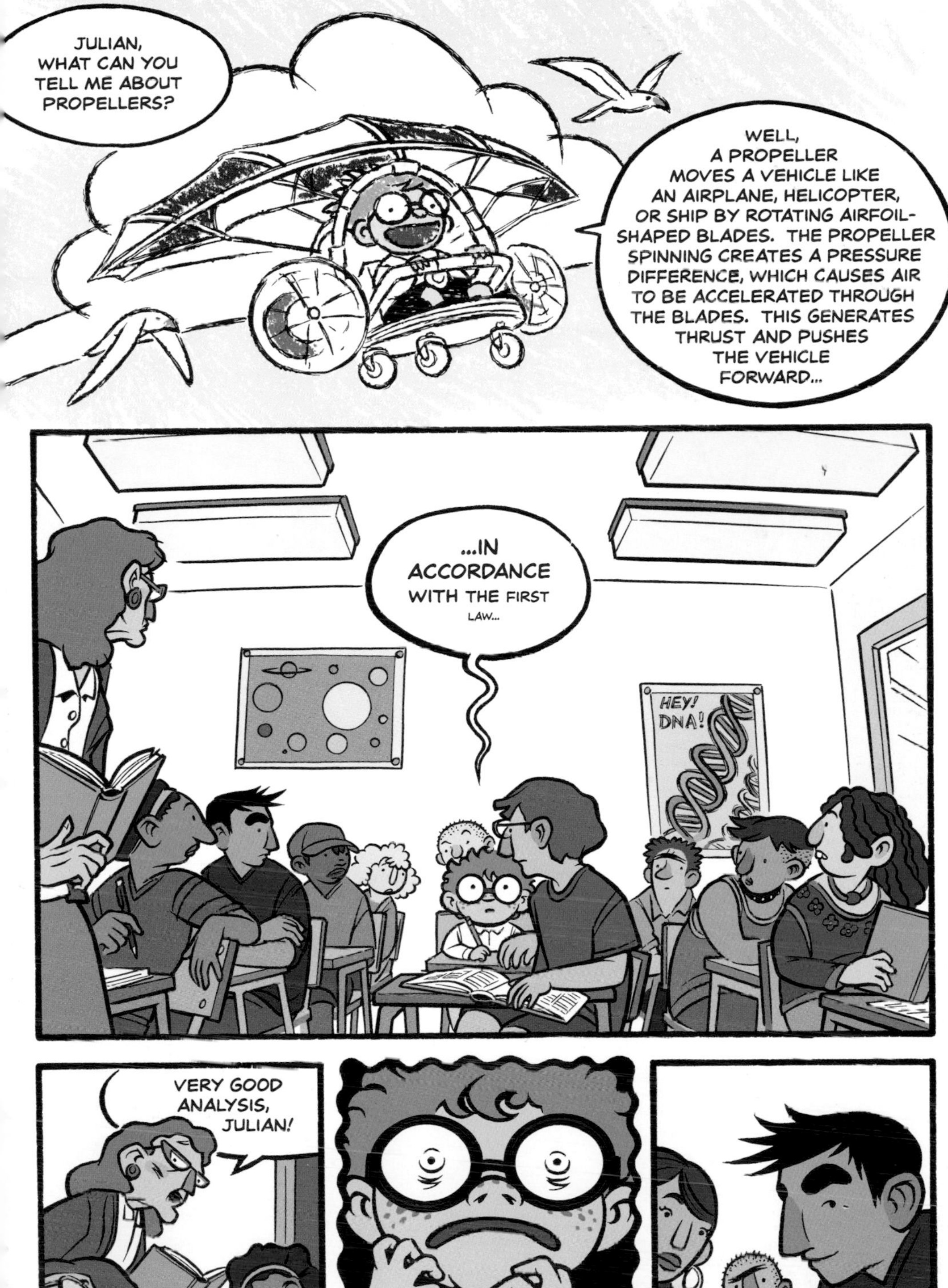
JULIAN, WHAT CAN YOU TELL ME ABOUT PROPELLERS?
WELL, A PROPELLER MOVES A VEHICLE LIKE AN AIRPLANE, HELICOPTER, OR SHIP BY ROTATING AIRFOIL-SHAPED BLADES. THE PROPELLER SPINNING CREATES A PRESSURE DIFFERENCE, WHICH CAUSES AIR TO BE ACCELERATED THROUGH THE BLADES. THIS GENERATES THRUST AND PUSHES THE VEHICLE FORWARD...
...IN ACCORDANCE WITH THE FIRST LAW...
HEY! DNA!
VERY GOOD ANALYSIS, JULIAN!

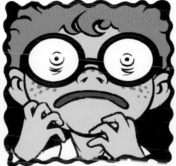

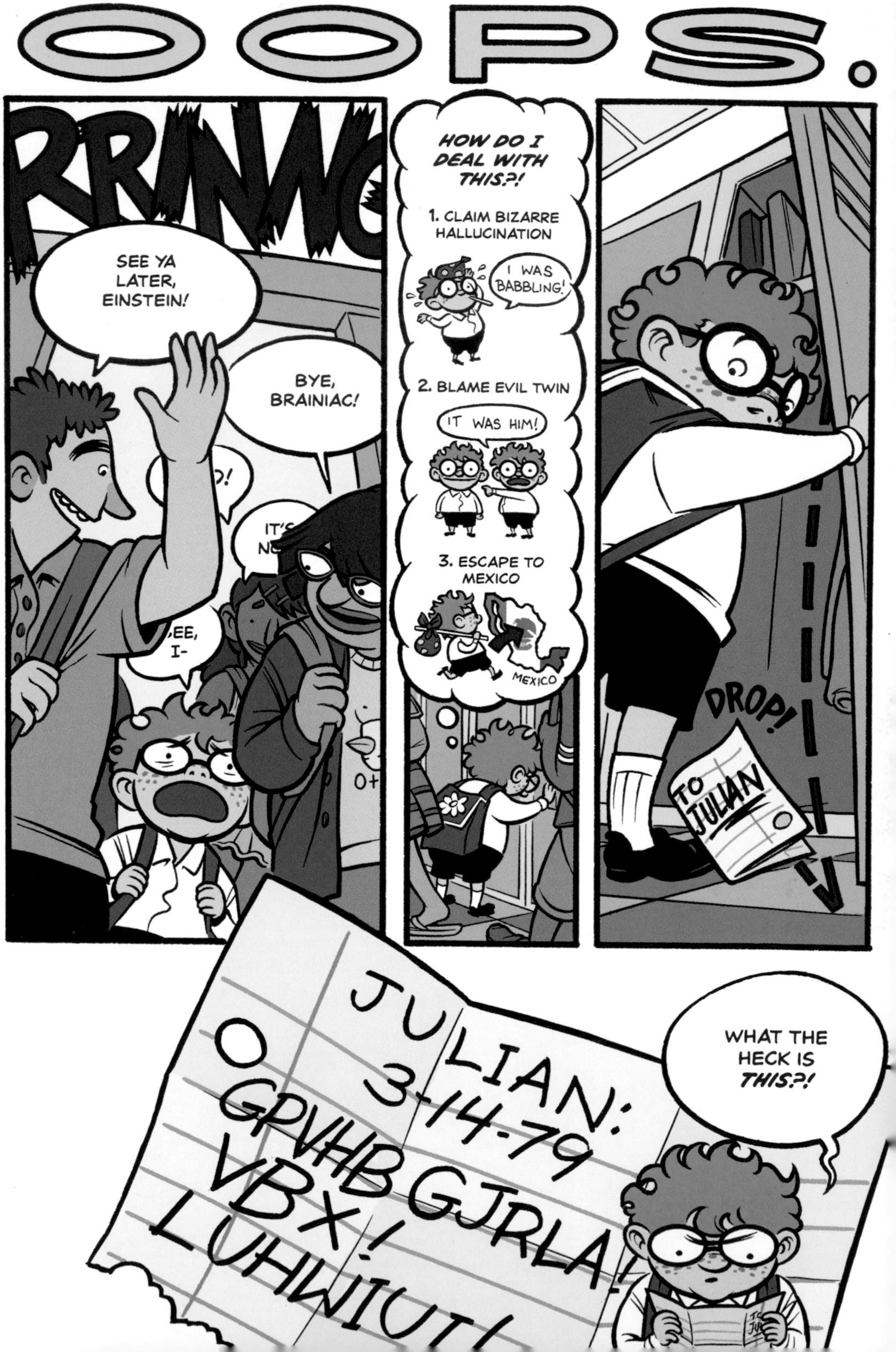
OOPS.
SEE YA LATER, EINSTEIN!
BYE, BRAINIAC!
HOW DO I DEAL WITH THIS?!
1. CLAIM BIZARRE HALLUCINATION
I WAS BABBLING!
2. BLAME EVIL TWIN
IT WAS HIM!
3. ESCAPE TO MEXICO
MEXICO
DROP!
TO JULIAN
JULIAN: 3-14-79
GPVHB GJRLA! VBX! LUHWIUT!
WHAT THE HECK IS THIS?!

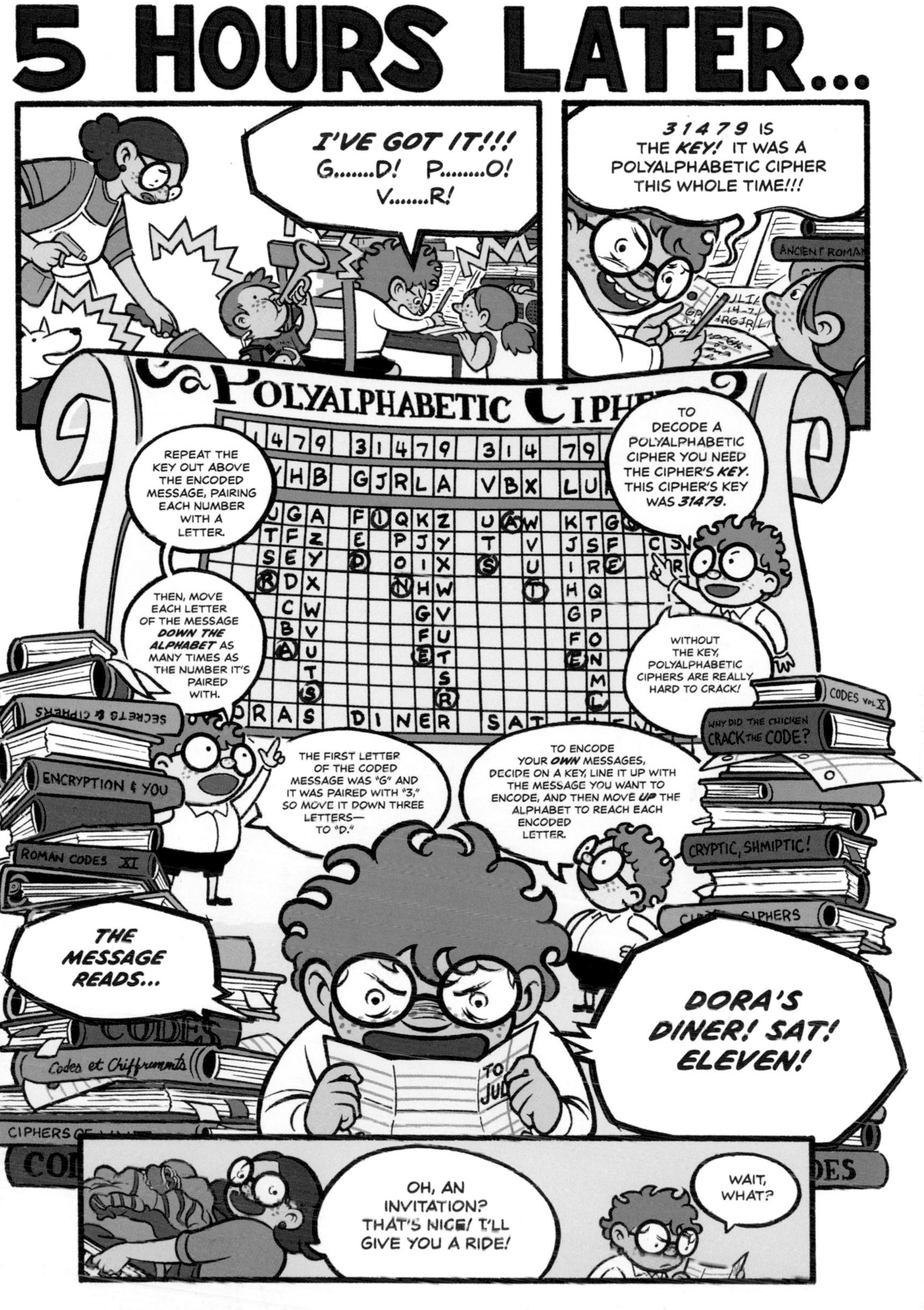
5 HOURS LATER...
I'VE GOT IT!!! G.......D! P........O! V.......R!
31479 IS THE KEY! IT WAS A POLYALPHABETIC CIPHER THIS WHOLE TIME!!!
ANCIENT ROMAN
POLYALPHABETIC
TO DECODE A POLYALPHABETIC CIPHER YOU NEED THE CIPHER'S KEY. THIS CIPHER'S KEY WAS 31479.
REPEAT THE KEY OUT ABOVE THE ENCODED MESSAGE, PAIRING EACH NUMBER WITH A LETTER.
THEN, MOVE EACH LETTER OF THE MESSAGE DOWN THE ALPHABET AS MANY TIMES AS THE NUMBER IT'S PAIRED WITH.
WITHOUT THE KEY, POLYALPHABETIC CIPHERS ARE REALLY HARD TO CRACK!
THE FIRST LETTER OF THE CODED MESSAGE WAS "G" AND IT WAS PAIRED WITH "3," SO MOVE IT DOWN THREE LETTERS— TO "D."
TO ENCODE YOUR OWN MESSAGES, DECIDE ON A KEY, LINE IT UP WITH THE MESSAGE YOU WANT TO ENCODE, AND THEN MOVE UP THE ALPHABET TO REACH EACH ENCODED LETTER.
SECRETS & CIPHERS
ENCRYPTION & YOU
ROMAN CODES XI
CODES
Codes et Chiffrements
CODES VOL X
WHY DID THE CHICKEN CRACK THE CODE?
CRYPTIC, SHMIPTIC!
THE MESSAGE READS...
DORA'S DINER! SAT! ELEVEN!
OH, AN INVITATION? THAT'S NICE! I'LL GIVE YOU A RIDE!
WAIT, WHAT?

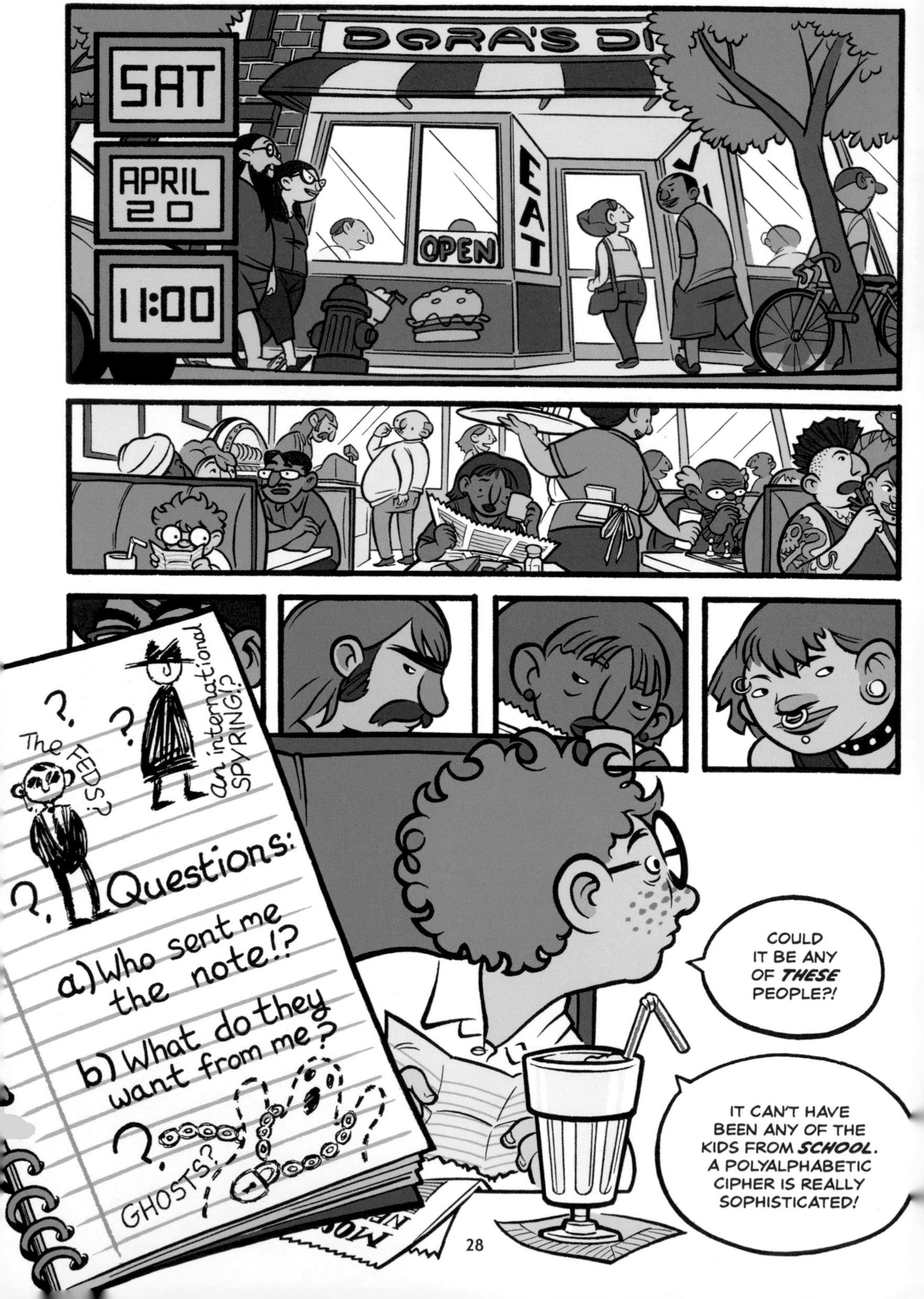
SAT
APRIL 20
11:00
DORA'S DI
OPEN
EAT
The FEDS?
an international SPYRING!?
Questions:
a) Who sent me the note!?
b) What do they want from me?
GHOSTS?
COULD IT BE ANY OF THESE PEOPLE?!
IT CAN'T HAVE BEEN ANY OF THE KIDS FROM SCHOOL. A POLYALPHABETIC CIPHER IS REALLY SOPHISTICATED!

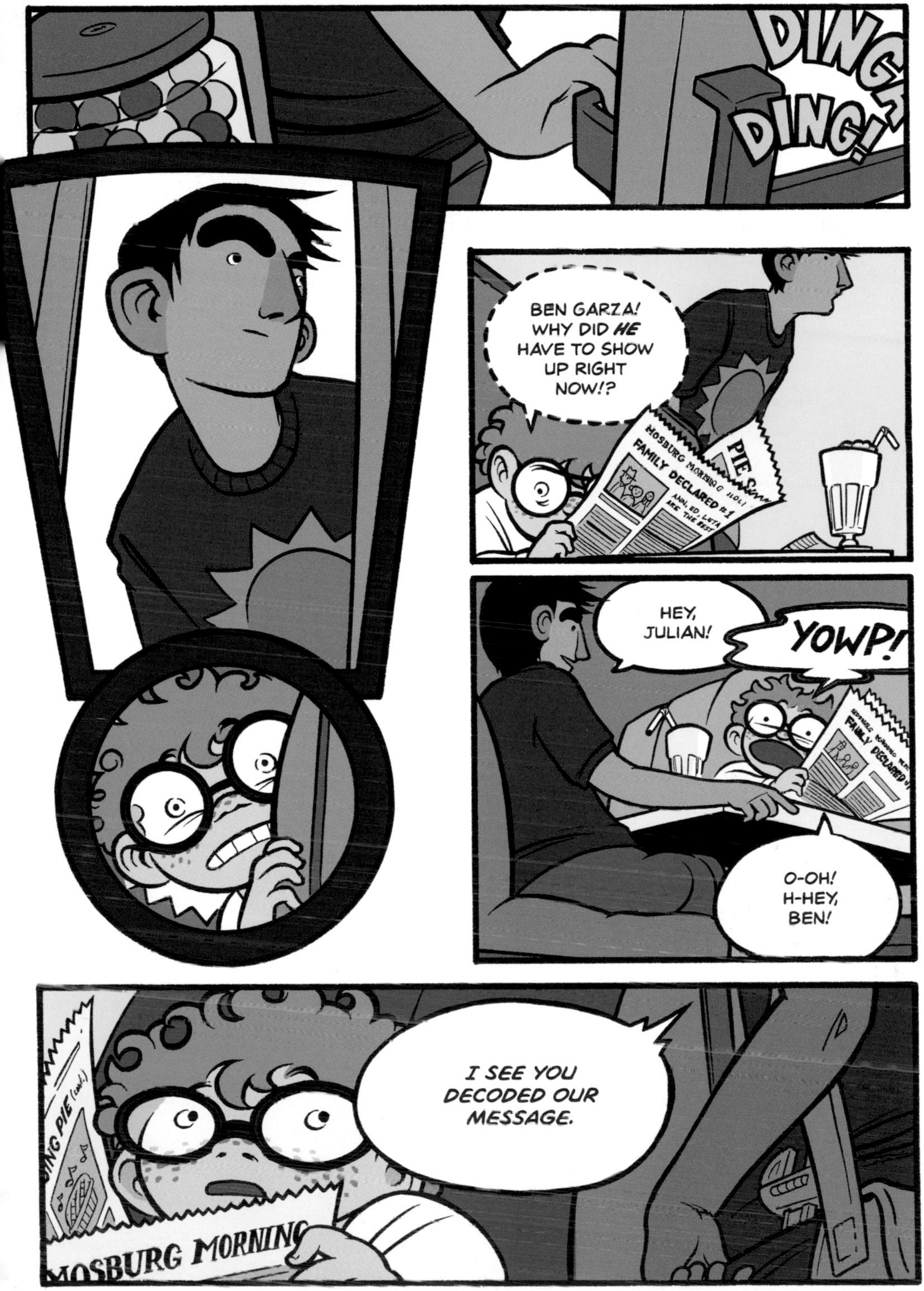
DING! DING!
BEN GARZA! WHY DID *HE* HAVE TO SHOW UP RIGHT NOW!?
MOSBURG MORNING (LOL)
FAMILY DECLARED #1
ANN, ED, LETA ARE THE BEST
HEY, JULIAN!
YOWP!
O-OH! H-HEY, BEN!
I SEE YOU DECODED OUR MESSAGE.
MOSBURG MORNING

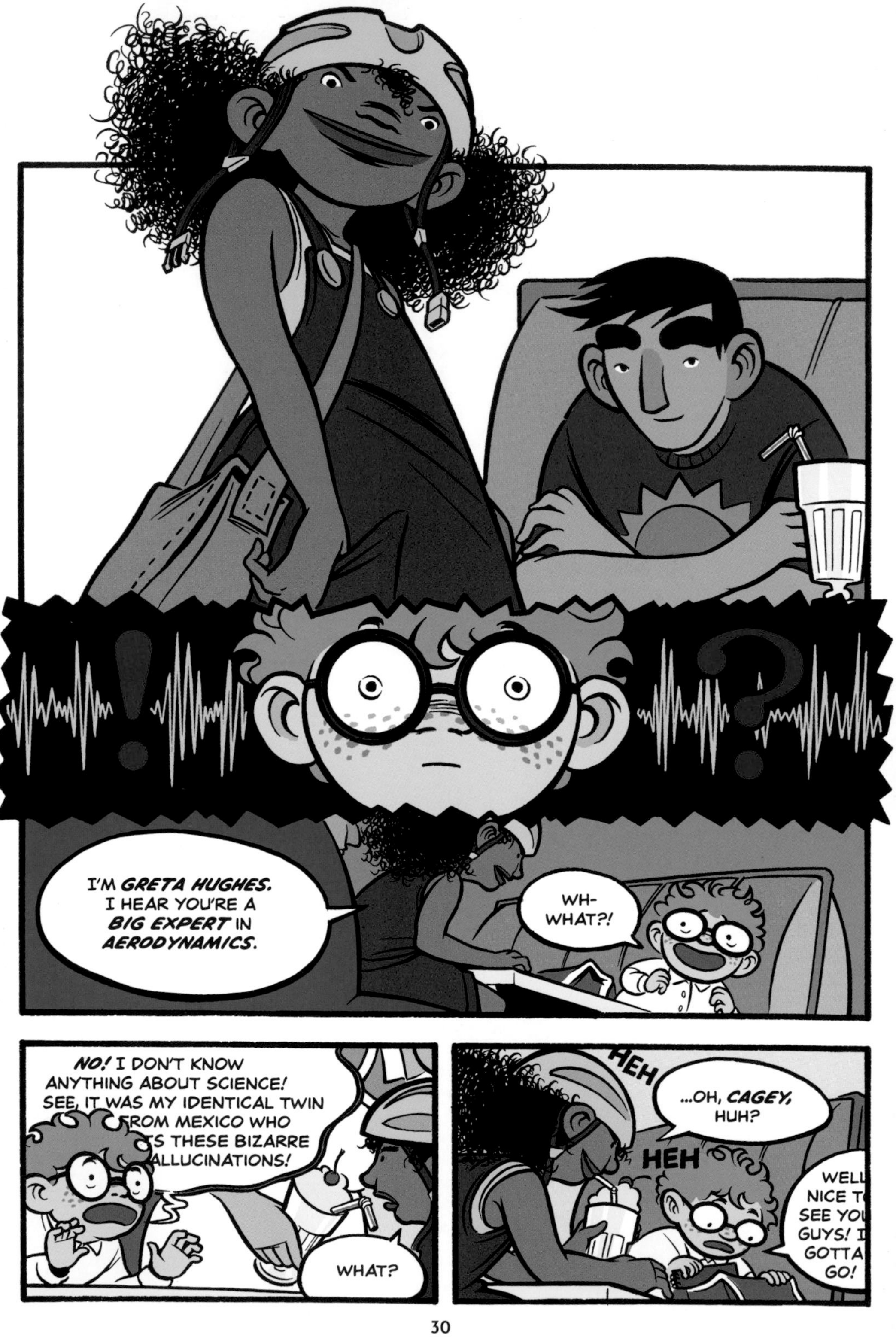
I'M GRETA HUGHES. I HEAR YOU'RE A BIG EXPERT IN AERODYNAMICS.
WH- WHAT?!
NO! I DON'T KNOW ANYTHING ABOUT SCIENCE! SEE, IT WAS MY IDENTICAL TWIN FROM MEXICO WHO TS THESE BIZARRE ALLUCINATIONS!
WHAT?
HEH
...OH, CAGEY, HUH?
HEH
WELL NICE T SEE YOU GUYS! I GOTTA GO!

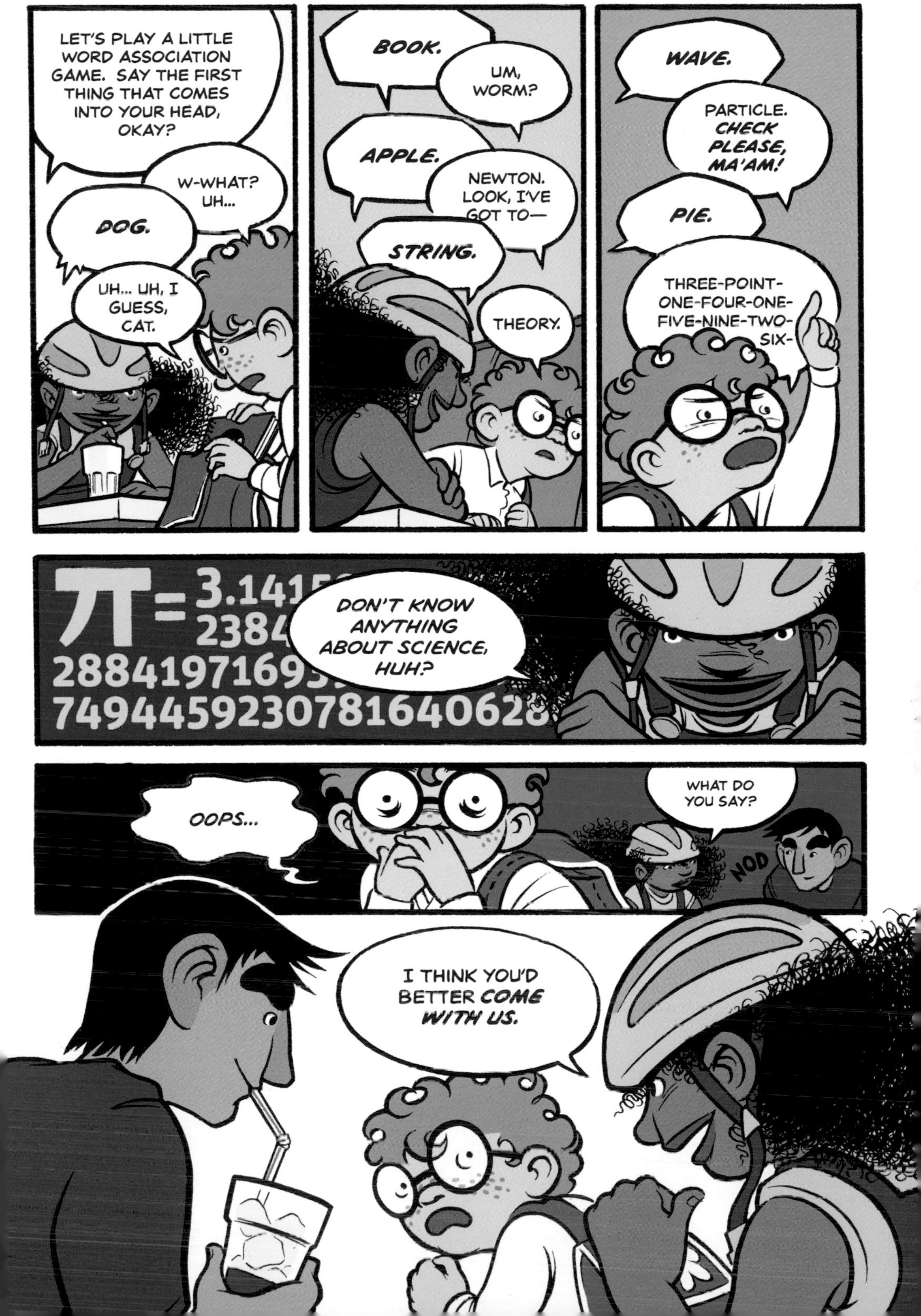
LET'S PLAY A LITTLE WORD ASSOCIATION GAME. SAY THE FIRST THING THAT COMES INTO YOUR HEAD, OKAY?
W-WHAT? UH...
DOG.
UH... UH, I GUESS, CAT.
BOOK.
UM, WORM?
APPLE.
NEWTON. LOOK, I'VE GOT TO—
STRING.
THEORY.
WAVE.
PARTICLE. CHECK PLEASE, MA'AM!
PIE.
THREE-POINT-ONE-FOUR-ONE-FIVE-NINE-TWO-SIX-
π=3.1415
2384
2884197169
7494459230781640628
DON'T KNOW ANYTHING ABOUT SCIENCE, HUH?
OOPS...
WHAT DO YOU SAY?
NOD
I THINK YOU'D BETTER COME WITH US.

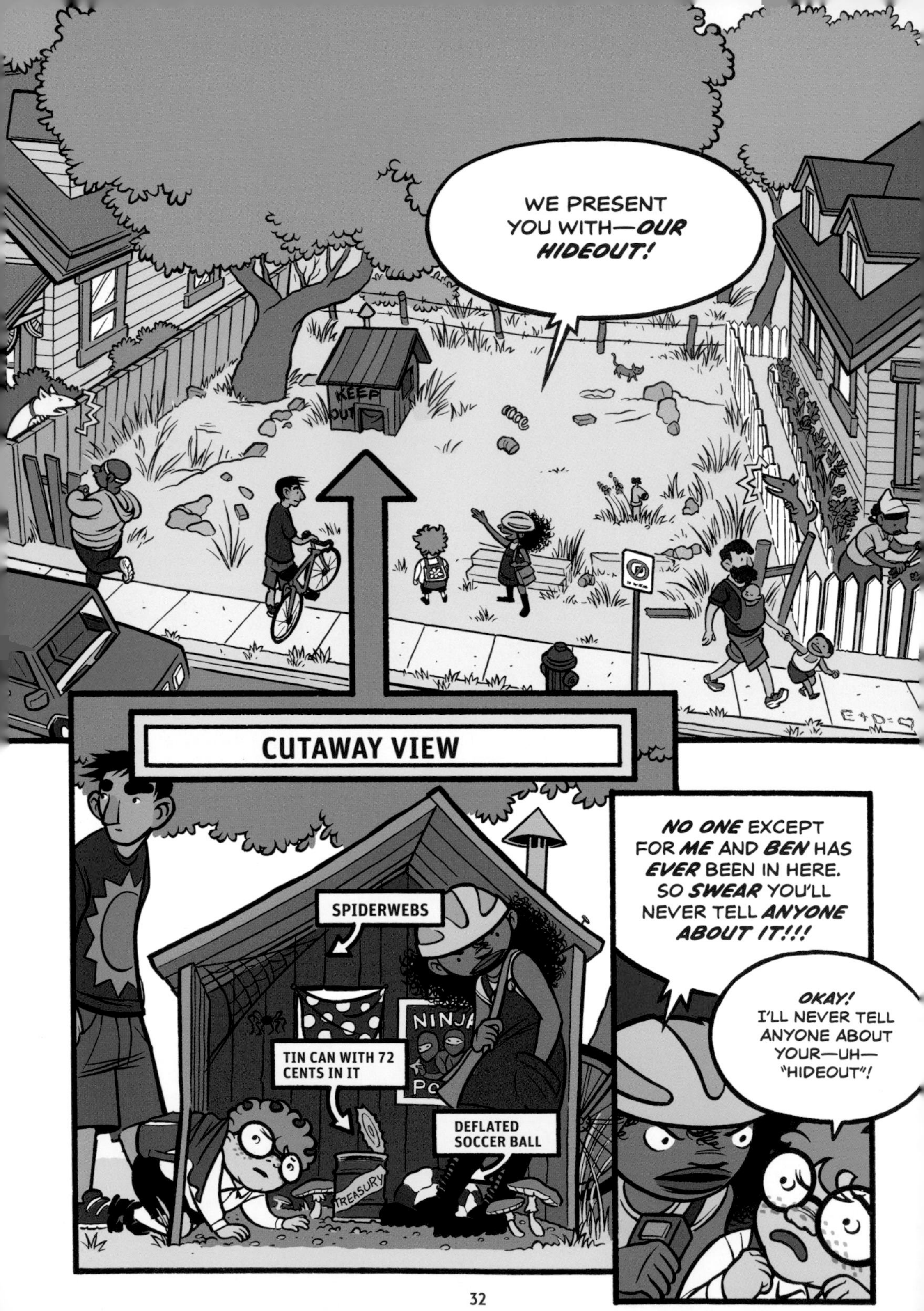

WE PRESENT YOU WITH—OUR HIDEOUT!
KEEP OUT
E+D=♡
CUTAWAY VIEW
SPIDERWEBS
TIN CAN WITH 72 CENTS IN IT
TREASURY
NINJA
DEFLATED SOCCER BALL
NO ONE EXCEPT FOR ME AND BEN HAS EVER BEEN IN HERE. SO SWEAR YOU'LL NEVER TELL ANYONE ABOUT IT!!!
OKAY! I'LL NEVER TELL ANYONE ABOUT YOUR—UH—"HIDEOUT"!

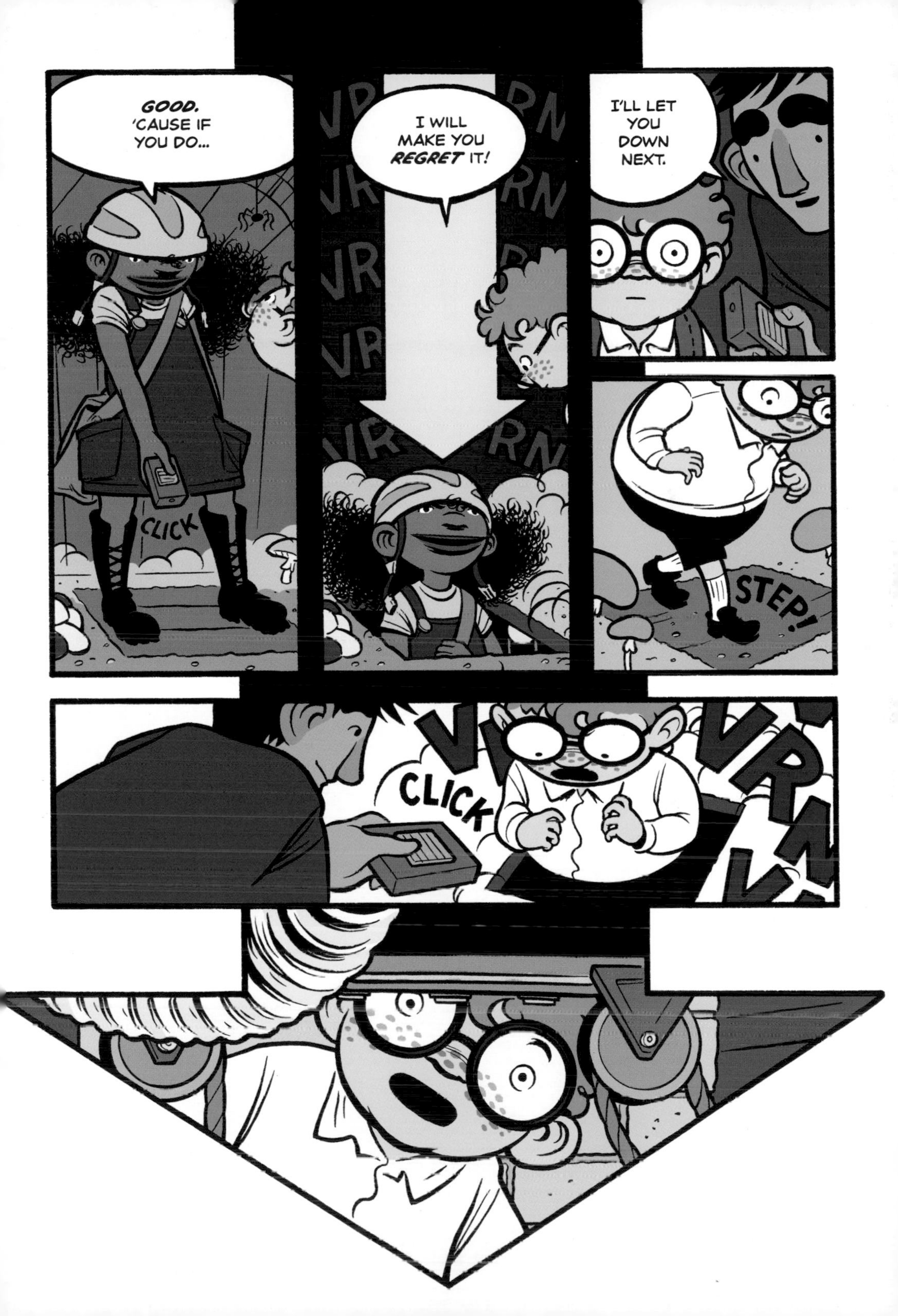
GOOD. 'CAUSE IF YOU DO...
CLICK
I WILL MAKE YOU REGRET IT!
VRRN VRRN VRRN
I'LL LET YOU DOWN NEXT.
STEP!
CLICK
VRRN

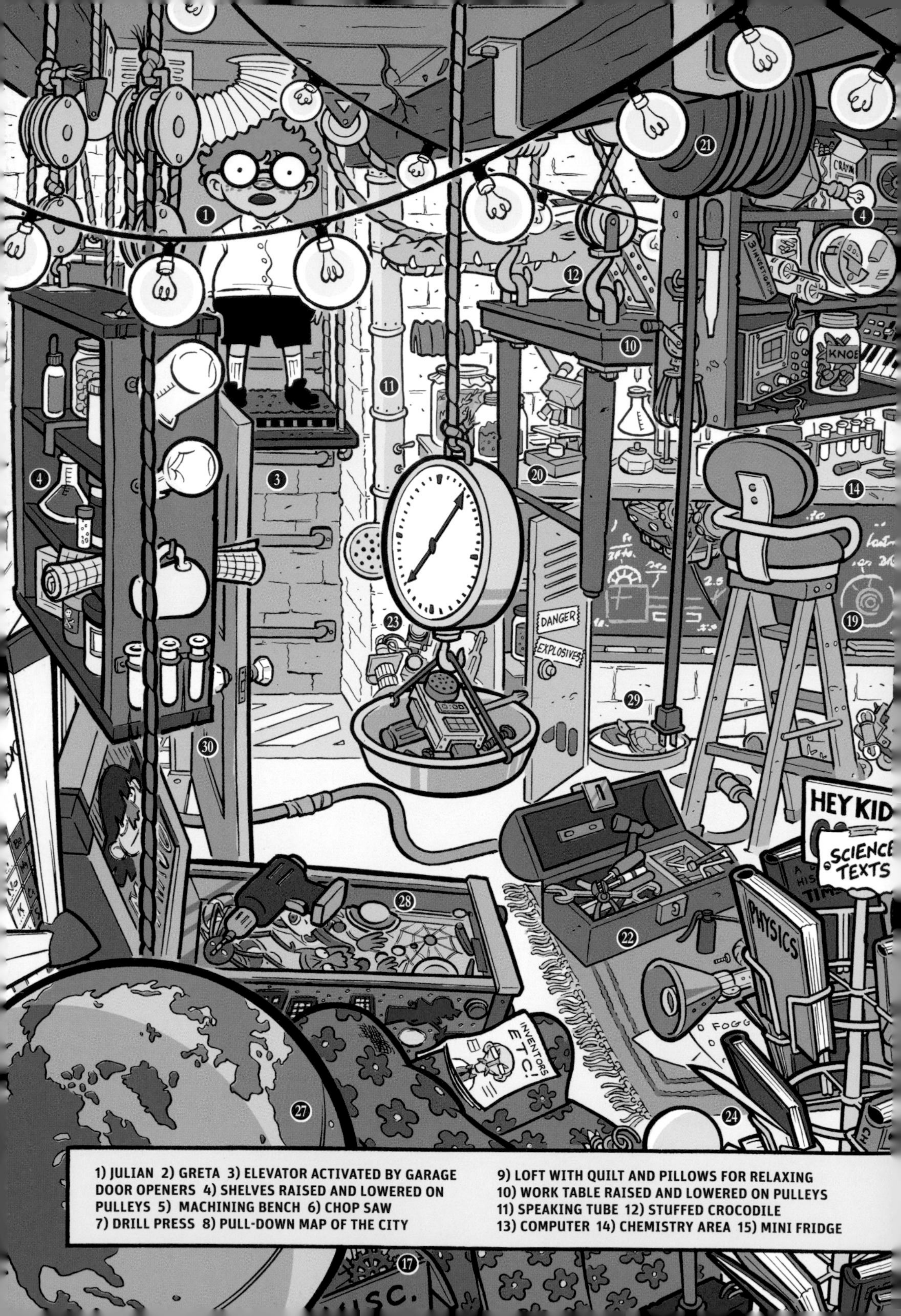
DANGER
EXPLOSIVES
HEY KID
SCIENCE TEXTS
PHYSICS
INVENTORS ETC!
MISC.

1) JULIAN 2) GRETA 3) ELEVATOR ACTIVATED BY GARAGE DOOR OPENERS 4) SHELVES RAISED AND LOWERED ON PULLEYS 5) MACHINING BENCH 6) CHOP SAW 7) DRILL PRESS 8) PULL-DOWN MAP OF THE CITY

9) LOFT WITH QUILT AND PILLOWS FOR RELAXING 10) WORK TABLE RAISED AND LOWERED ON PULLEYS 11) SPEAKING TUBE 12) STUFFED CROCODILE 13) COMPUTER 14) CHEMISTRY AREA 15) MINI FRIDGE

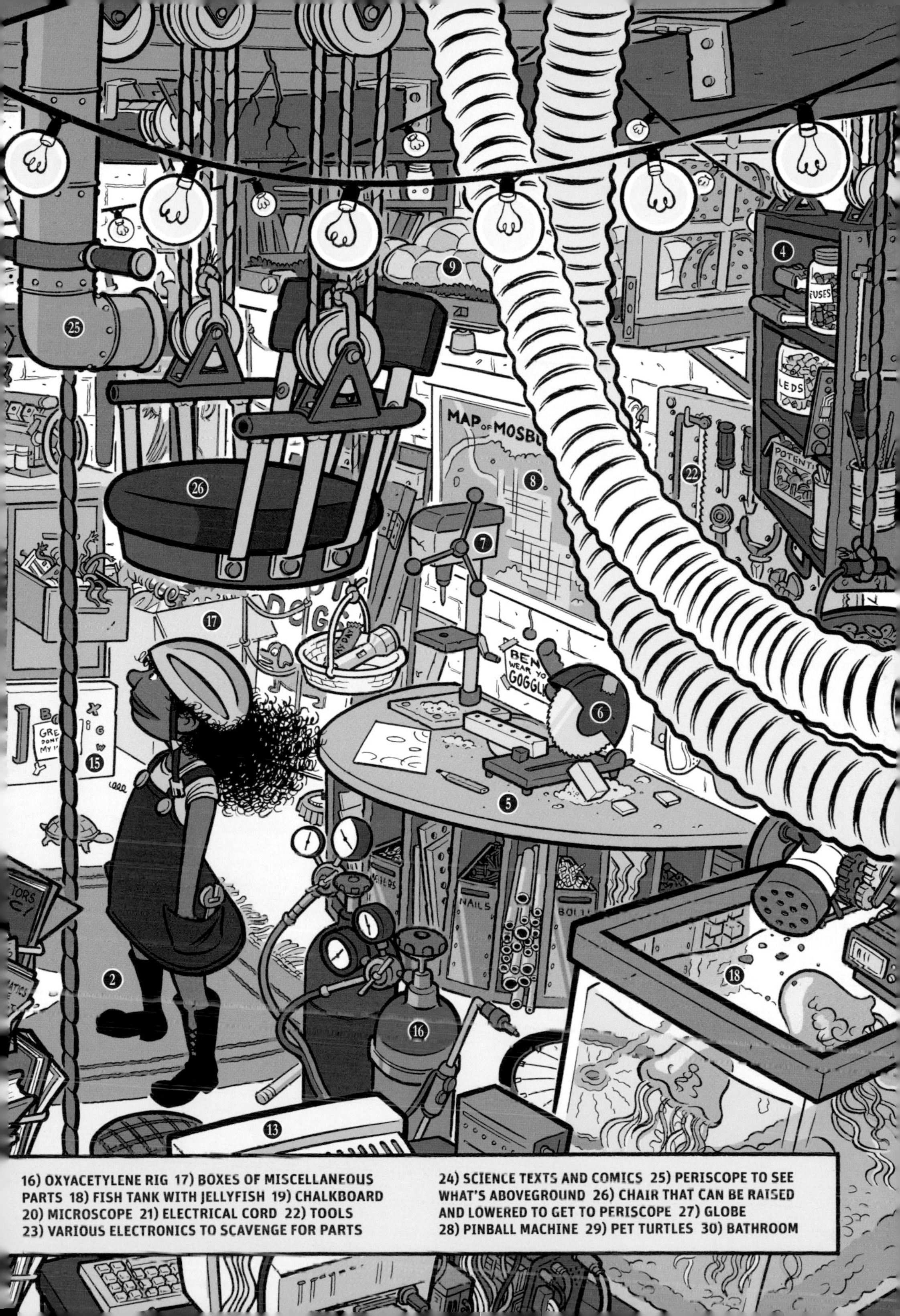
FUSES
LEDS
NAILS

16) OXYACETYLENE RIG 17) BOXES OF MISCELLANEOUS PARTS 18) FISH TANK WITH JELLYFISH 19) CHALKBOARD 20) MICROSCOPE 21) ELECTRICAL CORD 22) TOOLS 23) VARIOUS ELECTRONICS TO SCAVENGE FOR PARTS 24) SCIENCE TEXTS AND COMICS 25) PERISCOPE TO SEE WHAT'S ABOVEGROUND 26) CHAIR THAT CAN BE RAISED AND LOWERED TO GET TO PERISCOPE 27) GLOBE 28) PINBALL MACHINE 29) PET TURTLES 30) BATHROOM

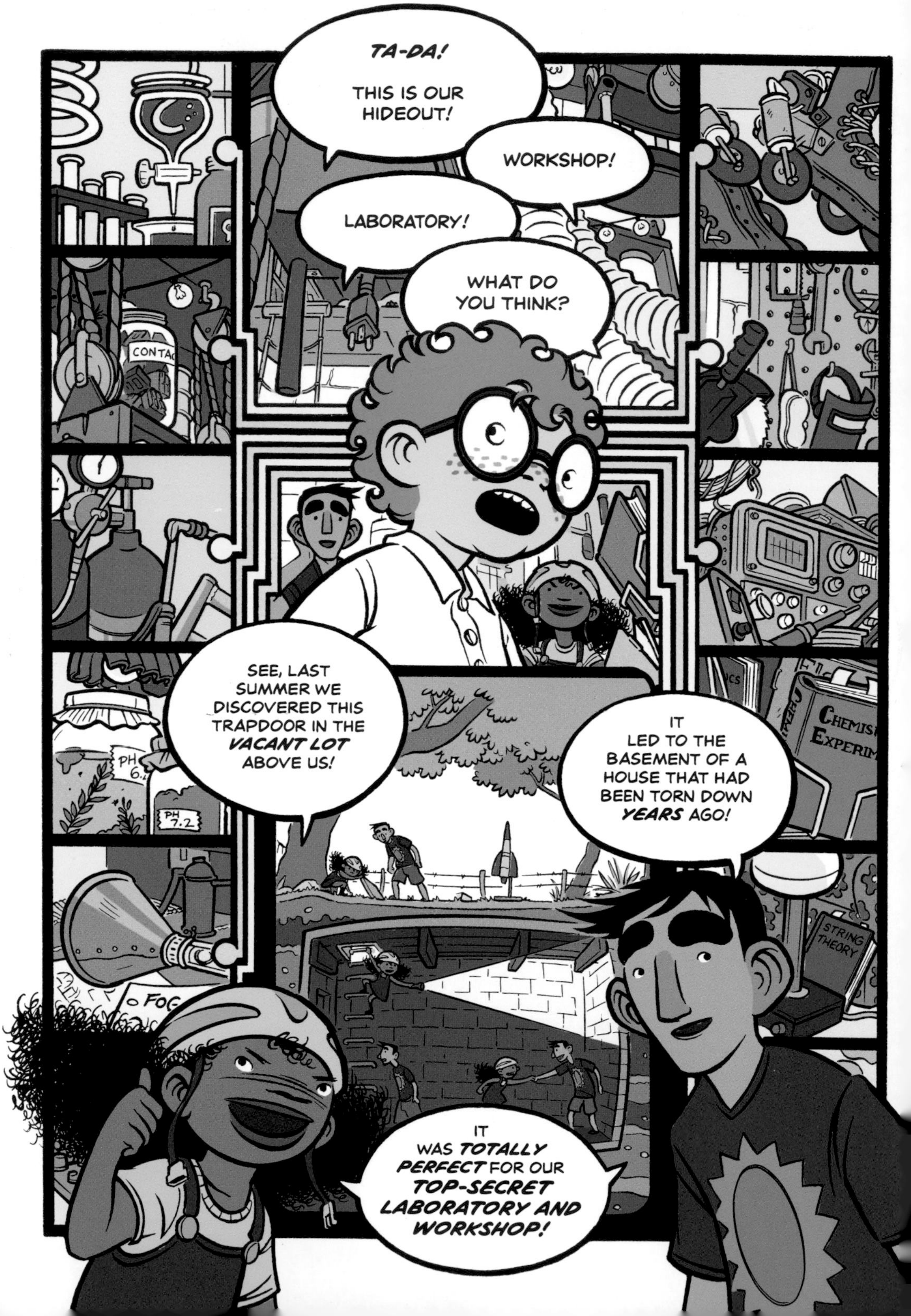
TA-DA!
THIS IS OUR HIDEOUT!
WORKSHOP!
LABORATORY!
WHAT DO YOU THINK?
SEE, LAST SUMMER WE DISCOVERED THIS TRAPDOOR IN THE VACANT LOT ABOVE US!
IT LED TO THE BASEMENT OF A HOUSE THAT HAD BEEN TORN DOWN YEARS AGO!
IT WAS TOTALLY PERFECT FOR OUR TOP-SECRET LABORATORY AND WORKSHOP!
CONTAC
PH 6.
PH 7.2
FOG
CHEMIS EXPERIM
STRING THEORY

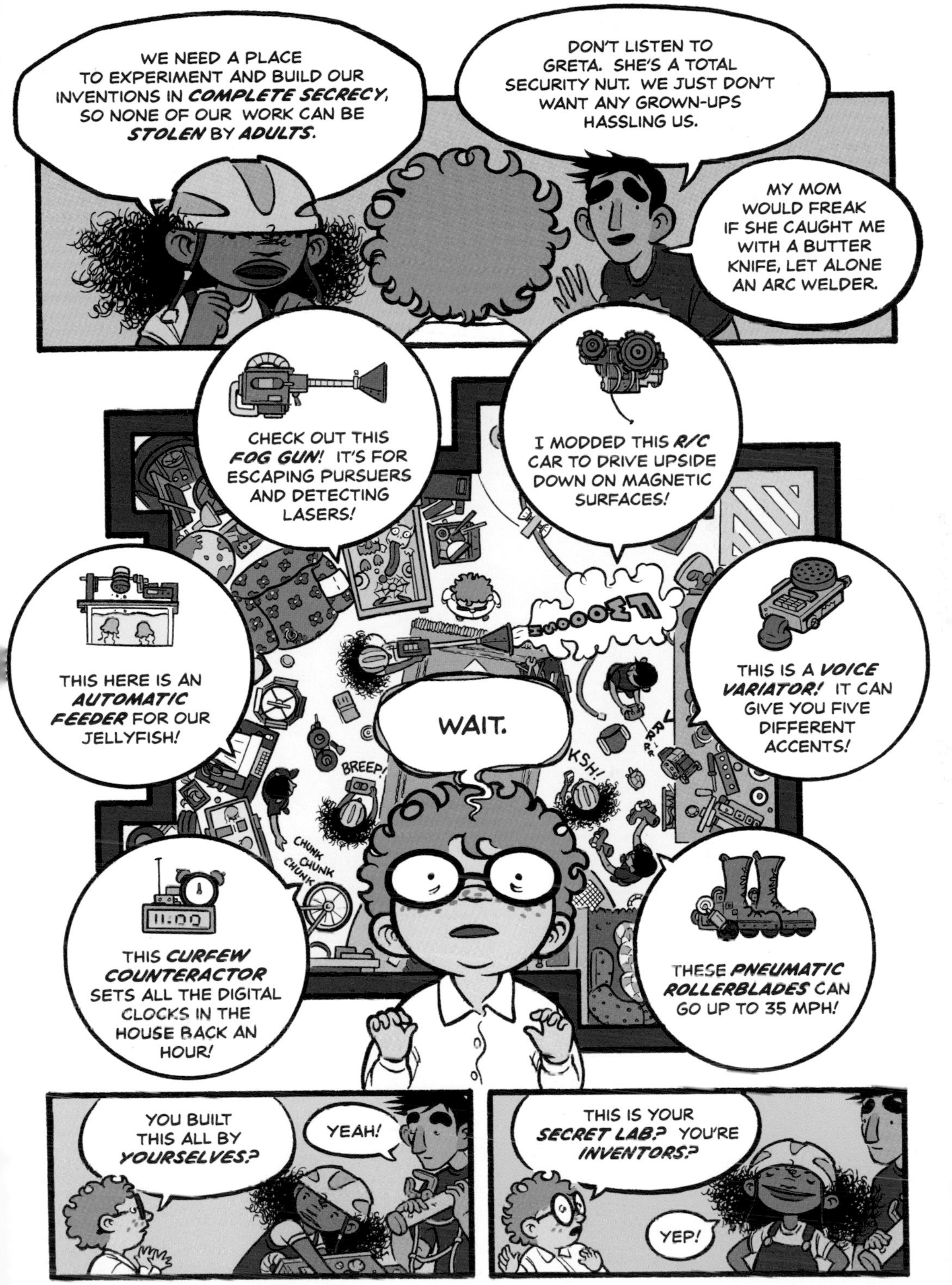
WE NEED A PLACE TO EXPERIMENT AND BUILD OUR INVENTIONS IN COMPLETE SECRECY, SO NONE OF OUR WORK CAN BE STOLEN BY ADULTS.
DON'T LISTEN TO GRETA. SHE'S A TOTAL SECURITY NUT. WE JUST DON'T WANT ANY GROWN-UPS HASSLING US.
MY MOM WOULD FREAK IF SHE CAUGHT ME WITH A BUTTER KNIFE, LET ALONE AN ARC WELDER.
CHECK OUT THIS FOG GUN! IT'S FOR ESCAPING PURSUERS AND DETECTING LASERS!
I MODDED THIS R/C CAR TO DRIVE UPSIDE DOWN ON MAGNETIC SURFACES!
THIS HERE IS AN AUTOMATIC FEEDER FOR OUR JELLYFISH!
THIS IS A VOICE VARIATOR! IT CAN GIVE YOU FIVE DIFFERENT ACCENTS!
WAIT.
BREEP!
KSH!
CHUNK CHUNK CHUNK
11:00
THIS CURFEW COUNTERACTOR SETS ALL THE DIGITAL CLOCKS IN THE HOUSE BACK AN HOUR!
THESE PNEUMATIC ROLLERBLADES CAN GO UP TO 35 MPH!
YOU BUILT THIS ALL BY YOURSELVES?
YEAH!
THIS IS YOUR SECRET LAB? YOU'RE INVENTORS?
YEP!

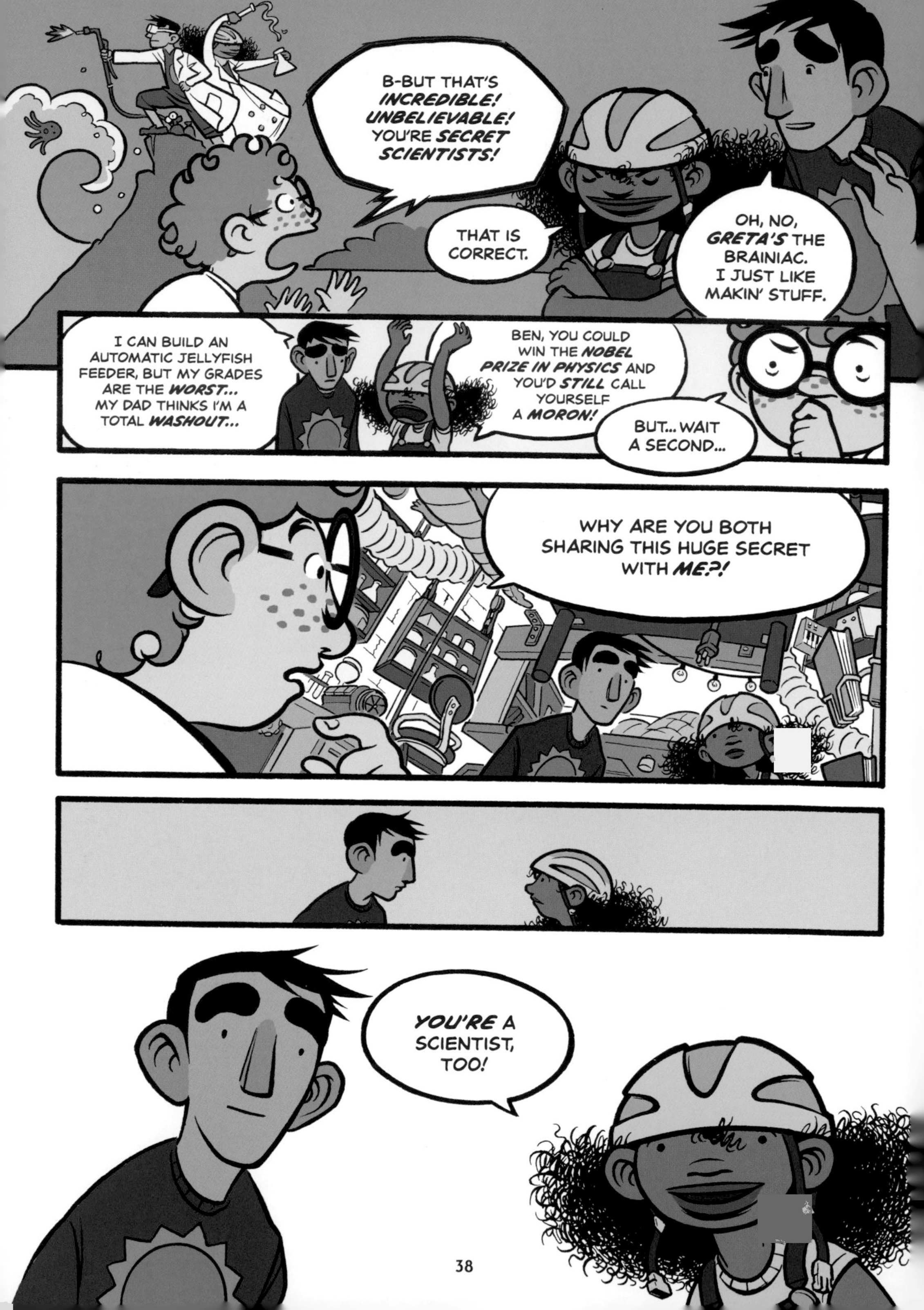
B-BUT THAT'S INCREDIBLE! UNBELIEVABLE! YOU'RE SECRET SCIENTISTS!
THAT IS CORRECT.
OH, NO, GRETA'S THE BRAINIAC. I JUST LIKE MAKIN' STUFF.
I CAN BUILD AN AUTOMATIC JELLYFISH FEEDER, BUT MY GRADES ARE THE WORST... MY DAD THINKS I'M A TOTAL WASHOUT...
BEN, YOU COULD WIN THE NOBEL PRIZE IN PHYSICS AND YOU'D STILL CALL YOURSELF A MORON!
BUT... WAIT A SECOND...
WHY ARE YOU BOTH SHARING THIS HUGE SECRET WITH ME?!
YOU'RE A SCIENTIST, TOO!

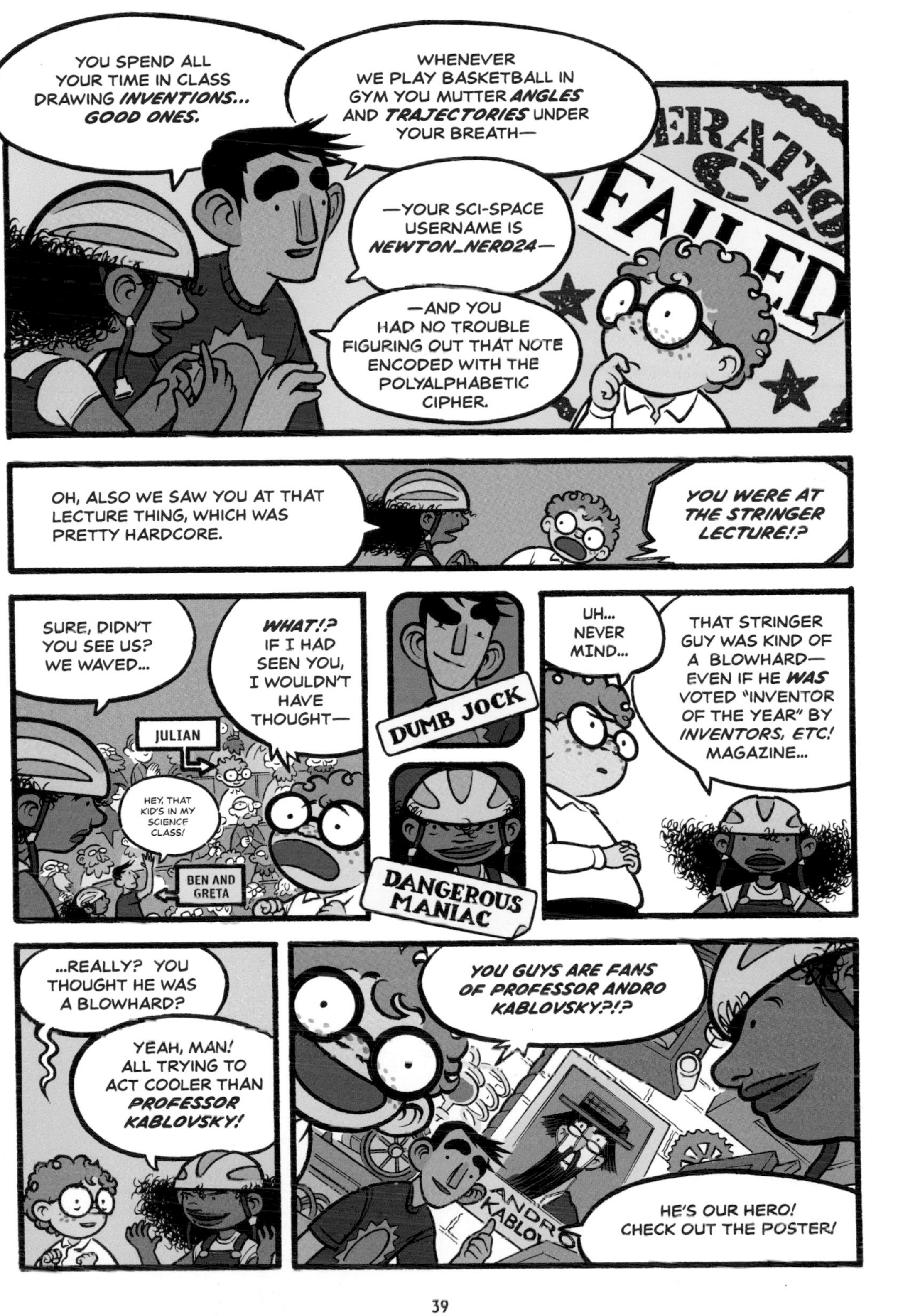
YOU SPEND ALL YOUR TIME IN CLASS DRAWING *INVENTIONS... GOOD ONES.*
WHENEVER WE PLAY BASKETBALL IN GYM YOU MUTTER *ANGLES* AND *TRAJECTORIES* UNDER YOUR BREATH—
—YOUR SCI-SPACE USERNAME IS *NEWTON_NERD24*—
—AND YOU HAD NO TROUBLE FIGURING OUT THAT NOTE ENCODED WITH THE POLYALPHABETIC CIPHER.
FAILED
OH, ALSO WE SAW YOU AT THAT LECTURE THING, WHICH WAS PRETTY HARDCORE.
YOU WERE AT THE STRINGER LECTURE!?
SURE, DIDN'T YOU SEE US? WE WAVED...
WHAT!? IF I HAD SEEN YOU, I WOULDN'T HAVE THOUGHT—
JULIAN
HEY, THAT KID'S IN MY SCIENCE CLASS!
BEN AND GRETA
DUMB JOCK
DANGEROUS MANIAC
UH... NEVER MIND...
THAT STRINGER GUY WAS KIND OF A BLOWHARD— EVEN IF HE *WAS* VOTED "INVENTOR OF THE YEAR" BY *INVENTORS, ETC!* MAGAZINE...
...REALLY? YOU THOUGHT HE WAS A BLOWHARD?
YEAH, MAN! ALL TRYING TO ACT COOLER THAN *PROFESSOR KABLOVSKY!*
YOU GUYS ARE FANS OF PROFESSOR ANDRO KABLOVSKY?!?
HE'S OUR HERO! CHECK OUT THE POSTER!

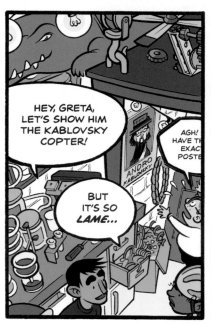

ANDRO KABLOVSKY
HEY, GRETA, LET'S SHOW HIM THE KABLOVSKY COPTER!
AGH! HAVE TH EXACT POSTE
BUT IT'S SO *LAME*...
MAYBE JULIAN CAN GIVE US SOME *ADVICE*—
HE'S THE *EXPERT IN AERODYNAMICS*, REMEMBER?
THE KABLOVSKY COPTER!
THAT'S *AMAZING!* DOES IT *FLY?*
WE *WISH.*
ALLOW GRETA TO DEMONSTRATE.
SRINK!
VWOOP
CHUNK

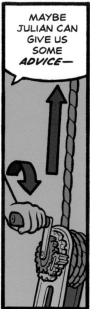

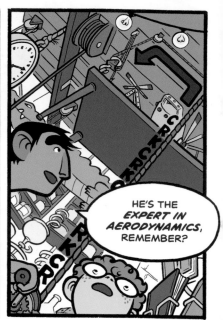

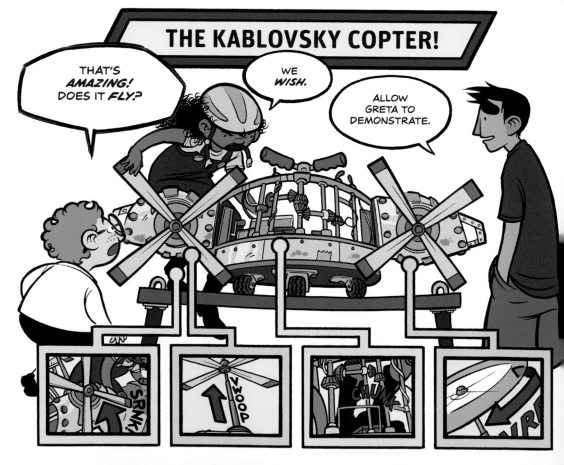

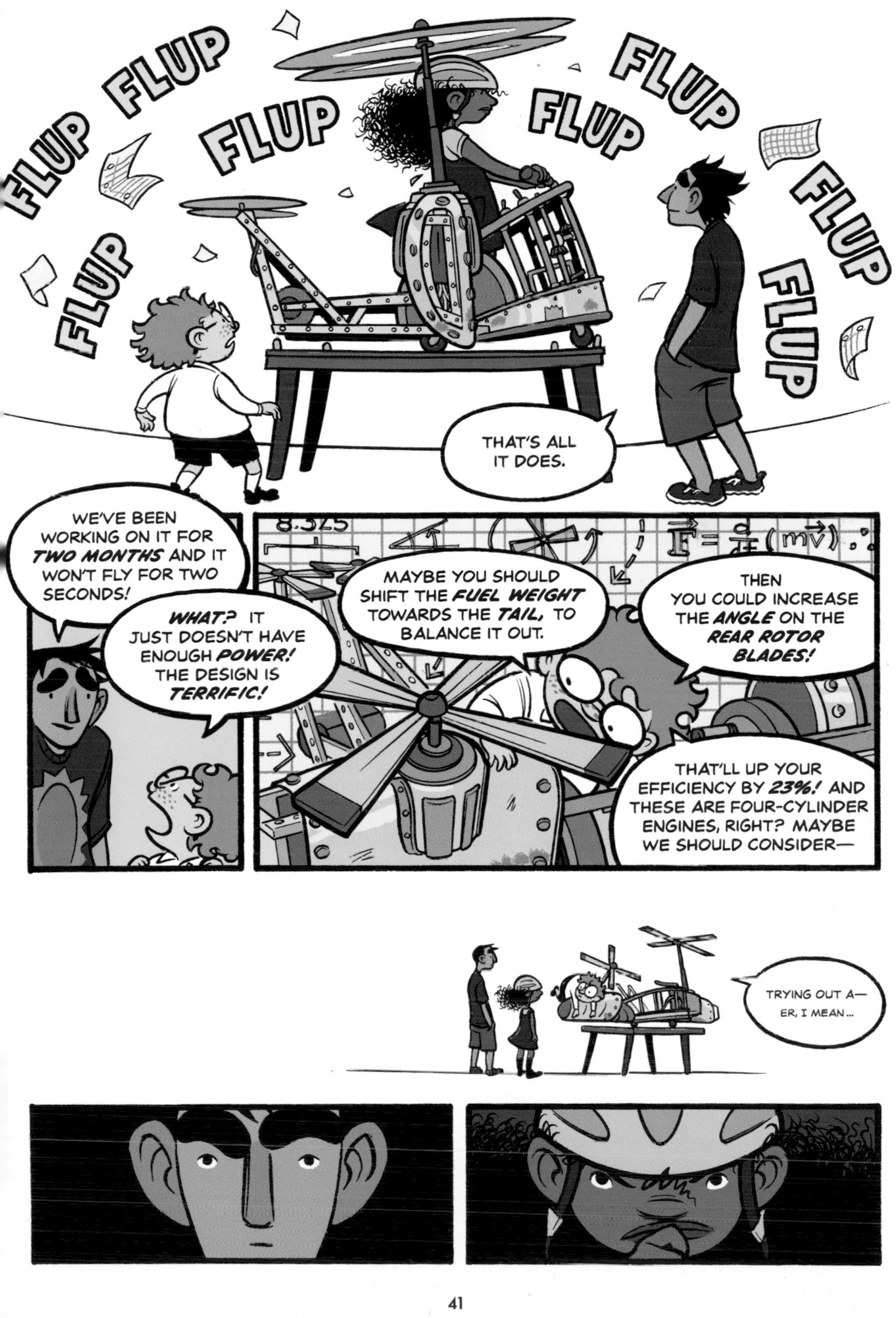
FLUP FLUP FLUP FLUP FLUP FLUP FLUP FLUP
FLUP
THAT'S ALL IT DOES.
WE'VE BEEN WORKING ON IT FOR TWO MONTHS AND IT WON'T FLY FOR TWO SECONDS!
WHAT? IT JUST DOESN'T HAVE ENOUGH POWER! THE DESIGN IS TERRIFIC!
MAYBE YOU SHOULD SHIFT THE FUEL WEIGHT TOWARDS THE TAIL, TO BALANCE IT OUT.
THEN YOU COULD INCREASE THE ANGLE ON THE REAR ROTOR BLADES!
THAT'LL UP YOUR EFFICIENCY BY 23%! AND THESE ARE FOUR-CYLINDER ENGINES, RIGHT? MAYBE WE SHOULD CONSIDER—
TRYING OUT A— ER, I MEAN...

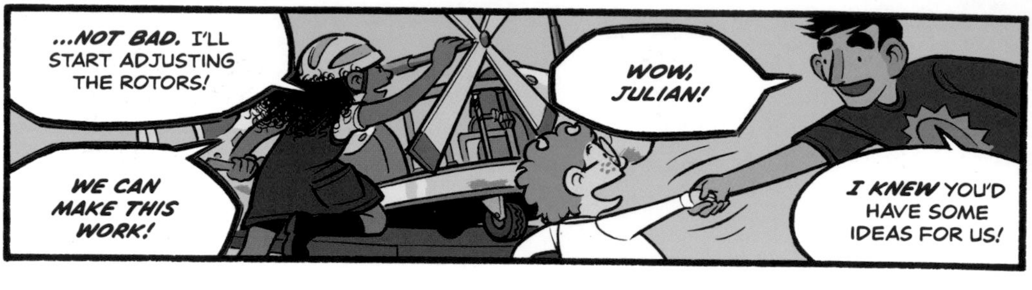
...NOT BAD. I'LL START ADJUSTING THE ROTORS!
WE CAN MAKE THIS WORK!
WOW, JULIAN!
I KNEW YOU'D HAVE SOME IDEAS FOR US!

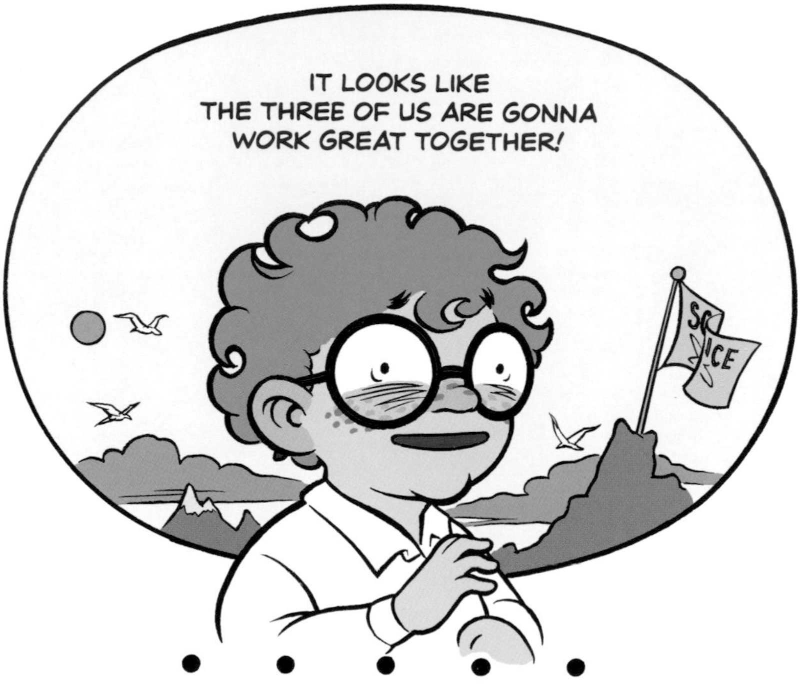
IT LOOKS LIKE THE THREE OF US ARE GONNA WORK GREAT TOGETHER!

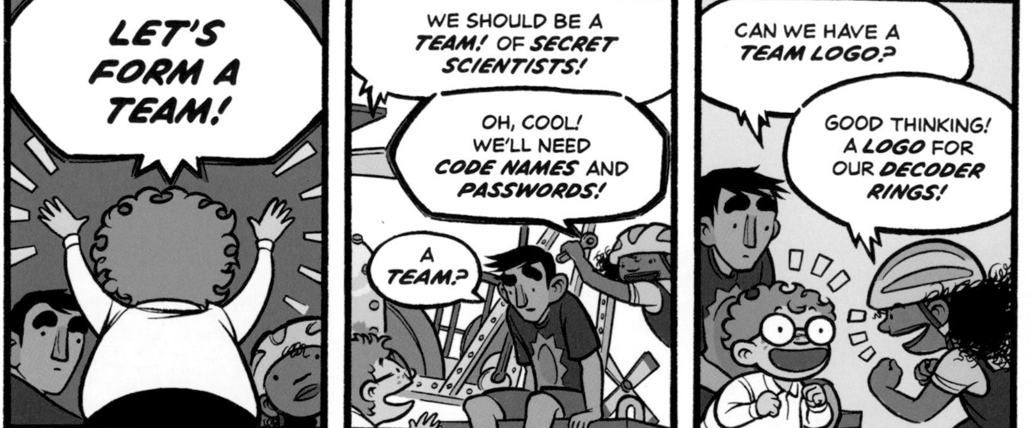
LET'S FORM A TEAM!
WE SHOULD BE A TEAM! OF SECRET SCIENTISTS!
OH, COOL! WE'LL NEED CODE NAMES AND PASSWORDS!
A TEAM?
CAN WE HAVE A TEAM LOGO?
GOOD THINKING! A LOGO FOR OUR DECODER RINGS!

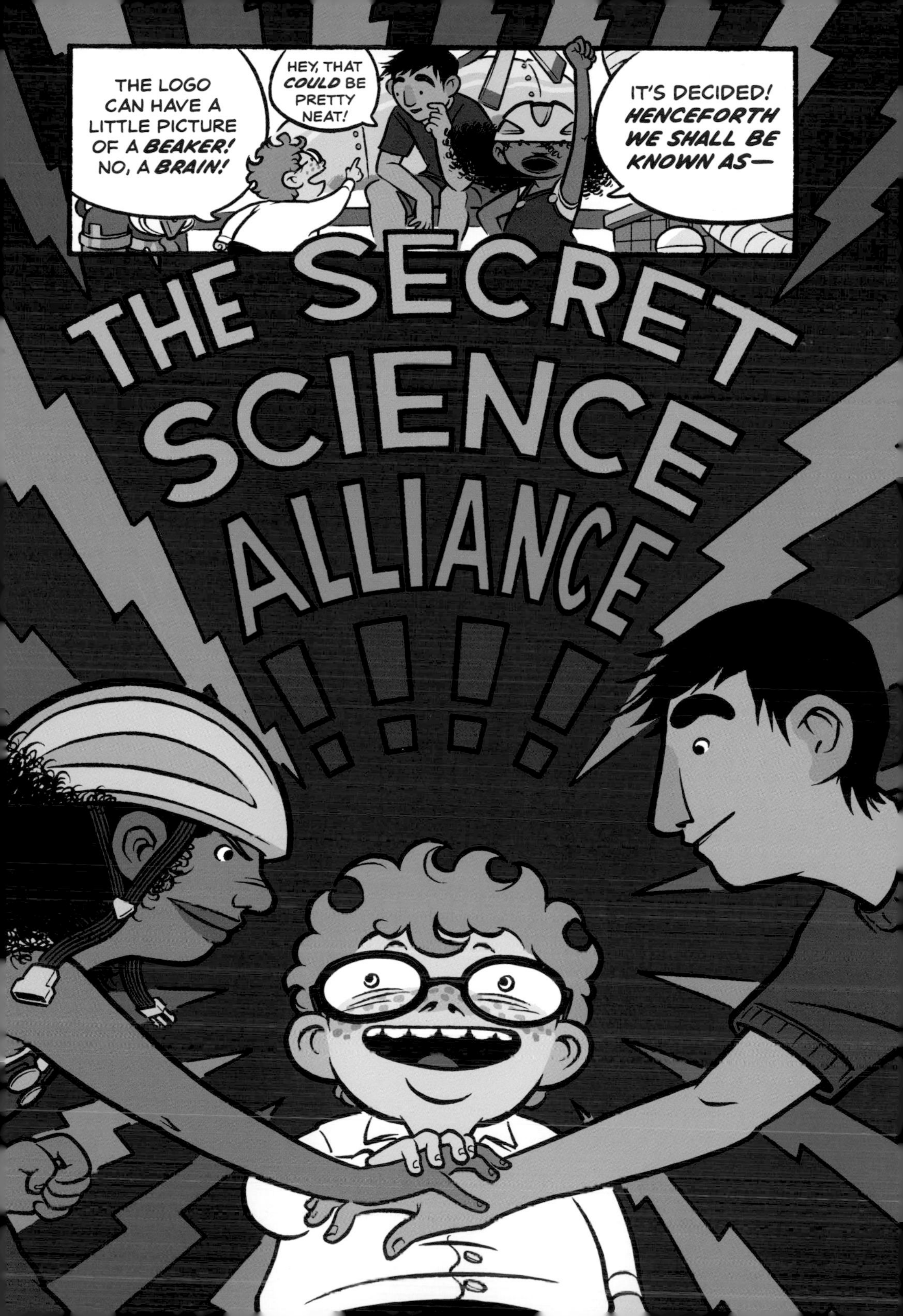
THE LOGO CAN HAVE A LITTLE PICTURE OF A *BEAKER!* NO, A *BRAIN!*
HEY, THAT *COULD* BE PRETTY NEAT!
IT'S DECIDED! *HENCEFORTH WE SHALL BE KNOWN AS—*
THE SECRET SCIENCE ALLIANCE!!!!

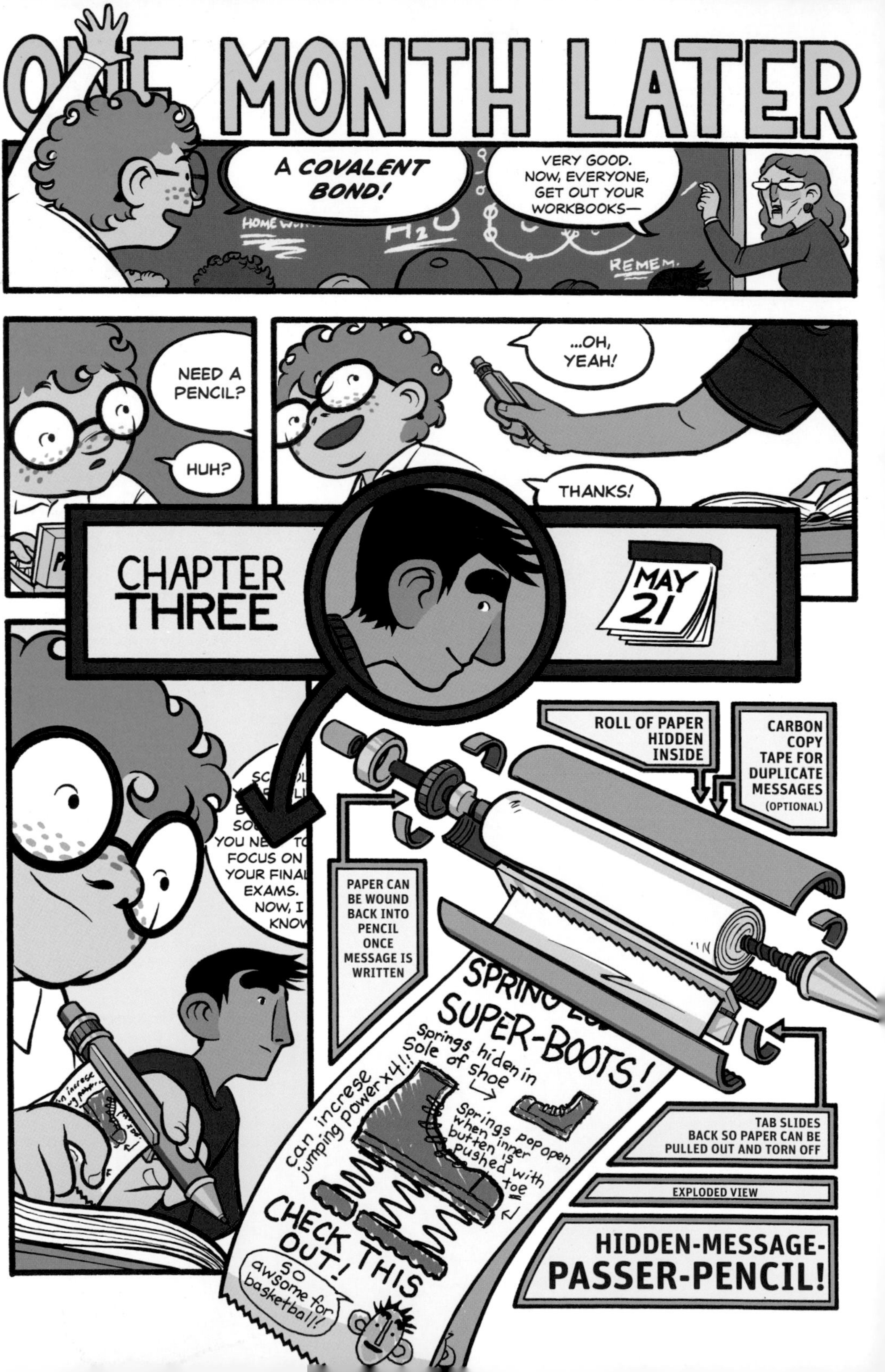

ONE MONTH LATER
A COVALENT BOND!
VERY GOOD. NOW, EVERYONE, GET OUT YOUR WORKBOOKS—
NEED A PENCIL?
HUH?
...OH, YEAH!
THANKS!
CHAPTER THREE
MAY 21
YOU NE TO FOCUS ON YOUR FINAL EXAMS. NOW, I KNOW
ROLL OF PAPER HIDDEN INSIDE
CARBON COPY TAPE FOR DUPLICATE MESSAGES (OPTIONAL)
PAPER CAN BE WOUND BACK INTO PENCIL ONCE MESSAGE IS WRITTEN
SPRING
SUPER-BOOTS!
Springs hiden in Sole of shoe
can increse jumping power x4!!
Springs pop open when inner butten is pushed with toe
CHECK THIS OUT!
SO awsome for basketball!!
TAB SLIDES BACK SO PAPER CAN BE PULLED OUT AND TORN OFF
EXPLODED VIEW
HIDDEN-MESSAGE-PASSER-PENCIL!

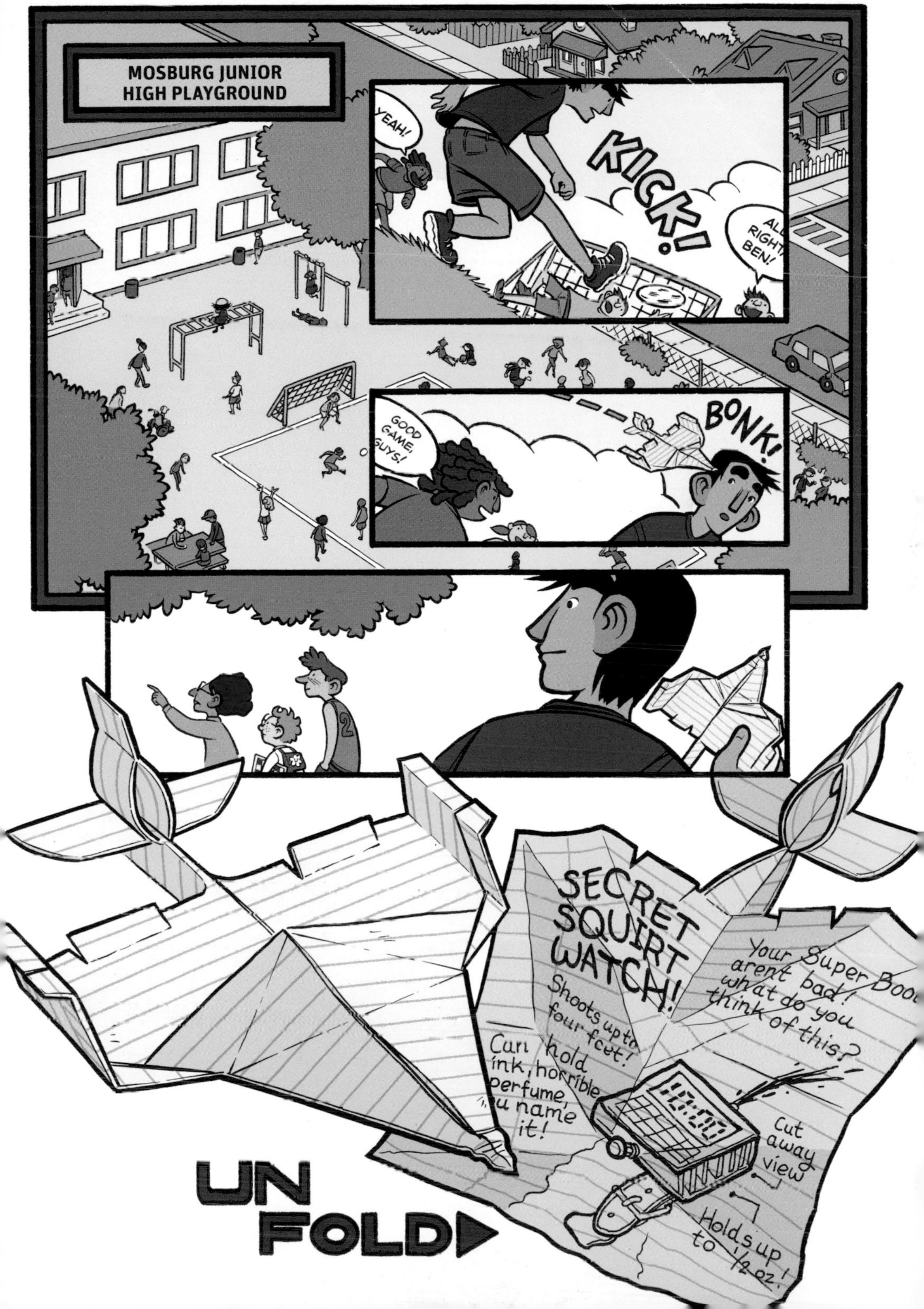
MOSBURG JUNIOR HIGH PLAYGROUND
YEAH!
KICK!
AL RIGHT BEN!
GOOD GAME, GUYS!
BONK!
SECRET SQUIRT WATCH!
Your Super Boo arent bad! what do you think of this?
Shoots up to four feet!
Can hold ink, horrible perfume, u name it!
Cut away view
Holds up to 1/2 oz!
UN FOLD

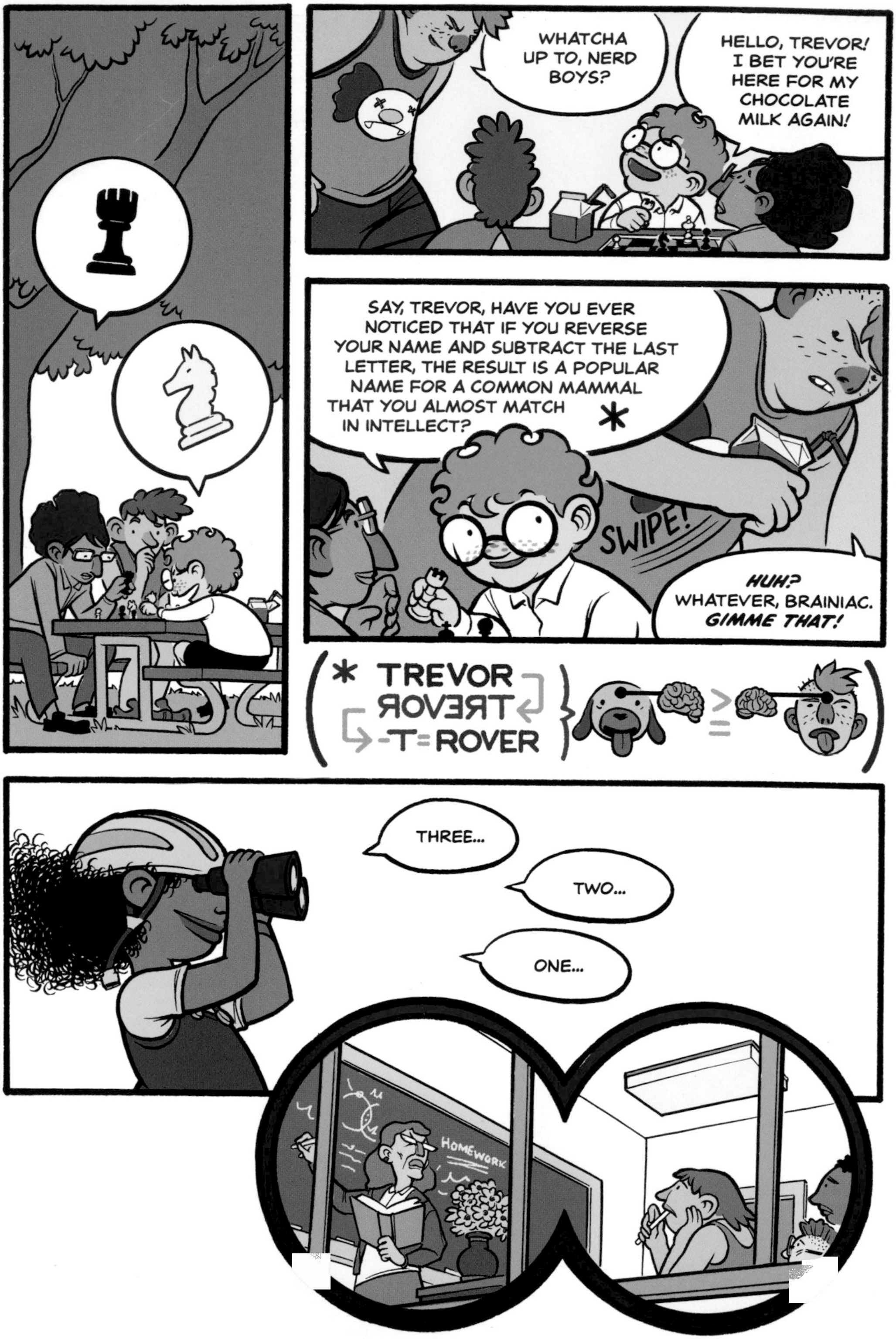
WHATCHA UP TO, NERD BOYS?
HELLO, TREVOR! I BET YOU'RE HERE FOR MY CHOCOLATE MILK AGAIN!
SAY, TREVOR, HAVE YOU EVER NOTICED THAT IF YOU REVERSE YOUR NAME AND SUBTRACT THE LAST LETTER, THE RESULT IS A POPULAR NAME FOR A COMMON MAMMAL THAT YOU ALMOST MATCH IN INTELLECT? *
SWIPE!
HUH? WHATEVER, BRAINIAC. GIMME THAT!
* TREVOR
ROVERT
-T=ROVER
THREE...
TWO...
ONE...
HOMEWORK

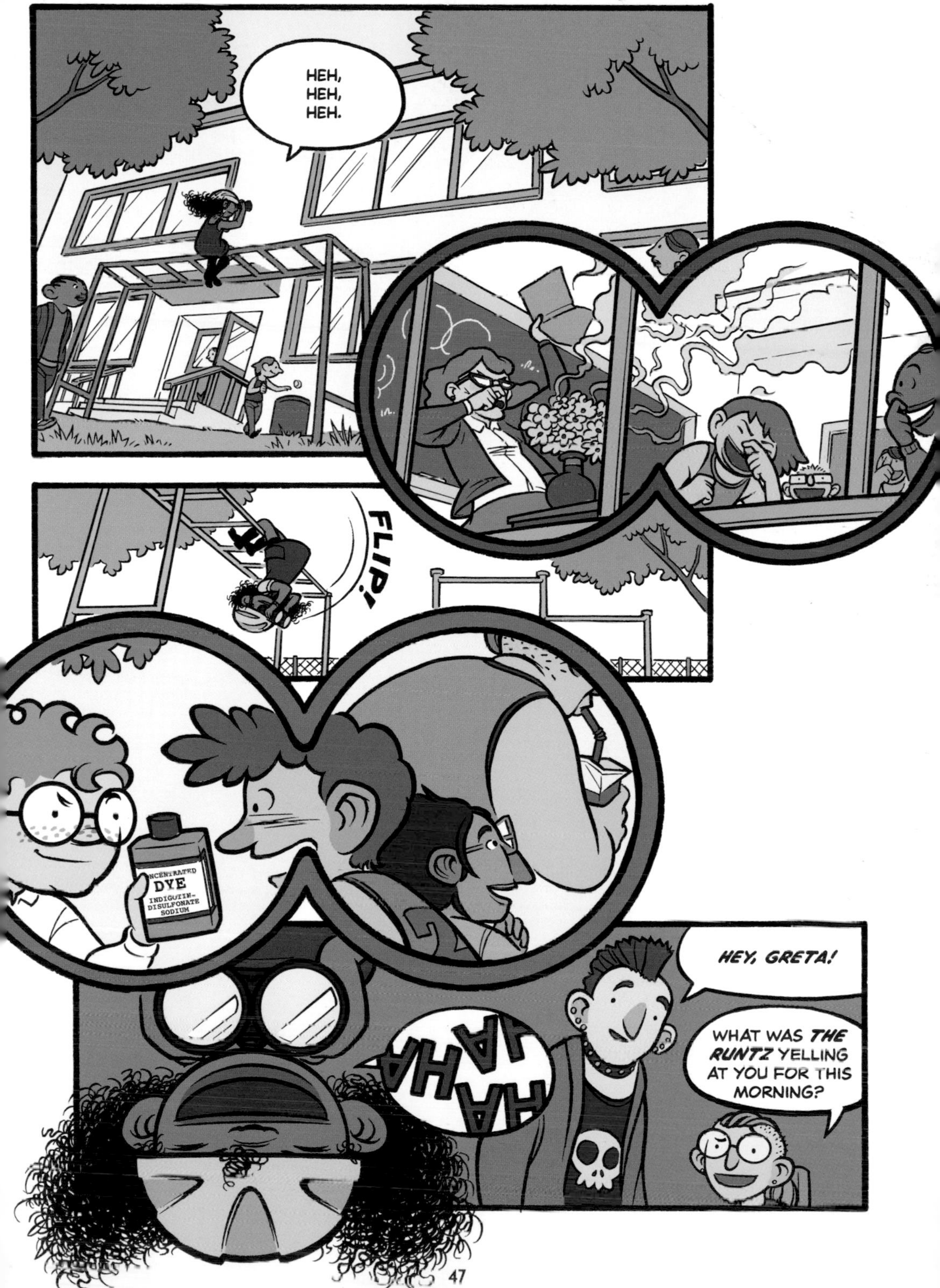
HEH, HEH, HEH.
FLIP!
DYE
INDIGOTIN-DISULFONATE SODIUM
HAHAHA
HEY, GRETA!
WHAT WAS *THE RUNTZ* YELLING AT YOU FOR THIS MORNING?

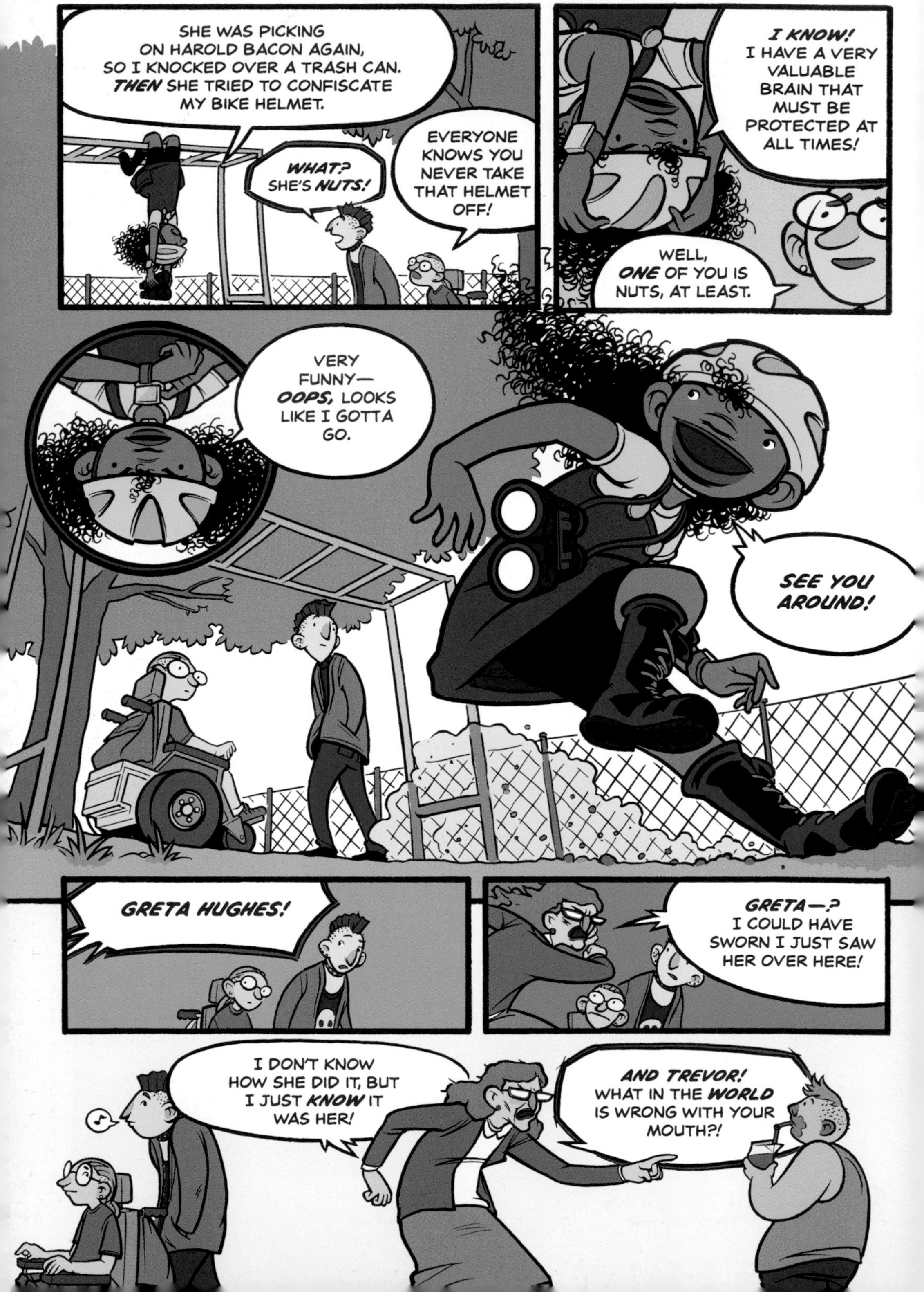

SHE WAS PICKING ON HAROLD BACON AGAIN, SO I KNOCKED OVER A TRASH CAN. *THEN* SHE TRIED TO CONFISCATE MY BIKE HELMET.
WHAT? SHE'S *NUTS!*
EVERYONE KNOWS YOU NEVER TAKE THAT HELMET OFF!
I KNOW! I HAVE A VERY VALUABLE BRAIN THAT MUST BE PROTECTED AT ALL TIMES!
WELL, *ONE* OF YOU IS NUTS, AT LEAST.
VERY FUNNY— *OOPS,* LOOKS LIKE I GOTTA GO.
SEE YOU AROUND!
GRETA HUGHES!
GRETA—? I COULD HAVE SWORN I JUST SAW HER OVER HERE!
I DON'T KNOW HOW SHE DID IT, BUT I JUST *KNOW* IT WAS HER!
AND TREVOR! WHAT IN THE *WORLD* IS WRONG WITH YOUR MOUTH?!

AFTER SCHOOL

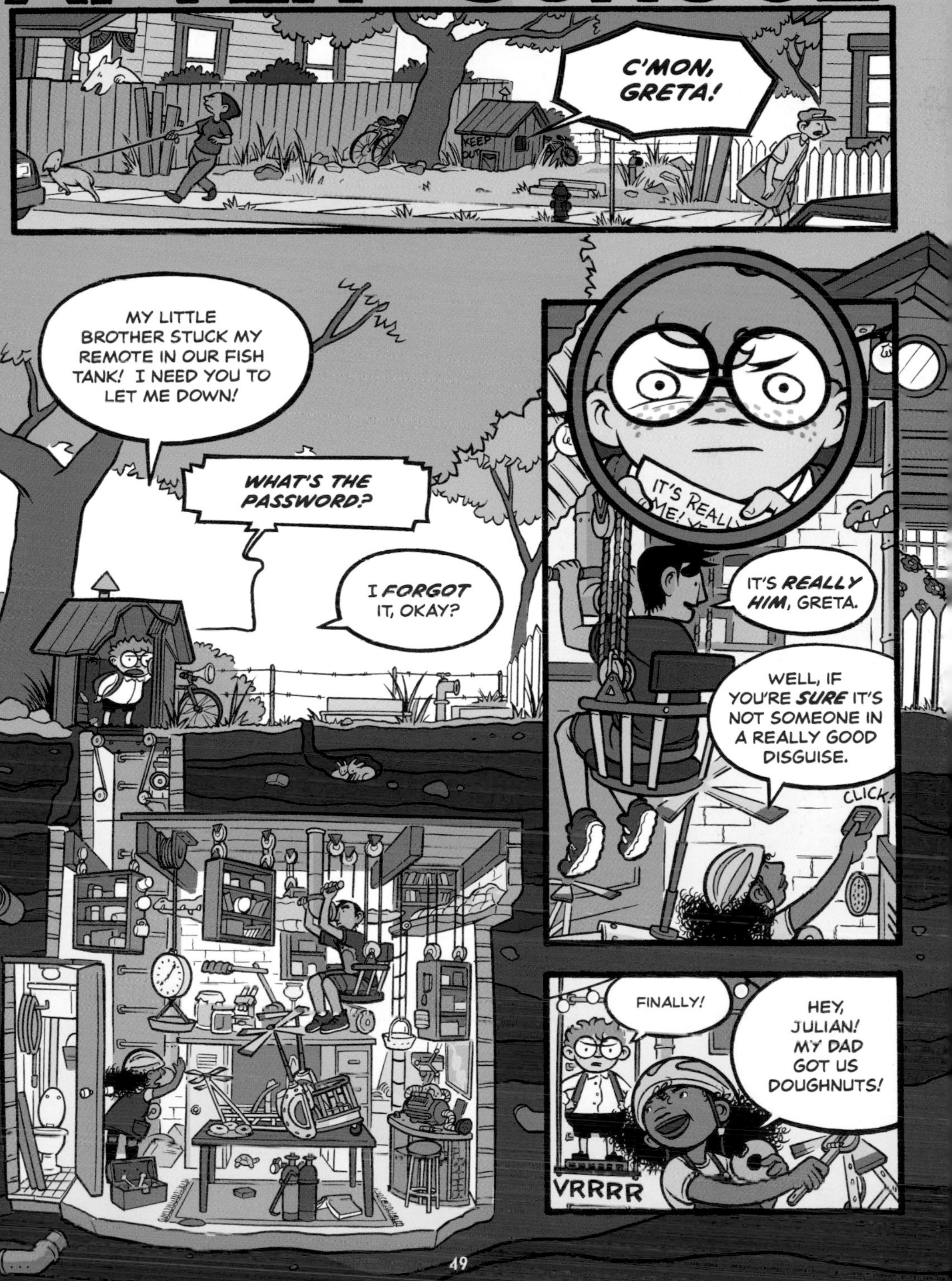
KEEP OUT
C'MON, GRETA!
MY LITTLE BROTHER STUCK MY REMOTE IN OUR FISH TANK! I NEED YOU TO LET ME DOWN!
WHAT'S THE PASSWORD?
I *FORGOT* IT, OKAY?
IT'S *REALLY HIM*, GRETA.
WELL, IF YOU'RE *SURE* IT'S NOT SOMEONE IN A REALLY GOOD DISGUISE.
CLICK!
FINALLY!
HEY, JULIAN! MY DAD GOT US DOUGHNUTS!
VRRRR

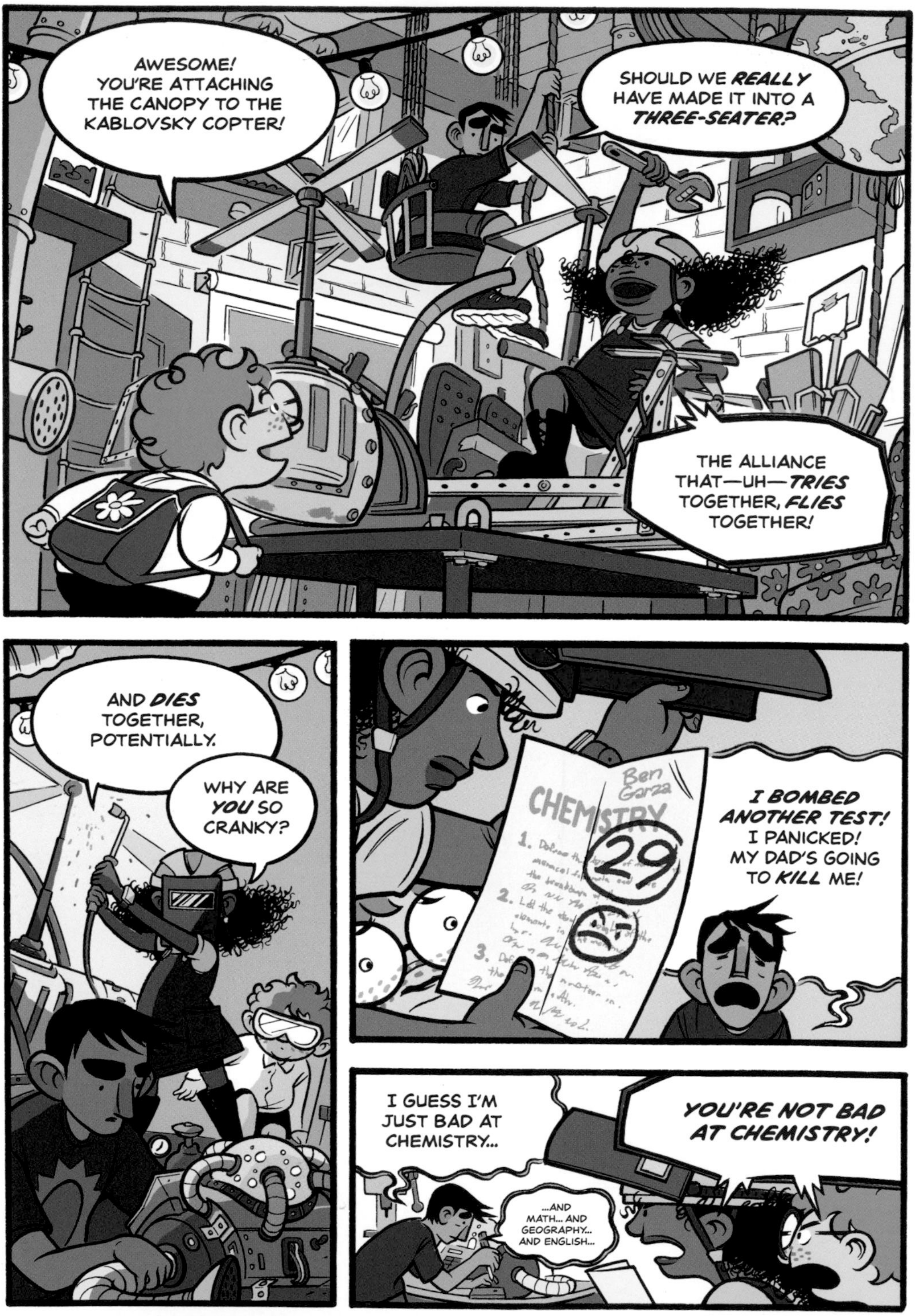
AWESOME! YOU'RE ATTACHING THE CANOPY TO THE KABLOVSKY COPTER!
SHOULD WE *REALLY* HAVE MADE IT INTO A *THREE-SEATER?*
THE ALLIANCE THAT—UH—*TRIES* TOGETHER, *FLIES* TOGETHER!
AND *DIES* TOGETHER, POTENTIALLY.
WHY ARE *YOU* SO CRANKY?
Ben Garza
CHEMISTRY
29
I BOMBED ANOTHER TEST! I PANICKED! MY DAD'S GOING TO *KILL* ME!
I GUESS I'M JUST BAD AT CHEMISTRY...
...AND MATH... AND GEOGRAPHY... AND ENGLISH...
YOU'RE NOT BAD AT CHEMISTRY!

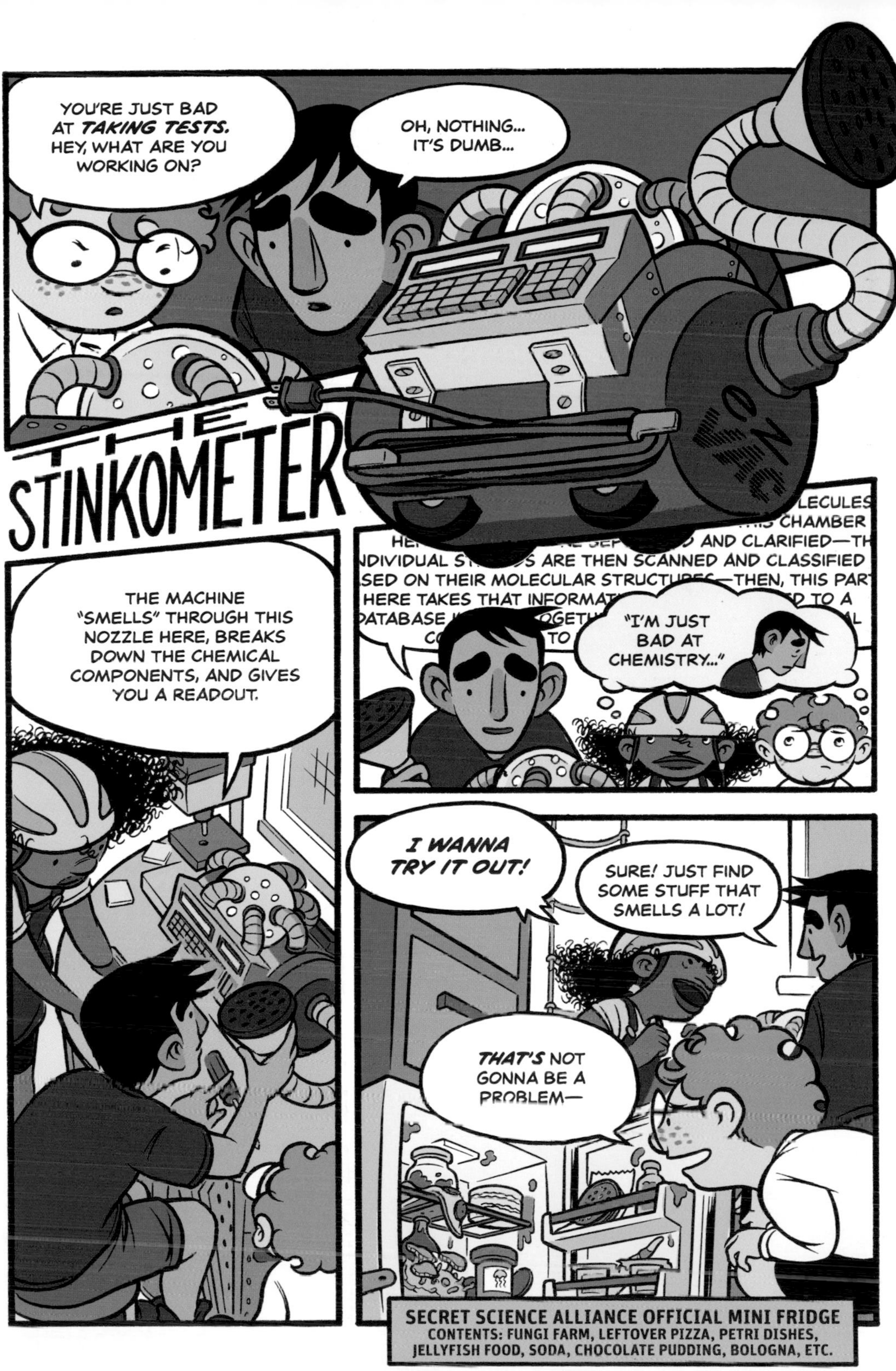
YOU'RE JUST BAD AT *TAKING TESTS.* HEY, WHAT ARE YOU WORKING ON?
OH, NOTHING... IT'S DUMB...
THE STINKOMETER
THE MACHINE "SMELLS" THROUGH THIS NOZZLE HERE, BREAKS DOWN THE CHEMICAL COMPONENTS, AND GIVES YOU A READOUT.
...LECULES ...THIS CHAMBER ...AND CLARIFIED—TH... ...NDIVIDUAL ST... ARE THEN SCANNED AND CLASSIFIED ...SED ON THEIR MOLECULAR STRUCTURES—THEN, THIS PART HERE TAKES THAT INFORMAT... TO A DATABASE ...
"I'M JUST BAD AT CHEMISTRY..."
I WANNA TRY IT OUT!
SURE! JUST FIND SOME STUFF THAT SMELLS A LOT!
THAT'S NOT GONNA BE A PROBLEM—
SECRET SCIENCE ALLIANCE OFFICIAL MINI FRIDGE
CONTENTS: FUNGI FARM, LEFTOVER PIZZA, PETRI DISHES, JELLYFISH FOOD, SODA, CHOCOLATE PUDDING, BOLOGNA, ETC.

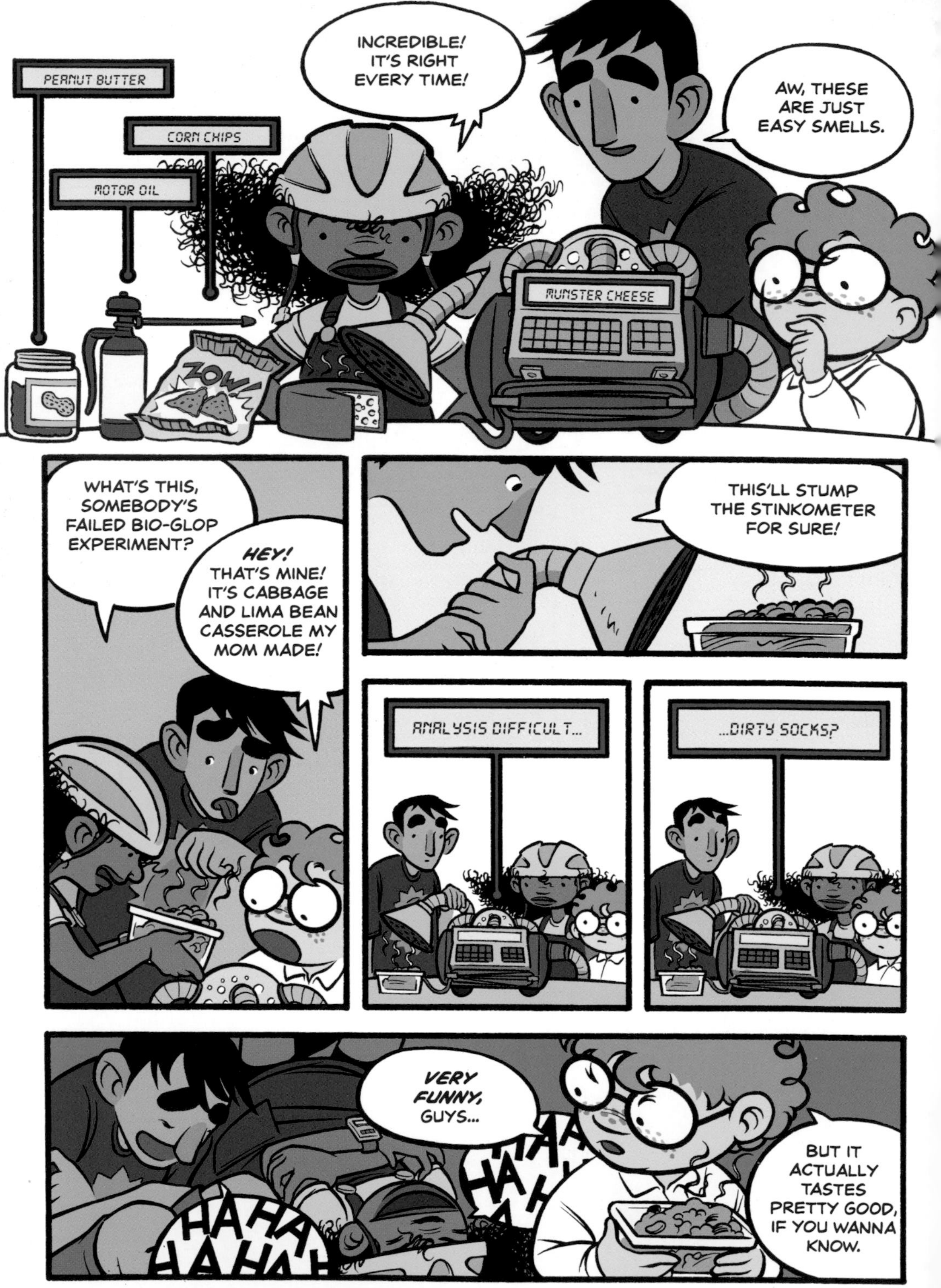

PEANUT BUTTER
CORN CHIPS
MOTOR OIL
INCREDIBLE! IT'S RIGHT EVERY TIME!
AW, THESE ARE JUST EASY SMELLS.
ZOW!
MUNSTER CHEESE
WHAT'S THIS, SOMEBODY'S FAILED BIO-GLOP EXPERIMENT?
HEY! THAT'S MINE! IT'S CABBAGE AND LIMA BEAN CASSEROLE MY MOM MADE!
THIS'LL STUMP THE STINKOMETER FOR SURE!
ANALYSIS DIFFICULT...
...DIRTY SOCKS?
VERY FUNNY, GUYS...
HAHAHA
HAHAHA
HAHAHAH
BUT IT ACTUALLY TASTES PRETTY GOOD, IF YOU WANNA KNOW.

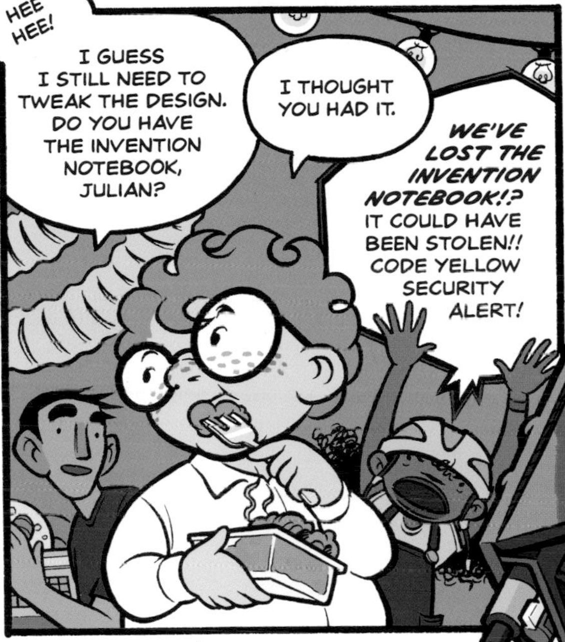
HEE HEE!
I GUESS I STILL NEED TO TWEAK THE DESIGN. DO YOU HAVE THE INVENTION NOTEBOOK, JULIAN?
I THOUGHT YOU HAD IT.
WE'VE LOST THE INVENTION NOTEBOOK!? IT COULD HAVE BEEN STOLEN!! CODE YELLOW SECURITY ALERT!

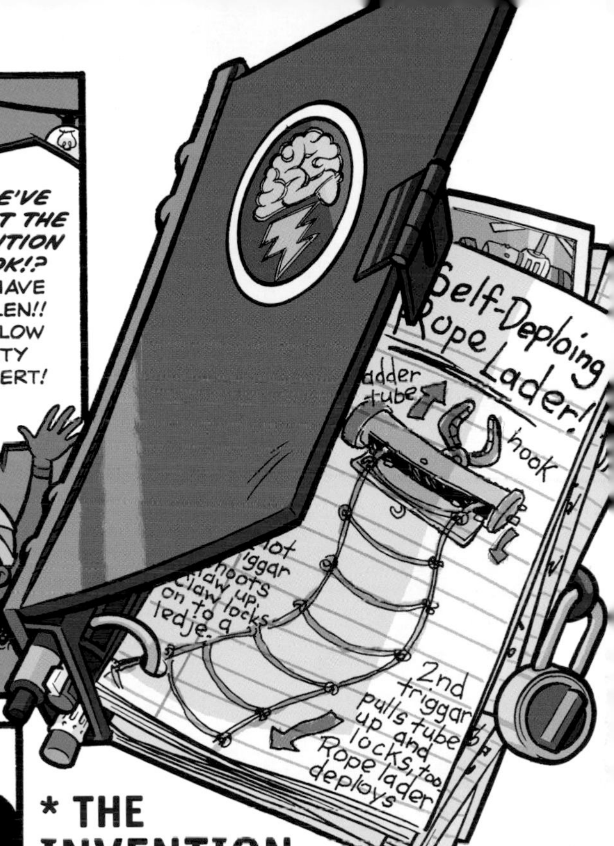
Self-Deploing Rope Lader!
adder tube
hook
ot triggar shoots claw up, locks on to a ledje.
2nd triggar pulls tube up and locks, too Rope lader deploys

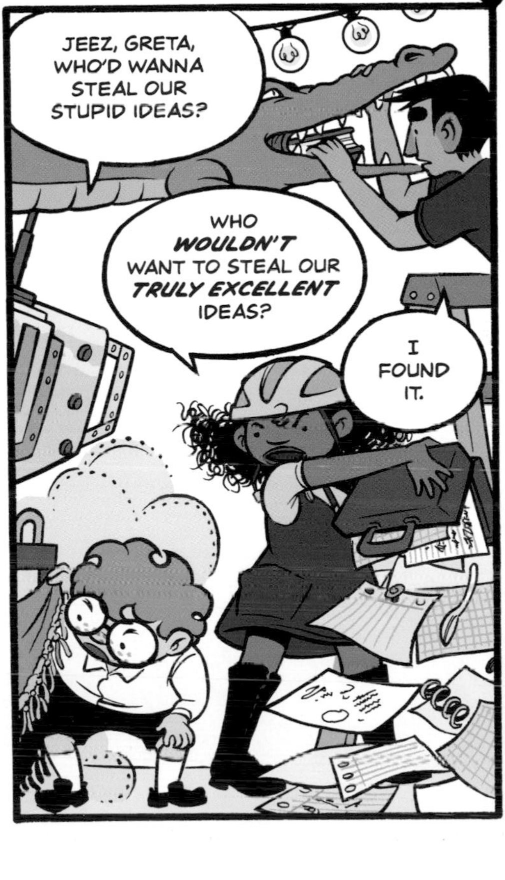
JEEZ, GRETA, WHO'D WANNA STEAL OUR STUPID IDEAS?
WHO *WOULDN'T* WANT TO STEAL OUR *TRULY EXCELLENT* IDEAS?
I FOUND IT.

* THE INVENTION NOTEBOOK!

THE NOTES AND DIAGRAMS FOR EVERY SCI-ALLI INVENTION ARE CONTAINED WITHIN THIS HIGHLY VALUABLE VOLUME. FOR THIS REASON THE INVENTION NOTEBOOK IS THE SECRET SCIENCE ALLIANCE'S MOST CLOSELY GUARDED POSSESSION!

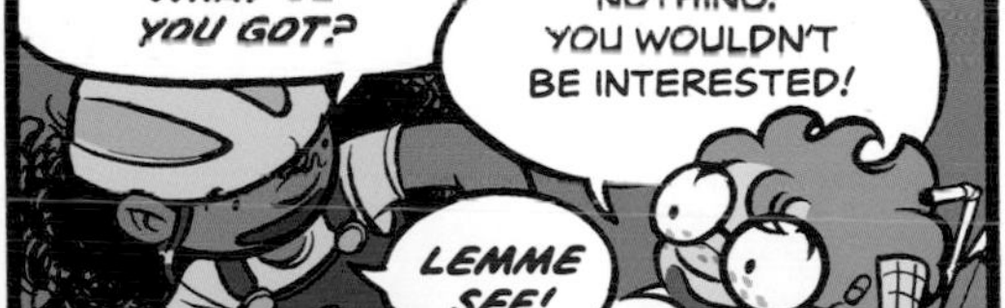
NOW IT SMELLS WEIRD...
I HAVE SOME STUFF TO RECORD!

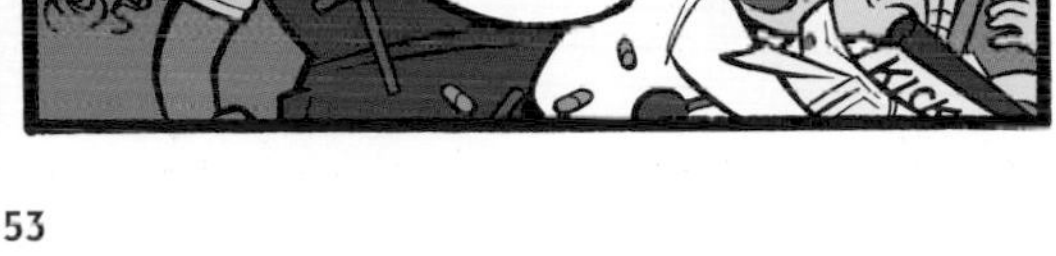
WHAT'VE YOU GOT?
NOTHING! YOU WOULDN'T BE INTERESTED!
LEMME SEE!

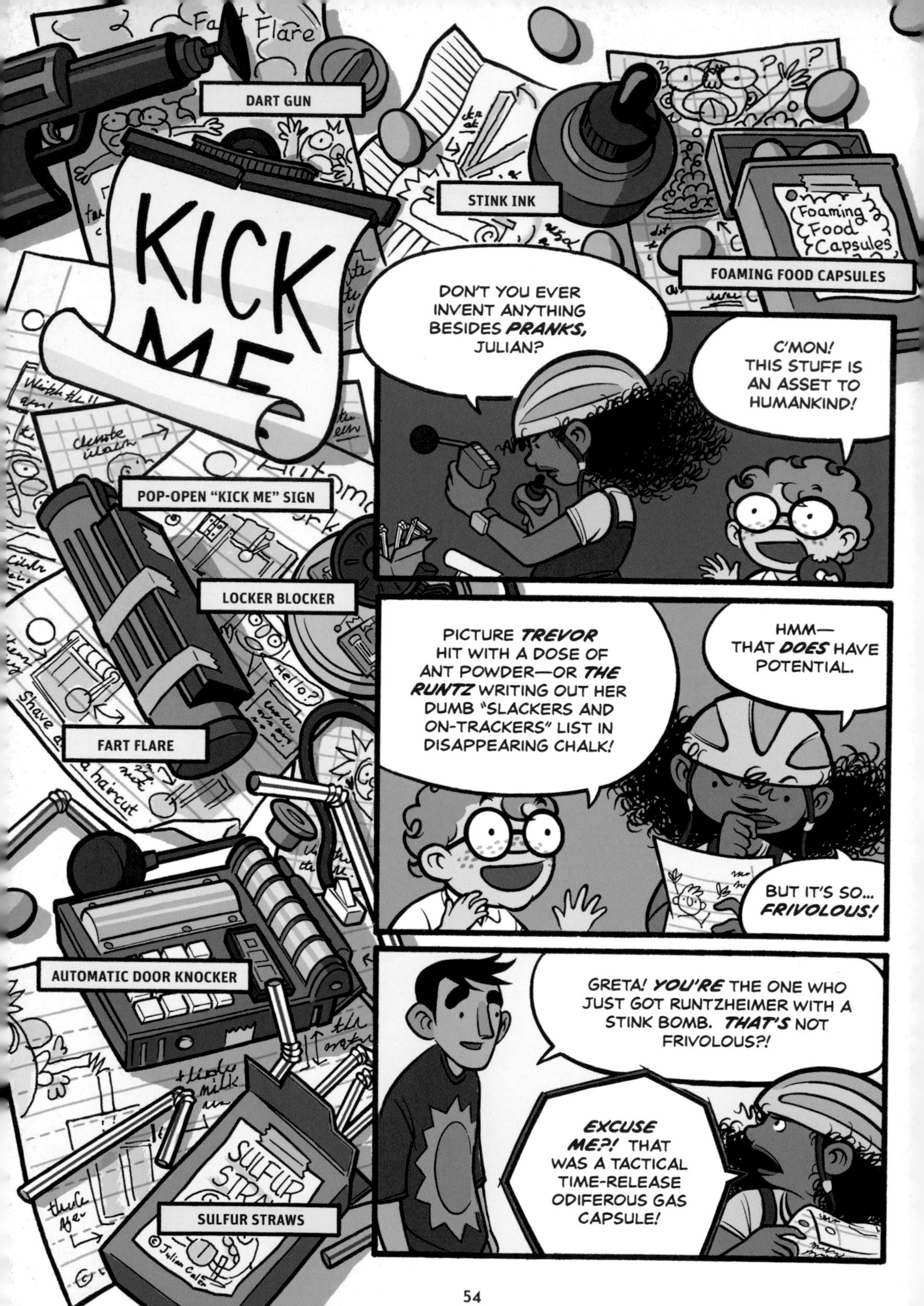
DART GUN
STINK INK
FOAMING FOOD CAPSULES
POP-OPEN "KICK ME" SIGN
LOCKER BLOCKER
FART FLARE
AUTOMATIC DOOR KNOCKER
SULFUR STRAWS
DON'T YOU EVER INVENT ANYTHING BESIDES PRANKS, JULIAN?
C'MON! THIS STUFF IS AN ASSET TO HUMANKIND!
PICTURE TREVOR HIT WITH A DOSE OF ANT POWDER—OR THE RUNTZ WRITING OUT HER DUMB "SLACKERS AND ON-TRACKERS" LIST IN DISAPPEARING CHALK!
HMM— THAT DOES HAVE POTENTIAL.
BUT IT'S SO... FRIVOLOUS!
GRETA! YOU'RE THE ONE WHO JUST GOT RUNTZHEIMER WITH A STINK BOMB. THAT'S NOT FRIVOLOUS?!
EXCUSE ME?! THAT WAS A TACTICAL TIME-RELEASE ODIFEROUS GAS CAPSULE!

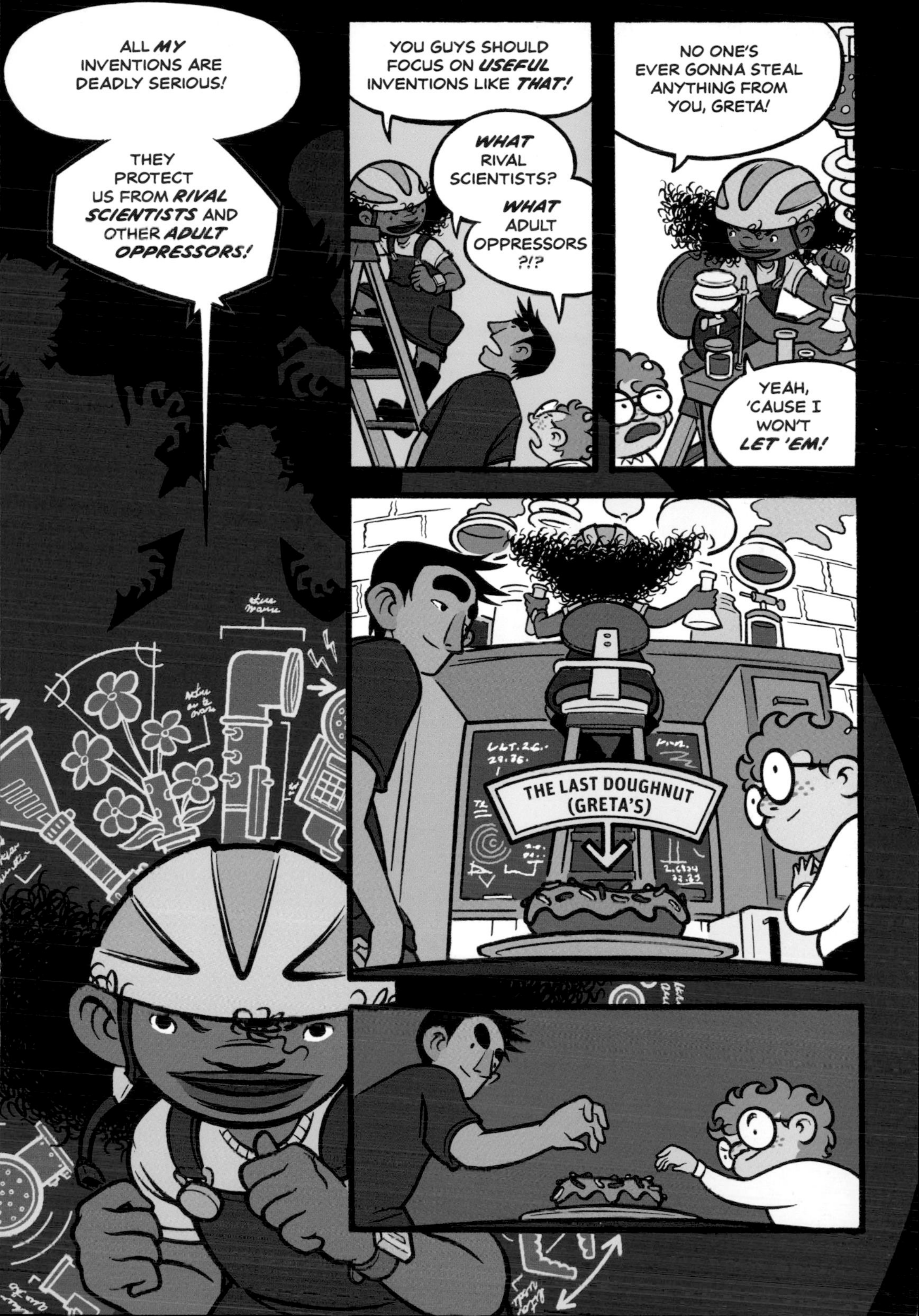
ALL *MY* INVENTIONS ARE DEADLY SERIOUS!
THEY PROTECT US FROM *RIVAL SCIENTISTS* AND OTHER *ADULT OPPRESSORS!*
YOU GUYS SHOULD FOCUS ON *USEFUL* INVENTIONS LIKE *THAT!*
WHAT RIVAL SCIENTISTS?
WHAT ADULT OPPRESSORS ?!?
NO ONE'S EVER GONNA STEAL ANYTHING FROM YOU, GRETA!
YEAH, 'CAUSE I WON'T *LET 'EM!*
THE LAST DOUGHNUT (GRETA'S)

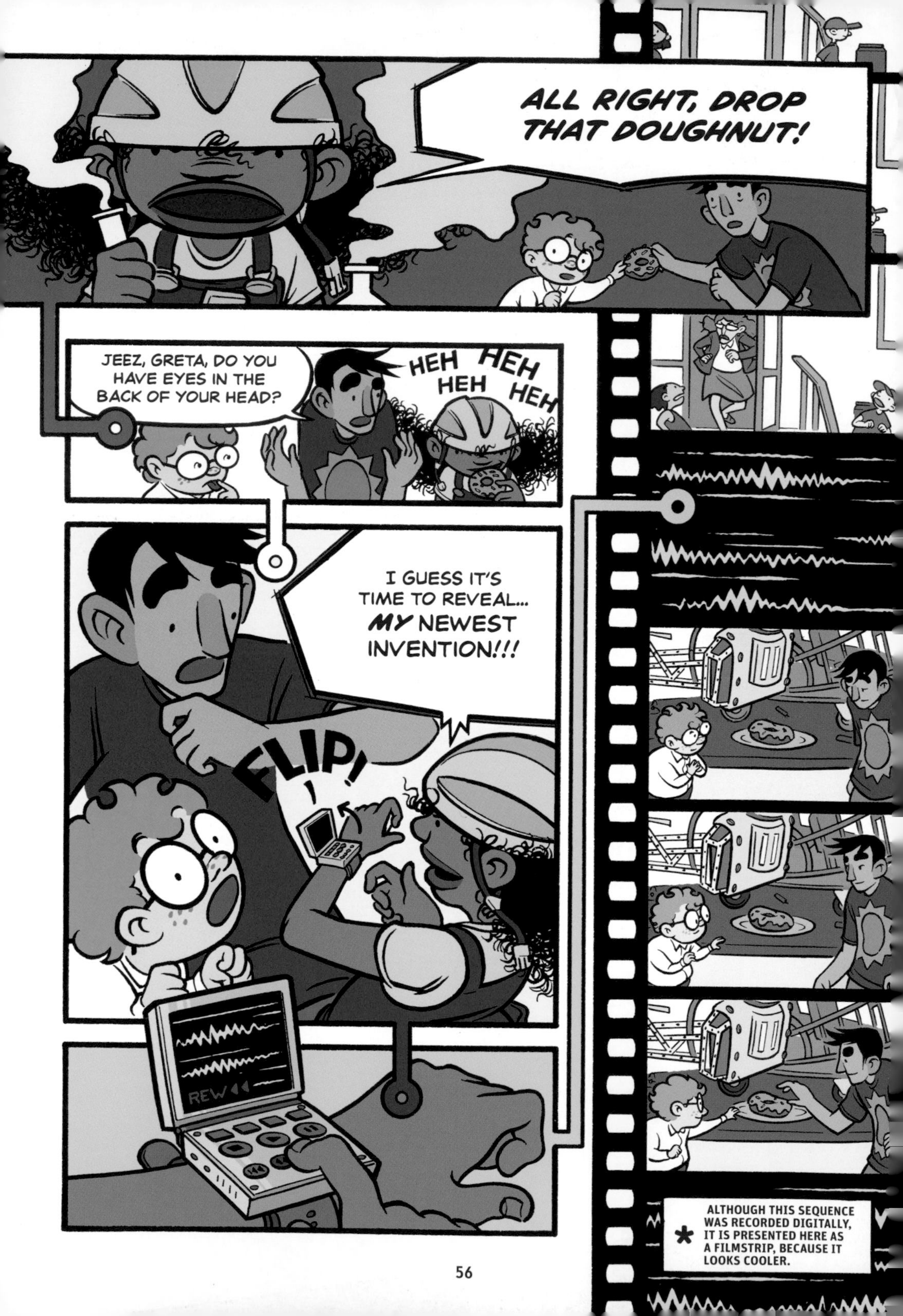
ALL RIGHT, DROP THAT DOUGHNUT!
JEEZ, GRETA, DO YOU HAVE EYES IN THE BACK OF YOUR HEAD?
HEH HEH HEH HEH
I GUESS IT'S TIME TO REVEAL... MY NEWEST INVENTION!!!
FLIP!
REW
ALTHOUGH THIS SEQUENCE WAS RECORDED DIGITALLY, IT IS PRESENTED HERE AS A FILMSTRIP, BECAUSE IT LOOKS COOLER.

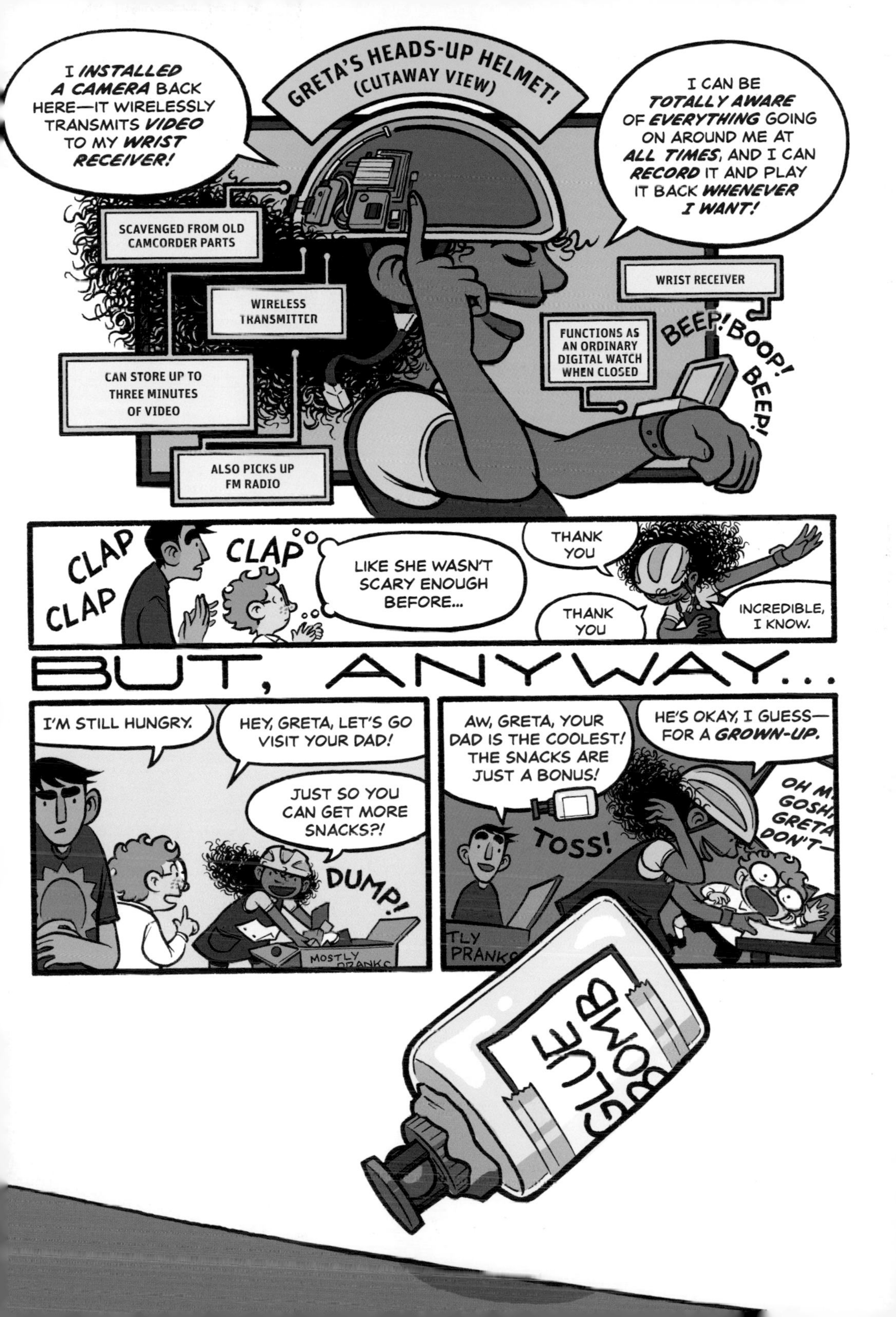
GRETA'S HEADS-UP HELMET! (CUTAWAY VIEW)
I INSTALLED A CAMERA BACK HERE—IT WIRELESSLY TRANSMITS VIDEO TO MY WRIST RECEIVER!
I CAN BE TOTALLY AWARE OF EVERYTHING GOING ON AROUND ME AT ALL TIMES, AND I CAN RECORD IT AND PLAY IT BACK WHENEVER I WANT!
SCAVENGED FROM OLD CAMCORDER PARTS
WIRELESS TRANSMITTER
CAN STORE UP TO THREE MINUTES OF VIDEO
ALSO PICKS UP FM RADIO
WRIST RECEIVER
FUNCTIONS AS AN ORDINARY DIGITAL WATCH WHEN CLOSED
BEEP! BOOP! BEEP!
CLAP CLAP CLAP
LIKE SHE WASN'T SCARY ENOUGH BEFORE...
THANK YOU
THANK YOU
INCREDIBLE, I KNOW.
BUT, ANYWAY...
I'M STILL HUNGRY.
HEY, GRETA, LET'S GO VISIT YOUR DAD!
JUST SO YOU CAN GET MORE SNACKS?!
DUMP!
MOSTLY PRANKS
AW, GRETA, YOUR DAD IS THE COOLEST! THE SNACKS ARE JUST A BONUS!
HE'S OKAY, I GUESS—FOR A GROWN-UP.
TOSS!
OH M GOSH GRETA DON'T—
TLY PRANKS
GLUE BOMB

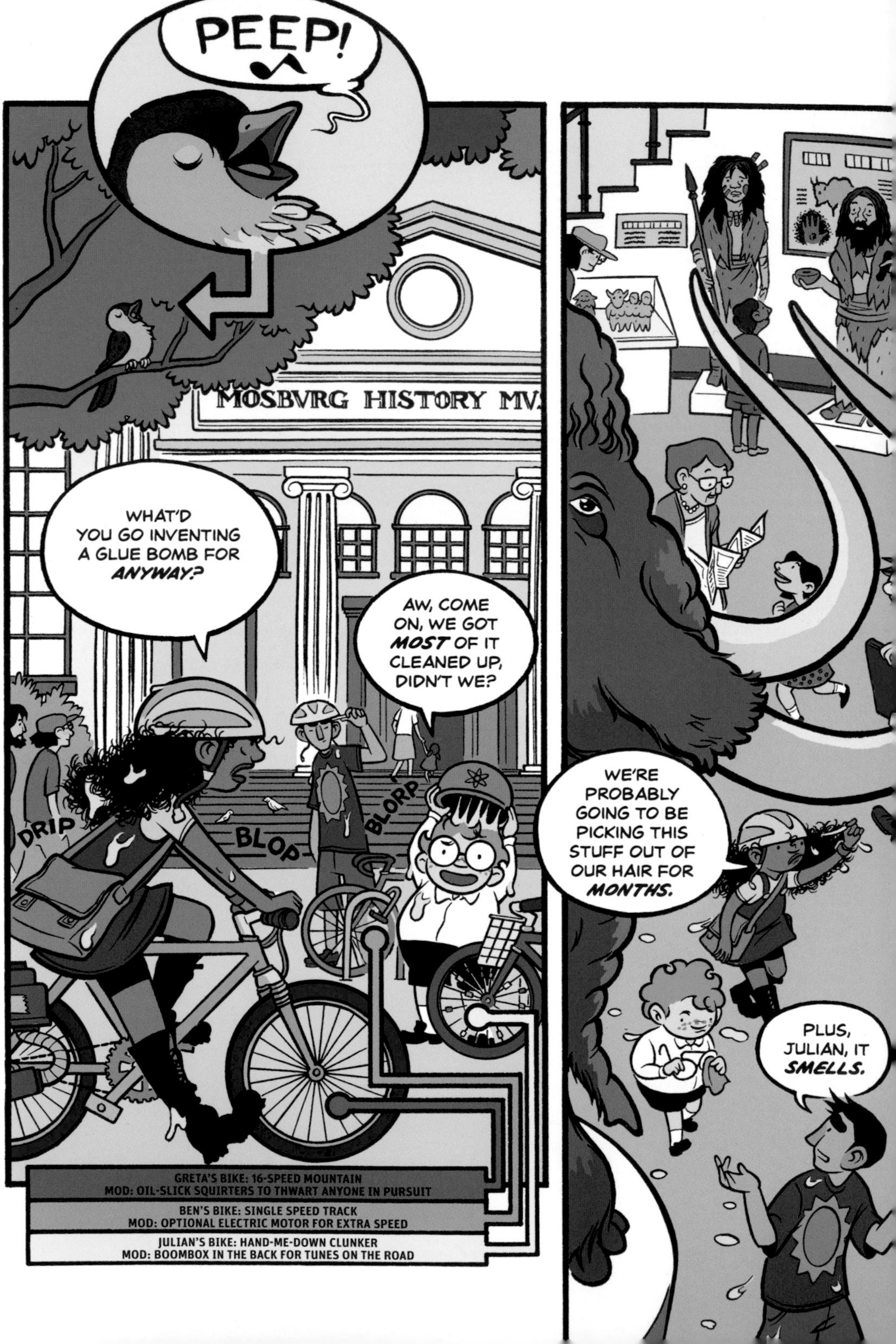
PEEP!
MOSBVRG HISTORY MV
WHAT'D YOU GO INVENTING A GLUE BOMB FOR *ANYWAY?*
AW, COME ON, WE GOT *MOST* OF IT CLEANED UP, DIDN'T WE?
DRIP
BLOP
BLORP
GRETA'S BIKE: 16-SPEED MOUNTAIN
MOD: OIL-SLICK SQUIRTERS TO THWART ANYONE IN PURSUIT
BEN'S BIKE: SINGLE SPEED TRACK
MOD: OPTIONAL ELECTRIC MOTOR FOR EXTRA SPEED
JULIAN'S BIKE: HAND-ME-DOWN CLUNKER
MOD: BOOMBOX IN THE BACK FOR TUNES ON THE ROAD
WE'RE PROBABLY GOING TO BE PICKING THIS STUFF OUT OF OUR HAIR FOR *MONTHS.*
PLUS, JULIAN, IT *SMELLS.*

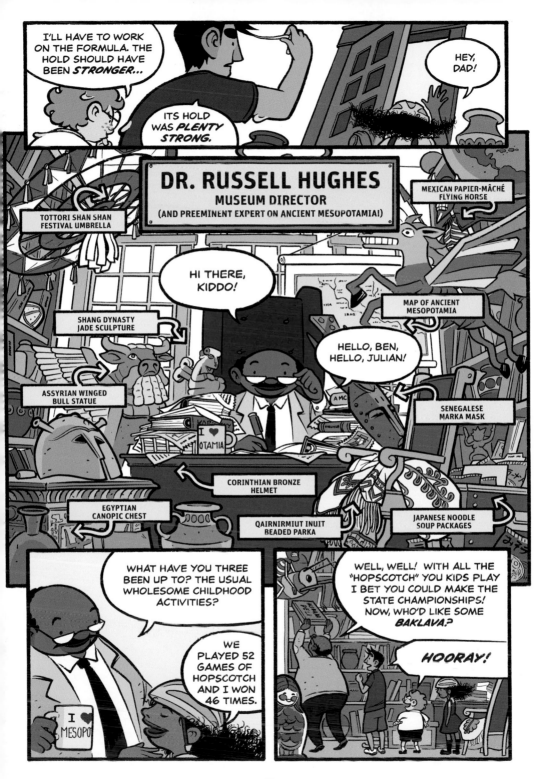

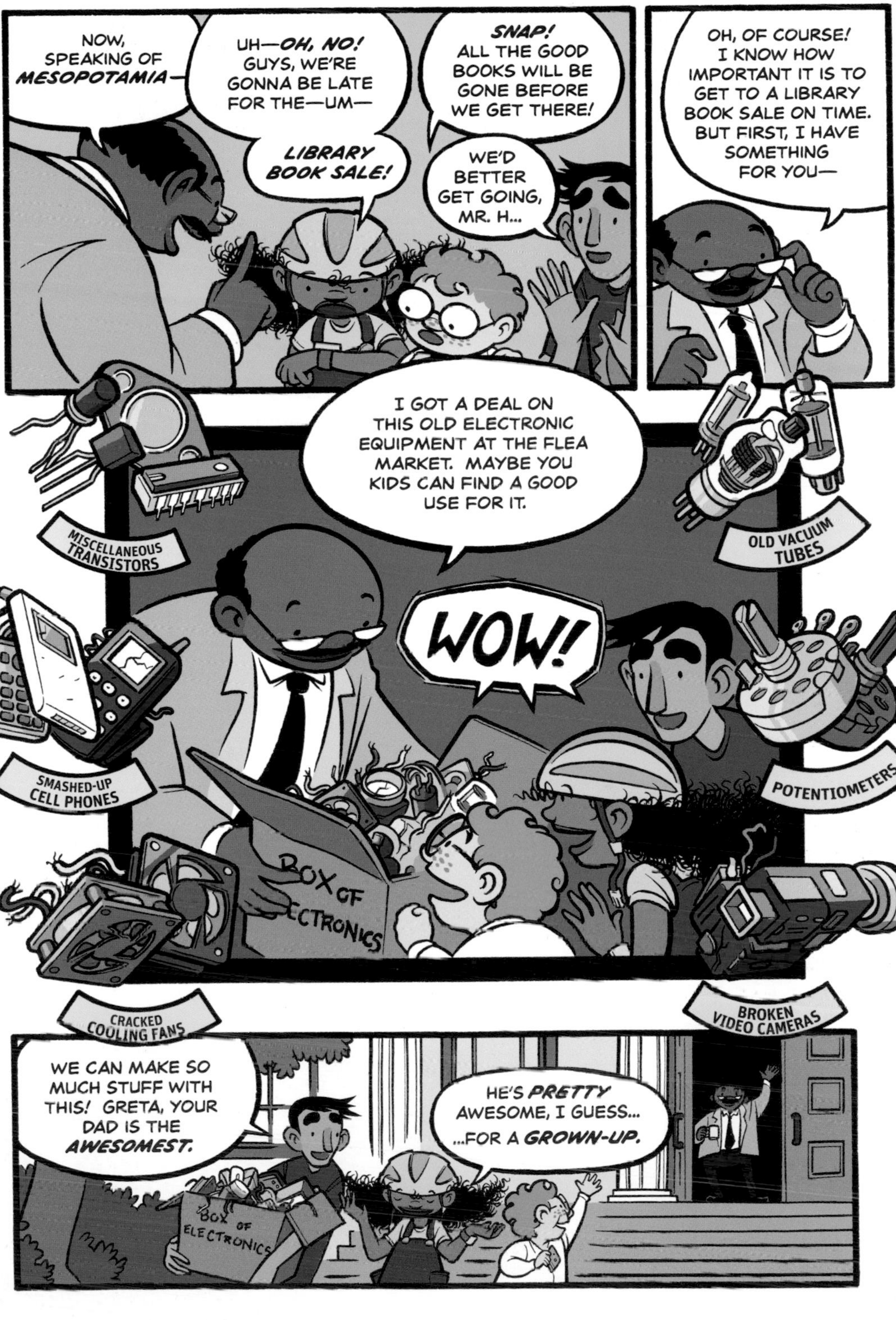
NOW, SPEAKING OF *MESOPOTAMIA*—
UH—*OH, NO!* GUYS, WE'RE GONNA BE LATE FOR THE—UM—
LIBRARY BOOK SALE!
SNAP! ALL THE GOOD BOOKS WILL BE GONE BEFORE WE GET THERE!
WE'D BETTER GET GOING, MR. H...
OH, OF COURSE! I KNOW HOW IMPORTANT IT IS TO GET TO A LIBRARY BOOK SALE ON TIME. BUT FIRST, I HAVE SOMETHING FOR YOU—
I GOT A DEAL ON THIS OLD ELECTRONIC EQUIPMENT AT THE FLEA MARKET. MAYBE YOU KIDS CAN FIND A GOOD USE FOR IT.
WOW!
MISCELLANEOUS TRANSISTORS
OLD VACUUM TUBES
SMASHED-UP CELL PHONES
POTENTIOMETERS
BOX OF ELECTRONICS
CRACKED COOLING FANS
BROKEN VIDEO CAMERAS
WE CAN MAKE SO MUCH STUFF WITH THIS! GRETA, YOUR DAD IS THE *AWESOMEST.*
HE'S *PRETTY* AWESOME, I GUESS... ...FOR A *GROWN-UP.*
BOX OF ELECTRONICS

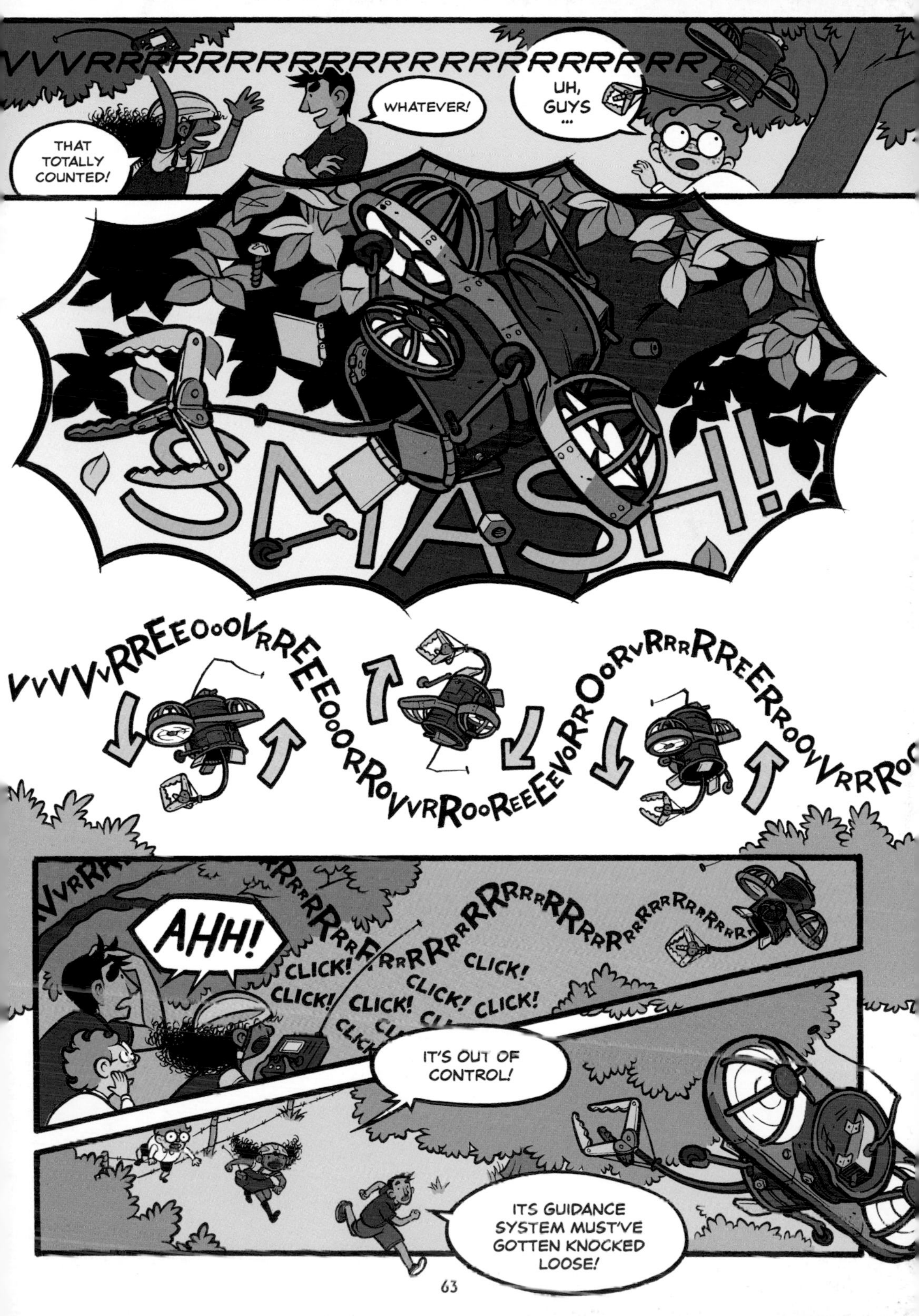
VVVVRRRRRRRRRRRRRRRRRRRRRRRR
THAT TOTALLY COUNTED!
WHATEVER!
UH, GUYS ...
SMASH!
VVVVVRREEOOOVRREEEEOOORROVVRROOREEEEVORROORVRRRRREERROOVVRRRO
AHH!
CLICK! CLICK! CLICK! CLICK! CLICK! CLICK!
IT'S OUT OF CONTROL!
ITS GUIDANCE SYSTEM MUST'VE GOTTEN KNOCKED LOOSE!

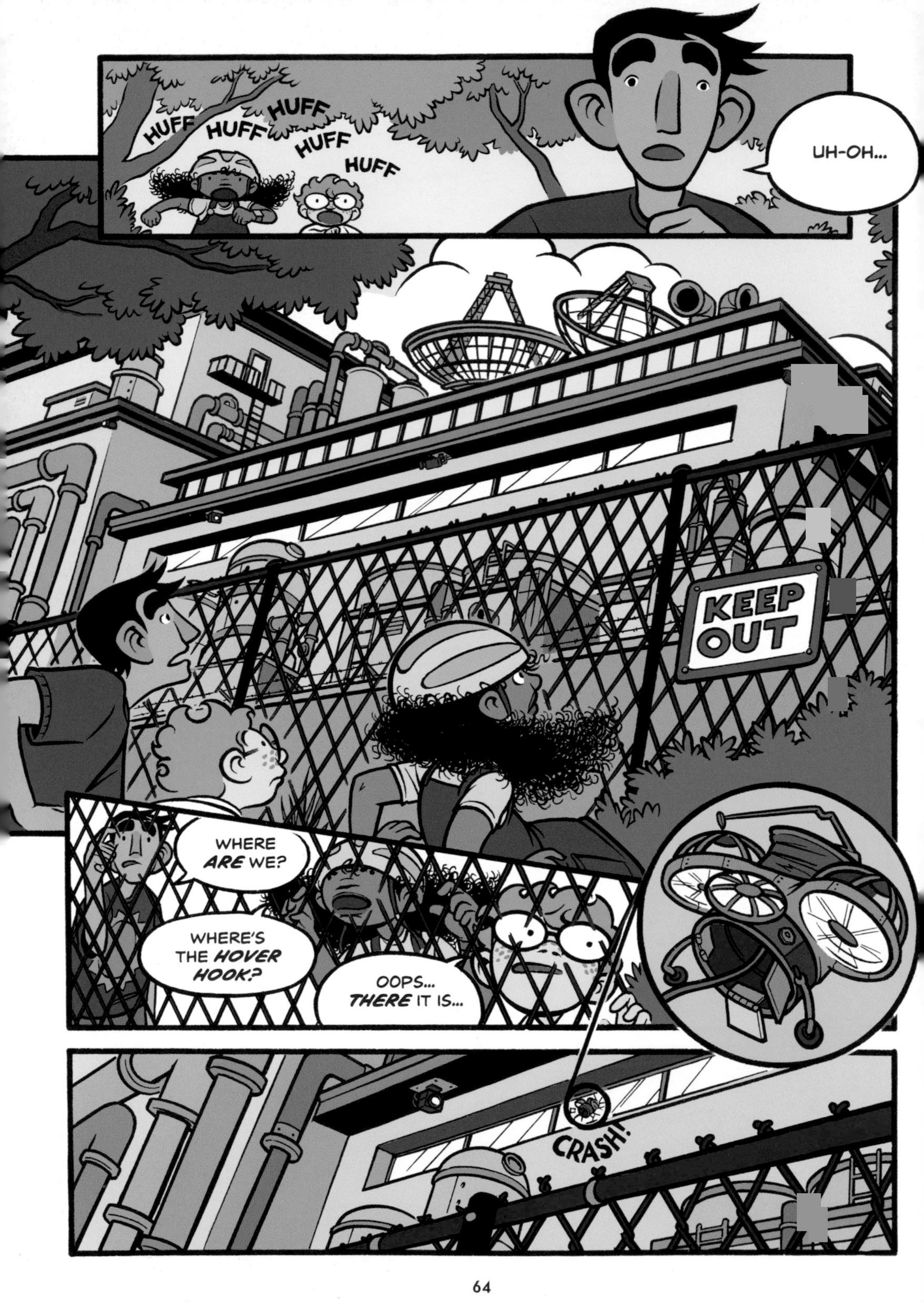
HUFF
HUFF
HUFF
HUFF
HUFF
UH-OH...
KEEP OUT
WHERE ARE WE?
WHERE'S THE HOVER HOOK?
OOPS... THERE IT IS...
CRASH!

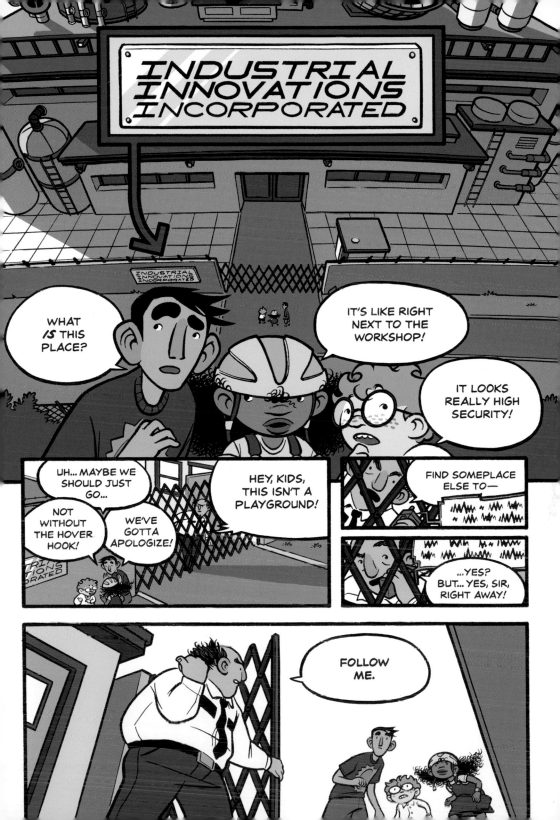

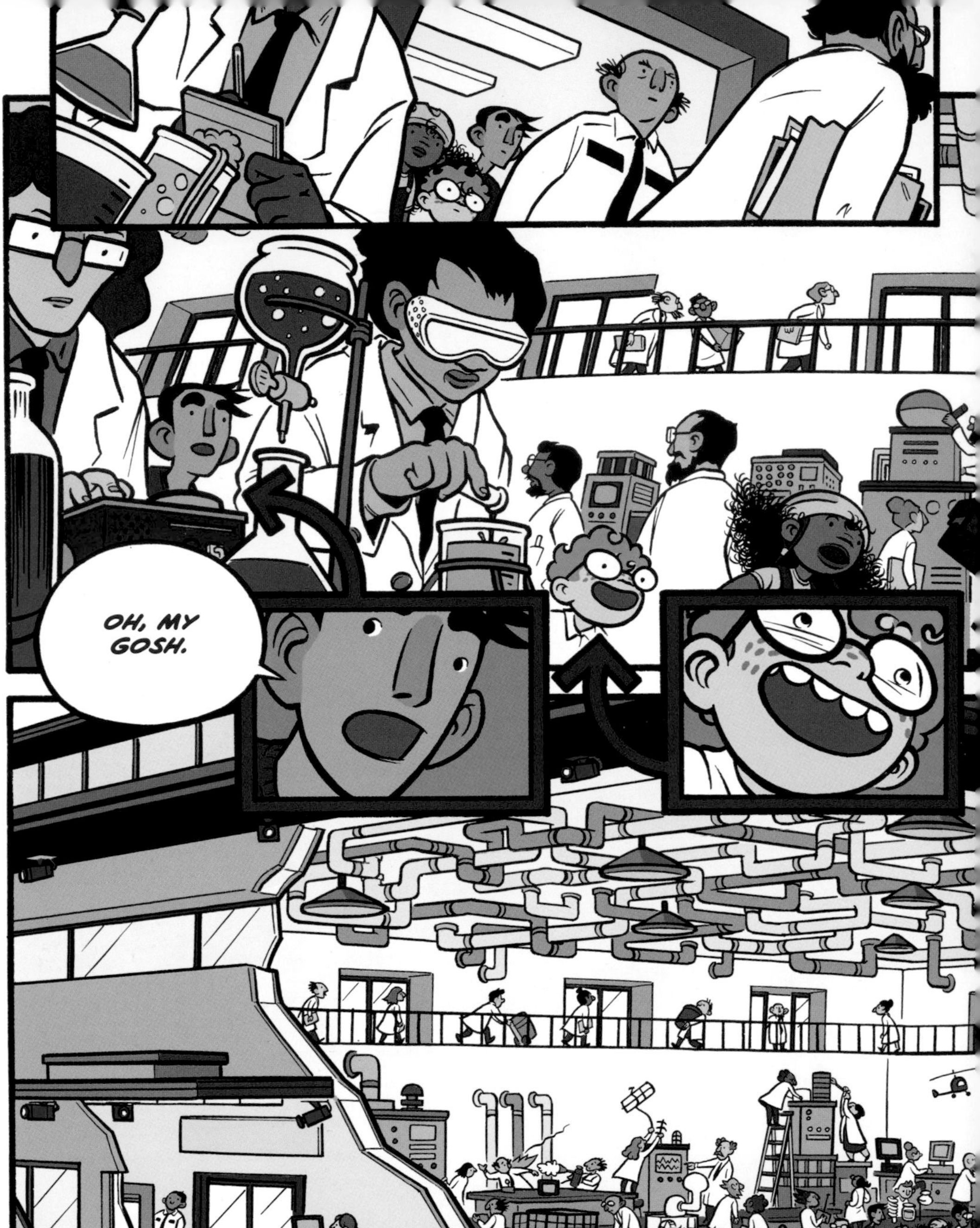
OH, MY GOSH.

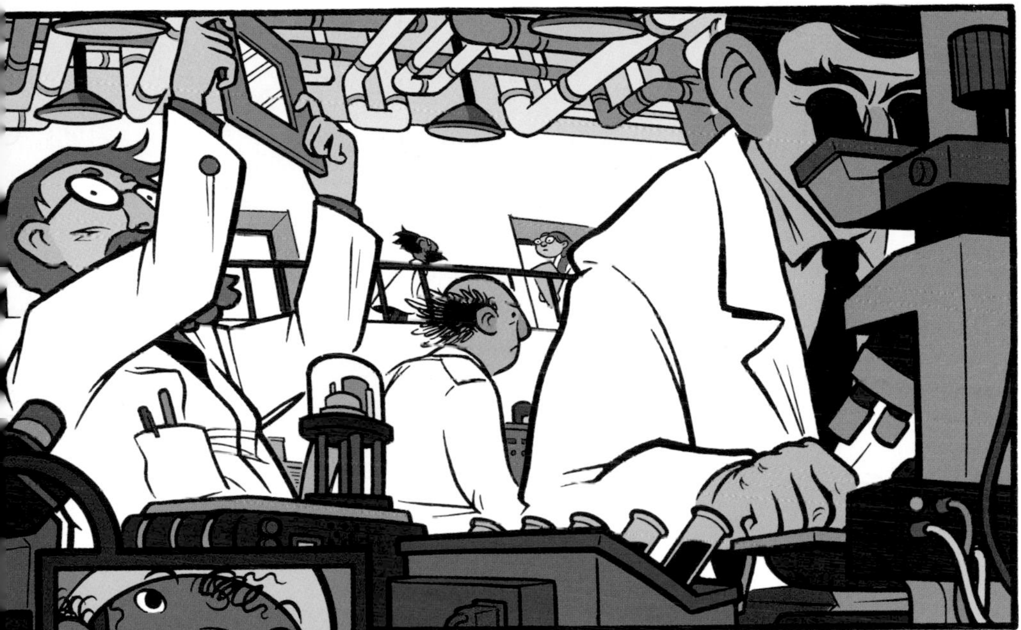

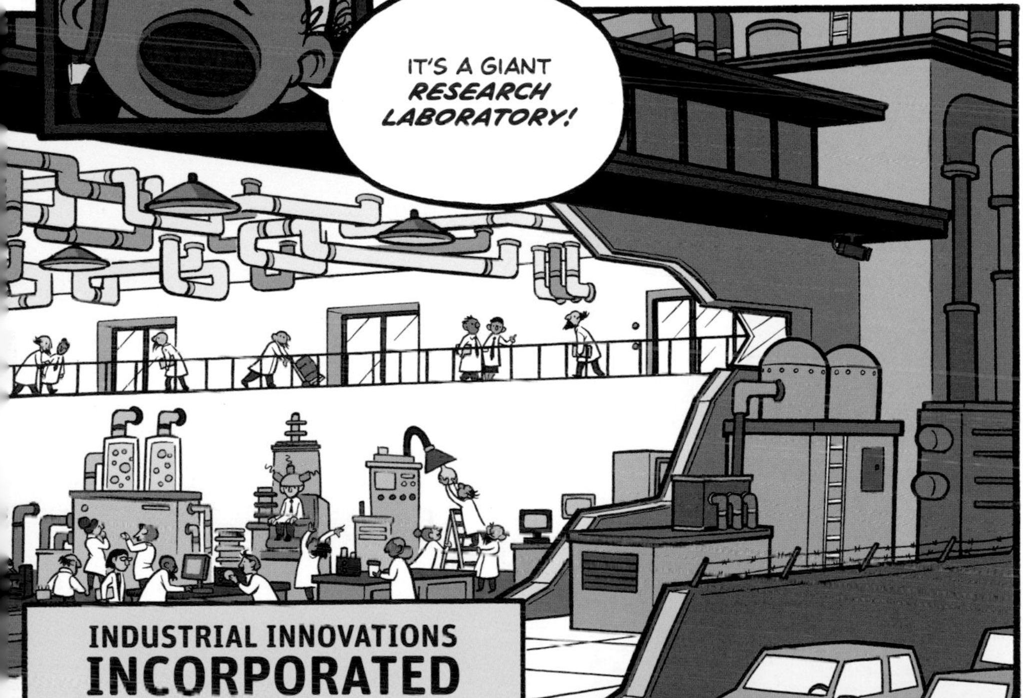
IT'S A GIANT *RESEARCH LABORATORY!*
INDUSTRIAL INNOVATIONS INCORPORATED CUTAWAY VIEW

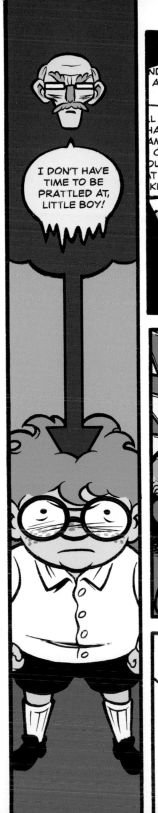

I DON'T HAVE TIME TO BE PRATTLED AT, LITTLE BOY!

...LY SORRY. ...D WE WERE FLYING IT ...ND AND IT CRASHED ...A TREE AND WENT HAYWIRE!

...LL PAY ...HATEVER ...AMAGES ...CAUSED ...OU'LL TELL ...T WAS ...KEN—

HMPH. A LIKELY STORY. ...AS FOR THIS... PIECE OF WORK...

WHERE DID YOU CHILDREN ACQUIRE SUCH AN—AH—ODD-LOOKING TOY?

W-WE MADE IT OURSELVES!

WELL! IT'S THE EXCITABLE BOY FROM MY LECTURE!

YOU LIKE TO PLAY AT INVENTOR, YOU SAID?

THIS IS YOUR HANDIWORK?

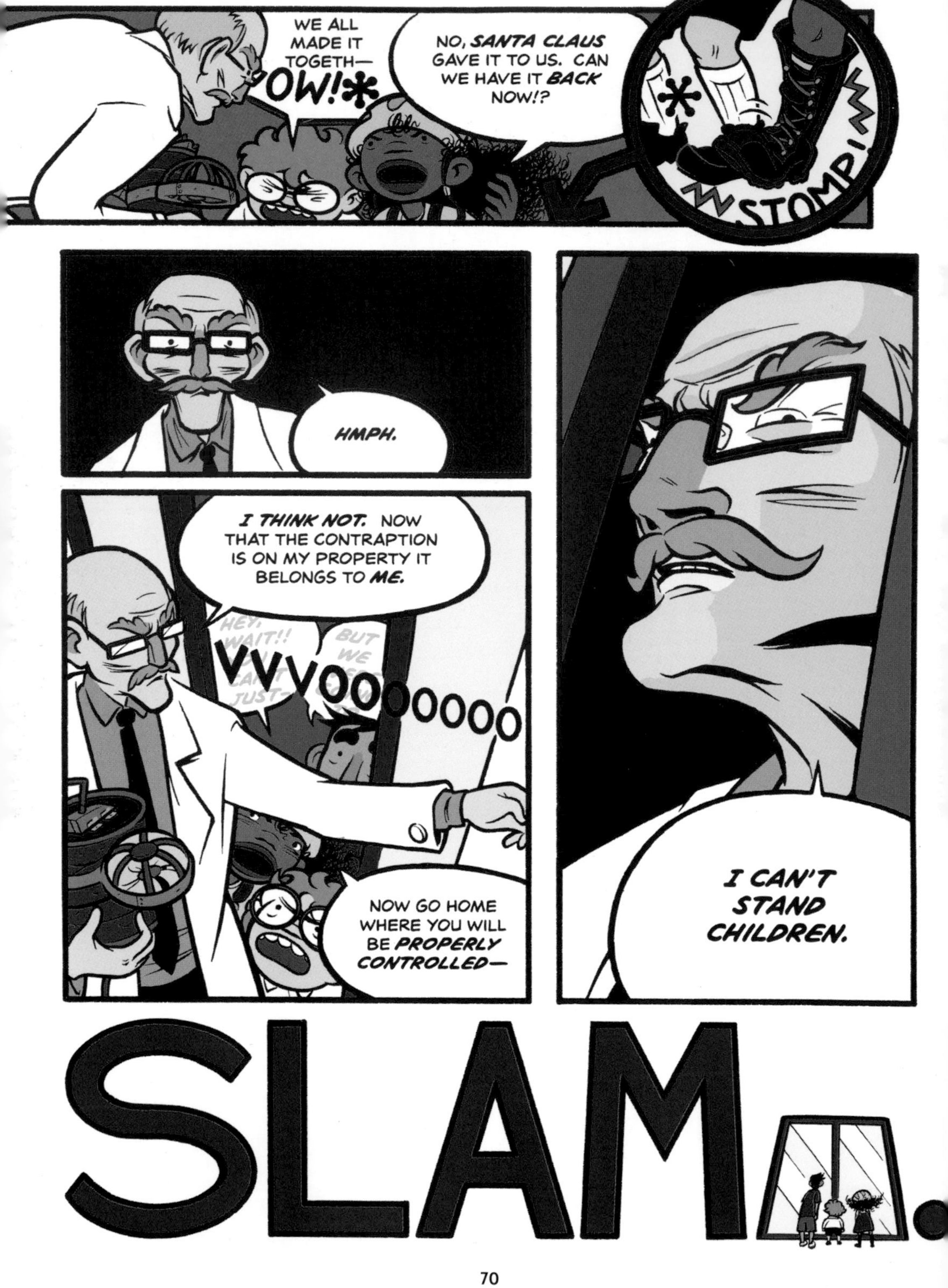
WE ALL MADE IT TOGETH—
OW!*
NO, SANTA CLAUS GAVE IT TO US. CAN WE HAVE IT BACK NOW!?
*
STOMP!
HMPH.
I THINK NOT. NOW THAT THE CONTRAPTION IS ON MY PROPERTY IT BELONGS TO ME.
HEY, WAIT!!
BUT WE
VVVOOOOOOO
NOW GO HOME WHERE YOU WILL BE PROPERLY CONTROLLED—
I CAN'T STAND CHILDREN.
SLAM.

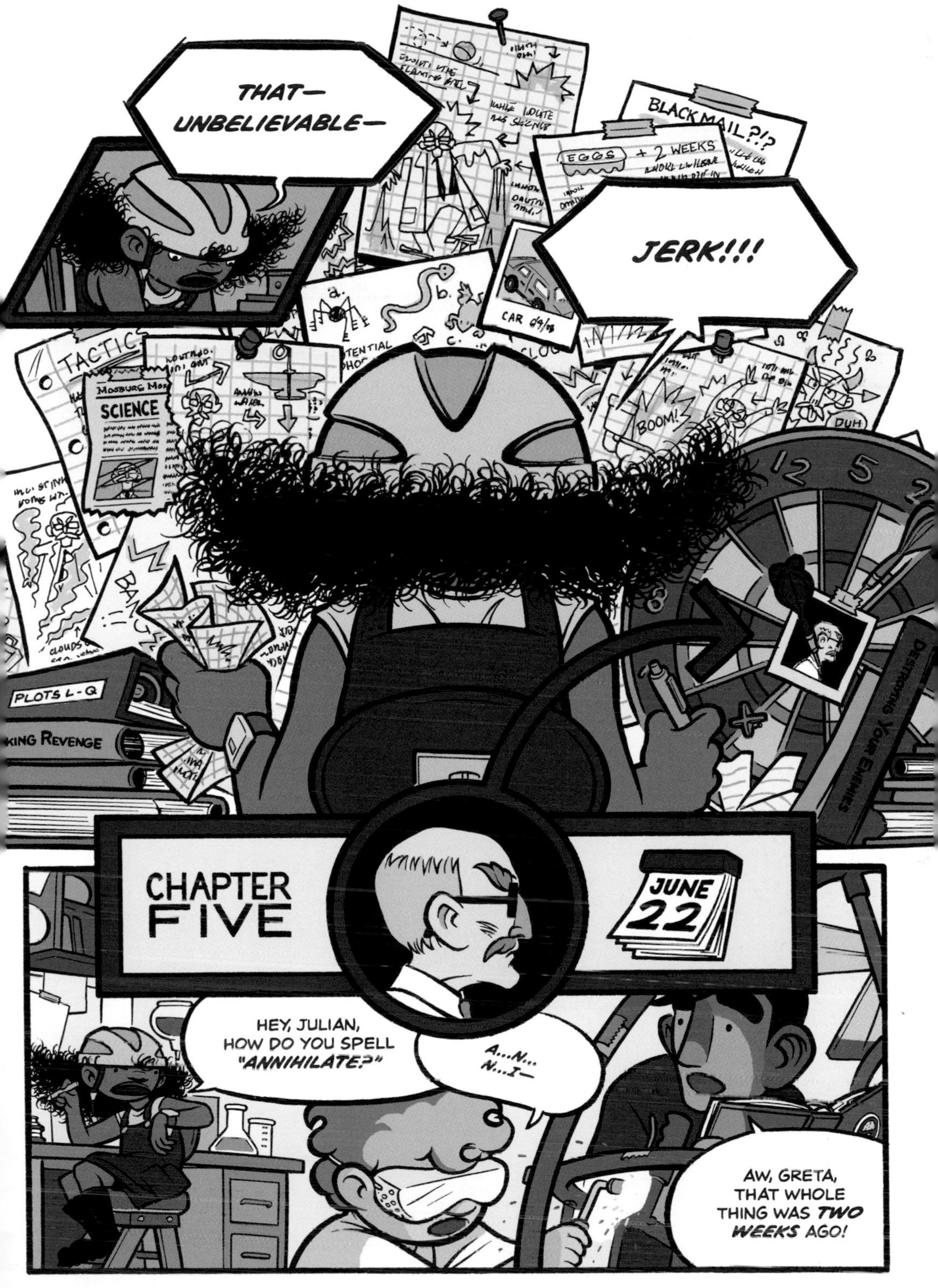
THAT—
UNBELIEVABLE—
BLACKMAIL?!?
EGGS + 2 WEEKS
JERK!!!
CAR
TACTIC
SCIENCE
BOOM!
DUH
PLOTS L-Q
KING REVENGE
DESTROYING YOUR ENEMIES
CHAPTER FIVE
JUNE 22
HEY, JULIAN, HOW DO YOU SPELL "ANNIHILATE?"
A...N... N...I—
AW, GRETA, THAT WHOLE THING WAS TWO WEEKS AGO!

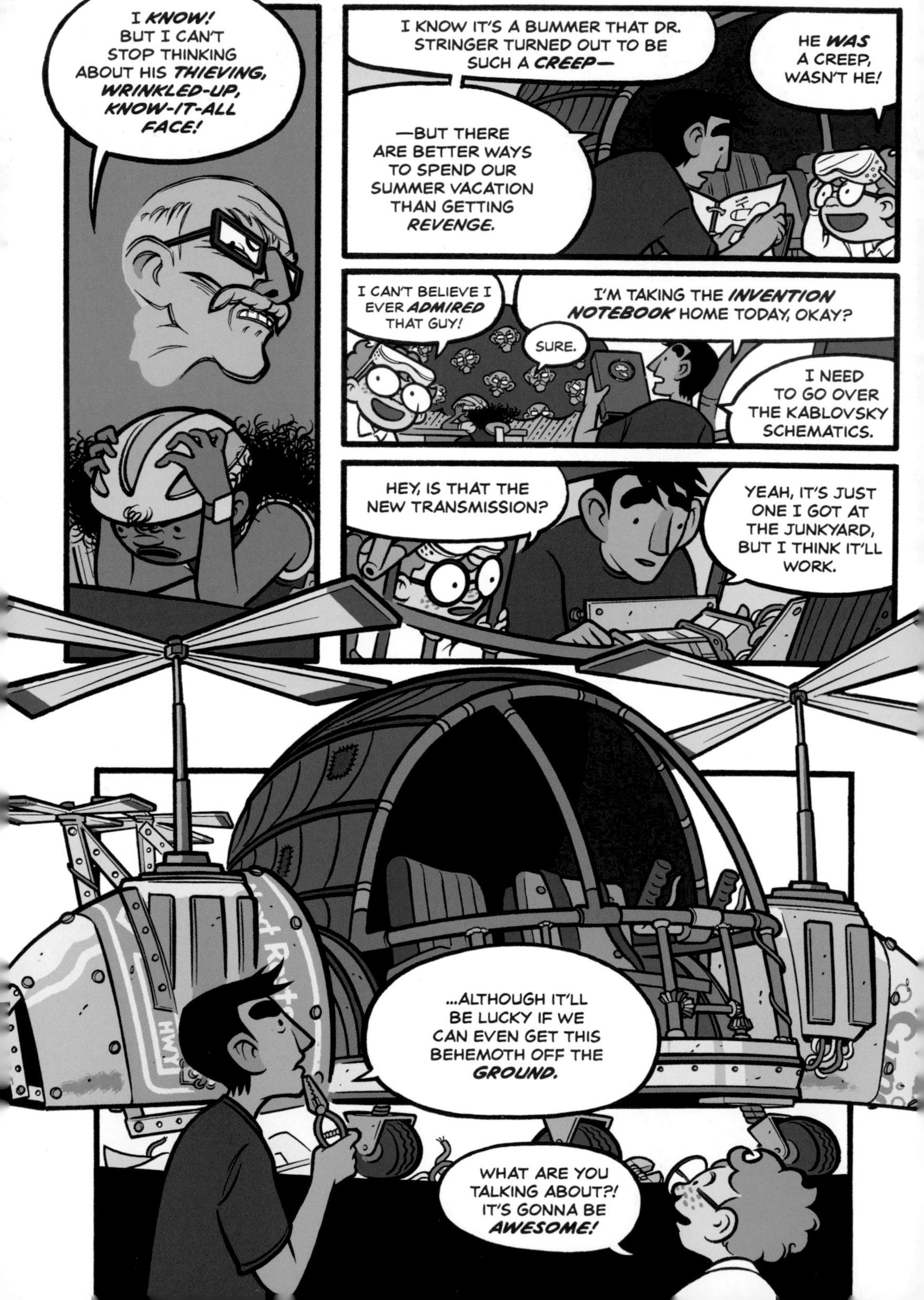

I *KNOW!* BUT I CAN'T STOP THINKING ABOUT HIS *THIEVING, WRINKLED-UP, KNOW-IT-ALL FACE!*
I KNOW IT'S A BUMMER THAT DR. STRINGER TURNED OUT TO BE SUCH A *CREEP*—
HE *WAS* A CREEP, WASN'T HE!
—BUT THERE ARE BETTER WAYS TO SPEND OUR SUMMER VACATION THAN GETTING *REVENGE.*
I CAN'T BELIEVE I EVER *ADMIRED* THAT GUY!
I'M TAKING THE *INVENTION NOTEBOOK* HOME TODAY, OKAY?
SURE.
I NEED TO GO OVER THE KABLOVSKY SCHEMATICS.
HEY, IS THAT THE NEW TRANSMISSION?
YEAH, IT'S JUST ONE I GOT AT THE JUNKYARD, BUT I THINK IT'LL WORK.
...ALTHOUGH IT'LL BE LUCKY IF WE CAN EVEN GET THIS BEHEMOTH OFF THE *GROUND.*
WHAT ARE YOU TALKING ABOUT?! IT'S GONNA BE *AWESOME!*

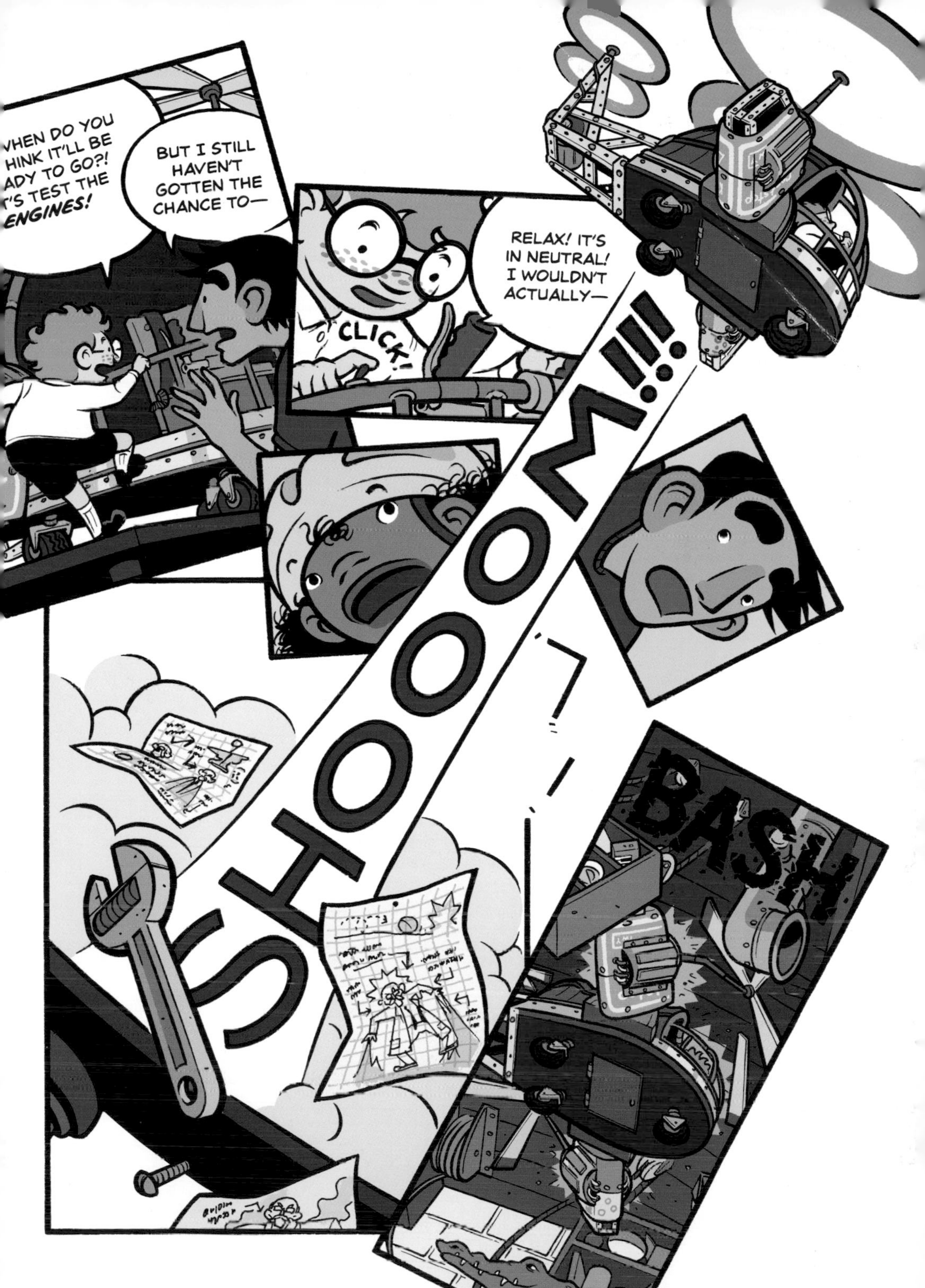

VHEN DO YOU HINK IT'LL BE ADY TO GO?! T'S TEST THE *ENGINES!*
BUT I STILL HAVEN'T GOTTEN THE CHANCE TO—
RELAX! IT'S IN NEUTRAL! I WOULDN'T ACTUALLY—
CLICK!
SHOOOOM!!!
BASH

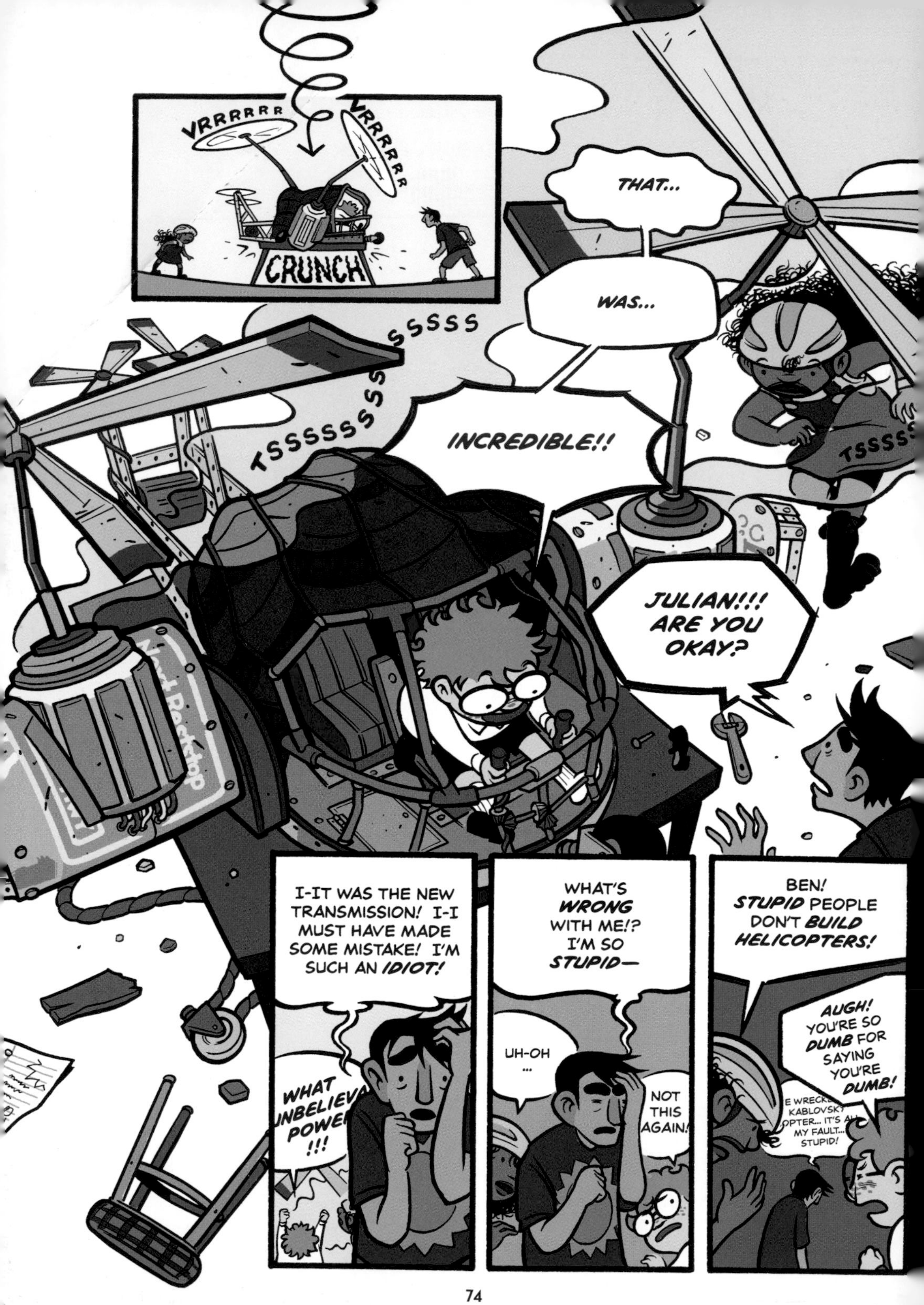
VRRRRRR
VRRRRRRR
CRUNCH
THAT...
WAS...
INCREDIBLE!!
SSSSS
TSSSSSSSSS
TSSSS
JULIAN!!! ARE YOU OKAY?
I-IT WAS THE NEW TRANSMISSION! I-I MUST HAVE MADE SOME MISTAKE! I'M SUCH AN *IDIOT!*
WHAT UNBELIEVA POWE !!!
WHAT'S *WRONG* WITH ME!? I'M SO *STUPID—*
UH-OH ...
NOT THIS AGAIN!
BEN! *STUPID* PEOPLE DON'T *BUILD HELICOPTERS!*
AUGH! YOU'RE SO *DUMB* FOR SAYING YOU'RE *DUMB!*
E WRECK KABLOVSKY OPTER... IT'S A MY FAULT... STUPID!

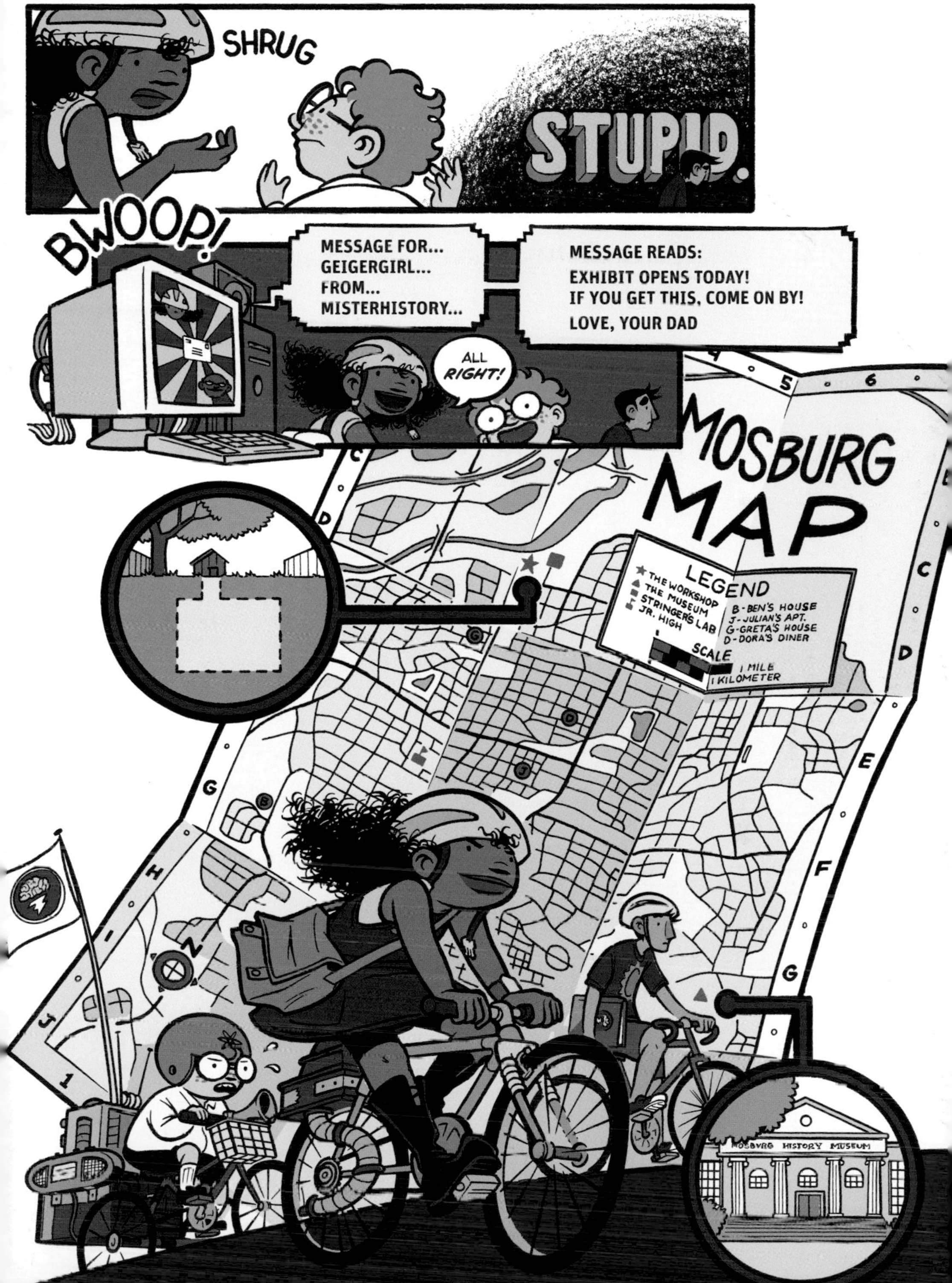
SHRUG
STUPID.
BWOOP!
MESSAGE FOR... GEIGERGIRL... FROM... MISTERHISTORY...
MESSAGE READS:
EXHIBIT OPENS TODAY!
IF YOU GET THIS, COME ON BY!
LOVE, YOUR DAD
ALL RIGHT!
MOSBURG MAP
LEGEND
THE WORKSHOP
THE MUSEUM
STRINGER'S LAB
JR. HIGH
B-BEN'S HOUSE
J-JULIAN'S APT.
G-GRETA'S HOUSE
D-DORA'S DINER
SCALE
1 MILE
1 KILOMETER
MOSBURG HISTORY MUSEUM

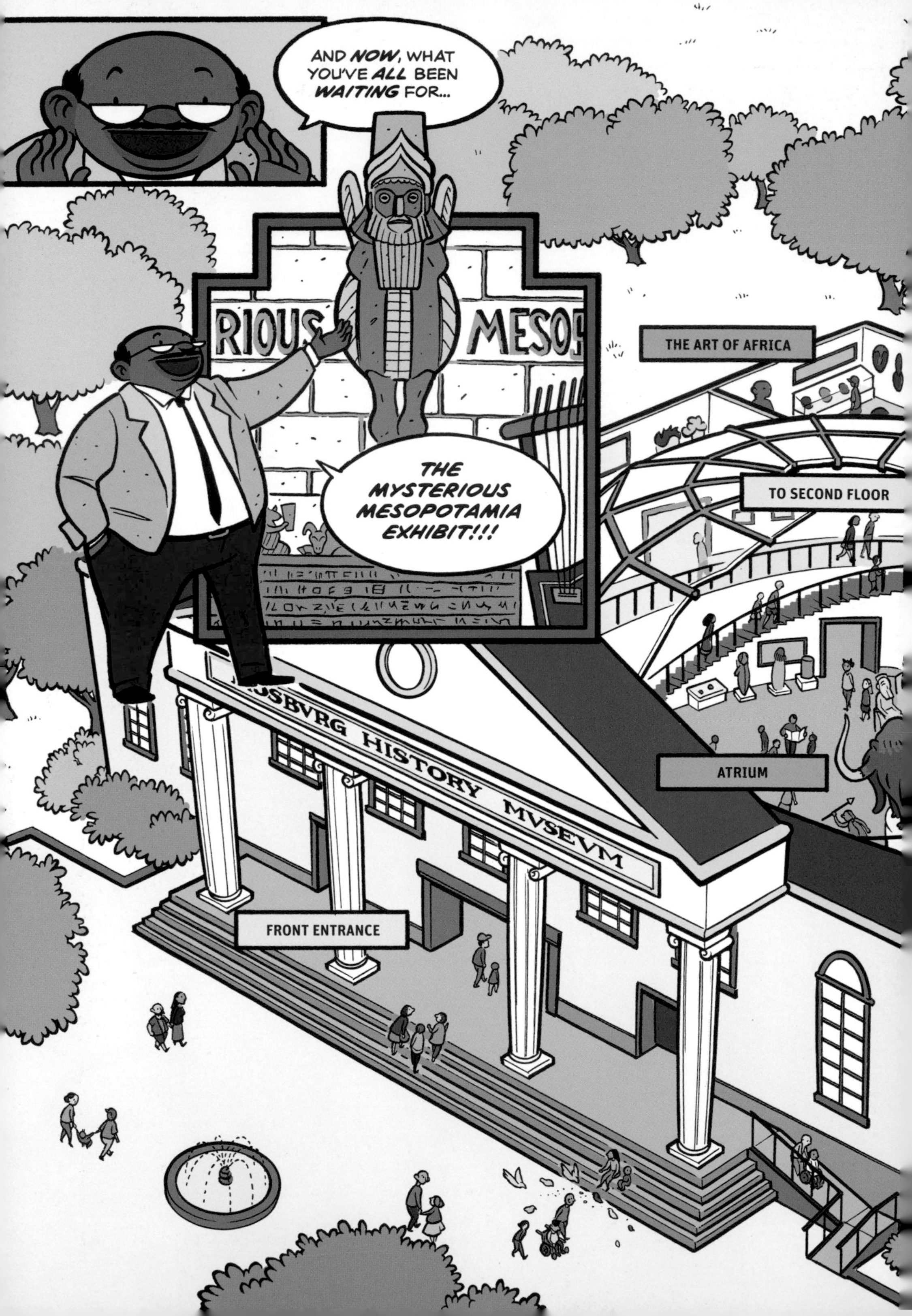
AND NOW, WHAT YOU'VE ALL BEEN WAITING FOR...
THE MYSTERIOUS MESOPOTAMIA EXHIBIT!!!
RIOUS MESO
THE ART OF AFRICA
TO SECOND FLOOR
ATRIUM
HISTORY MVSEVM
FRONT ENTRANCE

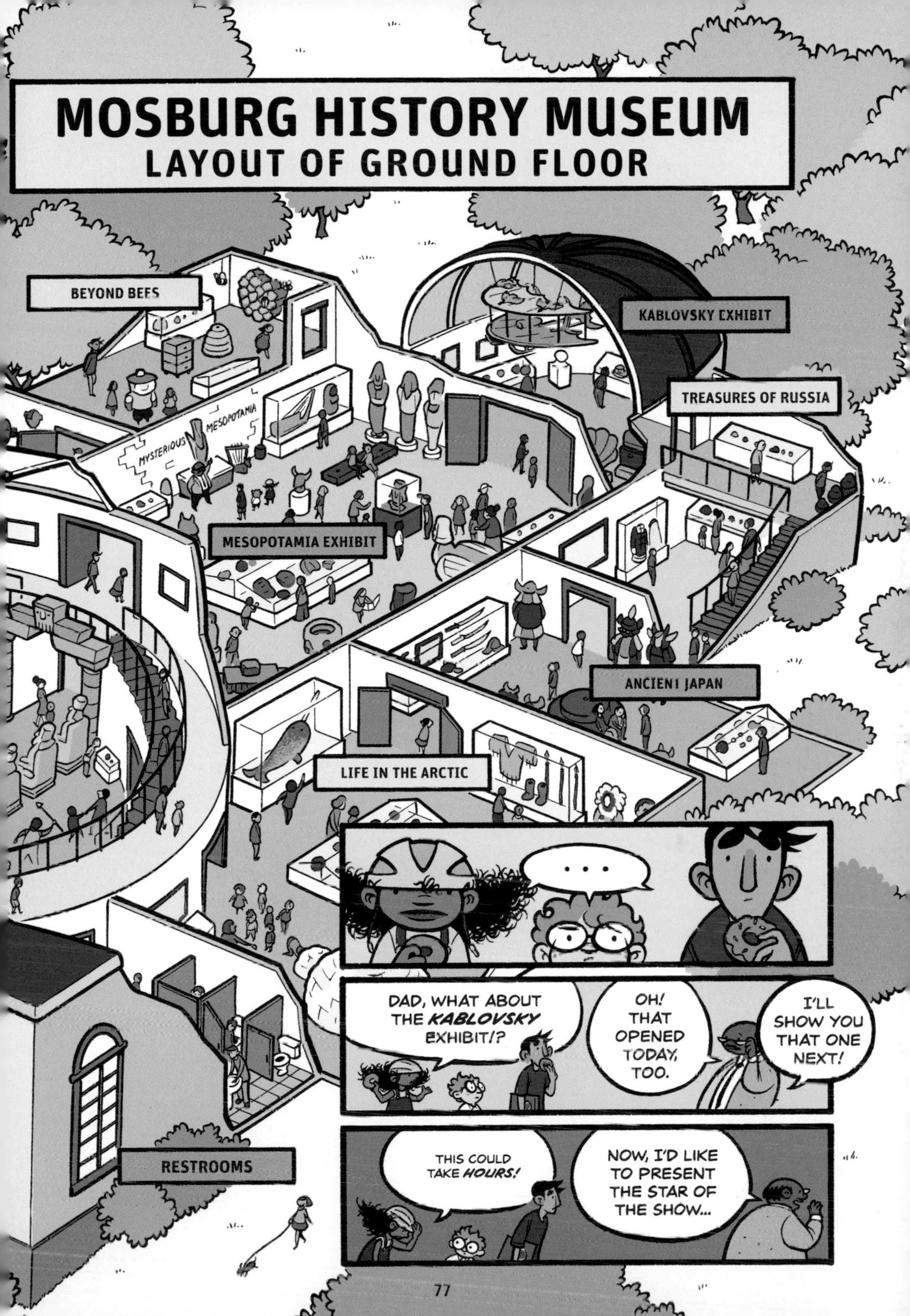

MOSBURG HISTORY MUSEUM
LAYOUT OF GROUND FLOOR
BEYOND BEES
KABLOVSKY EXHIBIT
TREASURES OF RUSSIA
MYSTERIOUS MESOPOTAMIA
MESOPOTAMIA EXHIBIT
ANCIENT JAPAN
LIFE IN THE ARCTIC
RESTROOMS
...
DAD, WHAT ABOUT THE *KABLOVSKY* EXHIBIT!?
OH! THAT OPENED TODAY, TOO.
I'LL SHOW YOU THAT ONE NEXT!
THIS COULD TAKE *HOURS!*
NOW, I'D LIKE TO PRESENT THE STAR OF THE SHOW...

...THE GOLDEN BUST OF ASHURBANIPAL, ON LOAN FROM THE SMITHSONIAN!!!

MADE OF HAMMERED GOLD AND INSET WITH SHELL AND LAPIS LAZULI, THIS BUST IS THE MOST PRICELESS THING IN THE WHOLE MUSEUM!

SNIFF!

PRESENTING MOSBURG WITH SUCH AN ASTONISHING PIECE OF ANCIENT ART HAS BEEN ONE OF THE PROUDEST ACHIEVEMENTS OF MY CAREER.

ISN'T THE MUSEUM KIND OF *LOW SECURITY* FOR SOMETHING SO VALUABLE??

OF COURSE *YOU'D* ASK ABOUT THAT, GRETA! DON'T WORRY—WE HAD A SPECIAL LASER ALARM INSTALLED TO PROTECT THIS ENTIRE ROOM.

I DON'T THINK THAT AN ADEQ MOUNT SECURIT DAD!

NOW, THIS SHELL HERE IS NOT NATIVE TO THE PERSIAN GULF. HOW DID IT MAKE ITS WAY TO NINEVEH, YOU ASK? WELL, COMPLEX TRADE ROUTE WERE ESTAB BETWE

1 HOUR 45 MINUTES LATER

DID WE GO OVER THE SMELTING METHODS THEY USED? THERE IS SOME CONTROVERSY AS TO EXACTLY HOW T LD HAVE

YES.

YES.

YES.

HOW ABOU THE ENGRAVI RECENTLY TH WAS A FASCINA DISCUSSION AB WHETHER TH ULD HAVE U E METHODS

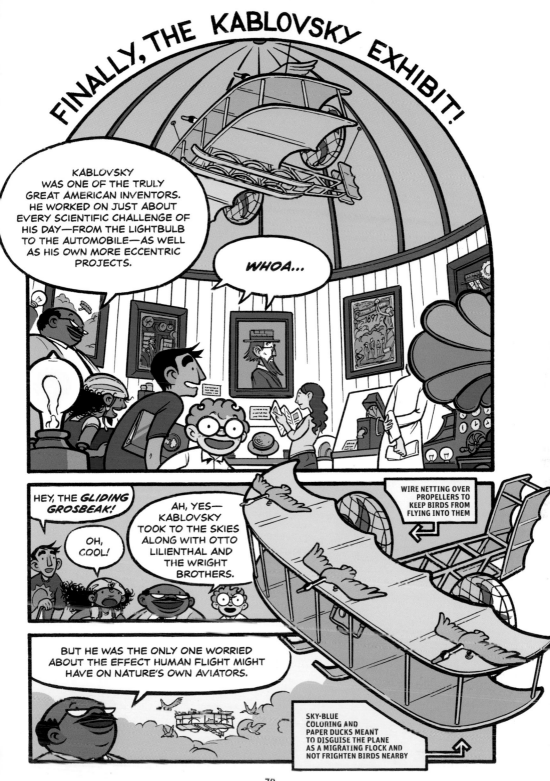

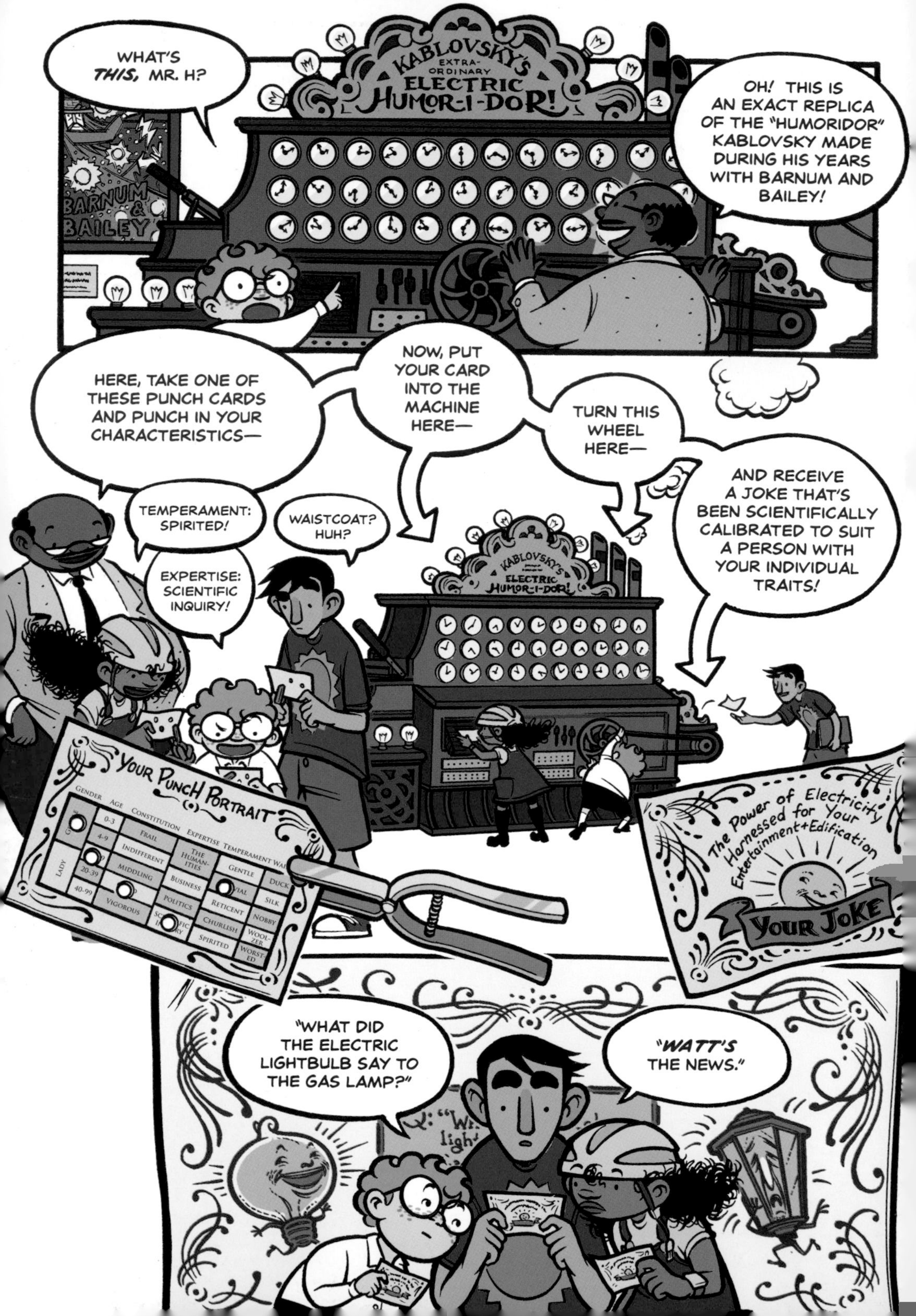
WHAT'S *THIS,* MR. H?
KABLOVSKY'S EXTRA-ORDINARY ELECTRIC HUMOR-I-DOR!
OH! THIS IS AN EXACT REPLICA OF THE "HUMORIDOR" KABLOVSKY MADE DURING HIS YEARS WITH BARNUM AND BAILEY!
BARNUM & BAILEY
HERE, TAKE ONE OF THESE PUNCH CARDS AND PUNCH IN YOUR CHARACTERISTICS—
NOW, PUT YOUR CARD INTO THE MACHINE HERE—
TURN THIS WHEEL HERE—
AND RECEIVE A JOKE THAT'S BEEN SCIENTIFICALLY CALIBRATED TO SUIT A PERSON WITH YOUR INDIVIDUAL TRAITS!
TEMPERAMENT: SPIRITED!
EXPERTISE: SCIENTIFIC INQUIRY!
WAISTCOAT? HUH?
KABLOVSKY'S ELECTRIC HUMOR-I-DOR!
YOUR PUNCH PORTRAIT
GENDER AGE CONSTITUTION EXPERTISE TEMPERAMENT
LADY
0-3
4-9
20-39
40-99
FRAIL
INDIFFERENT
MIDDLING
VIGOROUS
THE HUMANITIES
BUSINESS
POLITICS
GENTLE
RETICENT
CHURLISH
SPIRITED
DUCK
SILK
NOBBY
WORSTED
The Power of Electricity Harnessed for Your Entertainment+Edification
YOUR JOKE
"WHAT DID THE ELECTRIC LIGHTBULB SAY TO THE GAS LAMP?"
"*WATT'S* THE NEWS."

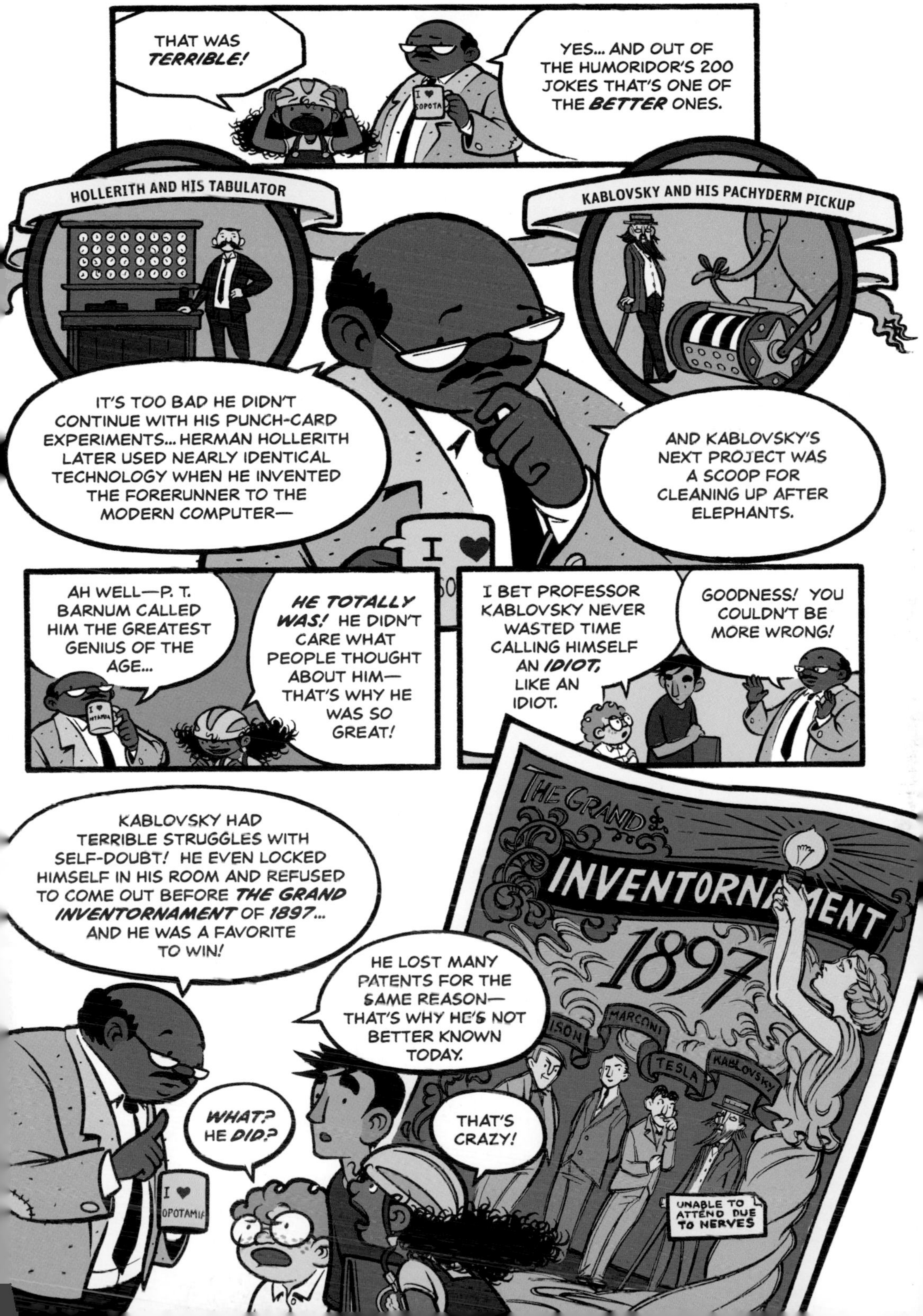

THAT WAS *TERRIBLE!*
YES... AND OUT OF THE HUMORIDOR'S 200 JOKES THAT'S ONE OF THE *BETTER* ONES.
HOLLERITH AND HIS TABULATOR
KABLOVSKY AND HIS PACHYDERM PICKUP
IT'S TOO BAD HE DIDN'T CONTINUE WITH HIS PUNCH-CARD EXPERIMENTS... HERMAN HOLLERITH LATER USED NEARLY IDENTICAL TECHNOLOGY WHEN HE INVENTED THE FORERUNNER TO THE MODERN COMPUTER—
AND KABLOVSKY'S NEXT PROJECT WAS A SCOOP FOR CLEANING UP AFTER ELEPHANTS.
AH WELL—P. T. BARNUM CALLED HIM THE GREATEST GENIUS OF THE AGE...
HE TOTALLY WAS! HE DIDN'T CARE WHAT PEOPLE THOUGHT ABOUT HIM—THAT'S WHY HE WAS SO GREAT!
I BET PROFESSOR KABLOVSKY NEVER WASTED TIME CALLING HIMSELF AN *IDIOT,* LIKE AN IDIOT.
GOODNESS! YOU COULDN'T BE MORE WRONG!
KABLOVSKY HAD TERRIBLE STRUGGLES WITH SELF-DOUBT! HE EVEN LOCKED HIMSELF IN HIS ROOM AND REFUSED TO COME OUT BEFORE *THE GRAND INVENTORNAMENT* OF 1897... AND HE WAS A FAVORITE TO WIN!
THE GRAND INVENTORNAMENT 1897
MARCONI
TESLA
KABLOVSKY
UNABLE TO ATTEND DUE TO NERVES
HE LOST MANY PATENTS FOR THE SAME REASON—THAT'S WHY HE'S NOT BETTER KNOWN TODAY.
WHAT? HE *DID?*
THAT'S CRAZY!

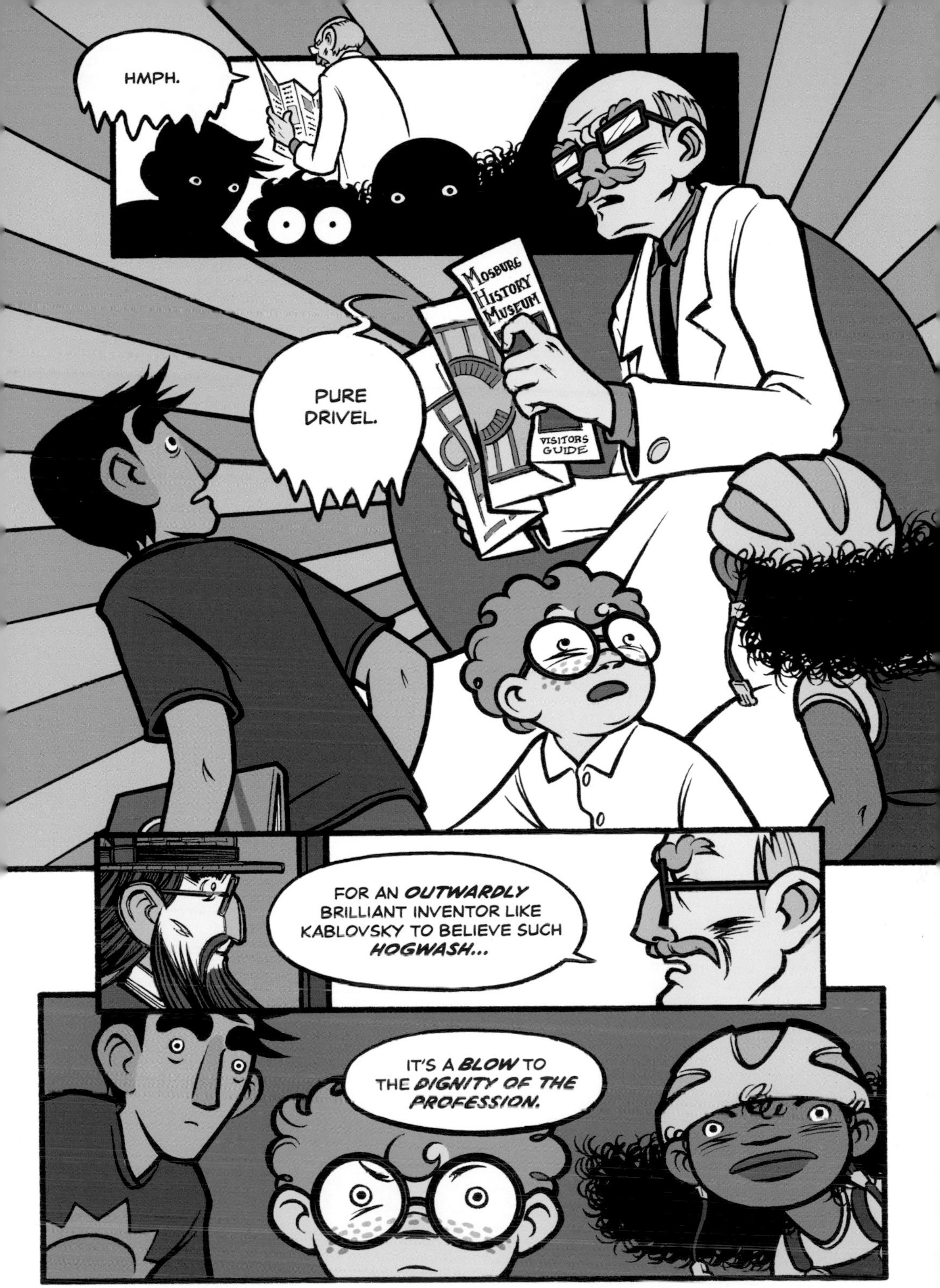
HMPH.
MOSBURG HISTORY MUSEUM
VISITORS GUIDE
PURE DRIVEL.
FOR AN *OUTWARDLY* BRILLIANT INVENTOR LIKE KABLOVSKY TO BELIEVE SUCH *HOGWASH*...
IT'S A *BLOW* TO THE *DIGNITY OF THE PROFESSION.*

ONE WEEK LATER

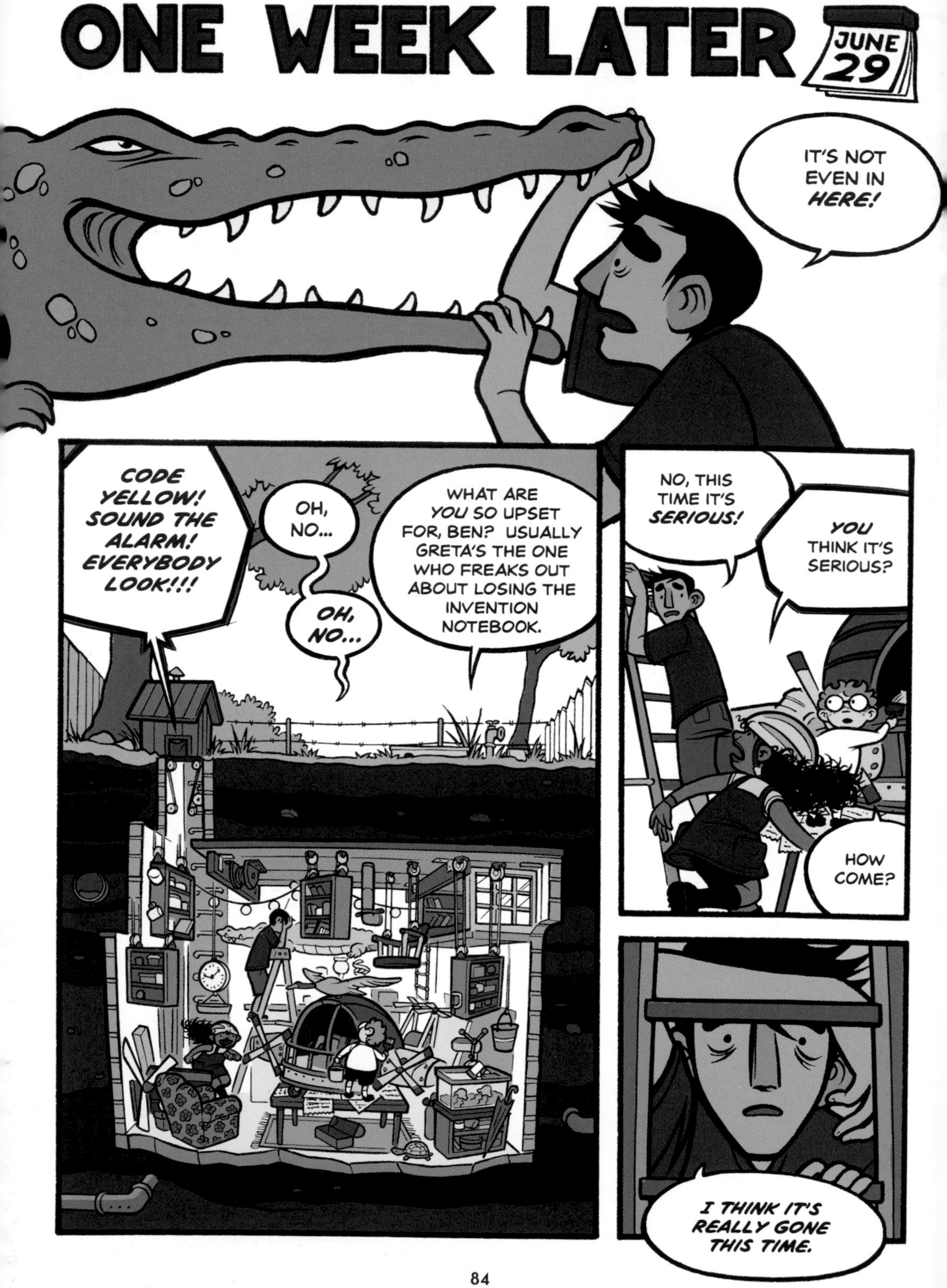
JUNE 29
IT'S NOT EVEN IN *HERE!*
CODE YELLOW! SOUND THE ALARM! EVERYBODY LOOK!!!
OH, NO...
OH, NO...
WHAT ARE *YOU* SO UPSET FOR, BEN? USUALLY GRETA'S THE ONE WHO FREAKS OUT ABOUT LOSING THE INVENTION NOTEBOOK.
NO, THIS TIME IT'S *SERIOUS!*
YOU THINK IT'S SERIOUS?
HOW COME?
I THINK IT'S REALLY GONE THIS TIME.

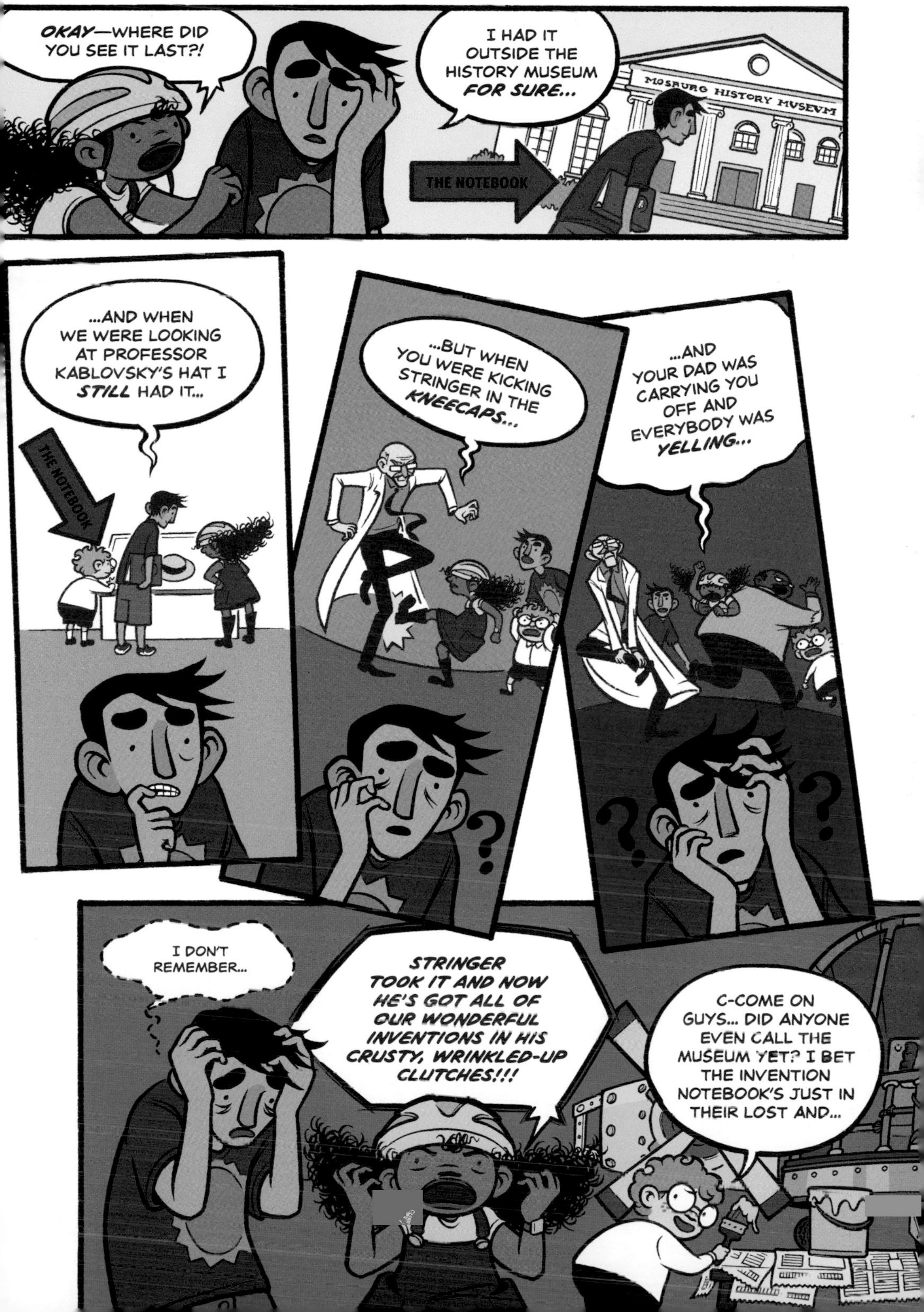
OKAY—WHERE DID YOU SEE IT LAST?!
I HAD IT OUTSIDE THE HISTORY MUSEUM FOR SURE...
MOSBURG HISTORY MUSEUM
THE NOTEBOOK
...AND WHEN WE WERE LOOKING AT PROFESSOR KABLOVSKY'S HAT I STILL HAD IT...
THE NOTEBOOK
...BUT WHEN YOU WERE KICKING STRINGER IN THE KNEECAPS...
...AND YOUR DAD WAS CARRYING YOU OFF AND EVERYBODY WAS YELLING...
I DON'T REMEMBER...
STRINGER TOOK IT AND NOW HE'S GOT ALL OF OUR WONDERFUL INVENTIONS IN HIS CRUSTY, WRINKLED-UP CLUTCHES!!!
C-COME ON GUYS... DID ANYONE EVEN CALL THE MUSEUM YET? I BET THE INVENTION NOTEBOOK'S JUST IN THEIR LOST AND...

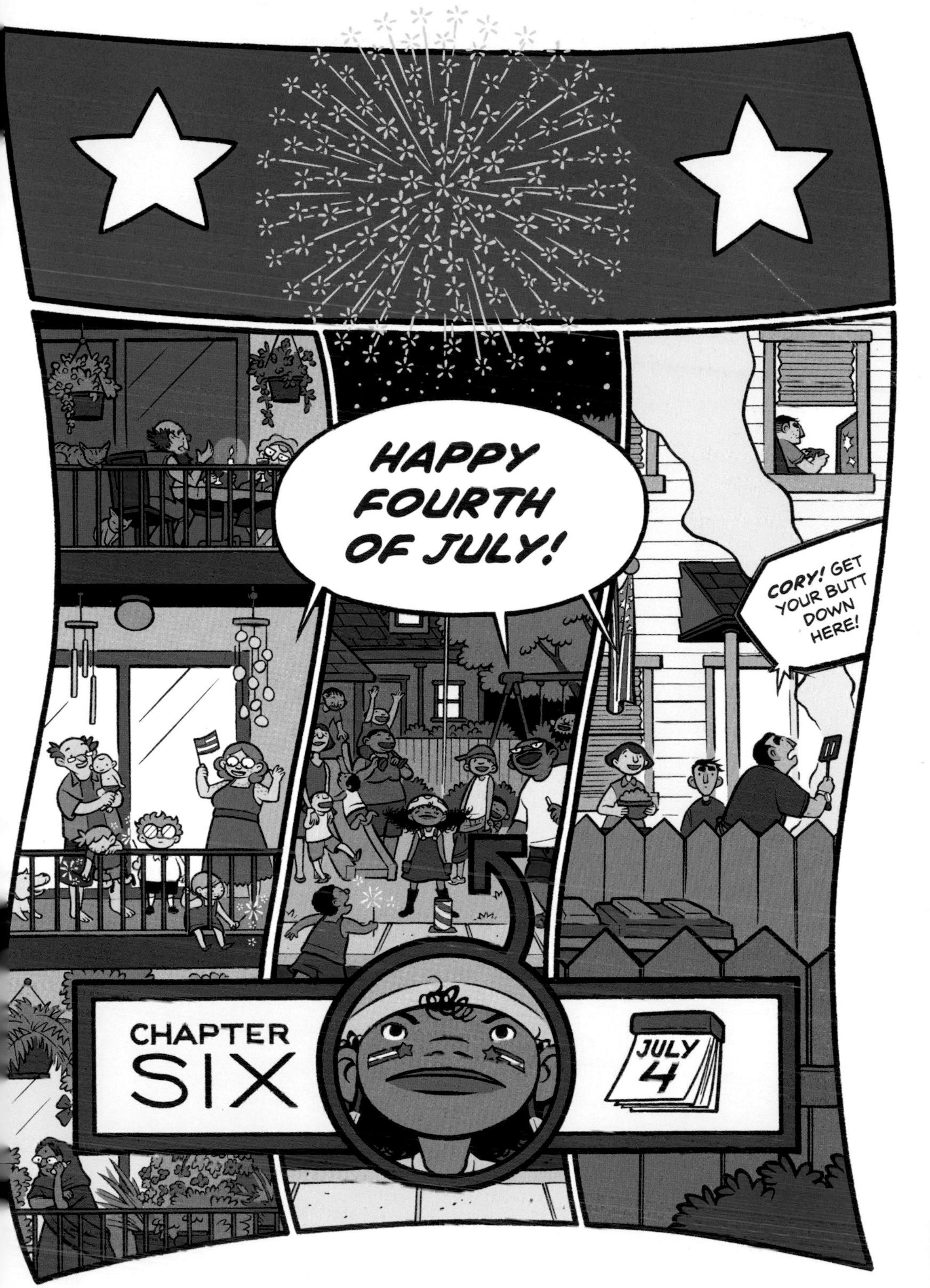
HAPPY FOURTH OF JULY!
CORY! GET YOUR BUTT DOWN HERE!
CHAPTER SIX
JULY 4

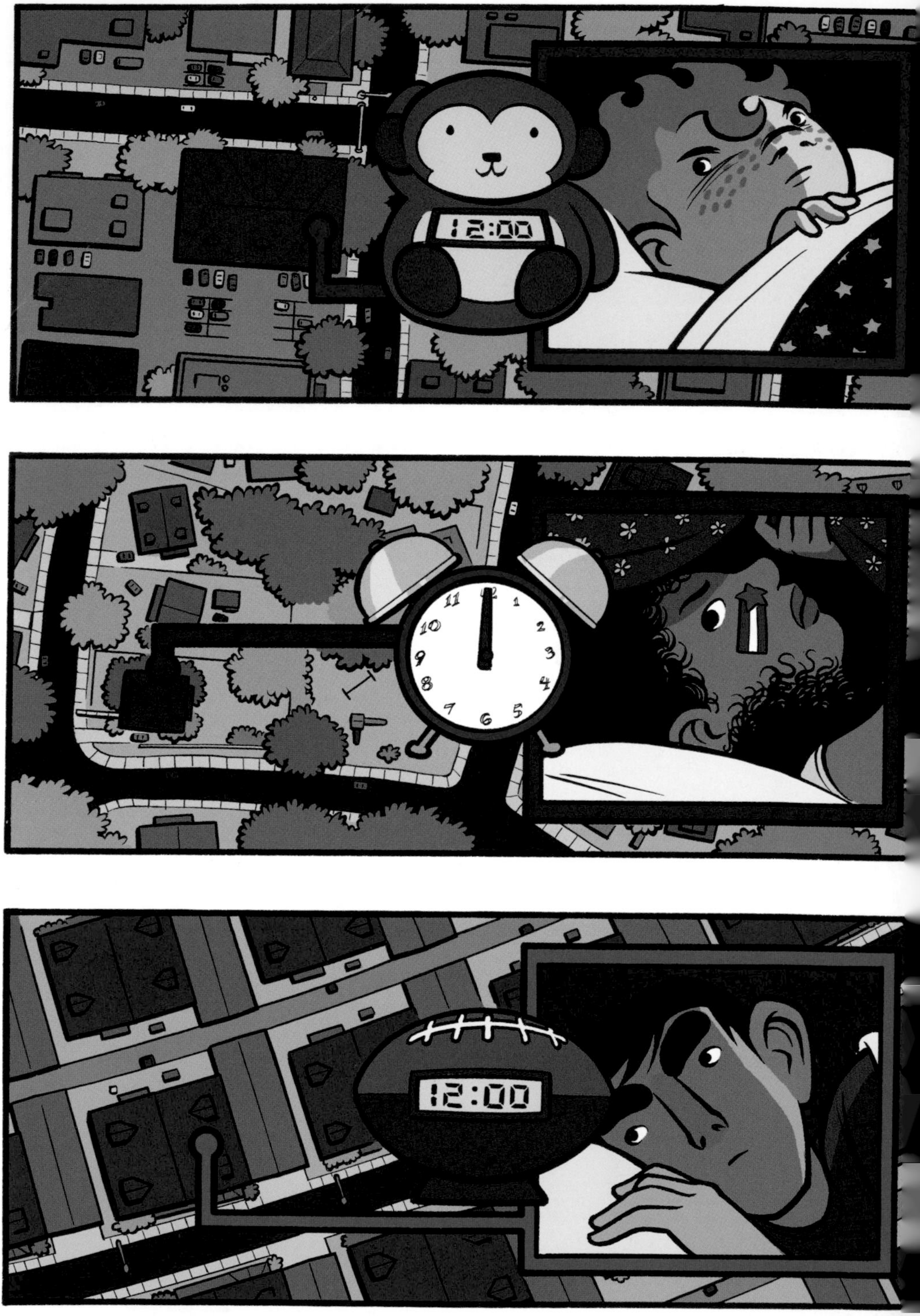
12:00
12:00

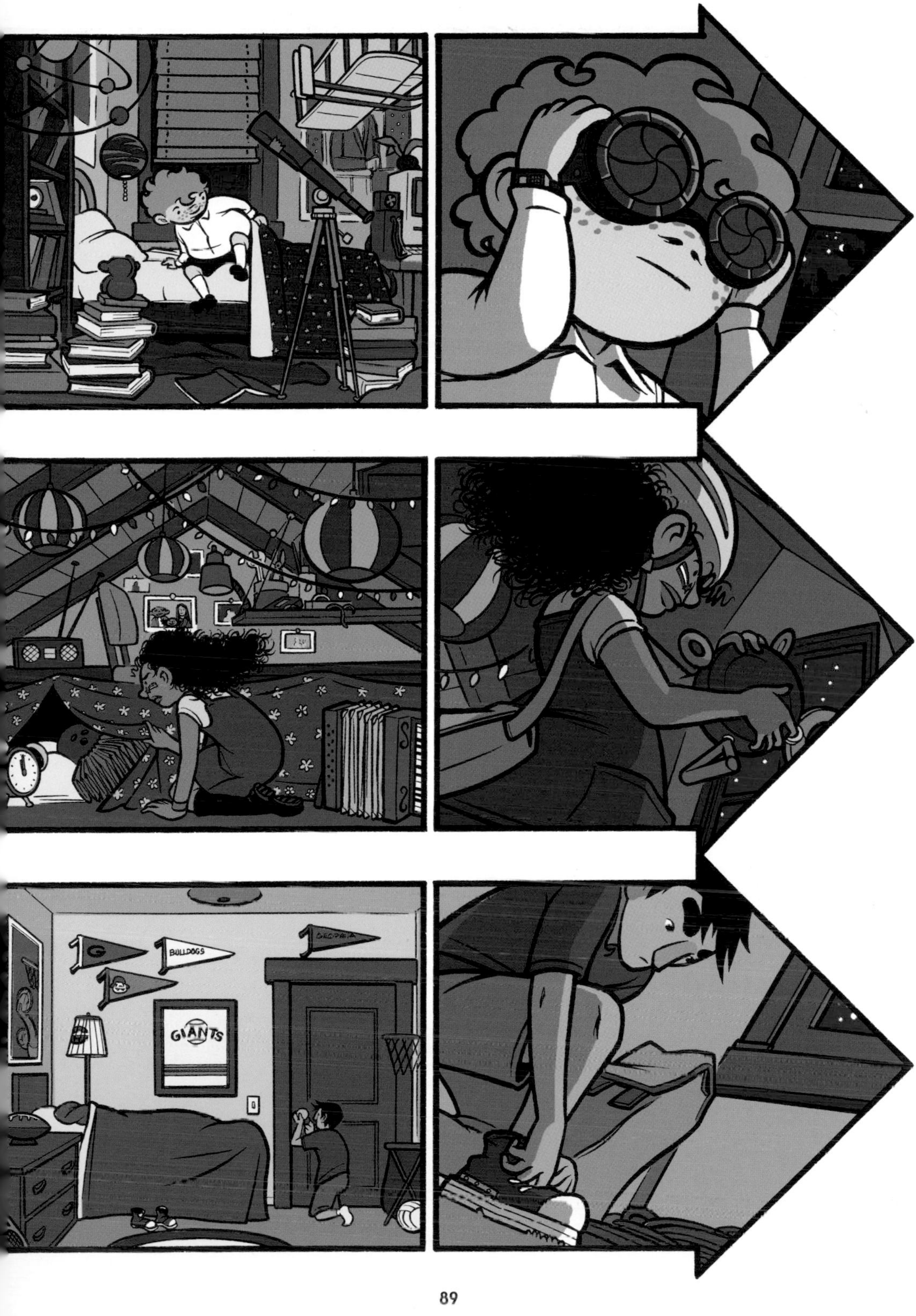
G
BULLDOGS
GIANTS

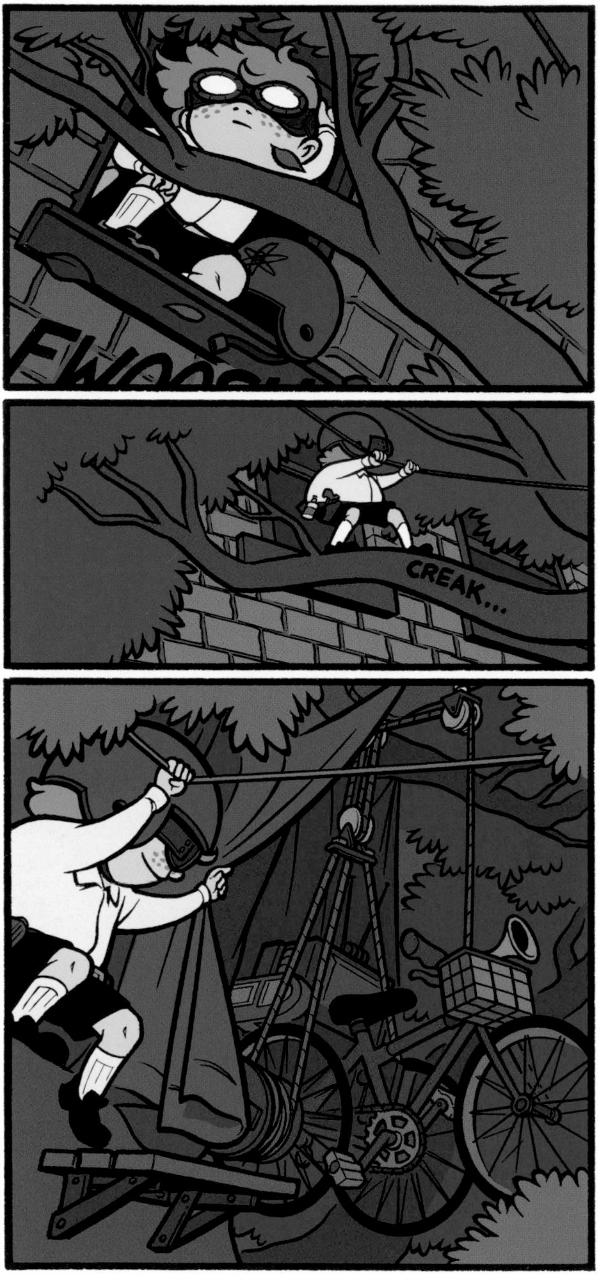
CREAK...

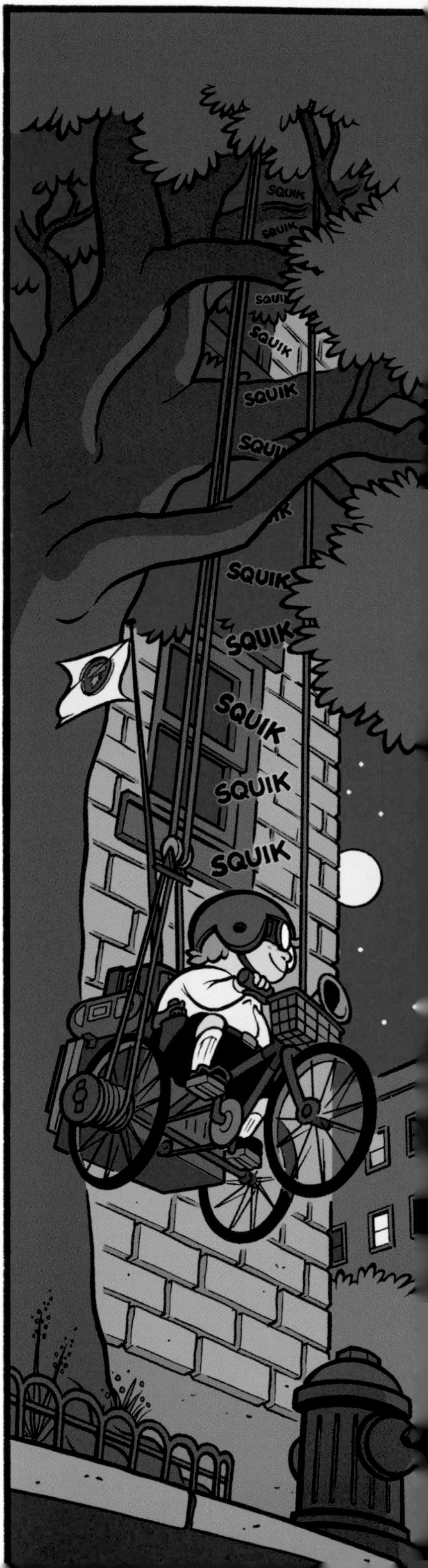
SQUIK
SQUIK
SQUIK
SQUIK
SQUIK
SQUIK
SQUIK
SQUIK
SQUIK
SQUIK

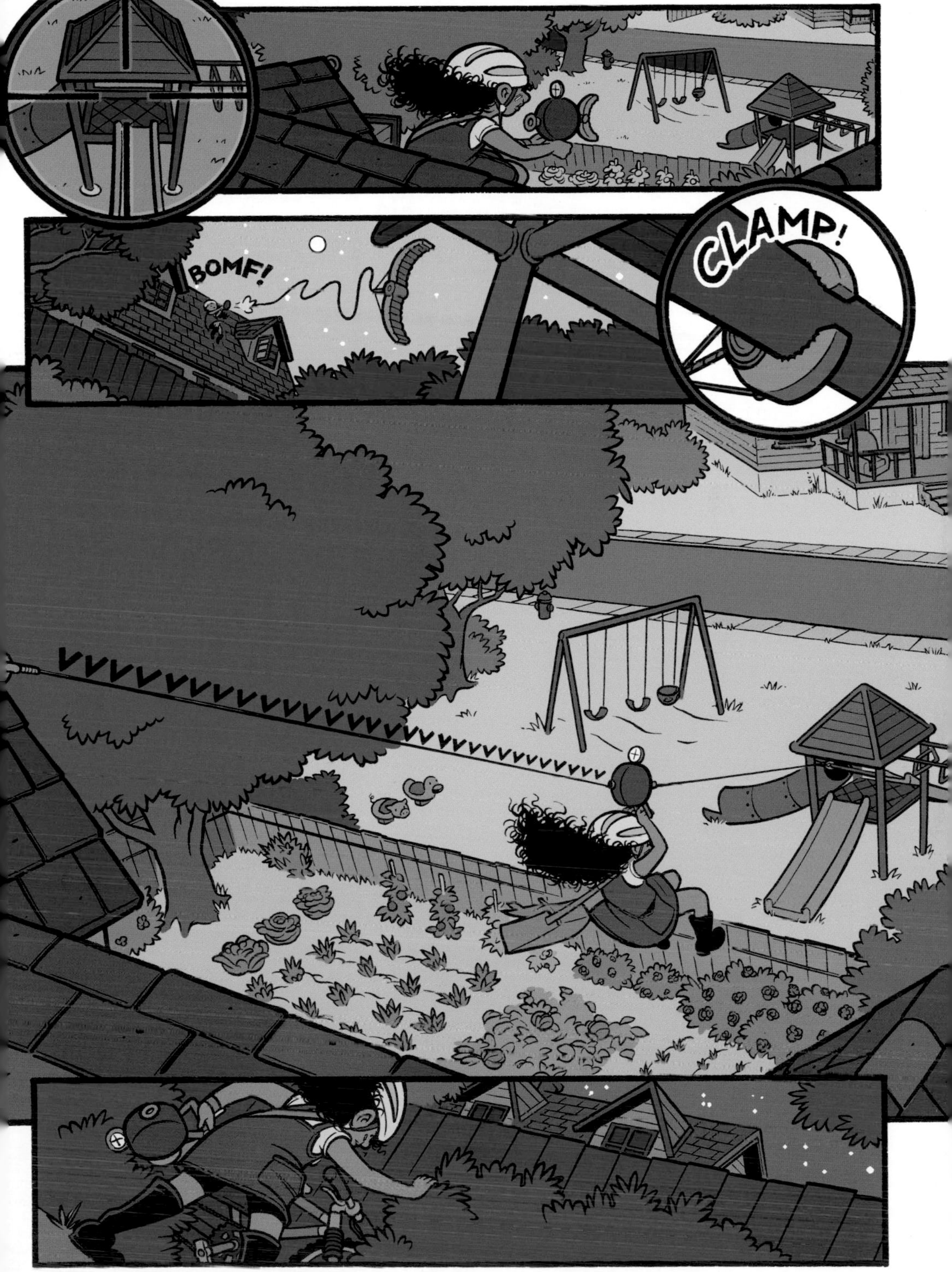
BOMF!
CLAMP!
VVVVVVVVVVVVVVVVVVVVVVVVVVVVV

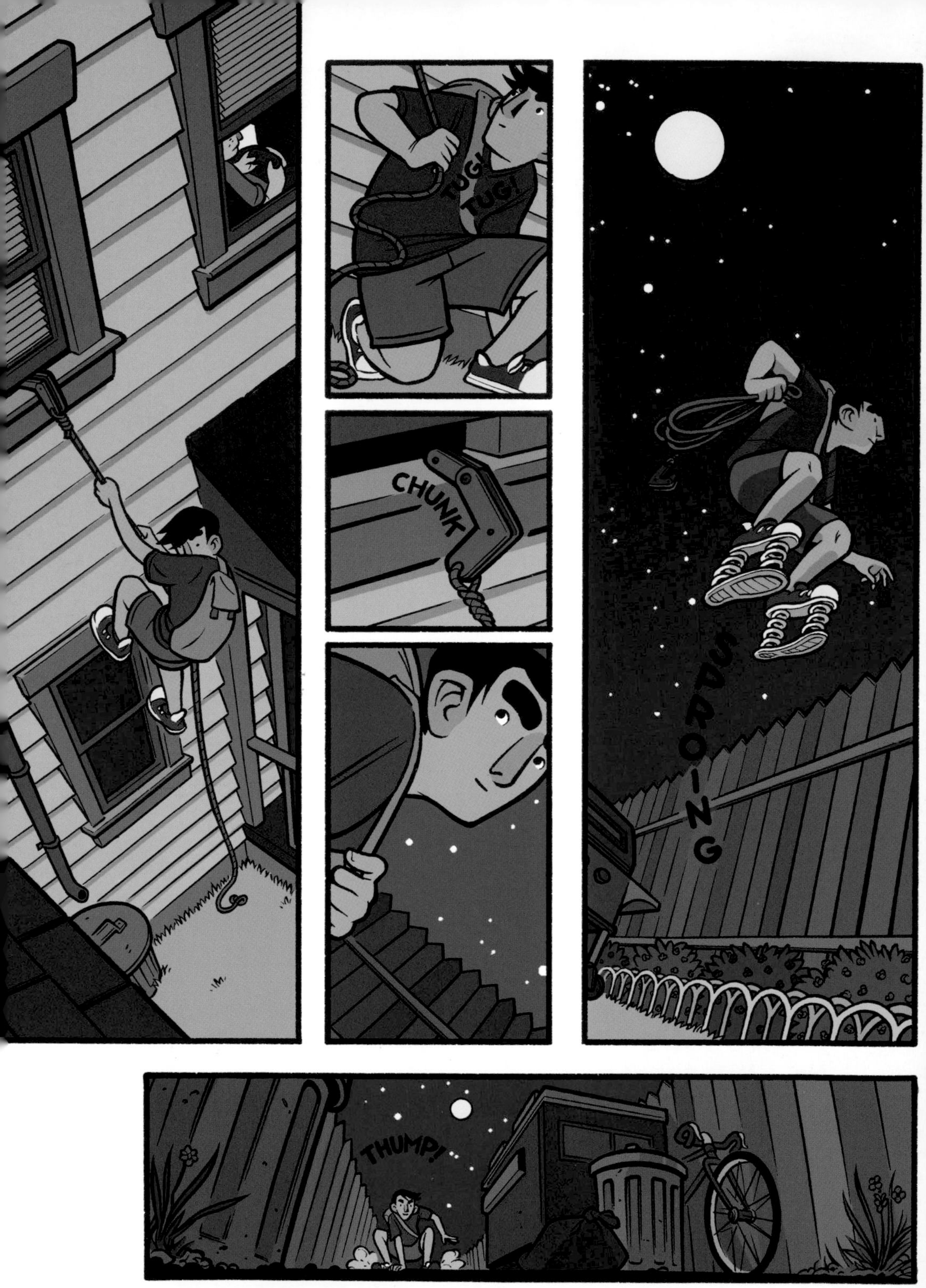
TUG! TUG!
CHUNK
SPROING
THUMP!

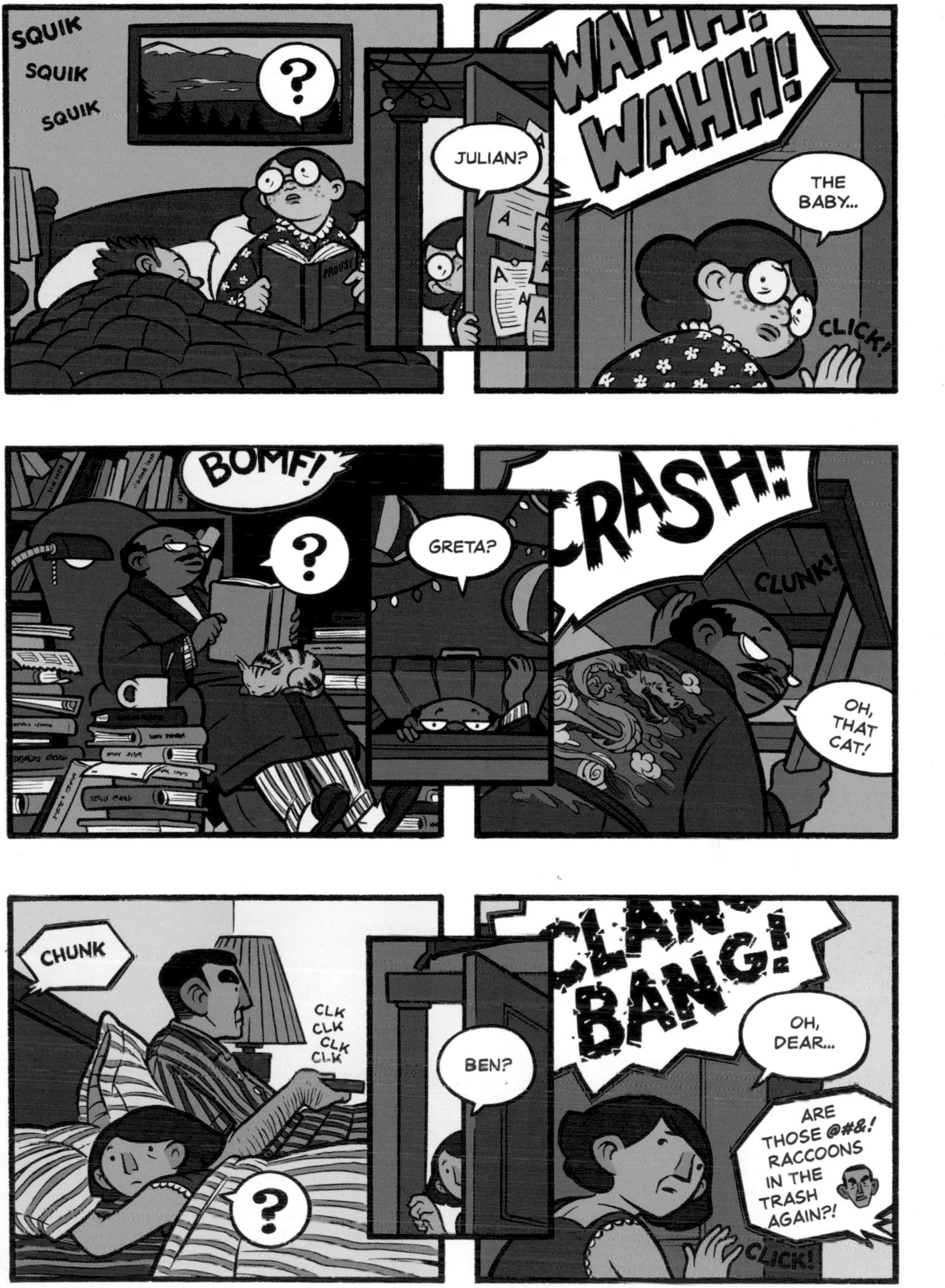
SQUIK
SQUIK
SQUIK
?
PROUST
JULIAN?
WAHH! WAHH!
THE BABY...
CLICK!
BOMF!
?
GRETA?
CRASH!
CLUNK!
OH, THAT CAT!
CHUNK
CLK
CLK
CLK
CLK
?
BEN?
BANG!
OH, DEAR...
ARE THOSE @#&! RACCOONS IN THE TRASH AGAIN?!
CLICK!

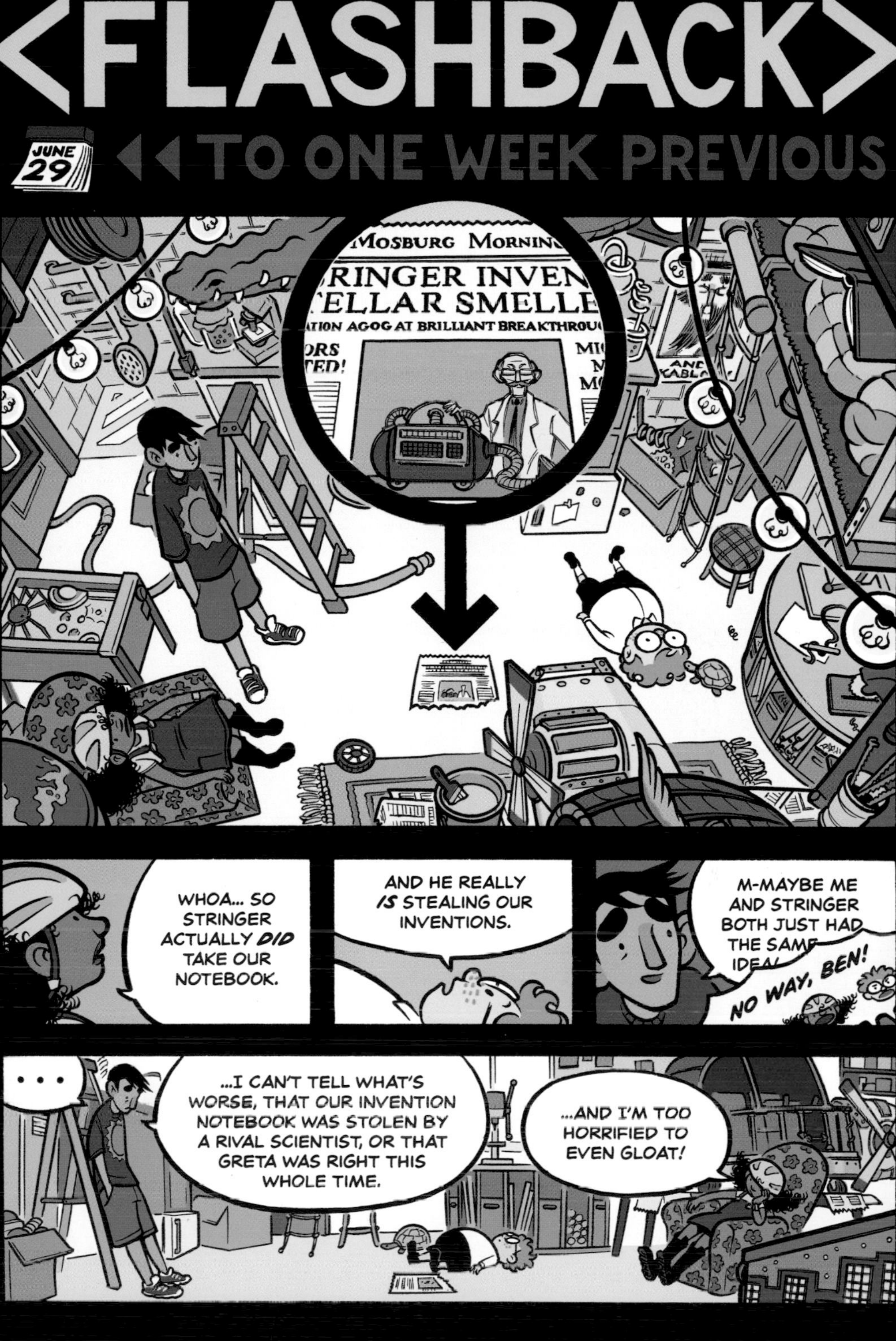

<FLASHBACK>
JUNE 29
TO ONE WEEK PREVIOUS
MOSBURG MORNIN
RINGER INVEN
ELLAR SMELLE
ATION AGOG AT BRILLIANT BREAKTHROU
WHOA... SO STRINGER ACTUALLY *DID* TAKE OUR NOTEBOOK.
AND HE REALLY *IS* STEALING OUR INVENTIONS.
M-MAYBE ME AND STRINGER BOTH JUST HAD THE SAME IDEA
NO WAY, BEN!
...
...I CAN'T TELL WHAT'S WORSE, THAT OUR INVENTION NOTEBOOK WAS STOLEN BY A RIVAL SCIENTIST, OR THAT GRETA WAS RIGHT THIS WHOLE TIME.
...AND I'M TOO HORRIFIED TO EVEN GLOAT!

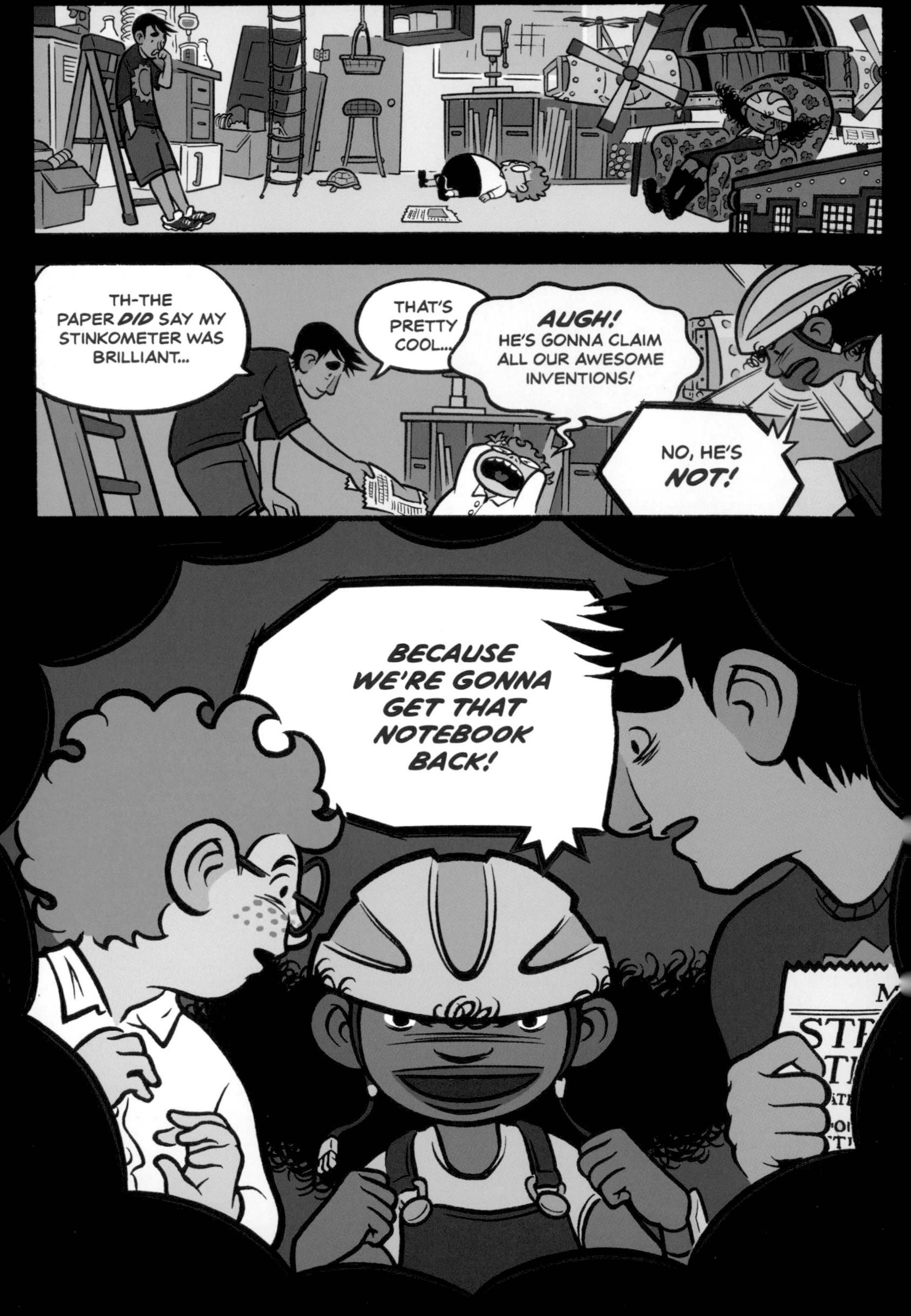
TH-THE PAPER DID SAY MY STINKOMETER WAS BRILLIANT...
THAT'S PRETTY COOL...
AUGH! HE'S GONNA CLAIM ALL OUR AWESOME INVENTIONS!
NO, HE'S NOT!
BECAUSE WE'RE GONNA GET THAT NOTEBOOK BACK!

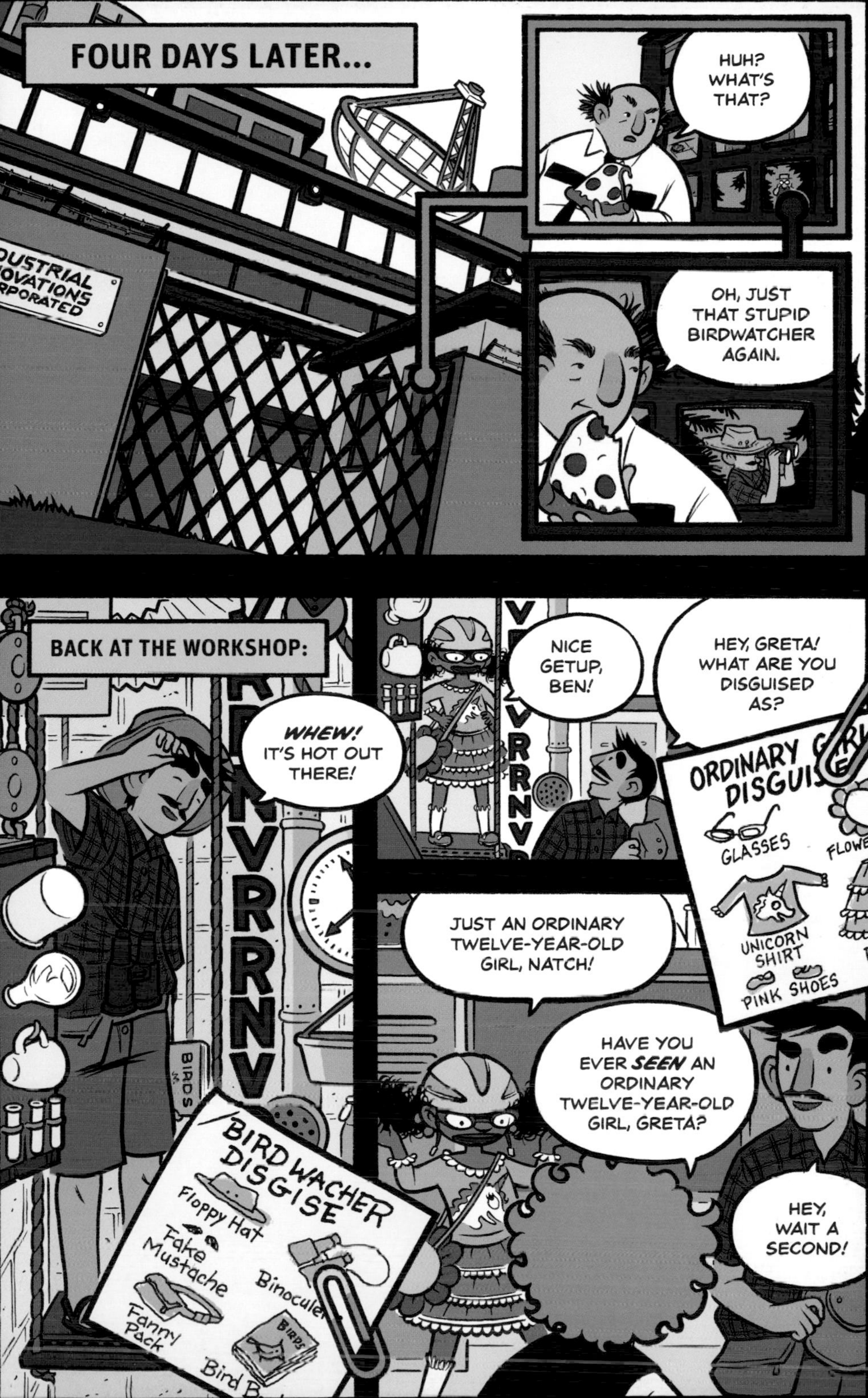

FOUR DAYS LATER...
HUH? WHAT'S THAT?
OH, JUST THAT STUPID BIRDWATCHER AGAIN.
BACK AT THE WORKSHOP:
WHEW! IT'S HOT OUT THERE!
NICE GETUP, BEN!
HEY, GRETA! WHAT ARE YOU DISGUISED AS?
JUST AN ORDINARY TWELVE-YEAR-OLD GIRL, NATCH!
HAVE YOU EVER SEEN AN ORDINARY TWELVE-YEAR-OLD GIRL, GRETA?
HEY, WAIT A SECOND!
ORDINARY GIRL DISGUISE
GLASSES
FLOWER PURSE
UNICORN SHIRT
RUFFLED SKIRT
PINK SHOES
BIRD WACHER DISGISE
Floppy Hat
Fake Mustache
Binoculers
Fanny Pack
BIRDS

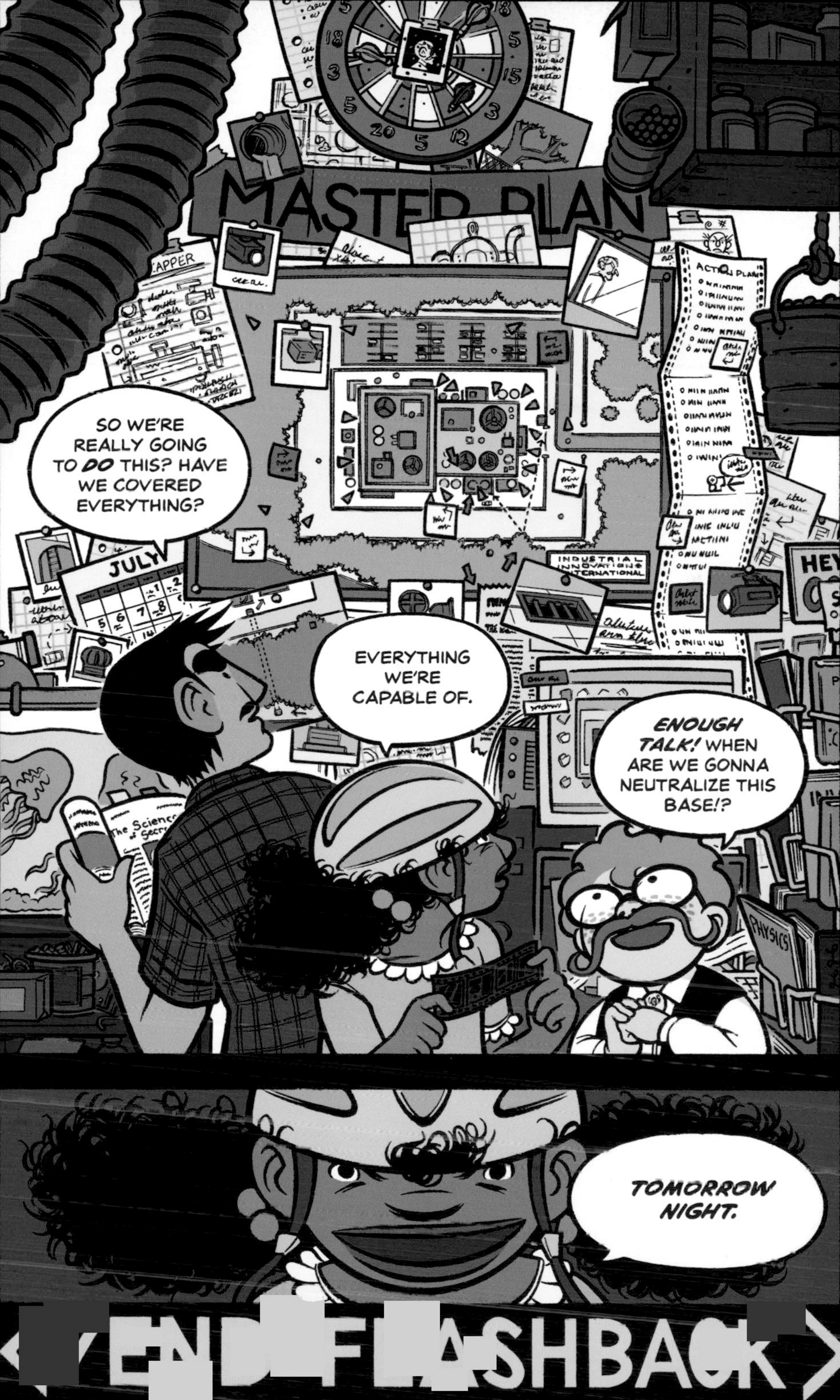
MASTER PLAN
ZAPPER
ACTION PLAN
JULY
INDUSTRIAL INNOVATIONS INTERNATIONAL
SO WE'RE REALLY GOING TO *DO* THIS? HAVE WE COVERED EVERYTHING?
EVERYTHING WE'RE CAPABLE OF.
ENOUGH TALK! WHEN ARE WE GONNA NEUTRALIZE THIS BASE!?
The Science of Secrecy
PHYSICS
TOMORROW NIGHT.
[redacted]END FLASHBAC[redacted]

CHAPTER SEVEN

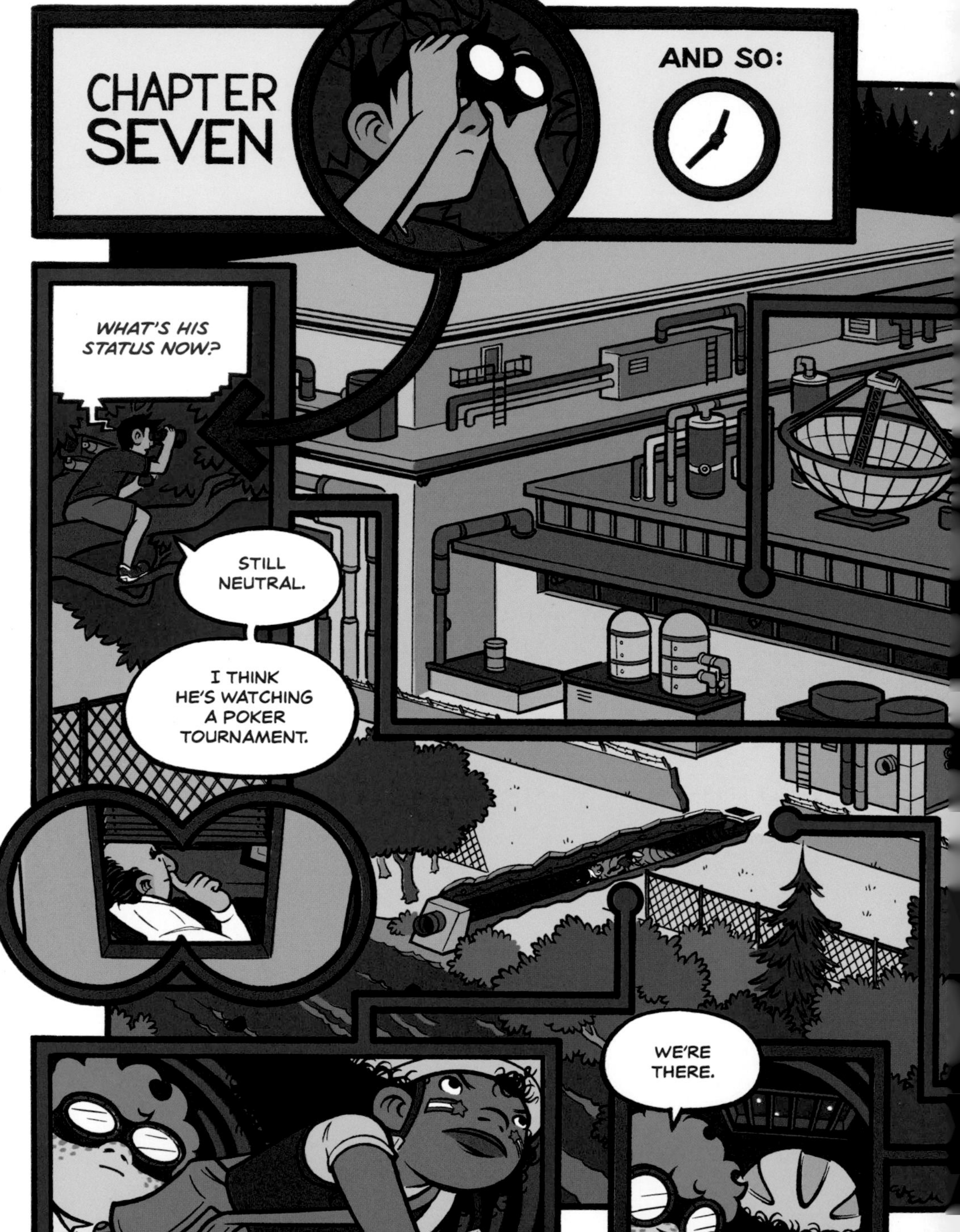
AND SO:
WHAT'S HIS STATUS NOW?
STILL NEUTRAL.
I THINK HE'S WATCHING A POKER TOURNAMENT.
WE'RE THERE.

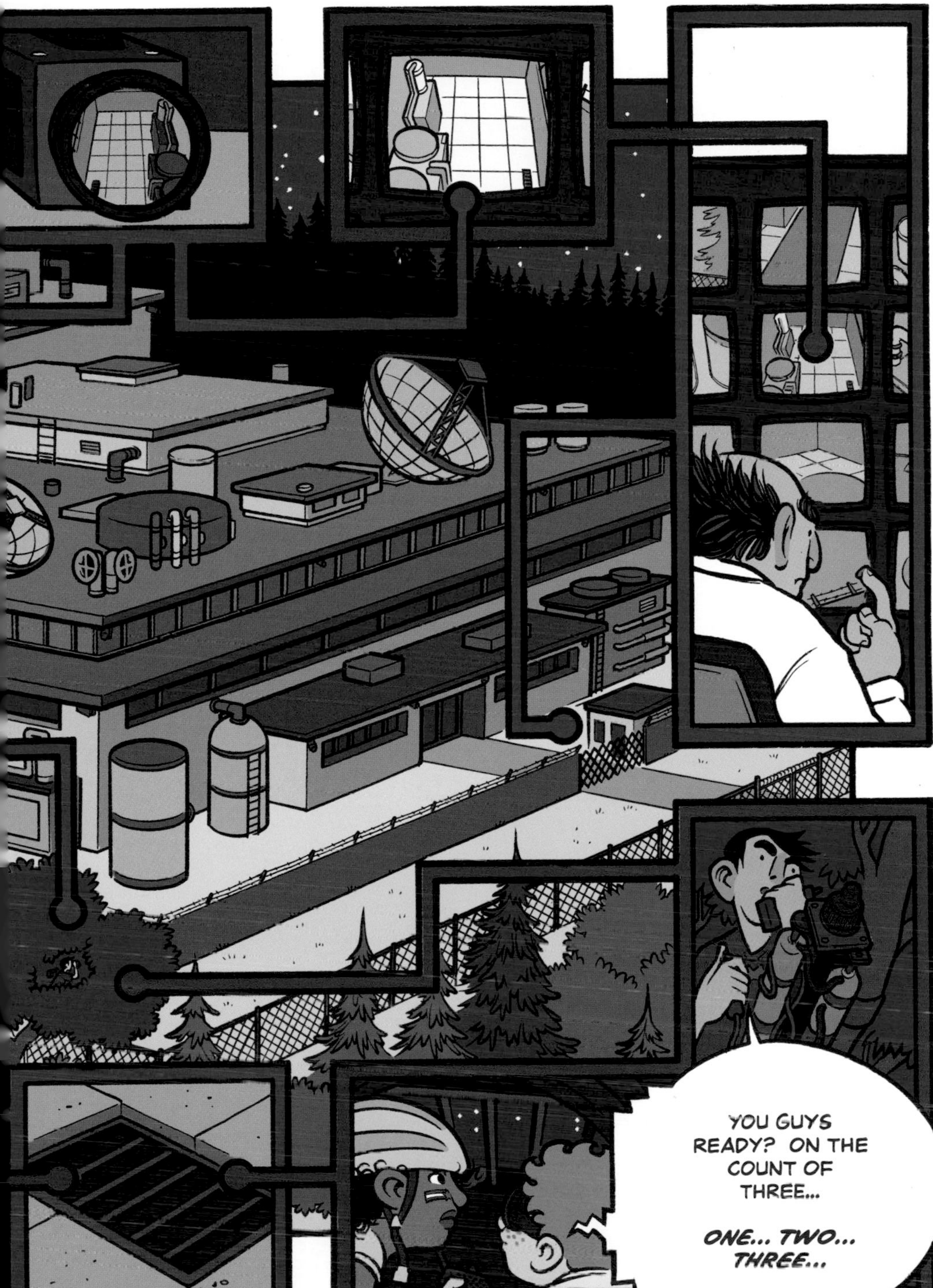
YOU GUYS READY? ON THE COUNT OF THREE...
ONE... TWO... THREE...

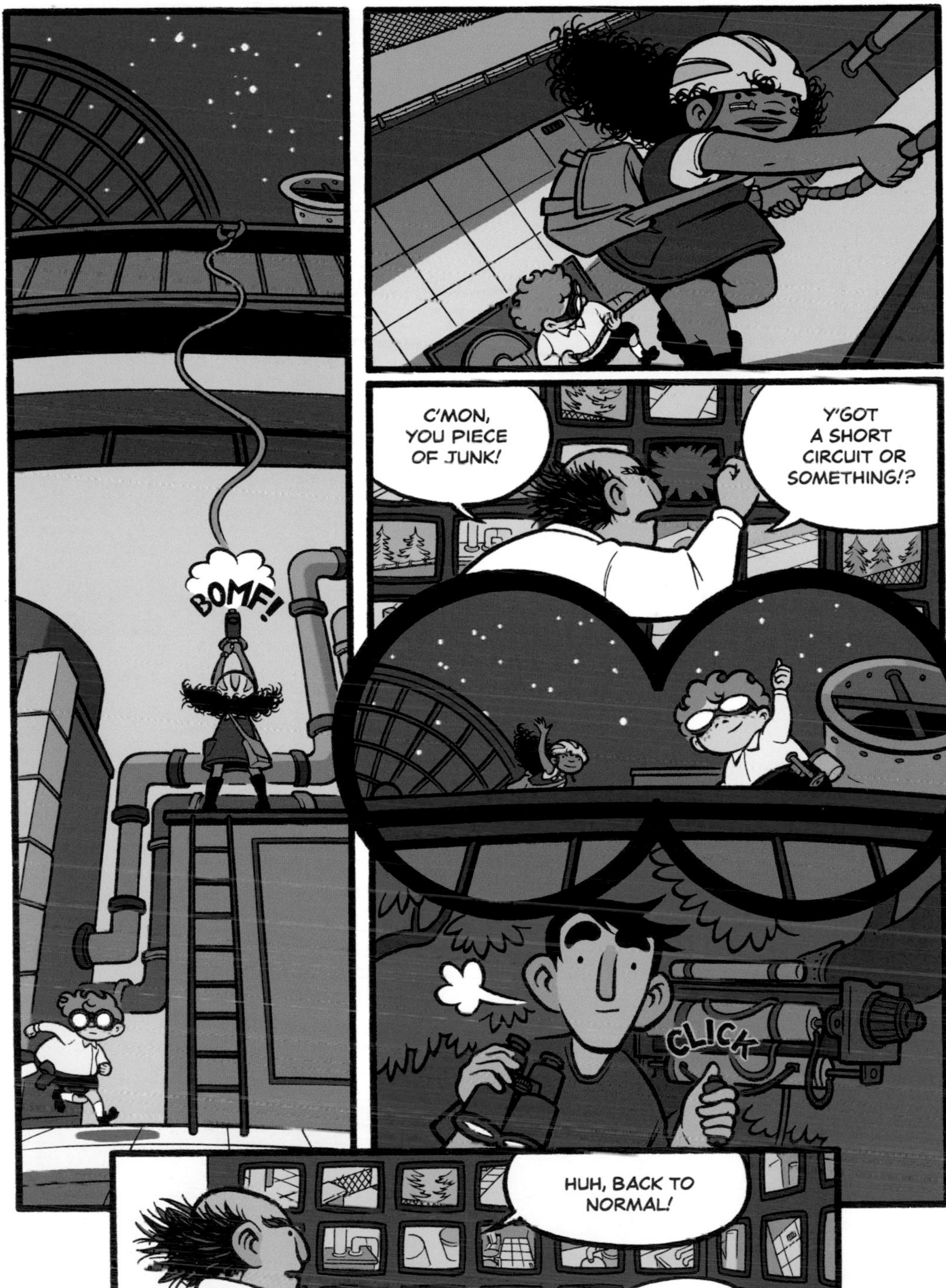
BOMF!
C'MON, YOU PIECE OF JUNK!
Y'GOT A SHORT CIRCUIT OR SOMETHING!?
CLICK
HUH, BACK TO NORMAL!
GOOD.

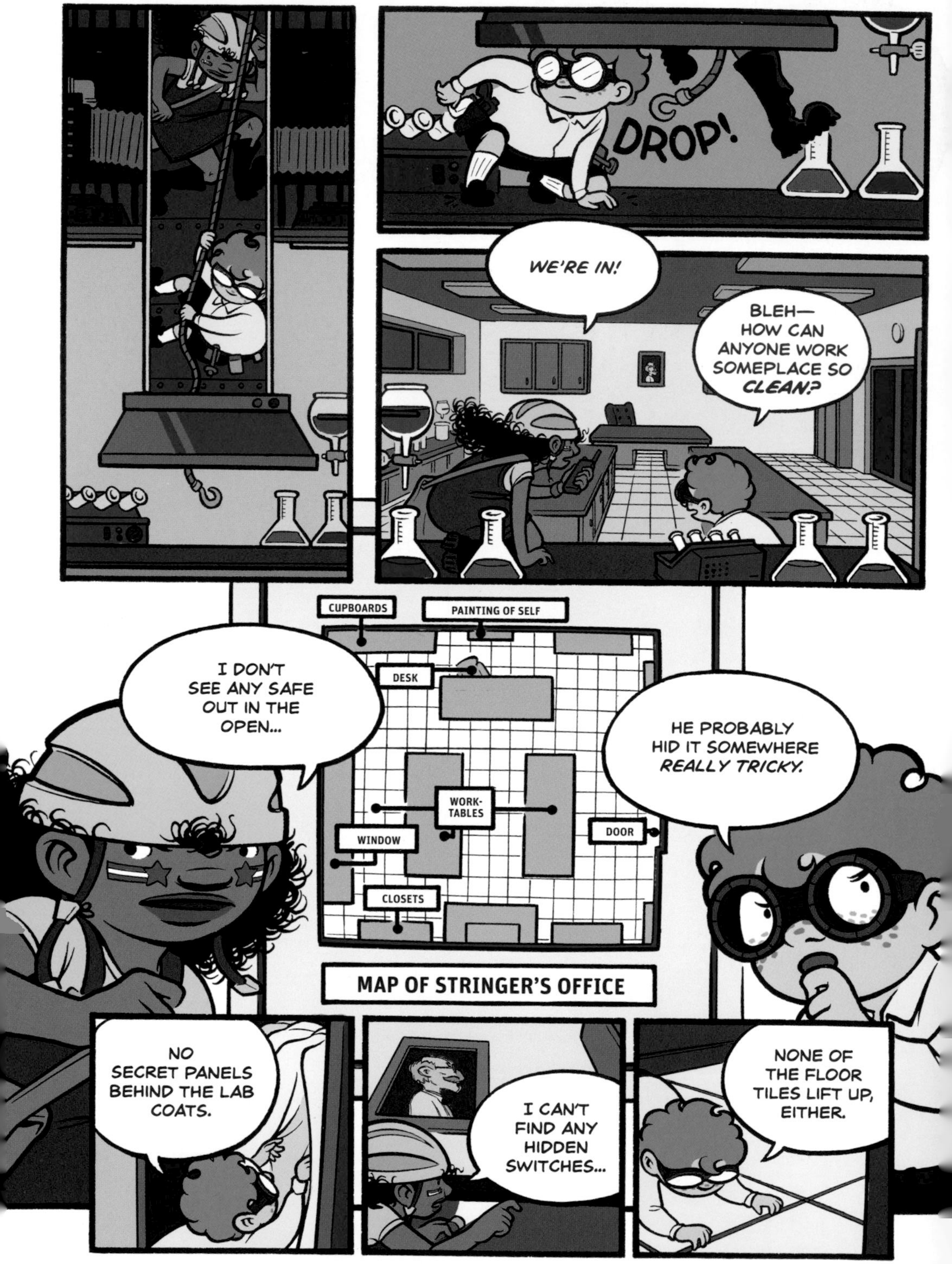
DROP!
WE'RE IN!
BLEH—HOW CAN ANYONE WORK SOMEPLACE SO *CLEAN?*
I DON'T SEE ANY SAFE OUT IN THE OPEN...
CUPBOARDS
PAINTING OF SELF
DESK
WORK-TABLES
WINDOW
DOOR
CLOSETS
MAP OF STRINGER'S OFFICE
HE PROBABLY HID IT SOMEWHERE *REALLY TRICKY.*
NO SECRET PANELS BEHIND THE LAB COATS.
I CAN'T FIND ANY HIDDEN SWITCHES...
NONE OF THE FLOOR TILES LIFT UP, EITHER.

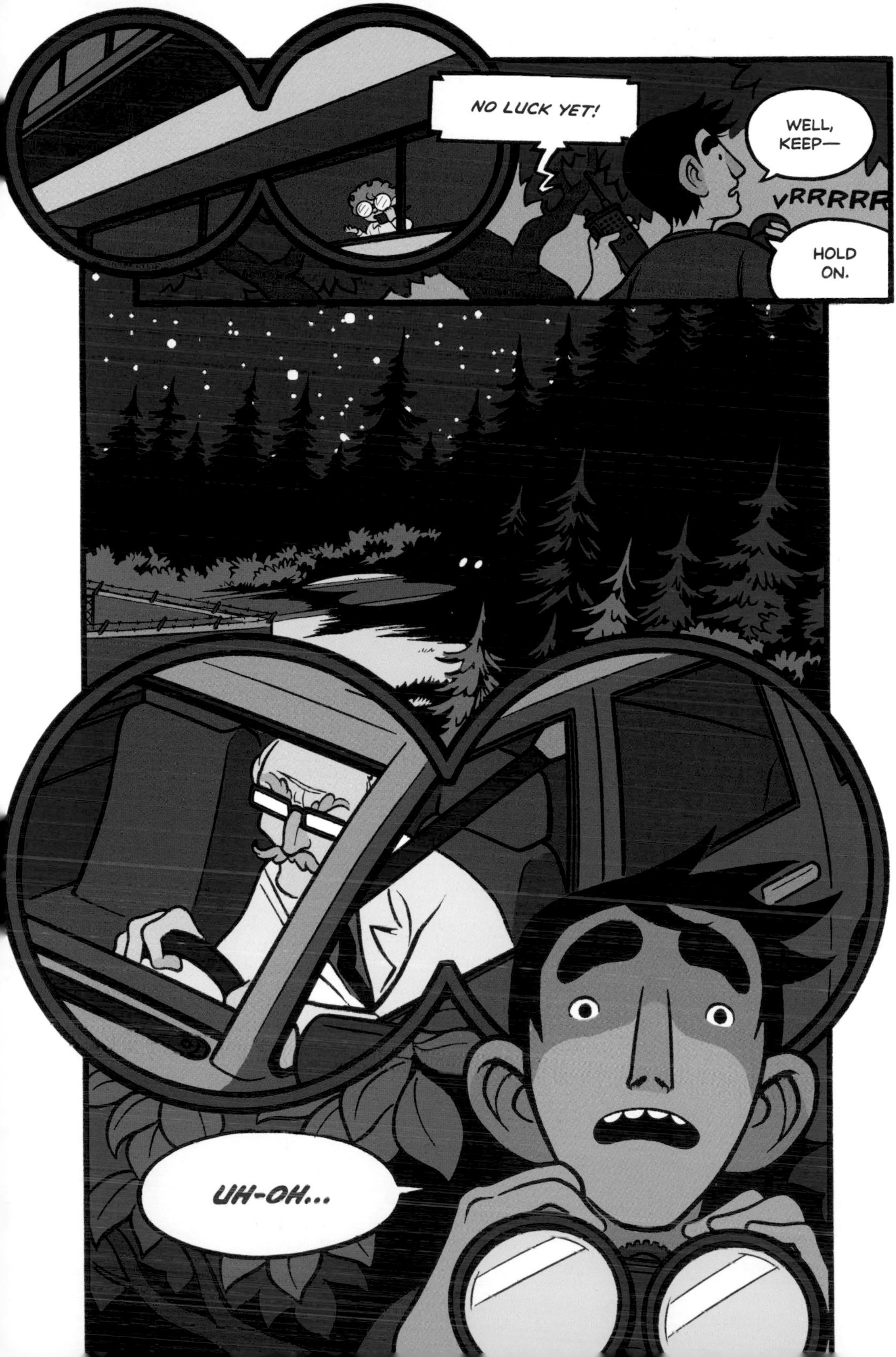
NO LUCK YET!
WELL, KEEP—
VRRRRR
HOLD ON.
UH-OH...

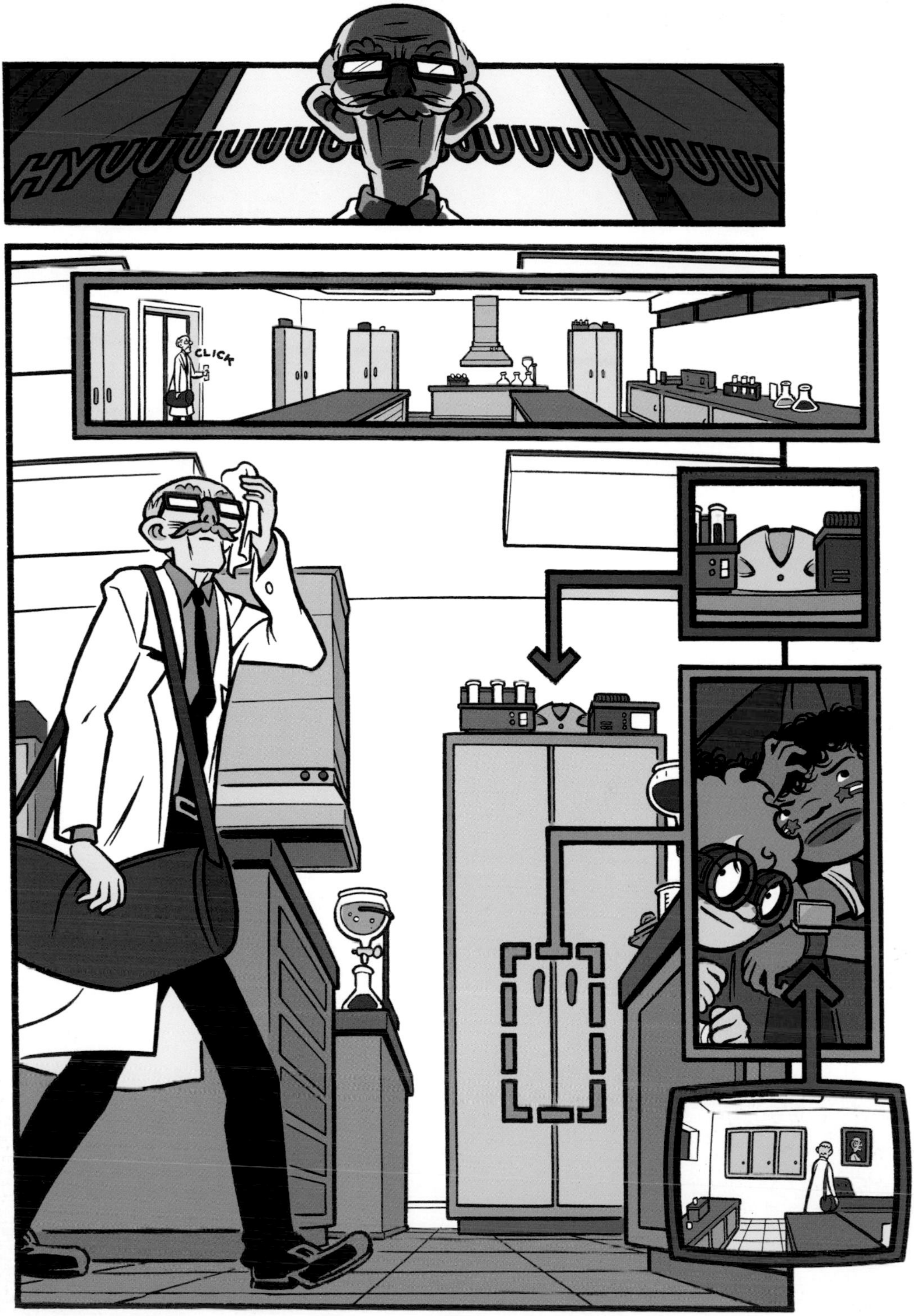
HYUUUUUUUUUUUUUUUU
CLICK

WHAT WAS **THAT** ALL ABOUT?

114

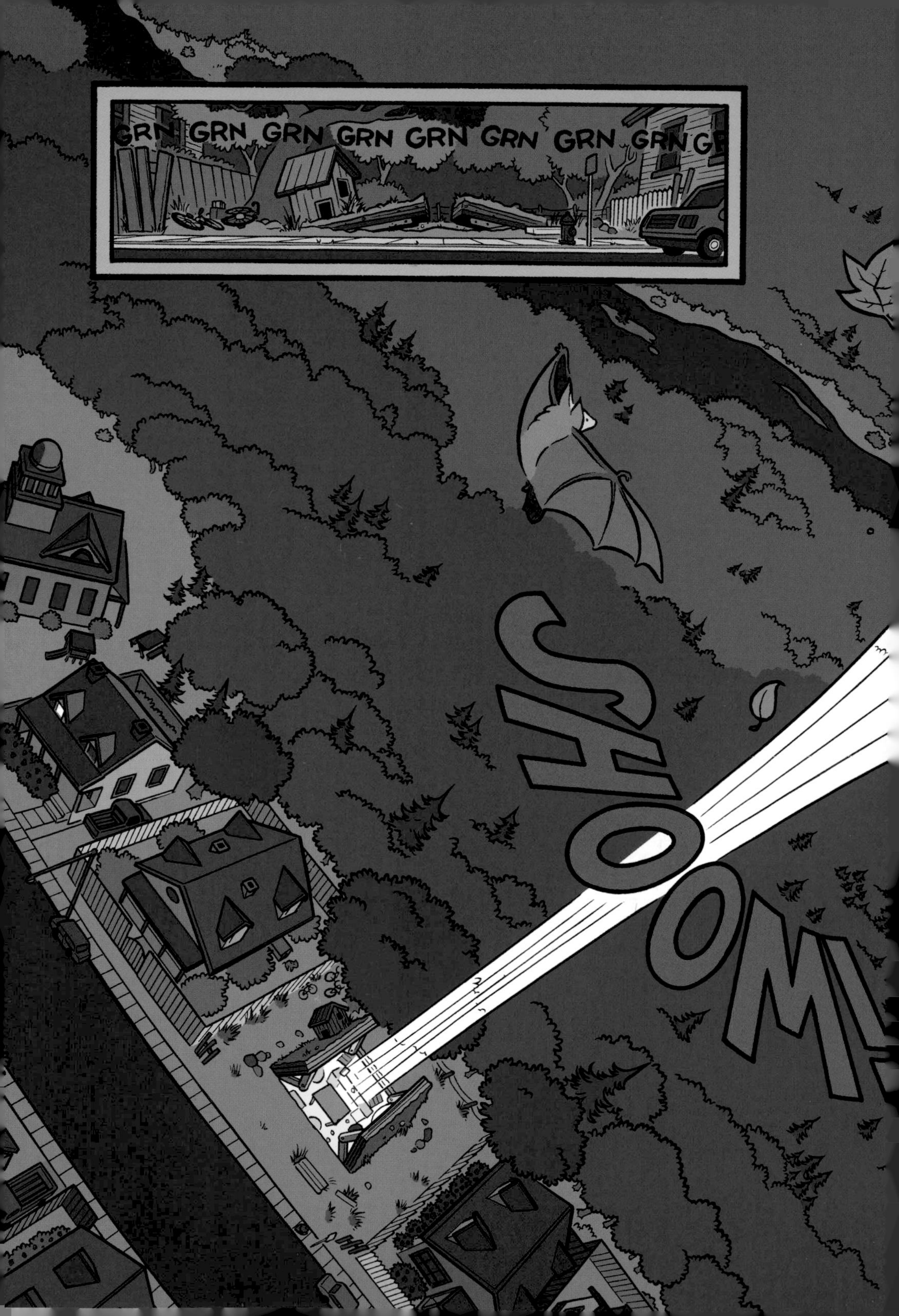
GRN GRN GRN GRN GRN GRN GRN GRN
SHOOM!

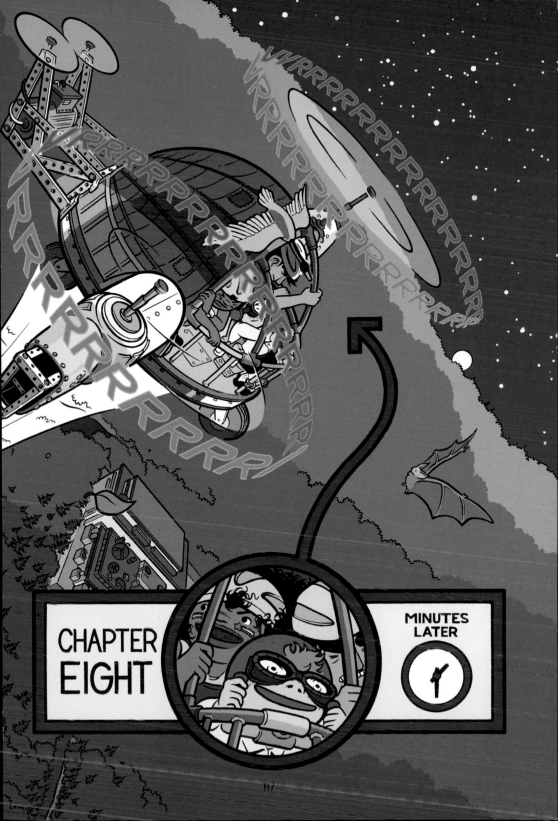

CHAPTER
EIGHT

MINUTES
LATER

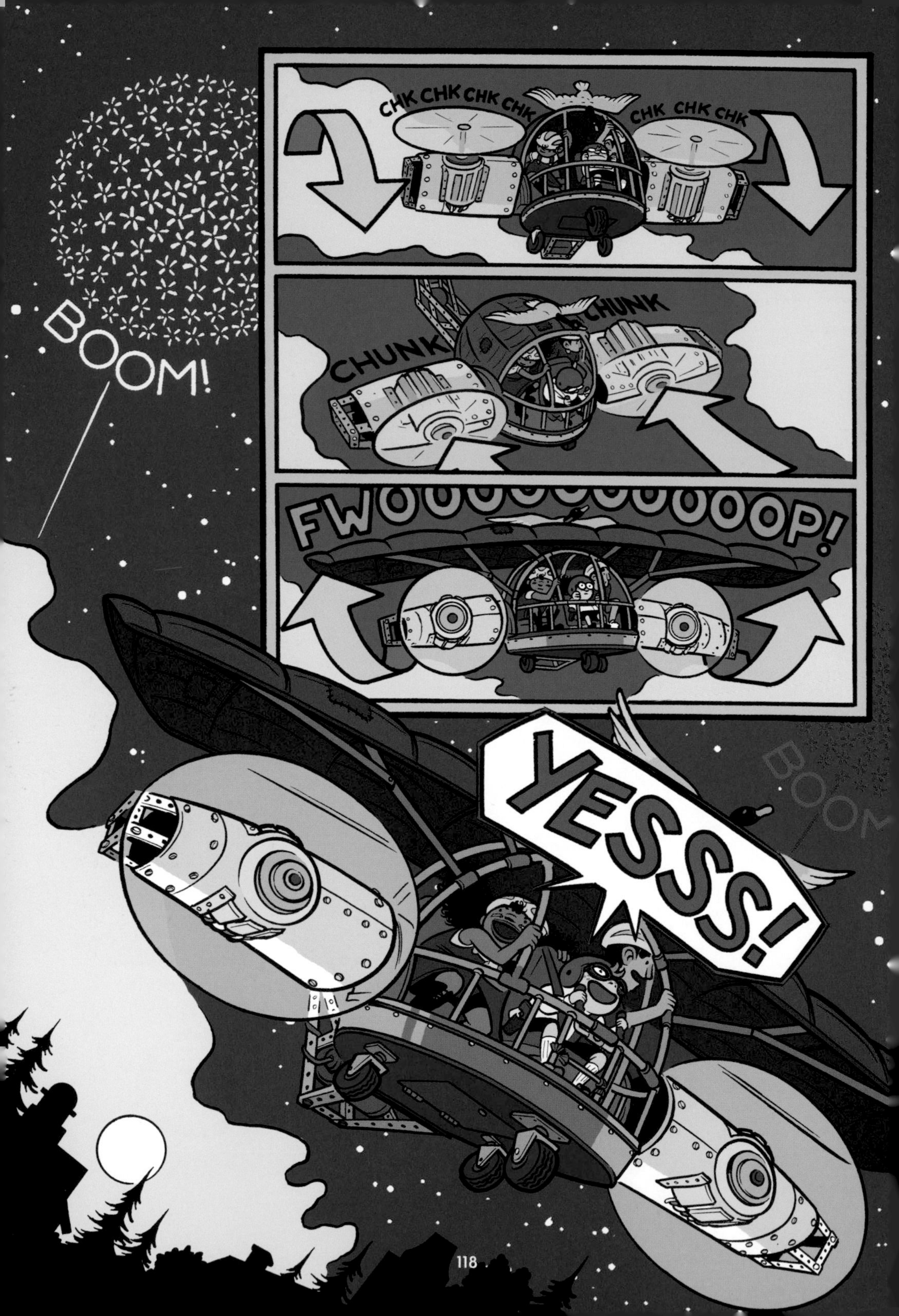
CHK CHK CHK CHK
CHK CHK CHK
BOOM!
CHUNK
CHUNK
FWOOOOOOOOOOOP!
YESSS!
BOOM

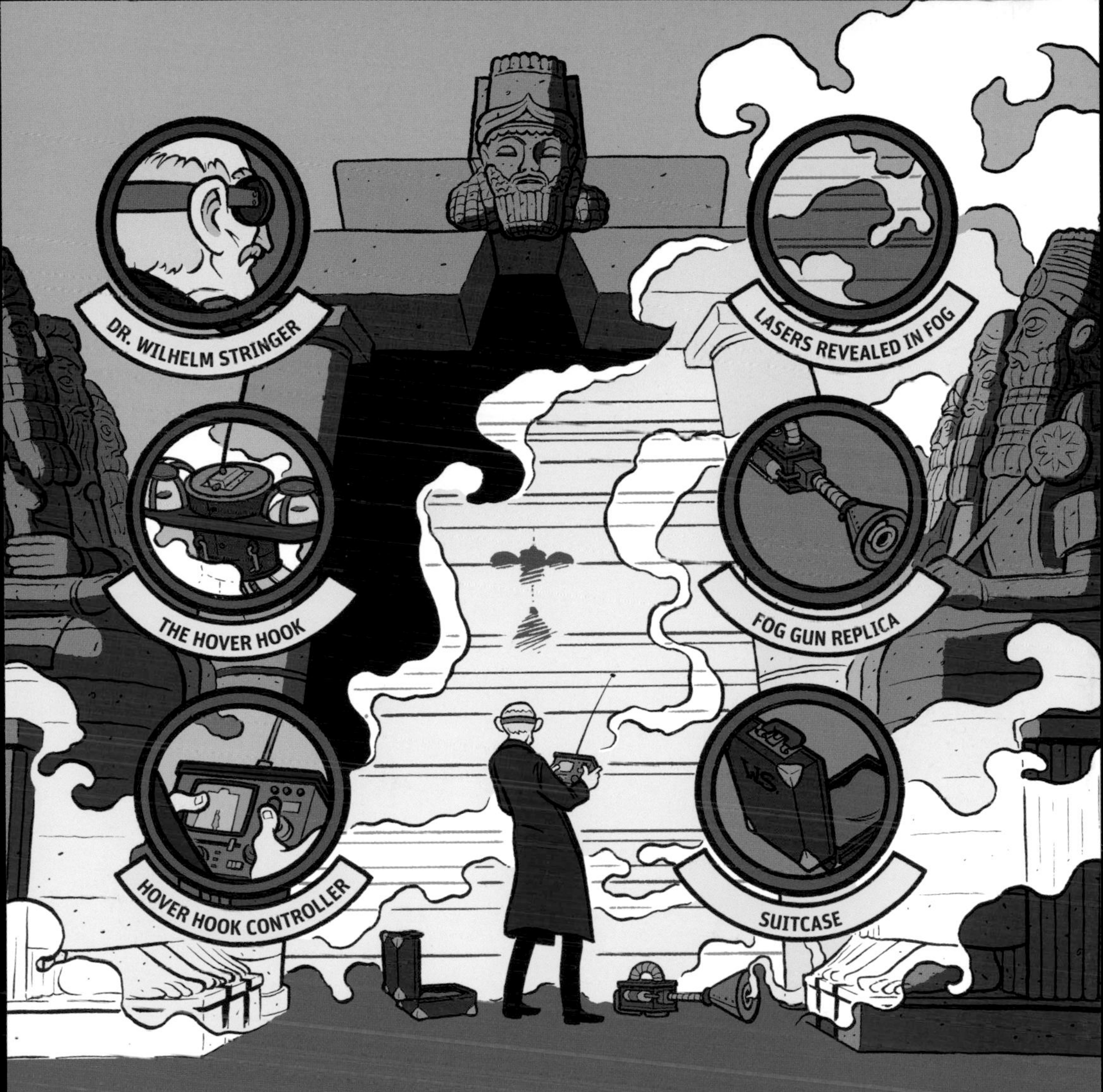
DR. WILHELM STRINGER
LASERS REVEALED IN FOG
THE HOVER HOOK
FOG GUN REPLICA
HOVER HOOK CONTROLLER
SUITCASE

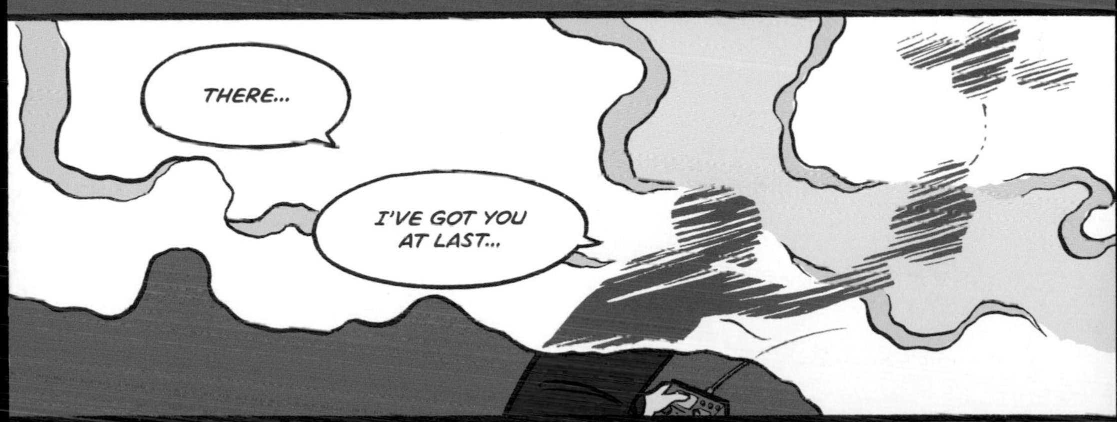
THERE...
I'VE GOT YOU AT LAST...

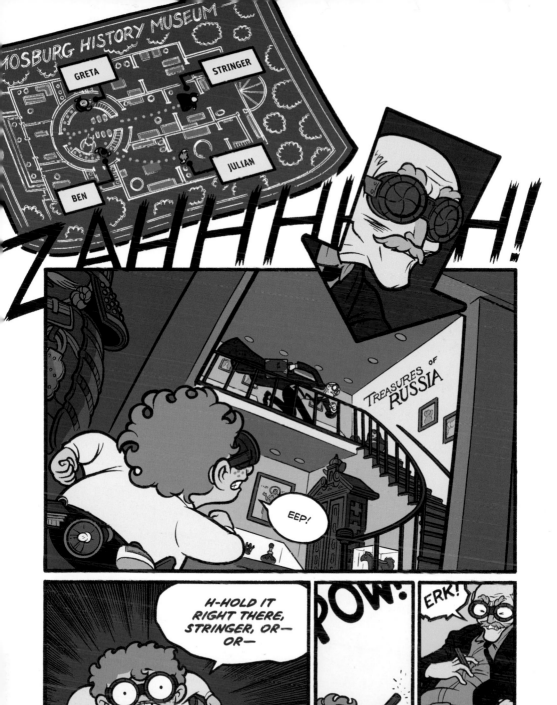

125

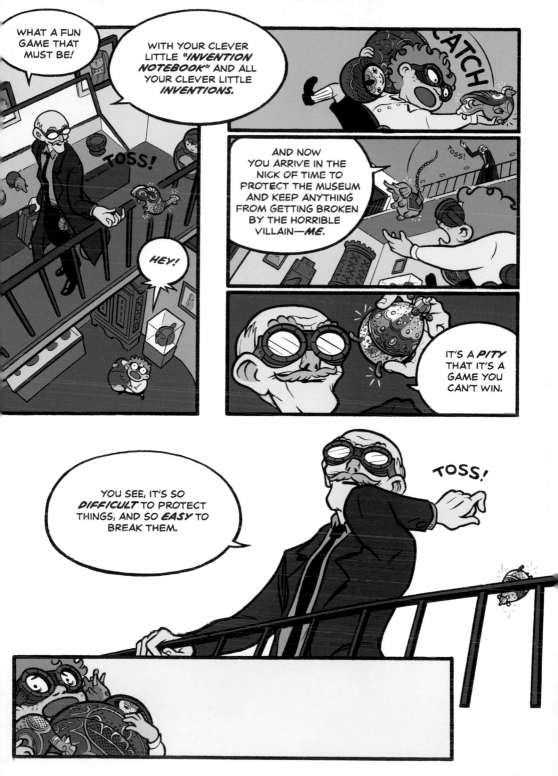

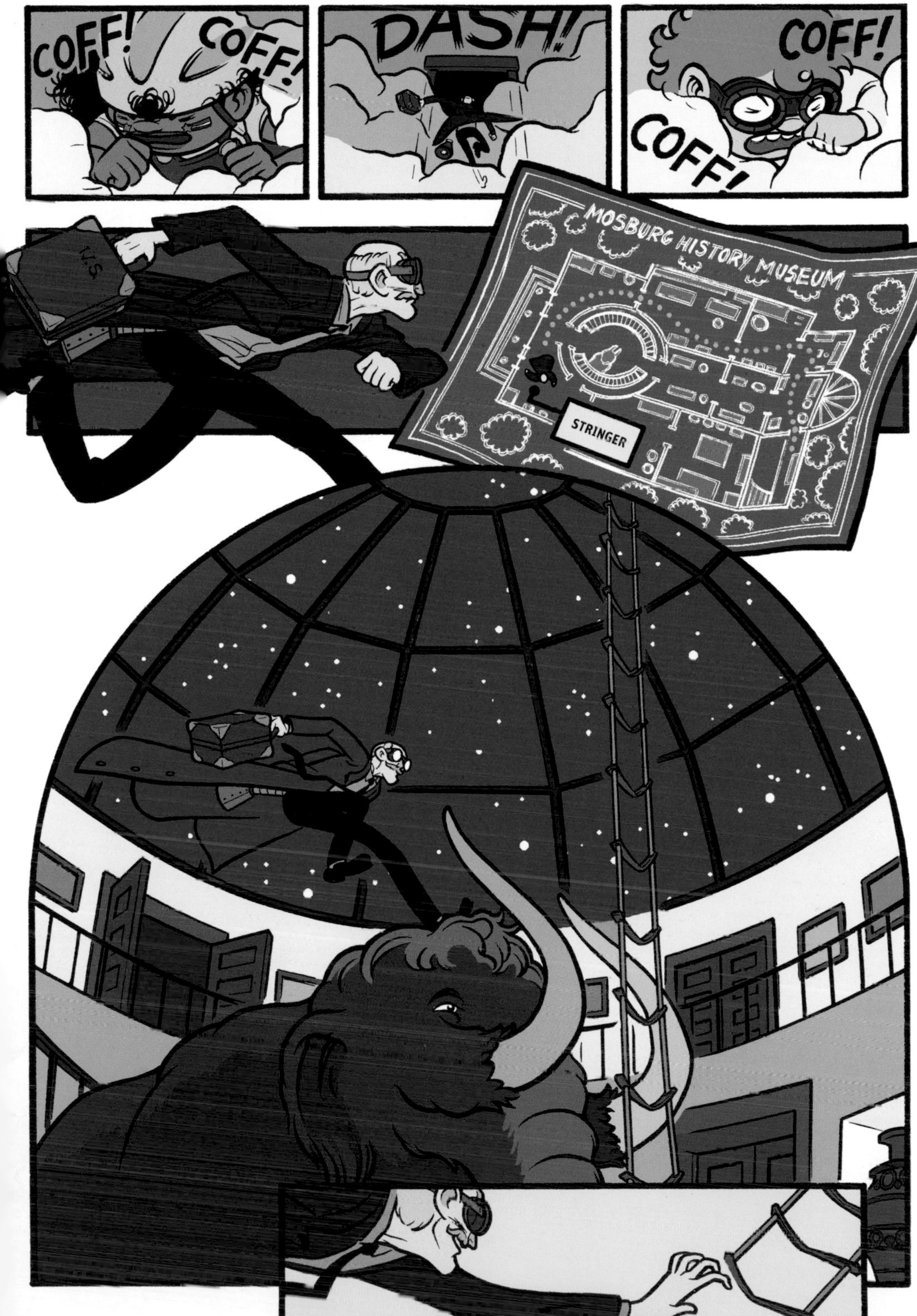
COFF!
COFF!
DASH!
COFF!
COFF!
MOSBURG HISTORY MUSEUM
STRINGER

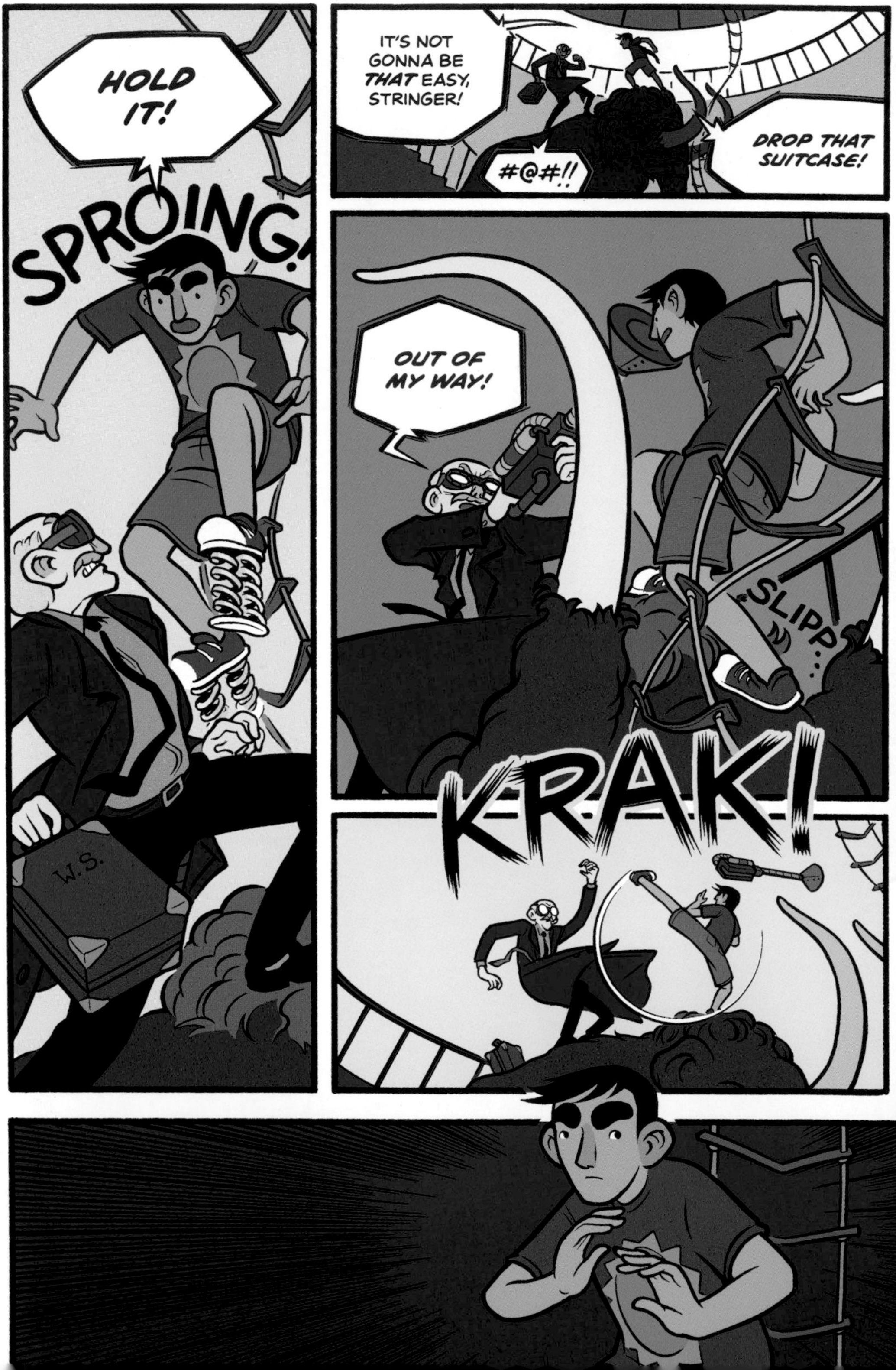
HOLD IT!
SPROING!
IT'S NOT GONNA BE THAT EASY, STRINGER!
#@#!!
DROP THAT SUITCASE!
OUT OF MY WAY!
SLIPP...
KRAK!
W.S.

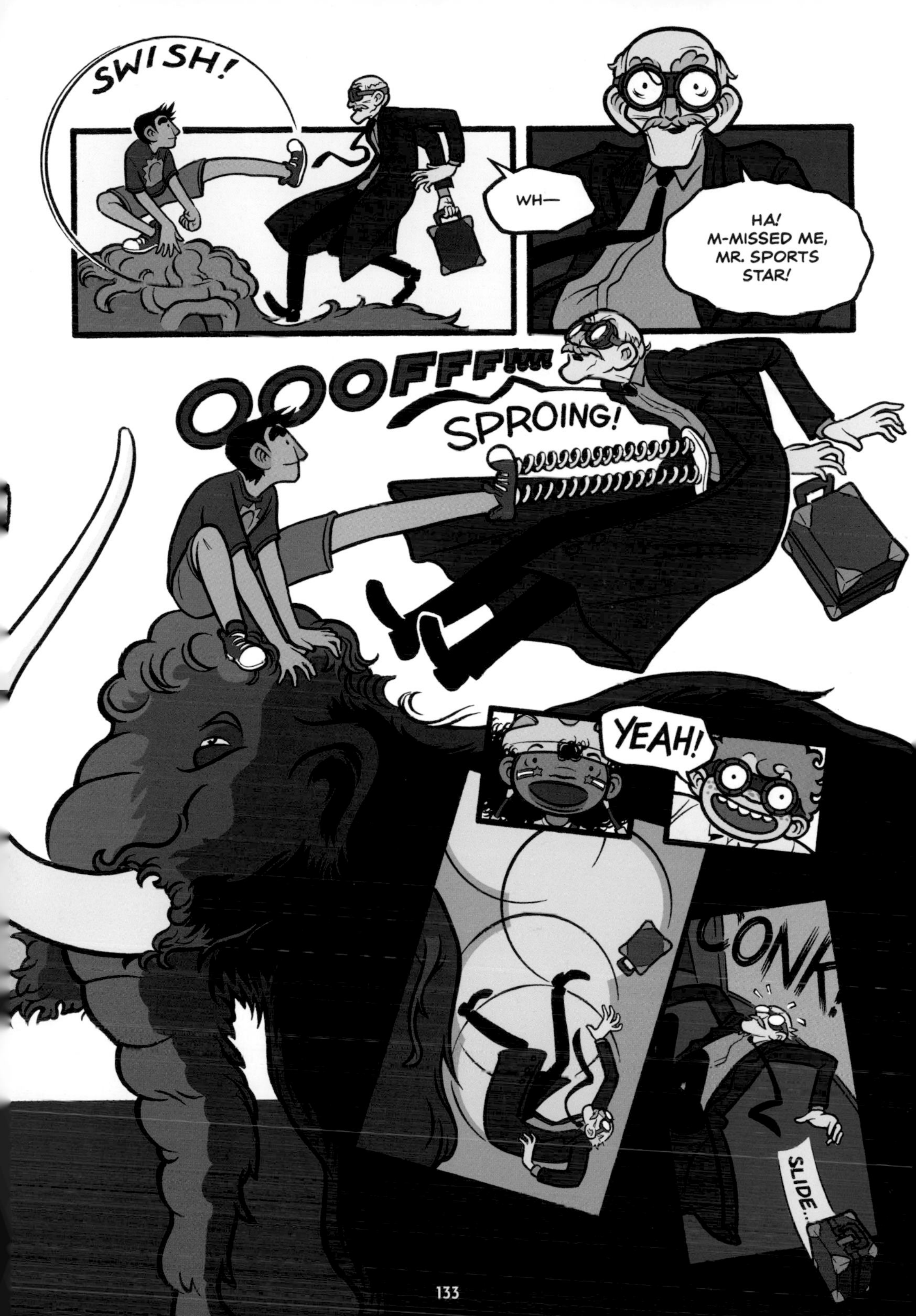
SWISH!
WH—
HA! M-MISSED ME, MR. SPORTS STAR!
OOOFFF!!!!
SPROING!
YEAH!
CONK!
SLIDE...

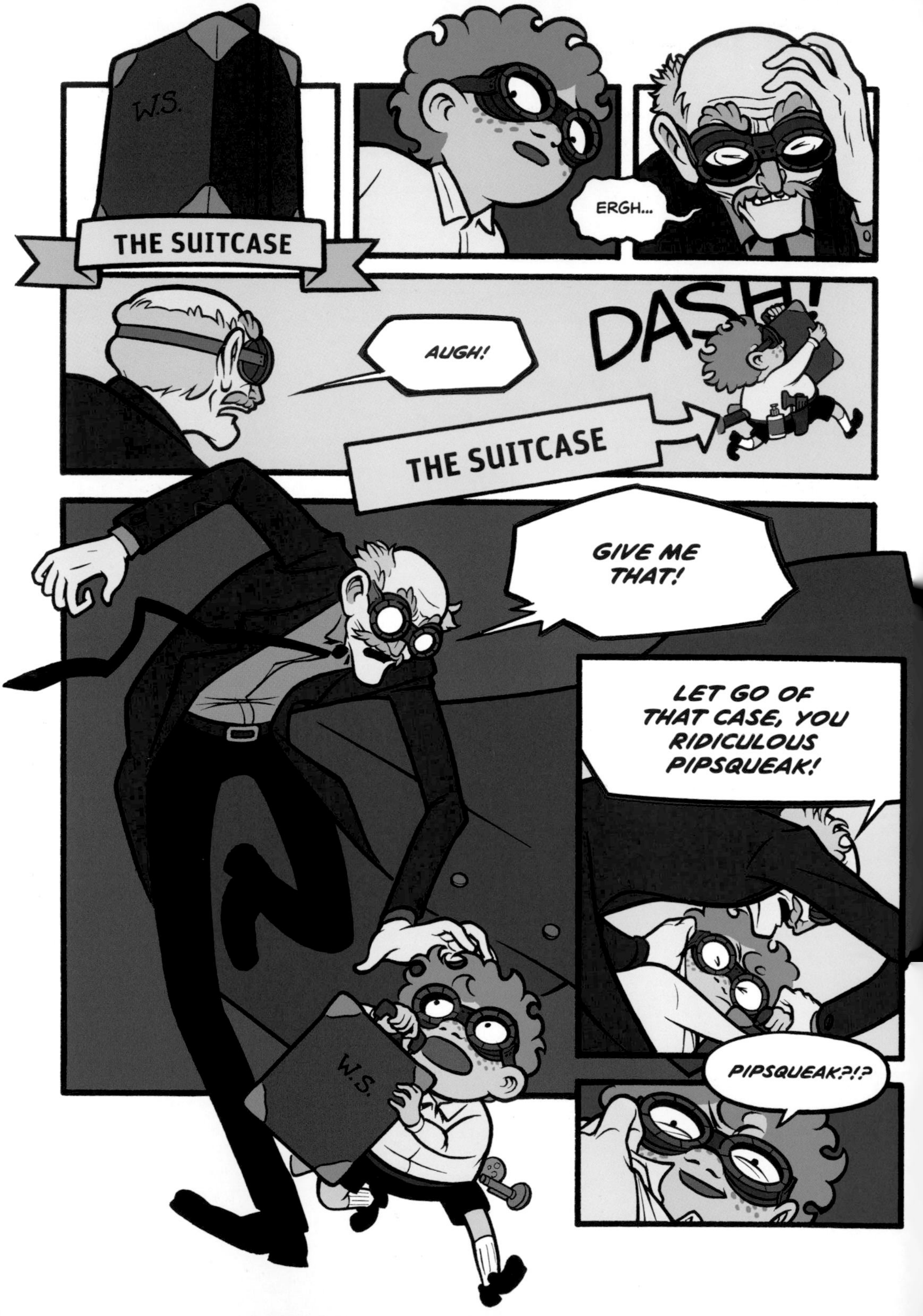
THE SUITCASE
W.S.
ERGH...
AUGH!
DASH!
THE SUITCASE
GIVE ME THAT!
LET GO OF THAT CASE, YOU RIDICULOUS PIPSQUEAK!
W.S.
PIPSQUEAK?!?

135

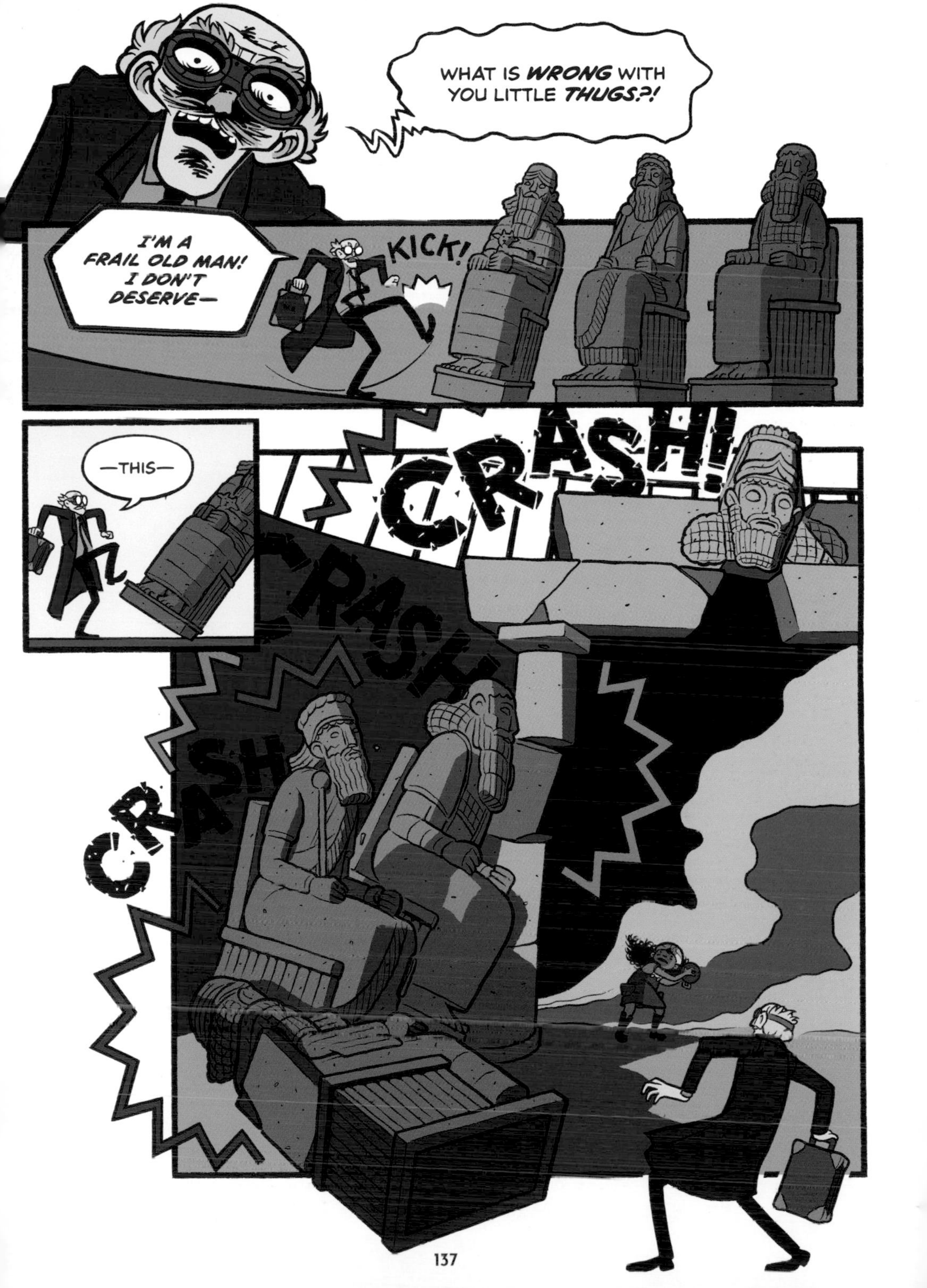
WHAT IS WRONG WITH YOU LITTLE THUGS?!
I'M A FRAIL OLD MAN! I DON'T DESERVE—
KICK!
—THIS—
CRASH!
CRASH!
CRASH!

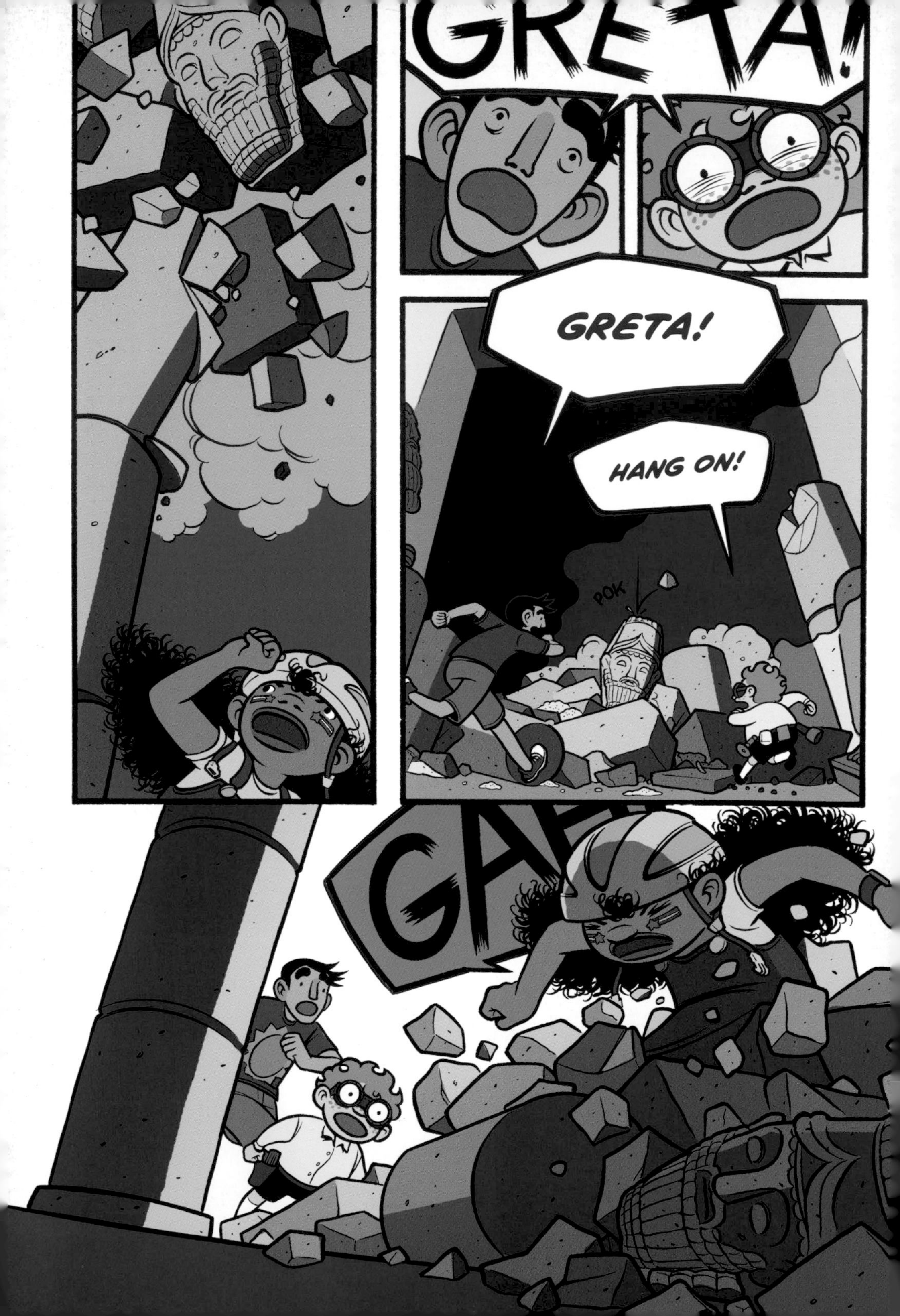
GRETA!
GRETA!
HANG ON!
POK
GA

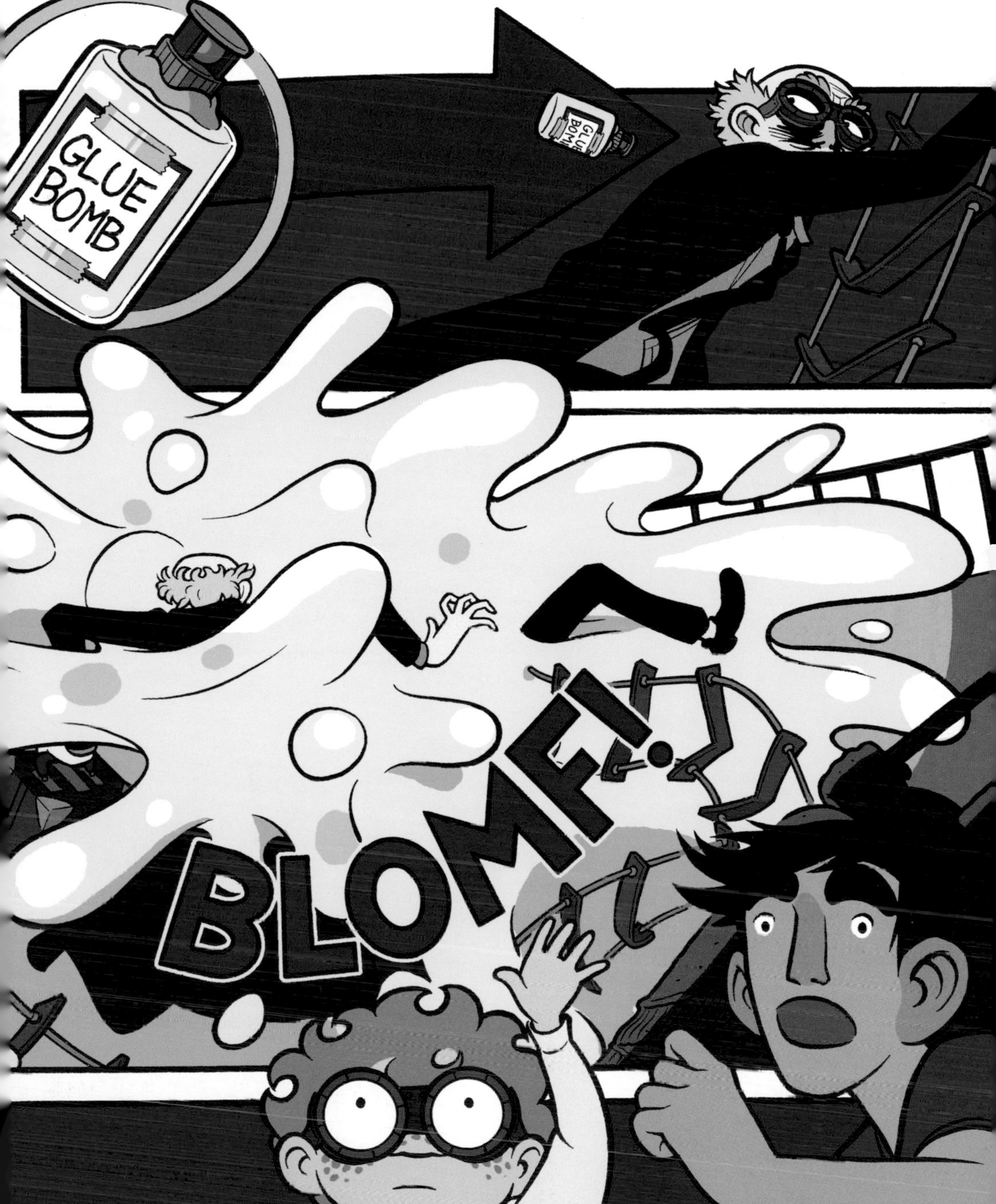
GLUE BOMB
GLUE BOMB
BLOMF!

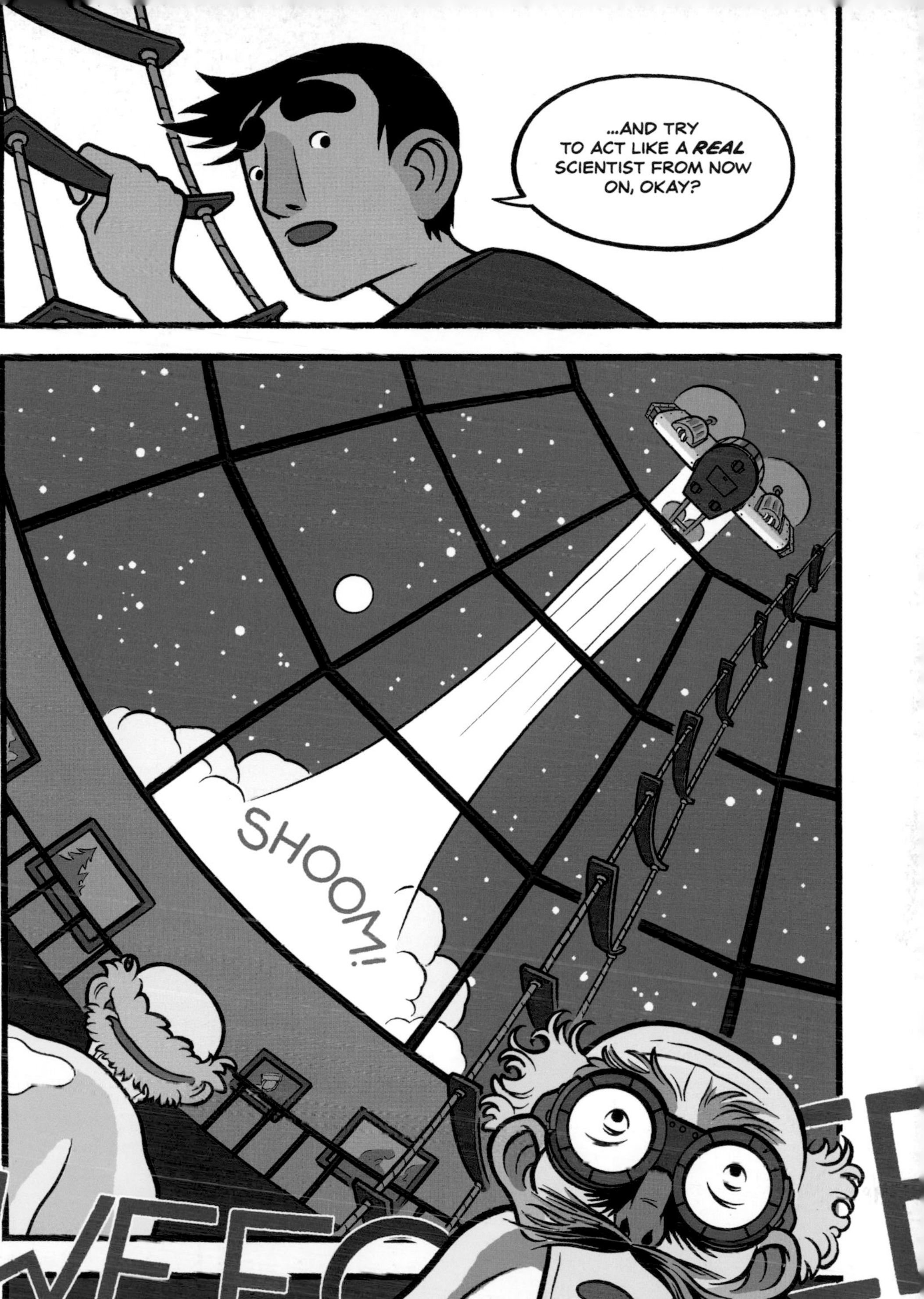
...AND TRY TO ACT LIKE A *REAL* SCIENTIST FROM NOW ON, OKAY?
SHOOM!

WHEN YOU WEREN'T IN YOUR BED, I FIGURED YOU'D BE WHERE THE MOST TROUBLE WAS.

I'M SORRY I SCARED YOU, DAD.

LORD KNOWS I'M USED TO IT BY NOW.

AND OF COURSE, HERE'S BEN AND JULIAN AS WELL. RIDICULOUS.

HERE THEY COME!

UM, HELLO, MR. H.

HI

THEY'VE GOT SOMEBODY!

IT'S AN OLD GUY!

IT'S THAT SCIENTIST! STRINGER OR SOMETHING!

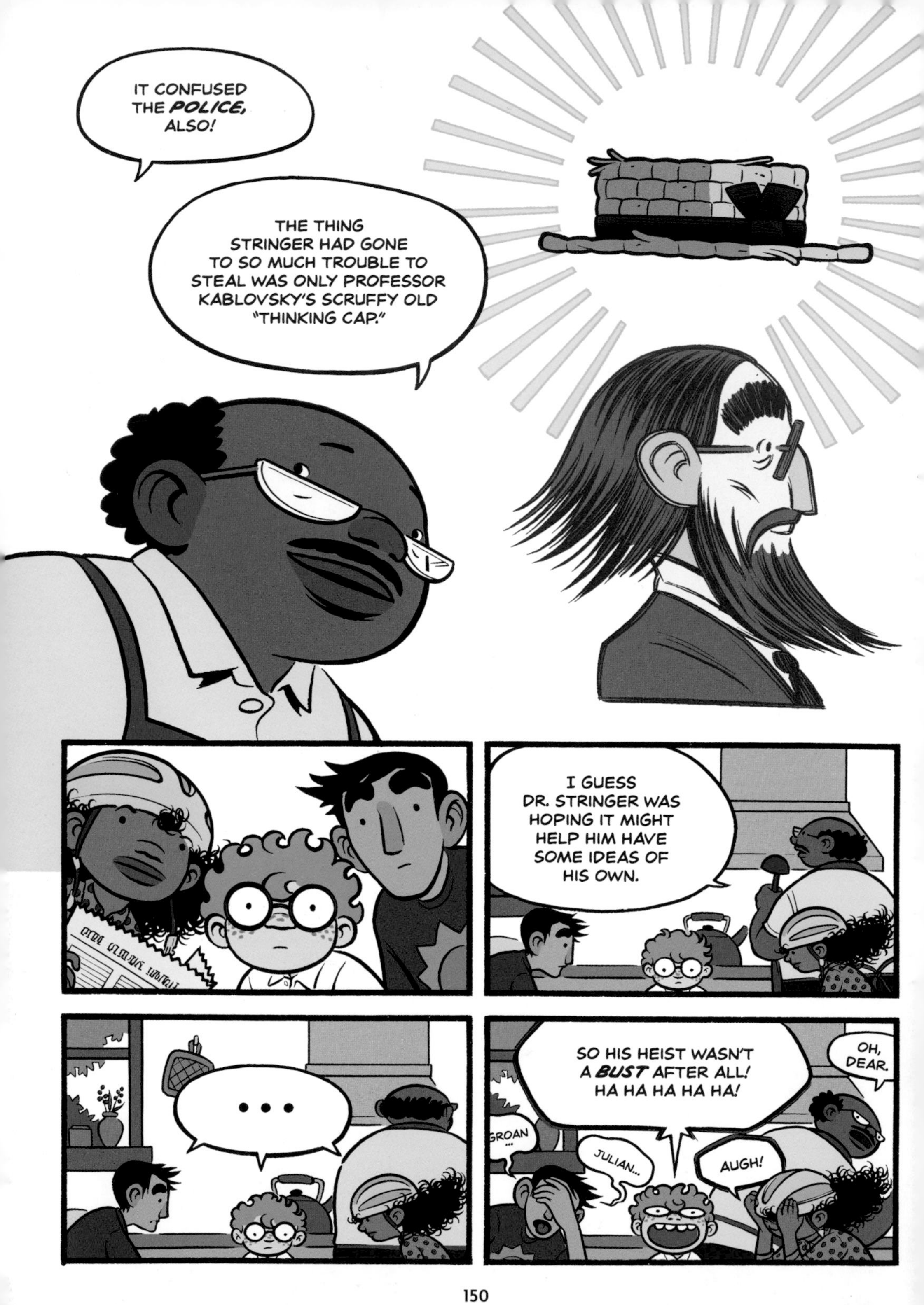
IT CONFUSED THE *POLICE,* ALSO!
THE THING STRINGER HAD GONE TO SO MUCH TROUBLE TO STEAL WAS ONLY PROFESSOR KABLOVSKY'S SCRUFFY OLD "THINKING CAP."
I GUESS DR. STRINGER WAS HOPING IT MIGHT HELP HIM HAVE SOME IDEAS OF HIS OWN.
...
SO HIS HEIST WASN'T A *BUST* AFTER ALL! HA HA HA HA HA!
OH, DEAR.
GROAN...
JULIAN...
AUGH!

ACKNOWLEDGMENTS

Thank you to the awesome team at Bloomsbury who've worked on SSA (both current and past)—Melanie Cecka, Margaret Miller, Donna Mark, Deb Shapiro, Liz Schonhorst, Julie Romeis, and Victoria Wells Arms, among countless others in production and sales. I'm continually astonished by and thankful for all that you do!

To Joey Weiser, Michele Chidester, Bryant Paul Johnson, John Lind, and Denis Kitchen, profuse thanks and high fives!

Thanks and love to Adam Aylard and my parents, Ann and Ed Davis, for slogging through miles of scrubby thumbnails and giving advice.

For general help, support, love, feedback, blurbs, and a million other things: Françoise Mouly, Tony and Angela DiTerlizzi, Scott McCloud, my grandmother Sue Ellen Groover Davis, my sister Leta Davis, the Davis and McCutcheon families in general, Kate Guillen, Nate Neal, the Savannah crowd of friends and mentors, the Athens crowd ditto, and—nerdily—the LJ comics support team.

And finally, there is no way to adequately thank my husband and partner, Drew Weing. Thank you for getting dragged into being coauthor and coartist of our book. Thank you for tireless months and years of work, and thank you for your inhuman patience. But most of all, thank you for bemusedly loving—and wholeheartedly believing in—Julian, Greta, and Ben.